A World Bathed in Fire

Eldritch monsters stalk the streets, the demon cultists are in
a murderous frenzy, and the Guildpact is torn by dissension.
Every guild is on its own. Divided, they will fall. Lucky for
Ravnica, on a world where ghosts linger, being dead isn't half
the excuse Kos would like it to be.

**Cory J. Herndon concludes the thrilling tale of heroism,
adventure, and deception he began in Ravnica.**

EXPERIENCE THE MAGIC

Ravnica Cycle · Book III

DISSENSION

Cory J. Herndon

Ravnica Cycle, Book III

DISSENSION

©2006 Wizards of the Coast, Inc.

Cover art by Zoltan Boros and Gabor Szikszai
First Printing: April 2006
Library of Congress Catalog Card Number: 2005932335

9 8 7 6 5 4 3 2 1

ISBN-10: 0-7869-4001-8
ISBN-13: 978-0-7869-4001-1
620-95532740-001-EN

U.S., CANADA,
ASIA, PACIFIC, & LATIN AMERICA
Wizards of the Coast, Inc.
P.O. Box 707
Renton, WA 98057-0707
+1-800-324-6496

EUROPEAN HEADQUARTERS
Hasbro UK Ltd
Caswell Way
Newport, Gwent NP9 0YH
GREAT BRITAIN
Save this address for your records.

Visit our web site at www.wizards.com

Dedication

For cousin Erik, my collaborator on many an unpublished monster comic.

Acknowledgements

The following good people helped make this book possible:
Susan J. Morris, editor
Brady Dommermuth, *Magic* creative director
Peter Archer, executive editor of Wizards of the Coast Books
Matt Cavotta, *Magic* creative writer
Jeremy Cranford, *Magic* art director
Scott McGough, wise guy
the creators of *Magic: the Gathering* in all its incarnations
and the crew of the *Behemoth* (1977-1979)

Special thanks to the unsinkable S.P. Miskowski,
the unflappable Bayliss, and the unstoppable Remo.

CHAPTER 1

Possession is nine-tenths of the law—we take care of the other tenth. Capobar and Associates specializes in object retrieval. No job too small, too big, or too dangerous. Satisfaction guaranteed. Fee negotiable, consultancy available (100 zinos/day plus expenses). 15017 Funnel Street, Midtown, Center of Ravnica. In-person meeting required. Expenses not negotiable. Everyone is looking for something. Send a falcon to us for an appointment today!

—Long-running classified advertisement,
Ravnican Guildpact-Journal

29 Cizarm 10012 Z.C.

Evern Capobar, master thief, hadn't been out on a job in almost ten years. The last one had taken him into the undercity of Old Rav, where he had almost lost several limbs to Devkarin bandits before getting away with one of their more sacred relics. He hadn't been on a job outside the City of Ravnica for almost three decades. This new job had the potential to be even stranger, and more dangerous, than a journey into the depths of Golgari territory, but Capobar was not worried. All jobs were strange in their own way, even if this one wasn't his usual cup of bumbat. Near as he could tell, he wouldn't so much be stealing something as retrieving it—and long-running classified advertisements aside, stealing was generally the job for which one hired a master thief. "Retrieval" was, of course, a convenient euphemism.

Capobar had people for this sort of thing, assuming you stretched your definition of "people." For this job, his personal attention had been requested, and fortunately the basic skill set for treasure hunter and thief were remarkably similar. Capobar had crossed that line on several occasions.

As the primary stakeholder of one of the most successful independent, fully licensed thieveries in the metropolitan center of the plane, Capobar rarely saw the need for personal risk and even less for passing through the city gates to the world beyond. He was not a coward, or fearful for his life, but he was realistic. He wasn't as nimble as he used to be, and truth be told, he had taken to his office more and more of late. Well into his eighties Capobar had been the best thief in the whole section. Now he had the books to oversee and face-to-face negotiations to lead. Those were the heart of his business as he entered his 101st year. Fortunately he had an excellent eye for talent, so Capobar and Associates was doing as well—if not better—than it had when he took on most jobs alone.

The exceptions were those clients who, for whatever reason, wanted Capobar to do a job personally and were willing to pay extra to ensure that the master oversaw the operation. For the right price, the right client, and the right job, Capobar would occasionally come out of semiretirement to add that personal touch. He still had a few tricks he hadn't taught his employees. More than once he'd even accepted jobs involving said employees, honor among thieves being relative. He would never have told the client, but even if Capobar's personal participation had not been requested he might well have gone ahead and done it anyway. You didn't get to be a master thief without a powerful sense of curiosity, and he was mighty curious about this job. For one thing, his client was a guildmaster. By definition, one of the ten—no, nine, he corrected himself—most powerful and wealthy beings on the entire plane of Ravnica.

For that kind of coin, Capobar would accommodate quite a bit. He would honor the client's odd demands and travel hundreds of miles from his urban stomping grounds to this far-flung reclamation zone.

He stood at this moment inside the ribcage of a creature that provided excellent cover from the still-noisy township and gave Capobar a glimpse of what he could expect inside the ruins. The blackened bones were all that was left of the massive corpse that had crashed and literally burned three weeks ago. Half a mile north, a similar jumble of charred skeletal remains marked the final resting place of the second dragon.

Rare as they were, these skeletons were not his objective. The rotting, corroded bones were useless to his client and therefore useless to him. They'd been set ablaze by the locals, it seemed, to ensure there was no chance either still lived. The black smoke coming from the region for weeks had spread as far as the city, and reports of the Utvarans torching the corpses had been on the front page of the newssheets the next day. For a short time, there were fears that the smoke would bring the dreaded *kuga* plague along with it, but Simic biomages had reassured the public that they detected no trace of the pathogen. The plague had been wiped out, or so it seemed, by a cure some *other* Simic dropped on the population. He'd been glad to hear that, though he kept protective gear and a couple of 'drops on his belt. Just in case.

He contemplated retrieving that gear when the smell began to burn his sinuses but decided to hold off. His partner wouldn't be much longer. Partner on the job, that is, since the shadewalker worked for Capobar. The bones had begun to corrode and filled the air with a metallic tang. Putrid, gelatinized marrow oozed from within. A drop fell from the dead dragon's tenth rib and sizzled as it melted into the stone near his right foot. If he hadn't been on a schedule, he would have found a way to collect some—it certainly would have made a potent poison and a simple, if pungent, way to get through most any lock. But dragon skeletons and acidic marrow were not what he'd been hired to find and retrieve.

What Capobar *had* been hired to retrieve rested in the center of a ring of ruined architecture built over a simmering volcanic caldera. He pulled a black bandanna over his nose and mouth to fight the odor of decaying dragon bones. He could move as soon as his scout returned from—

"The path to the ruin is clear," a disembodied voice whispered over his right shoulder. The sound, as usual, came without warning—not even footsteps marked the shadewalker's passage, one of the reasons he and his kind were paid so well. Another was near-perfect invisibility, which prevented any but the shadewalker himself from knowing exactly what a shadewalker's "kind" really was. Capobar, for all his sources, had never been able to find out whether that invisibility was some kind of ability inherent to the shadewalker's species or if the stealthy operator was simply a human with remarkable skills of deception.

"Well done," Capobar whispered. "No sign of the plague?"

"I would have smelled it," the shadewalker replied. "The air is clear as well." The invisible stalker added, "Clear of plague, at least. There is much death, and the scavengers have not yet taken it all away."

"Perhaps the scavengers are among the dead," Capobar observed.

"If by 'scavengers' you mean Gruul, I would say you are right. They number among the more distant corpses. Many, in the hills."

"You're talkative," Capobar said. "Nervous?"

"Hardly," the voice replied. "May I ask your instructions?"

"Stick with the plan," the thief replied, a little nervous himself. He wasn't a stickler for rank in this informally organized business, but it was peculiar, and a little unnerving, that none of the shadewalkers he employed at quite handsome rates had ever used the slightest of honorifics when speaking to their employer. No "sir," no "boss." Capobar might even have been content with "Mr. Capobar."

The master thief kept three shadewalkers on retainer (as far as he knew—getting a head count was tricky, and he was only *paying* three of them), but had not worked much with them personally. He didn't even know this one's name. It wasn't like he could tell them apart. Shadewalkers lived in a state of natural invisibility. Certain tricks could reveal them—though Capobar pitied anyone who tried to toss powder or paint on one—but no living eye could detect them without magical assistance.

They always took payment in cash. Cash that disappeared, literally, from Capobar's hands. He wondered what they did with it. Presumably they had to eat, but what else did they buy with the zinos?

The shadewalker's heightened senses were only one reason the master thief had brought the invisible agent along. From his vantage point at the edge of the Husk, the glowspheres of Utvara's main thoroughfare still flickered, and the noises of a typical evening's debaucheries continued. A great many of the miners on the flats continued to work through the darkness or hired graveyard shifts of nomadic laborers to do it for them, and there was little cover between Capobar and the remains of the Cauldron.

The flats were the real problem. They were not endless by any means, ringed as they were by the Husk (and beyond that, mile after mile of architecture), but they were huge enough. An open wasteland now, at some time in the distant past it had been a grandiose pavilion, paved with brick and stone. Beneath that stone were layers of ancient, abandoned civilization littered with treasure, or so the fortune-seekers working their scattered islands of prospecting activity testified.

The target was sitting smack in the middle of it. Anyone who cared to glance might spot him at some point, no matter how many precautions he took. Capobar had never trusted invisibility magic, personally—it could be quite dangerous when applied by unskilled hands—which made the shadewalker instrumental.

He had to work under the assumption he would be seen, but Capobar still had to personally retrieve the booty according to the doubly enchanted, thrice-signed, and virtually unbreakable contract. Then the shade would move the actual item back to the office in the City of Ravnica. Just because the client had hired him to personally retrieve it didn't mean he had to transport it all three hundred miles back to the city. Success relied on two factors. Capobar had to reach the target quickly—he had that covered—and any response from the locals had to be slow. They might reach him by the time he was heading back out, but by then the shadewalker would be slipping into the foothills on the way to delivering the financial future of Capobar and Associates. According to his inquiries, new settlers were flocking to the area. A new face wouldn't be overtly surprising. Capobar reasoned he could put off any serious inquiries by simply claiming to be new in town and curious about the ruins.

More dangerous than the miners in the township were the tribal Gruul who laid claim to a ring of crumbling hills that bordered the small region on all sides. The Husk—the ring of corroded hill country surrounding the Utvara township—was their sovereign territory since the battle weeks earlier, from that day and on into perpetuity (though that word, "perpetuity," had many different dimensions and definitions when it came to Orzhov contracts). Capobar had no doubt that at this very moment one or more Gruul scouts watched him even as he watched the township, the flats, and the ruins. Just as he was counting on the local constabulary, such as they were, to respond with midnight lethargy to a lone man walking into the Cauldron, he had done enough research into the area to learn that the Gruul didn't give a wooden zib what you did in the flats. If they cared they would already have been on him. Judging from what the shadewalker had said they weren't in any shape to show an interest even if they wanted to. But if he tried to cut through the Husk on his way out, the trespass alone would mean the end of the venture, even if their numbers were reduced.

He slipped a pair of mana-goggs from his forehead to the bridge of his nose and tapped the refraction crystal several times to get a look at the entire spectrum of magical auras. The old magelord's djinns and elementals, even his goblins, had long since abandoned the place or, perhaps, been driven away by the same townsfolk who had incinerated the dragons's corpses. On the lowest and highest refractions he thought he could make out a haze over the path ahead, perhaps a magical fog, but with so much mana recently burned away here, that was to be expected. The small swath of farmland to the west looked gray under the moonlight but glowed green in his crystallized vision. Elsewhere, other spots of magic appeared on the inner lenses—the reddish shape of a miner in a strength-enhancing liftsuit, the streaking white line of a passing falcon enchanted for speed, and the olive-gray wall surrounding two structures that looked like dorms for zombie labor.

A month ago, Capobar knew little of Utvara. It was just another reclamation zone, one of many such areas all over the world, places where the old, crumbling infrastructure of civilization was flattened and rebuilt anew. It was a process long since perfected, in theory. Then the dragons had come, which had, of course, been big news even in the central city. Two of them had torn out of the still-smoldering ruins that stood a half mile away from him. They'd flown, they'd fought, and they had killed each other. Most blamed the Izzet magelord who had built the collapsed power station and adjoining superstructure, though it was widely reported that some damn fools had tried to *ride* the things.

Capobar's client said that there had been three dragons, and only two had made it out of the caldera. And whether it was simple superstition or a real concern about safety, the ruins of the Cauldron had lain undisturbed for three weeks and change. The townsfolk had no idea of the treasure that lay within or its value. The Orzhov baroness certainly didn't or it wouldn't still be there.

And it was definitely there, suffused with a blazing orange and blue aura, sitting in the ruins. It was so bright he had to tap the goggles again to bring it into focus.

Capobar adjusted his cloak as he stood and stretched his legs, wincing involuntarily at the popping joints. He was dressed in dark, unassuming clothes that didn't scream out "master thief" but didn't draw attention to him either. Capobar tapped the mana-goggs until the refraction field settled on the higher spectrum of magic that had shown the "fog" and left it there.

The thief pulled his hood down tightly over his head, popped his knuckles inside his fingerless gloves, turned over his shoulder, and whispered, "Stay ten paces behind me until I have it. Make the exchange without a word. Wait for me at the office, and don't even think about running out on me." He added the last almost by reflex as he leaned down and pressed his palms against his outer thighs, over the twin swiftfoot magemarks tattooed on his legs. The magical markings were relatively new features on his aging body and had cost him a pretty zib. He whispered the activation words and potent magic rushed into his muscles, bones, and circulatory system all at once. They would not last long, but in twenty-four hours (give or take) he could use them again. Not that he expected the need to arise. In twenty-four hours Capobar intended to be sipping hyzdeberry wine and counting the take from this little adventure.

"The thought occurs that if you did not trust me, you did not need to hire me."

"The thought also occurs that I'm not paying you to think," Capobar said. He shuddered before making a small hop that almost sent him crashing headfirst into the half-arch of a blackened rib.

It always took him a few minutes to get used to the magemarks' effects. "From here, the only real danger is falling rocks and cooling lava. In fact, between you and me, the paycheck on this job makes even less sense now that I see this place. The road is clear, and there are no guards at all." He tapped his foot, which made a sound like a hummingbird and looked a bit like one too. A craving not unlike thirst was settling into his bones thanks to the magical tattoos. Capobar needed to *run*.

"Of course my fee is nonnegotiable," the shadewalker whispered.

"Of course," Capobar snapped. "Your *salary* is the same as always. And," he added before the shade could reply, "the bonus will be waiting back at the office."

In his accelerated state, Capobar saw the fog slowly form sharp edges all around him. A second later the ground rocked and knocked him off of his feet.

It sounded like an enormous footstep, while the impact felt like an underground explosion. Capobar curled and came down ready to spring, expecting to see—well, something. He managed to stay upright when the second "footstep" came, and he realized why there was nothing to see. Whatever was making the footsteps was "walking" (or pounding) on the underside of the ground Capobar stood upon.

It sounded big, and it sounded like it wanted out.

He pushed the mana-goggs back onto his forehead. The magical field was blinding. Whatever was down there was practically sweating mana into the air. Through solid rock. Another crashing thump sounded beneath him, and this time a radial crack in the stone before him appeared.

"Strike what I said. That fee is making more and more sense every second," he muttered, then said a little louder to make sure the shadewalker heard him, "But there's no way I'm going back empty-handed. You still with me?"

"I am uncertain why we are waiting," the shadewalker replied.

"Uncertain why—" Capobar began, but a fourth thump cut him off. The cracked ground took on a vaguely conical shape. "Never mind. This is a distraction. Let's go."

Capobar bolted forward just as the biggest crash yet struck the flats from below. A single accelerated step took him more than twelve paces, and he caught the sole of one foot on a rising slab of stone that erupted ahead of him to form a rapidly elevating ramp. The spring-loaded thief used the stone's momentum to launch himself into the air like an acrobat. He risked a look down as he soared faster than a speeding bamshot over the center of a split in the earth.

In the center of the crack, a single yellow eye with a pupil like a cat's blinked at him once. The alien glare hit Capobar with a palpable wave of malice, like a sucker punch to the soul. The wave made him forget to roll when he landed on the far side of what was rapidly turning into a crater. He regained his footing at a dead run with all of his bones intact only because of the quick reaction time afforded by the magemarks. He didn't look back, nor did he call for the shadewalker. Capobar just ran as fast as he could for the Cauldron. In a corner of his mind, he was already adding an astronomical amount of hazard pay to the day's expenses.

The master thief spun in midrun and ran backward, feet blurring beneath him and wind whistling past his hood. He pulled the mana-goggs back on and cast his eyes about for the shadewalker, tapping the refraction until he spotted the ghostly blue shape of his partner dashing down the path beside him. Reason number one Capobar had plunked down so many zinos for this particular piece of equipment: Invisibility was in the eye of the beholder. The mana-goggs let him keep track of his entire staff, including shadewalkers.

As a side benefit, the mana-goggs also made it slightly easier to gaze at that baleful yellow eye. It had risen from the crater in the road and stared from atop a writhing mass of a long, scaly tentacle. The mottled appendage clutched the eye like it was a rubber ball, and through the focused goggs he could see it was misshapen, not like a true eye at all. Some kind of camouflage? Why would something that large need camouflage?

Not that this creature was his concern as long as it stayed put. The crashing seemed to have stopped, and the eye-that-wasn't-an-eye simply watched him run. The hair on the back of Capobar's neck stood on end, but as long as it only watched, it didn't change the original plan. Whatever the thing was, it hadn't disturbed the Utvara nightlife. It certainly wasn't another dragon, and though it was visible from the township no one there seemed the least bit concerned about it. The carousing continued beneath the glowposts, and the mining equipment continued to delve beneath the surface.

The master thief had known there were monsters in these parts but not that they were quite so big. But if it didn't bother the locals, it didn't bother him either. The thing certainly couldn't catch him if it wanted to, regardless. He could use it for any explanations he might need to give later, however—new in town, monster attack, took shelter in the nearest structure, even if it was a smoldering ruin.

It only took a few minutes for the fleet-footed master thief to reach the edge of the Cauldron. The heat and smoke grew more palpable and made him pull the bandanna back over his face, sweat beading on his forehead. The place might be a ruin, but it was still sitting atop an active geothermic vent. Nothing rose up to threaten him but the temperature.

Good enough.

He took a few slow breaths as the swiftfoot effect started to wear off. The magic was useful but didn't last long. It was with relief that he saw the shadewalker keeping pace.

There had once, it appeared, been two main entrances to the caved-in cone that remained of the Izzet magelord's massive Cauldron project. One of them still provided access to the interior—Capobar could tell from the way the target's magical aura brightened inside the shape of the arched door. With hardly a sound, he scrambled over the rocks and boulders that hid the access point from the rest of the flats and entered the Cauldron proper.

Upon seeing the interior of the ruined structure, he bit back a warning that had been forming on his lips. From the look of it, a loud voice might trigger one of two outcomes, neither desirable. One, the whole place might finish the slow process of caving in. Tangles of metal architecture and broken stone lay everywhere, illuminated by the soft, orange glow of the lava that made the place as hot and humid as a jungle. A huge disk, looking for all the world like a gigantic broken dinner plate, hung suspended on one end by the wreckage. The other edge of the platform rested atop the indisputably crushed remains of a gigantic egg. Strange geometric shapes were still visible on the disk's surface.

To Capobar's surprise, he and the shadewalker were not alone inside the ruin. And to his relief, he had not yet been spotted. The second possible outcome, and the more likely one in his estimation, would be death by monster.

A few taps of the mana-goggs showed that this giant had some kind of magical kinship with the tentacle-eye thing under the road. It was big but nowhere as large as the skeletal dragon—maybe about the size of a pair of good-sized wagons stacked on top of each other—but it might easily have swallowed him whole. Its body was shaped like a beetle's, though it had no carapace or wings. Its skin appeared disturbingly human, pink and fleshy, with a long tail and a flat, toothy face showing no eyes. It stood on four muscular legs that appeared to end in parodies of human hands, and it shifted back and forth on its hand-feet as it dug into what, for it, must have seemed like a feast—a smashed egg twice its size.

Unfortunately, that meant the eyeless thing's head was buried nose-deep in the bright glow of Capobar's target. Fortunately, it was a big target, and he still might avoid detection. The monster looked quite focused on its meal.

The Gruul called creatures like this "nephilim," but it wasn't the name of a species so much as a generic term for large, presumably dangerous, mutations that emerged from time to time from the caves in the Husk. They were as large as a cargo wagon, though the tribes claimed they had once been towering and godlike. Nor were the Gruul the only ones who believed it, though it was their name for the creatures that had stuck. Such monsters had been the stuff of both legends and history on Ravnica for as long as anyone could remember, but only in wilder regions like Utvara did one find them anymore. The Gruul also believed the nephilim to be immortal, but Capobar wasn't the sort to accept such claims. Magic was magic, and magic could do strange things, but magic was a tool first and foremost. Things lived, things died, sometimes they lingered, but nothing lived forever, of that he was fairly certain. No matter how magic they were. Not even the angels were still around. No guarantee that they were dead, but they *had* disappeared. Everyone knew that.

The nephilim shuffled toward Capobar to get a better angle on its food. The thief ducked behind a dromad-sized piece of some bizarre, twisted wreckage that had once been an assortment of polished Izzet contraptions.

If Capobar approached the broken egg from the far side, he could still make it out with the treasure. Summoning all the control he could muster, he willed himself to be perfectly silent.

The thief padded quietly around the nephilim's shuffling bulk without incident.

A smell like rotten eggs washed over him. The nephilim smelled as unpleasant as it looked, but compared to the corroding dragon bones it was almost refreshing. At least the nephilim's distinctive nasal signature wasn't likely to permanently destroy your nostrils and most of your face.

His eyes trained on the monster, Capobar almost stumbled over a goblin corpse. There were a few scattered here and there, workers who had been unable to escape. Curious that the nephilim hadn't touched them. He'd have thought the creature would find the corpses to be bite-sized morsels. Perhaps they were too cooked. A careful, silent leap took him over a bubbling seam in the floor that exposed more cooling lava.

Capobar almost collided with a second nephilim that was doing much the same as the first. Hunks of ruined machinery and the rocky lava dome that was the egg's nest had concealed it. This one was serpentine, with a tubular, coiled body covered in multihued scales and patches of the same pinkish skin he'd seen on the other two. It was impossible to tell exactly how long the creature was, but it sat atop several coils. Its head and upper body were one, and again the creature had a freakish resemblance to at least part of a human being. A pair of humanlike arms with clawed hands picked small pieces of dragon flesh from within the steely eggshell and popped them into a small mouth ringed by silvery teeth set in the navel of a torso-shaped head. In the center of the nephilim's chest-face was a single yellow eye that stared intently at the feast. It reminded the thief in an odd way of the flying snakes the Simic had set loose into the wild for the Decamillennial celebrations. Or a centaur that was all tail and eyeball.

This second feasting creature paid Capobar no more heed than the first. The remains of the egg must have been some good eating, he guessed, at least if you were a freakish mutant amalgamation. He just hoped they'd leave enough to satisfy his client.

He realized his heart was racing and reminded himself who he was. Evern Capobar was the master. *A* master, at least. So there were monsters. Big ones. He'd gotten around a monster or two in his day.

One exposed section of the egg was still clear. All he needed to do was get around this second monster undetected and he would be out of sight of both. He carefully slipped past a writhing tail as big as a tree trunk and over another desiccated goblin body, then risked a look up. The cyclopean snake-thing's claws continued to pick at the morsel. One of them snapped at the first nephilim, which growled. The two creatures were making short work of the stillborn dragon's remains.

Capobar raised a hand to signal the shadewalker. A few seconds later an empty silver cylinder about the length and circumference of his arm appeared in midair and dropped into his open hand. From his own pack, the thief screwed a sharp, hollow needle into the business end of the cylinder then raised it overhead like a soldier preparing to impale an enemy.

Capobar took no chances. Had he been caught before getting into the Cauldron he would have had difficulty explaining the implement.

The entire affair had gone unnoticed by the snacking nephilim. But not everyone had missed it.

"Human," a voice rumbled, and the thief almost dropped the syringe. The voice seemed to be coming from—

No, it was *definitely* coming from within the egg.

Capobar only waited a second before he replied, "Yes?"

"Human," the dragon repeated. Its voice was unnaturally deep, and it shook the master thief's bones. But it was obvious even to Capobar, who had never seen a living dragon in his life, that this one was incredibly weak. The thief doubted its words would carry to the ears of the nephilim, let alone outside the Cauldron ruins. And why shouldn't it be weak? It was being eaten alive.

Capobar had to hand it to the client. The timing was crucial for this particular retrieval, as he understood it, and it seemed to the thief that he had walked in at exactly the right time. Extraction had to take place before death, but preferably *just* before death, according to his instructions. He wondered if his client had known about the nephilim. Perhaps even sent them. Guildmasters—especially this one—could almost certainly manipulate such monstrous, if rather stupid, creatures.

The thief had expected the dragon to be alive. There was no point in being here otherwise. He had never expected the thing to speak to him.

"I am a human," Capobar whispered to the darkness inside the ruined egg. He took a silent step forward and looked deeper into the shell where he could make out the shape of a reptilian snout. A faint, red circle appeared in the shadows.

The eye blinked once, slowly, with the sound of sandpaper rubbing together.

"You hear me," the dragon wheezed. Even as it spoke, Capobar could also hear the two nephilim continuing to tear it apart. He was glad he'd skipped dinner. "You understand."

"Yes," Capobar whispered. "I'm trying to keep those two from knowing it though. Could you keep it down?"

If the dragon heard him, it didn't acknowledge the fact. "You will kill me," it said. Though truer words, Capobar reflected, had rarely been spoken in his presence, it did not sound like a prediction. The words were a command. A command painted with a hefty coat of plea.

"You want to die?" Capobar asked.

"You will kill me," the dragon repeated. It didn't falter even when the snake-thing ripped away one of its ribs.

"I will," Capobar said. He raised the syringe. "This is going to hur—"

His mouth froze in place as the red eye focused on him with a hint of blazing irritation, even at the end of life. The scrutiny was palpable. Evern Capobar loosened his collar absently.

"However you do it," the dragon wheezed, "do it. No time to waste."

"Could you lift—?" Capobar began and grimaced. "I'm sorry, but I'm helping you here, so maybe you could help me. This would be a lot easier if you could, maybe, stretch out your neck? Poke your head out a little bit?"

A gravelly, repetitive wheeze came from inside the crushed egg. The dragon was laughing. "You are small. You cannot see. I am trapped. My spine, crushed or gone. My flesh is being stripped. Consumed. My head is going nowhere, morsel."

No, I can definitely see that, Capobar thought. He tried to ignore that he'd just been called a "morsel." To the dragon, he whispered, "Then I guess I don't need to ask you to hold still." He tucked the huge syringe under one arm. With careful steps, he moved over the pieces of jagged eggshell and a fortune in dried dragon blood until he could see the massive disk resting just overhead. The red eye was right in front of his face.

"Why do you wait?" the dragon wheezed.

"Just need to make sure I hit the right spot—the gland is right . . . *there*," Capobar said as he raised the needle and drove it home just above the enormous glowing orb. He braced a foot against a stirrup bolted onto the side of the cylinder and pulled with all his might. After a few moments that threatened to throw his back out permanently, a pane of glass showed him that the syringe was filled with a thick grayish-red substance that pushed the definition of "liquid." A few seconds later he saw that the plunger had retracted as far as it was going to retract.

The needle slid free without a sound. Capobar unscrewed it and returned it to his pack. He slammed a cork stopper into the improvised canister and tucked it under his arm again—with the stopper extended it was the only way to carry the precious cargo.

"Thank you," the dragon said, and died.

* * * * *

The shadewalker had already left to meet Capobar at the edge of the ruins. He thought he heard the sounds of dromad hooves from the direction of the township. Sure enough, someone was coming to check him out. The enormous eye was nowhere to see or be seen.

"Now?" the shadewalker whispered over his shoulder when he arrived.

"Yes," Capobar said and held out the container that held the precious substance. An invisible hand took it from him, and the portable payday disappeared. "I'll see you back at the office," he added. Reiteration never hurt. "Plan on going with me to the client. I could use a little insurance."

"This is true," the voice said.

Then Capobar felt something like ice press against his chest. A tiny pinprick of cold just over his heart made him pull back with a start, and he felt himself caught by another pair of strong, invisible arms before he went over backward.

He knew he should never have hired shadewalkers. They were entirely too . . . shady.

* * * * *

The nephilim fed for hours. The two that Capobar had evaded became three. Three became four. When the fifth nephilim arrived, there was no longer enough room in the Cauldron to hold them.

Their bodies would not stop growing, so their hunger would not subside.

Each one was unique. One looked like living rock, a hunk of hillside on three crustaceanlike legs. The head of an ancient statue hovered over its center of gravity, a peculiar effect born of this nephilim's own magical nature and a recently ended four-century nap during which it had played the part of actual hillside a bit too well. Another resembled a six-legged cross between a salamander and a bloated fish: all arms, legs, and gullet. The bulbous throat of the beast writhed with what looked like a thousand tiny imitations of itself, some of which wriggled free of the thing's mouth and hopped into the streets, attacking fleeing Utvaran townsfolk. Finally, the burrower moved in, the thing that had ripped its way through the ground at the edge of the Husk and almost ended the master thief's latest exploit ahead of schedule. When fully exposed, it resembled a cross between an octopus, a jellyfish, and a freakish tree on tentacles. Smaller appendages supported eyestalks like the one that had watched Capobar flee. The creature ripped away bits of meat with barbed hooks lining its writhing arms and stuffed the flesh between light-sensitive eye sacs, there to be digested directly by an organ that had no known analog on the plane of Ravnica, a combination stomach and brain. It could see in every direction, and in seven dimensions.

At first, there was plenty of food for all concerned, and so all were content. Then things changed.

The four-legged one that looked like a walking mouth and tail was the first to realize that its body was pressing against the inside of the ruins. A few minutes later what remained of the Cauldron walls cracked and split. With a bold snap of its jaws, the tube-tail tore loose the last substantial hunk of dragon flesh and gulped it down whole. It roared into the night sky. The others followed suit with their own terrible cries, and the ground shook as the giant things circled each other, looking for advantages over the corpse. They were hungry, painfully hungry, and each one was both predator and potential prey.

Their bodies grew at an alarming rate, growing even larger as they moved from dragon flesh to dine on freshly caught Utvaran miner on the moonlit flats. The bigger the predator, the bigger the territory, the Gruul said, and the disappearing remains of the crushed dragon were gone. The nephilim would have to expand their territory outward, and they all seemed to realize it at once.

As their gargantuan bodies expanded and mutated, they looked about for something to eat or fight, preferably both. They clashed with each other in brief collisions that shook the ground like thunder, a counter to the terrible shrieks and roars that filled the early morning light. Others turned to the relatively tiny townsfolk and their puny homes, business, and outposts.

Within hours, the whole of Utvara was roiling with panic and chaos. Anything that could burn was burning amid fires that had erupted when the nephilim smashed the old Yorboff forge. The nephilim's footsteps and roars triggered landslides in the Husk that sent the Utvar Gruul bolting for cover as their wood-and-leather structures toppled. The nephilim snapped them up and devoured them whole, occasionally stopping to fight over the livestock that scattered across the foothills, fleeing the giants. Townsfolk bolted in every direction, driven by a wave of palpable terror that knocked the few vedalken in Utvara to the ground in pain.

In the less and less intact township square, a serpent sat coiled on its tail, its head and neck swaying easily to a rhythm only it could hear. It watched the nephilim turn toward the city and the tiny, shrieking things that infested it. The serpent knew all about infestations. Had any of the screaming people been paying attention, they would have noticed the serpent's head take on a peculiarly human shape, with the face of a small girl. The face smiled, melted into a writhing mass of bluish worms for the briefest of moments, and became reptilian again. Satisfied, the serpent slithered into the crowd to gather a complete report for its master.

* * * * *

The one person who might have been able to prevent the disaster in Utvara arrived hours too late to help. The goblin rocketed through the sky over the reclamation zone, clearing the cloud cover without the typical sonic boom that accompanied normal observosphere flight protocol. The goblin pilots assigned to observation duty by the Izzet magelords usually reveled in the sound, which more often than not was a precursor to an especially spectacular death.

This goblin had seen enough explosions recently, which made the sight of Utvara's ongoing ruin that much harder to take. The bubbling scar that stood where the Cauldron had so recently fed power and water into the small boomtown was especially jarring, she admitted to herself.

She was returning from a visit with the guildmaster, the dragon Niv-Mizzet. The dragon had appointed her head of the Cauldron, shattered as it was, but the goblin had plans she was certain would prove successful. Now her best chance for her own colloquy was gone, and a newly adopted home crumbled beneath the feet and tentacles of creatures that the goblin knew very well. Until a few weeks ago, she had been an Izzet courier and spent a great deal of time with the tribal Gruul who inhabited the Husk. She'd almost been killed by the nephilim.

They'd been smaller then.

The observosphere pilot tapped the smooth, faintly glowing, translucent white stones set into the flight panel, and the icy-crystal hummed to life. The shimmering, mirrorlike surface of the viewing pane materialized in thin air above the crystal and almost immediately reflected the features of a bald human woman in her early hundreds. She wore a tattoo in the shape of the Izzet guild sigil on her forehead, and her neutral face hardened into a stern scowl when she saw who was calling.

"This is—" the goblin gulped nervously. Her title was still more than a little grandiose for her mouth. The new, dragon-given syllables of her name felt stranger still. "This is Master Engineer Crixizix," the goblin said. "I hereby request the assistance of the Emergency Containment Corps. There is a disaster in progress in the Utvara reclamation zone that poses a much wider threat."

"Where is your magelord, goblin?" the woman said. "You are not authorized to use this ley frequency for frivolous—"

"This is not frivolous," Crixizix said as calmly as she could. "This is quite serious. And perhaps you did not hear me clearly. This is *Master* Engineer Crixizix. You will immediately send a containment team to the Utvara reclamation zone. Do you understand?"

Crixizix forced herself away from an impolitic but self-satisfied smirk when the emergency dispatcher's face displayed the clear fact that she had finally seen the sigil of the Firemind that, from her perspective, glowed clearly beneath Crixizix's chin.

"Yes," the dispatcher said. "Right away. How large a team will you need?"

The goblin took another look out of the observosphere's cockpit and belatedly activated a half-dozen small recording globes before she replied. "Large," she said, "And tell them to bring out the big bam-sticks. These things could, forgive my impertinence, give the Great Dragon a run for his zinos."

"How can you be certain that this is an Izzet-caused incident?" the dispatcher said. "This sounds like something you want to refer to the Simic authorities. Giant monsters are their—"

"It's plain as the tattoo on your forehead, madam," Crixizix said. "They consumed the remains of Zomaj Hauc's project. The results are what was always speculated but never attempted, due to concerns about heresies." Which was a polite way of saying that the first and last magelord to suggest to Niv-Mizzet that the dragon sacrifice so much as a scale from his crimson hide to feed to anyone or anything was reduced to ash and bone.

"Mobilization and deployment will take a few hours," the dispatcher said.

"A few *hours*?" the goblin said. "This is an emergency!"

"Then I suggest, Master Engineer," the woman replied, "that you do the best you can until we arrive." The floating mirror shimmered and disappeared.

"My best," Crixizix muttered, applying a braking angle to the flame-pods ringing the 'sphere's equator to keep from overshooting Utvara. What could she do? In truth, she was barely even an engineer, master or otherwise. The title was something she would be growing into. And an engineer wasn't a battalion of angels or even a Gruul horde, either of which looked to be necessary to mop up the mess the nephilim were making of Utvara. The reclamation zone was going to need reclaiming.

The Firemind had touched her when the Great Dragon gave her a title within the guild. Once given, that touch never left. Even at this distance, Crixizix could feel the Firemind. If she concentrated, the goblin could hear the low rumbling echoes of the Great Dragon's thoughts in a deep, dreamless slumber. She had heard the life churchers call the Firemind a form of fellowship like their own "song." Crixizix didn't know if that was true, but she did know that it was nothing like a song when you gave yourself over to the dragon's power. It was direct, baleful contact with an intellect and will that made even the mightiest magelord, let alone a newly entitled master engineer, feel small and obsequious.

Yet the link had been granted to the goblin for a reason. Technically she did have the right to call for his help. The dragon did not have to give it, but certainly a personal interest could bring him.

"There aren't any bigger bam-sticks than him," the goblin said out loud. She set the observosphere's automatic navigation aura for a course that should set her down on the most intact and unthreatened part of the remaining thoroughfare, then closed her eyes, seeking contact with that sleeping consciousness and hoping to Krokt that Niv-Mizzet didn't wake up too grumpy to listen to the details.

CHAPTER 2

Volunteers shall be given the full rights and responsibilities of commissioned wojeks while on duty. Academy training shall not be required for qualified volunteers who have five or more years experience in the approved organizations named in Subsection A.
　　　　—Wojek-Ledev Joint Operations Agreement, Section 2

No owl-folk need apply.
　　　　—Sign in the window of the Wojek Recruiting Office

30 Cizarm 10012 Z.C.

On the shadier, more run-down end of Tin Street—the largest marketway in the densely populated Tenth District that cut a ragged pie wedge from the central metropolis of Ravnica—a small pet shop had closed early for the day. The patrolling wojeks who arrived at the scene immediately saw that Zuza's Exotic Bestiary would not be opening again any time soon, unless it was under new management.

One of the wojeks had decades of experience on the streets of the city, while the other had more familiarity with the laws of Ravnica's open roads. Yet it was the older veteran who lost his composure, and a few ounces of his breakfast, when the two stepped through the door. Fortunately for the preservation of the possible crime scene—Zuza was well established with the Orzhov Guild, making this potential murder a punishable violation of commerce laws—the lieutenant had the presence of mind to vomit outside on the rainy street.

"They're *eating* her," Lieutenant Pijha said after he'd composed himself. His leathery face creased into a frown of distaste tinged with horror, and he pulled off his helmet to wipe sweat from his wrinkled brow.

"I can see that," his partner replied. "The question is, why?"

Nikos Pijha, a barrel-shaped bull of a man in a slightly older cut of wojek armor that no longer quite fit him, arched an eyebrow at the slim, youngish half-elf at his side. She wore both the Boros crest and the cloak pin of the Selesnya Conclave over a gleaming new wojek breastplate bearing a still-shiny ten-pointed star. A green cape contrasted with the red hanging from Pijha's shoulders, and she wore her golden hair tied in a simple tail that emerged from beneath a helmet that was not wojek regulation—it was the lightweight protective headgear of the Selesnyan ledev guard. The lieutenant's partner held the rank of auxiliary patrol officer, an "apo" from a division of the League of Wojek that had been formed after the Decamillennial from volunteers. Apos came mostly from the ledev and Azorius bailiffs, and career wojeks called them "half-timers," at least behind the backs of the apos. Truthfully, the half-elf mused, they probably said much worse.

The wojeks had lost a lot of good people at the Decamillennial, but the members of the League had no time to collectively grieve the losses—Ravnica needed them more than ever after that disaster. Still, veterans looked upon the apos with some resentment. Pijha was one of the welcome exceptions to that rule.

His apo partner's name was Fonn Zunich, and she didn't like the way 'jek-reg helmets affected her hearing. She'd had decades to train her softly pointed half-elf's ears to alert her to almost any danger.

Then again, all she heard at the moment was chewing and whistling. The chewing came from dozens of rats gnawing away at the dead pet-shop proprietor and the whistling from the veteran forensic labmage—a necrotician named Helligan—who used a sharp, pointed scoopknife to take samples from the corpse. He nodded at their approach and returned to delicately removing something half-eaten from the chest cavity of the dead woman.

"Field necrotopsy?" Pijha asked the labmage.

"It seemed more efficient than waiting for the exterminator to clear all of these fellows out," Helligan said with the grin of one who had long ago lost any sense of gravity around corpses, no matter what shape they were in. "They work fast." Fonn would not have been surprised to see him snacking on a bag of grubcrisps while he worked.

Fonn suppressed an instinctive shudder at the "fellows" Helligan was talking about. "What's so exotic about rats?" she asked no one in particular. "Sure, these ones are pretty big, but I've seen bigger in Old Rav."

"Lots of things," Pijha said. "Smart, rats are. And they have a highly organized society, it's said by some. My great-uncle Pollondo was an exterminator. Said he once found an entire rat city down in Old Rav. Turns out they'd organized a sort of giant hunting pack—are a lot of rats a pack? A mob, or a flock, or whatever—anyway, they were feeding on the zom— on the undead down there, you know, the slow ones. The shambling types. But thing is, it hadn't killed them. Everyone knows that anything that eats undead dies."

"Necrotic flesh is almost universally poisonous," Helligan agreed absently without looking up.

"But these rats of Uncle Poll's, they found a way to—"

"I believe you, sir," Fonn said. "That's not my point though. What I mean is, I don't see any *other* animals. Not everybody has an exterminator in the family. This place is called Zuza's Exotic *Bestiary,* right? It's not a . . . a rodentorium."

"Good point," Pijha said after some consideration. "That doesn't make much sense. If it was a diner, maybe I could see it. Lots of places serve rat."

"Really," Fonn said, feeling her own insides grow queasy. Blood was one thing, but . . .

"Rats make good eating too. So my uncle always said," Pijha continued. He shrugged. "How about this? She did sell rats but not exclusively. But then the rats, see, they ate the other pets. Then," he said, jerking his thumb at the presumed body of Zuza herself, "they caught her napping."

"Maybe. She must have been sleeping pretty hard if she didn't notice them biting her. But look around the place," Fonn said, adding another "sir" as an afterthought. She may have been a centuriad of the Ledev Guard in her "normal" life, but here her rank was well below the 'jek's. She was free to speak her mind, but some formality was required. "There are dozens of rats here and dozens of cages. All of them open. But the front door is unlocked. There was no reason for her to get cornered by them. She could have outrun rats."

"I still like my explanation," Pijha said good-naturedly, his nausea long since over. He was a bit thickheaded at times, but he was not a vindictive or particularly argumentative officer. Fonn got along with him well enough that they worked together often, though the half-elf only served in the League a few months out of the year. She suspected that most, if not all, of the time Pijha's slow intellect was an act anyway. Nothing lulled witnesses into revealing too much like a "dim" law officer. In the few years she'd served as an apo—first serving one week a month, then longer as the work grew on her—she'd met few like him in the League. Most were veteran street 'jeks. The generally younger, newly promoted officers making up the wojek brass tended to think more combatively, more militaristically, which was understandable after the losses they had suffered more than a decade earlier. Most any wojek who had joined the league in the last ten years—aside from apos, most of whom arrived with an understanding of different methods—thought little of roughing up suspected violators or even witnesses with extreme prejudice.

Still, Fonn suspected that this time the lieutenant was wide of the mark. The place didn't smell right. The only animal scent in the air was indeed rat. Thick, oily rat. The only blood in the room, her nose told her, was human.

"Where's the blood then?" Fonn said.

"There," Pijha said, pointing, "and there. All around her, really. Looks like the rats are helping themselves to that too. It's enough to make me reconsider lunch."

"But only around her," Fonn replied, circling the body and gingerly stepping over the scuttling rodents. A few snapped at her boots but were otherwise intent on fighting their kin for what was left of their meal.

"Watch your step, please," labmage Helligan said. "I'm still working here."

"Did you contact someone about collecting the rats?" Pijha asked the labmage, who was kneeling over the corpse of the pet-shop owner. "They can't all be exterminated. We'll need a few for evidence."

"Yes," Helligan said, focused on a wound that several rodents were intently making larger by the second. "And I told them there's no rush. This is fascinating, don't you think?"

"Fascinating or not, we need to collect a few, I'd think," Fonn said. "If they're responsible—"

"You wish to bring them to justice?" Helligan asked. "If anything, this was accidental. I'm sure I'll find she died of natural causes." He had apparently completed one of his delicate incisions and was taking a more active interest in the wojeks' conversation.

"She barely looks seventy," Pijha said.

"Indeed," Helligan agreed. "But I don't think they're going anywhere. What's left of her is. I need to collect enough to determine what killed her."

"The rats didn't kill her, Doctor?" Fonn prodded.

"Indeed not. Even if my initial necrotic observations didn't tell me that, all of this blood would have. See?" He poked it with the surgical tool, and the blood in the pool jiggled. "It's semicoagulated, but you can still see a faint impression of shape. This blood started to congeal while it was still inside her. Our friends here are the ones that let it out, but this blood—and this woman—were dead before that happened."

"So much for my theory," Pijha said. " 'Necrotic observations?' Like what?"

As if in reply, a shriek rang in the late-evening air, from the sound of it only a few alleys away. "That, for starters," Helligan said. "Woundseeker. I waited for it to leave before I began to work. Standard safety protocol, labmages aren't issued grounders. She didn't seem to want to hang around."

"I can't imagine she found the view appealing," Fonn said. "So the rats didn't kill her, but she *was* killed."

The labmage picked up one of the rats, and Fonn steeled herself for another natural-history lesson she hardly needed. Helligan fancied himself more than a simple labmage and rarely wasted a chance to demonstrate the breadth of his extracurricular studies.

"Your partner is correct, Officer Fonn. They are fascinating creatures," the labmage began. "No fear of us whatsoever. They easily outnumber every other form of life in the world, you know. Perhaps not if you include the undead, but then the definition of 'life' is such a—but I digress. My point is that I would hesitate to put anything out of the reach of their rodent brains, or their efficient little bodies." As if to emphasize Helligan's point, one of the feasting rodents chattered at him as he poked a small, hooked tool into an open wound on the woman's neck.

Fonn grimaced. She knew that joining the 'jeks would not always be simple. Today, it was outright disgusting.

In the wake of the Decamillennial, the League of Wojek had found its ranks decimated. Between the corrupted Selesnyan quietmen and their mad attack on every wojek fort in the city, and the disturbingly widespread lurker infiltration (still not a widely known fact outside the League), hundreds of wojek officers had been killed. Before the reckoning of wojek losses was even complete many more had left the service for higher-paying jobs in security. And some, like Fonn Zunich's troubled friend Agrus Kos, simply quit. This created a void that needed filling, and the League turned to similar organizations with other guilds that could help. Fonn's father had been a wojek, and she was one of the first ledev to volunteer for the auxiliary ranks. She took to the work easily. It was in her blood, perhaps even more than the open road.

Her blood and all of her instincts told her this was not as simple as it looked, but she could not tell exactly *why* it wasn't so simple. Pijha might be right.

"Not long ago," Pijha said, "this wouldn't even be worth our time. You know that, right? A simple murder like this, I mean. We might really be stretching the definition of guild commerce here. There was no sigil over the door."

"No, but look, she's got the collar pin of the Karlov family. She's connected, all right. And her customers might have been—" Fonn began. "Wait. Her customers. We need to check her sales records. The last person to buy something will be a possible suspect, or at the very least a witness."

"Rats ate that," Helligan said. "I think there are a few shreds over there in the corner where they're building a nest."

"Okay," Fonn ventured. "Then we can make an educated guess. No other animals here, so let's say we can assume she only sold rats. Rats are holy in many cultures. And the Rakdos Guild favors rats as pets, right?"

"Officers?" Helligan said.

"And maybe—maybe the Rakdos didn't like her prices," Pijha said. "They roughed her up a bit, but they're thrill-killers and couldn't resist. Except there's only one problem."

"Yeah," Fonn nodded with a grimace, "she still has blood left."

"Rakdos would have drunk it or smeared it all over the walls. They're not exactly known for restraint," Pijha said, rolling now. "So it wasn't Rakdos. Who else would—"

Helligan coughed and repeated more loudly, "Officers? Lieutenant?"

"What have you found?" Pijha said.

"Oh, nothing yet. I'll have to run tests first on these samples," the labmage said. "But there is a simple way to determine whether any of these rats consumed anything other than this woman, if that is something you wish to determine immediately. I think there are enough to spare for the alchemical sciences, since we'll be collecting extra." Helligan's empty hand shot out lightning quick and snapped up a fat, squealing rat by the tail. In the other hand he raised the surgical tool, currently configured as a razor scalpel.

"No, Doctor, that's really not—" Fonn said and finished with an involuntary "Ew."

Several seconds and several more sounds the half-elf apo would not soon forget later, the labmage shook his head. Surprise registered on his face, tempered with scientific curiosity. He tossed the rat corpse aside and took up another, then did the same with the new rat corpse, and another.

"Well, I'll be a dromad's mother," he said. "I admit it was a small and not particularly scientific sample, but all I'm finding are several semidigested chunks of Mrs. Zuza Uldossa, proprietor." He shook his head. "I'll have to try a few more to be sure, of course. But if they ate the birds, this one didn't get any."

"Birds?" Fonn said. She had picked up a faint avian scent in the air but had attributed it to the pigeons that lined the eaves of the roof outside, as they did almost everywhere in the city.

Helligan waved his bloody scalpel in a circle around his head. "Birdcages, if I don't miss my guess. And I found this." He produced a golden feather curiously free of blood.

"Where did you find that?" Fonn asked.

"In the dustpan," Helligan said, pointing to the corner where the dustpan in question rested on the floor next to an upright straw broom. "Aside from the obvious, this place is quite tidy. She must have swept up recently."

Pijha took the feather from the labmage and held it up to the light. He shook his head, shrugged, and handed it to Fonn, who did the same. "It's not pigeon," she said after a few seconds.

"It's not?" Pijha said.

"No," Fonn said. She gave the feather an experimental sniff, and her nose confirmed what her eyes told her. "This is a tail feather from a bird of paradise."

"Those are exceedingly rare," Helligan said. "I'd say it qualifies as 'exotic.' "

"It certainly does," Fonn agreed, and Pijha nodded.

"I'll send a falcon for a few extra hands," Helligan said. "We may need to collect more of these little fellows than I thought. If they ate a bird of paradise—"

"This investigation is going to expand too," Pijha said with a sigh. He was dedicated, but Fonn knew he also preferred his cases simple, like most career 'jeks, or at the very least free of interference from the brass. But the death of such a valuable creature would elevate the level of the crime, and the higher-ups would almost certainly take an interest once the assurors and other interested parties came to them demanding to know what was being done to protect the good, wealthy citizens of Ravnica.

Outside, a chorus of ringing bells interrupted Fonn's train of thought. She counted the tolls and grimaced.

"Lieutenant, I'm sorry," she said, "but I'm going to have to let you take it from here. I have a prior commitment."

Pijha's frown curved back into his usual amiable grin. "I remember. You mentioned it yesterday, and the week before, and the week before that. Say 'hello' to the kids for me. Helligan and I can hold down this fort until you get back. And if we figure this out before then, the first round will be on you."

"I don't doubt you will," Fonn said. "I'll see you in a few days."

* * * * *

Myczil Savod Zunich held his breath as his quarry shuffled past the makeshift hunting blind. He was eleven years old, but this was not his first venture into the wilds that fringed the underground metropolis of Old Rav. His father had made sure the boy could load a crossbow by the time he could walk. He had made his first kill at the age of five, a serpent-wurm hatchling that had fallen into a trap the precocious child had concocted himself and built with his father's help.

Jarad, the Devkarin guildmaster of the Golgari and the de facto lord of the undercity, was similarly silent, crouched beside his son with an ornately carved Devkarin spear gripped loosely in one hand. This was the first time he had taken the boy on a hunt for two-legged prey. Their quarry was a small gang of rebellious zombie deadwalkers who had taken to raiding the less-traveled roads into and out of Old Rav, where neither the ledev nor the wojeks bothered to keep order. Jarad preferred it that way. Keeping his own form of order in the undercity was a point of pride for the Golgari under his leadership. And whenever he could attend to security personally, he gladly did so.

Technically, these deadwalkers were Golgari, but they had

given up any rights to the name when they'd defied Jarad's edict that outlawed such activity.

The guildmaster did not know if his son would choose to follow in his footsteps or those of his mother. Perhaps the boy would choose neither path and find his own way, which was his right. But Jarad was a father as well as a guildmaster and naturally preferred to have his progeny carry on for him when his own time ended, as it inevitably would. So far, young Myc had always done him proud. The boy had matured rapidly, like those with elf blood did, and had already proven himself against beasts. Now he would be tested against more canny prey. Myc had formed his own plan for this hunt, and Jarad had approved, impressed. The boy had come up with a simple but quite effective plan, even if it wasn't as lethal as the one the guildmaster would have conceived.

Jarad blamed Myc's mother for that.

Seven, eight . . . in all, thirteen pairs of gray, skeletal feet shuffled past. The deadwalkers were still several paces away from springing the trap when Jarad heard Myc gasp, a sound that abruptly stopped short when the last zombie froze in its tracks. The Devkarin saw what had made his son gasp a moment later and scowled.

His ex-wife rounded the corner and rode boldly down the little used road at a trot, the hooves of her great dromad clopping on the moss-covered stones. The deadwalkers immediately turned to face her, well short of the pit that would have cast them all into a huge net and captured them easily in one fell swoop. As soon as she saw them, the dromad rider pulled the reins and stopped her mount short.

"Hello," the half-elf said, the silver crest of her ledev helm glinting in the blue light of the only glowsphere for half a mile in either direction. "I trust there will be no trouble. I am bound for Old Rav."

The thirteenth zombie, in the lead position as the pack reversed direction, shuffled ominously toward the dromad rider and hissed a simple reply. "No, yoush are nosht," the deadwalker managed through its toothless mouth.

Jarad felt a jab in his ribs and saw Myc looking up at him anxiously. He mouthed the words, *What now?*

The dromad rider dismounted easily and stepped between the animal and the deadwalkers, drawing a silver long sword as she did so. "Yes," she said calmly, "I am."

For the briefest of moments, Jarad remembered why he had pursued Fonn Zunich's heart, and felt a tinge of regret that things had turned so sour between them.

Courage or not, she was still outnumbered. Jarad turned to Myc and mouthed, *on three.* Myc nodded. When the entire gang had shuffled by and closed on Fonn, who remained as calm as ever despite a nervous whinny from her dromad, the Devkarin counted down silently. One. Two.

Myc tensed and nodded.

Three.

Father and son sprang from the blind simultaneously behind the zombies. The two rearmost deadwalkers whirled slowly on them. Devkarin steel cut down each one in turn.

"Good to see you both," Fonn said, breaking the zombies' stunned silence. "Friends of yours?"

"Hi, Mom," Myc said.

"Not friends," Jarad smirked. "Prey."

The deadwalkers were smart enough to understand the words— and the fact that their numbers had been quickly reduced from thirteen to eleven. On either side, slick, stone walls blocked their way, and in both directions drawn blades obviously wielded with some skill blocked the underground road.

The deadwalkers would react to this one of two ways, in Jarad's experience: They would turn on each other, or they would fight.

As one, the deadwalkers chose option two. Four charged toward Fonn, who beheaded one before blocking a series of ragged, uncoordinated strikes from the other zombies' rusty, makeshift weapons.

That was all Jarad saw of her before the remaining seven went after guildmaster and son. The Devkarin took the forearms off of the nearest with an upward swipe of his kindjal, and removed the top of the zombie's skull on the downward strike. Myc's smaller stature allowed him a different angle of attack, and the boy drove his own sword through the leg of a hissing deadwalker who was just within reach. The zombie toppled to one side, but two more took its place, forcing Myc to backpedal to his father's side.

A lucky strike from one of the deadwalkers knocked Fonn's blade free from her grip, and she backed into the dromad, which started to shuffle backward itself.

"Mom!" Myc cried and threw a look over one shoulder. "We've got to help her!"

"I'll be fine!" Fonn said. "Don't do anything—"

Myc was already moving, however, and Fonn's protest fell on deaf ears. It was all Jarad could do to keep up with the agile boy as he ducked around and under the deadwalkers, making his way to his mother's side as the swipes and snarls of the zombies followed.

The distraction was enough for Jarad to take out another pair of deadwalkers and incapacitate a third with a backward kick that shattered both of the zombie's kneecaps. Jarad followed that with a boot heel that crushed the thing's skull.

By the time Jarad returned his attention to Myc and Fonn, the other four lay in pieces on the road, twitching as their necrotic energy dissipated into the ground.

"Did you—?" Jarad said to Fonn, who shook her head.

"They were messing with my mom," Myc said. "Sorry, Dad. We'll have to capture them next time. Couldn't be helped."

Jarad had to suppress a grin that he knew would have brought grief from his ex-wife, which he preferred to avoid when in their son's presence.

Fonn, for whatever reason, wasn't so inclined at the moment. "So this is how you take care of my son?" Fonn said with sudden anger. "A zombie hunt?"

"It was my idea, Mom," Myc said. "I've been learning a lot, but I've always got more to learn, like you always say. And I thought—"

"Never mind," Fonn said with a sigh. She arched an eyebrow at Jarad. "We can talk about this later. Right now we've got a journey ahead of us. You're ready, Myc? Do you need to pick anything up from—"

"No," Myc said, but he looked questioningly at his father. "I'm ready to go?"

"You did well. Take pride in this hunt," Jarad said. "The ability to improvise is at least as important as the ability to plan—nothing can be completely foreseen."

"Yes, Dad," Myc said. The Devkarin instinctively concealed the unseemly disappointment he felt when he saw how easily the boy changed his focus to his ledev studies. Intellectually he knew that his son would ultimately be a better man for the scope of his training. The disappointment was more visceral. Jarad buried it as he always did. There was little point in dwelling on it.

"Fonn, it is good to see you," Jarad said formally.

"Right," Fonn said.

The Devkarin shrugged and pulled a white hunting mask, his symbol of office, over his face. "I will see you soon. I must summon hunters to clean up this mess." He placed a hand on Myc's shoulder then looked at Fonn and said, "You did very well today."

"Thank you," Fonn said with surprising sincerity. Then she turned from him. "Myc, the other scouts will be waiting."

"I know, I know," Myc said and gave his father a quick hug. "I'll see you soon too, Dad."

"Come on," Fonn said. "You can ride the dromad."

"I think I need to stretch my legs," Myc said. "You go ahead."

Jarad watched them go with a fading smile and returned Myc's final wave. He turned his mind to the immediate, messy task before him and the infinitely messier tasks waiting for him when he returned his full attention to running the guild. Usually, that would have been more than enough to keep his mind occupied until the next time he saw his son and actually got to enjoy himself in some small semblance of his old life, hunting and exploring the wilds.

This time, a nagging uncertainty refused to release its grip on his thoughts. Some Devkarin elves had the gift of prophecy, but Jarad had never been one of them. Yet he could not shake the feeling that the two people on all of Ravnica he truly cared about were headed into deep trouble.

CHAPTER 3

Don't say I have the face of an angel,
'Cause it's such an easy thing to do.
I would never want the face of an angel,
Not after seein' what an angel goes through.

       —*Face of an Angel,* by Shonya Bayle,
         the Balladrix of Tin Street

30 CIZARM 10012 Z.C.

Teysa Karlov shivered. She wished she had thought to wear
a heavier cloak over her ceremonial advokist's robes to this first
interview. The entire complex was still chilly from the night and
an unseasonable cold snap. The sun was only just peeking over
the towers outside when Teysa had stepped inside the Azorius
demesnes, and Prahv, the seat of law in the center of Ravnica,
was always a little chilly throughout its vaulted halls. The Azorius
employed a lot of vedalken, and they liked low temperatures—they
claimed the chill helped preserve their "superior intelligence."
Regardless of the reason, Teysa had already grown used to the
warm, desertlike conditions in her new barony. The young woman,
a scion of one of the three most powerful ruling families in the
Guild of Deals, ruled the reclamation zone of Utvara as baroness
(and soon as duly elected mayor, all the right gears having been
sufficiently oiled). She was also a fully licensed Orzhov advokist,
a lawmage of great acclaim, and she had returned to the city of
Ravnica to take on a new client she could hardly refuse.

Cases like this didn't come along every day, and she felt things
were well in hand back in Utvara. Zomaj Hauc was dead and gone,
and the Schism in the sky over her barony had faded to a barely

40

discernible distortion. There were mysteries yet to be unraveled about it, but one such mystery was intimately linked to this case.

The baroness brought her shivering under control with a silent, willful message to her Orzhov blood. It was not literal communication, but she found the blood responded better when she formed her will into words. Within seconds, the shaking subsided and her composure returned, though the room grew even colder when the guard shut the cell door.

Whatever the physical cause, the shiver left behind an odd feeling of uncertainty, unease, as it departed. She resolved to get in touch with her surrogates back home—odd that she was already thinking of the place as home, but the word had arisen in her mind automatically—as soon as she was out of here. The blood had been known to warn of impending danger, and for one of the ruling family unease could be a sign of much worse to come.

Teysa's cane, one of the prices exacted on her body by the blood, almost slipped on the floor. Not just chilly, *damp* and chilly. The parts of Prahv the public saw would never have allowed molds and other . . . things to grow wild, but in the holding cells janitorial duties were a fairly low priority, it seemed. It hadn't always been that way. She'd been in several such interview cells, and at one time they had shined. The Azorius were slipping. The Senate was filled with more and more sycophants and opportunists these days, seemingly more interested in long debate than in maintaining the façade of purity and justice Prahv had always shown to the world. They were becoming almost Orzhovlike.

The Baroness of Utvara struggled to ignore the variety of odd smells that clouded the confined space in an unpleasant pastiche. She limped the short distance from the door to the transparent barrier without using her cane and stood eye to eye with the last known angel on Ravnica.

Teysa had met this angel under different circumstances only a few weeks ago. The angel had emerged from the Schism while the baroness led a ragtag posse against the Izzet magelord who had tried to set dragons loose upon the world. The towering warrior, with timing typical, in Teysa's experience, of law enforcement, had arrived just a little too late. By the time Teysa met her, the angel was grieving for the old man who had died fighting the dragons, a retired wojek named Kos. Such attachment to a "mortal" was not generally considered an angelic trait, and Teysa had found it curious at the time and assumed the angel was simply using it as cover to avoid revealing why she alone was there and where the other angels had gone. Their disappearance at the time of the Decamillennial was known the world over, a reliable topic at most any corner table at the local watering hole. In Utvara alone, Teysa had already heard more than twelve distinct theories on the subject in Pivlic's tavern, which currently served as her base of operations.

What Teysa knew was that the angel had spoken at the wojek's funeral and disappeared a few days later, leaving even more questions behind. A few hours ago, the angel had reappeared, triggering the sequence of events that brought Teysa back to Prahv.

The baroness had the chance to get some answers, both to satisfy her professional obligations and her personal curiosity—the Schism still hung over Utvara, smaller but still inscrutable, and Teysa felt she needed to learn all she could about it, whatever its current size. Then there was the fact that the disappearance of the angels was one of the great mysteries of the last century, and the woman who uncovered the truth would become a legend. Teysa did not crave notoriety for its own sake, but it did open new avenues to power that the barony of Utvara did not.

That was the advokist talking, arguing the case of her natural ambition, and the advokist had a point. Teysa took the fastest zeppelid available back to the City of Ravnica as soon as the message from the angel had arrived in her office that morning, mulling over possible strategies and hypotheses the entire way.

The angel stood in shackles. A coil of heavy, silver chain ran through the braces on her wrists and ankles and through mizzium rings bolted to a section of solid mizzium flooring, giving the prisoner room to move while adding another layer of security to the already indestructible cell. It was far below the base of the third tower of Prahv. The towers contained many such cells, where those awaiting trial awaited it in complete physical isolation that still gave them the ability to communicate with the outside, provided the outside came to them. The Azorius and their Senate guard allowed the accused to speak to visitors through thick plates of sound-conducting invizomizzium.

The Guildpact was a harsh set of laws at times, but fair—if you could afford one, an advokist or lawmage would help argue your cause before the blind judges. The Senate prided itself on near-obsessive attention to such protocols. She wished it was more obsessive about the condition of this dungeon, but that was immaterial at the moment.

The ministers of Azorius, the upper-middle class bureaucrats that kept Prahv running and populated the lower house of the Senate, were bound and determined, it appeared, to ensure no breaches of protocol would come between the angelic prisoner and prosecution. The smaller and more proactive group of vedalken speakers that filled the upper house of the Senate—which still had less collective political power than the judges—were no doubt just as eager to question the lost angel as was everyone else, but the accused's advokist had the right to first interview once charges were brought. Even the judges couldn't interrogate before Teysa could.

Word had leaked quickly to the newssheets and the "holy prisoner of Prahv" was drawing people to the Azorius stronghold. For the most part, those spreading the rumors implied that the Azorius were making a mistake by imprisoning the angel and that no good could come of it. Teysa had passed a few small groups of praying pilgrims on the way in. By the time she left, they'd probably be singing around a burning effigy of Grand Arbiter Augustin IV. The Azorius were walking a fine line with this.

Teysa settled on an angle for the angel within moments. The prisoner no doubt expected questions and more questions about her vanished kin, so Teysa would do the opposite. Her face sharpened into number twenty-seven: irritated protest.

"Hello. Great to meet you. I want you to know that I should be back in Utvara," Teysa said to the prisoner. "I daresay in the time you spent with us there you learned that I'm no longer a practicing advokist. I'm semiretired. And no offense, ma'am, but I hardly know you. What made you request me? Do you even know what I charge for my services? Do you even have a zib to your name?"

No reaction. The angel just stood, hidden in shadow from the blue glowsphere that provided the only illumination.

"Excuse me, ma'am, I'm over here," she said.

Nothing. The feeling of unease knocked on the back of her mind, demanding attention, and she squelched it.

Then her eyes finally adapted to the darkness enough to clearly make out the angel in the shadows, and the shocking injuries she had suffered, protocols or no protocols. Even bound by the silver rings that made her golden wings hang paralyzed from her shoulder blades, her great angelic power largely suppressed, the tall prisoner was an imposing figure but also battered, bruised, and slashed. The wings made her look like a hunched and wounded raptor, especially once Teysa got a good look at the dried, spattered blood that glittered in the dull light of the cell's lone, sputtering glowsphere. "Look, Miss—Pierakor Az Vinrenn D'rav," Teysa added crisply—she'd memorized the name on the flight—"you'll need to work with me a little more than this."

The angel turned and covered the distance between the baroness and the invizomizzium with two steps. The heavy chain around her feet brought her up just short of the barrier with a clang, and Teysa took an involuntary step back. One of the angel's eyes blazed with rage and pain. The other was swollen completely shut beneath an untended wound that had cut to the bone. The gash ran from the center of her forehead to just above her left ear. A blood-soaked bandage was wrapped tightly around her ribs, another bound her right thigh, and a third, her left shoulder. The angel's left arm was in a simple prison-issue sling, and she wore a simple, gray prison tunic that had at best been made for someone shorter and much less . . . angelic. Her red tresses had been cropped close and short, from the look of it unintentionally and possibly with a torch. She was drawn and pallid. It was said angels were beings made of magic, but this angel was apparently also made of blood and tissue. If the baroness was any judge, the prisoner had lost a lot of the former in exchange for her injuries. Had the angel been human and not a semi-immortal physical manifestation of magical justice, Teysa would have suggested they begin by drawing up a last will and testament.

The eye that was still open locked with hers, and for one split second Teysa saw fire aimed at her own soul. Then just as quickly it was gone. The angel relaxed and even attempted a smile. "My apologies," she said. "I was thinking. You interrupted me, and I reacted instinctively. Confinement is a . . . peculiar state for me, especially at the moment. You are the Baroness of Utvara."

"And you're—well, you're hurt," Teysa said. "Are you sure you're up to this? I could fetch a healer, get you some teardrops. We can always meet later."

"No," the prisoner replied. "I will heal."

"You'd heal faster if—never mind," the baroness said. "Ma'am, may I call you Feather? We've met before, and at the time you said to call you Feather."

"You may," the angel said. "That has become my name."

Odd way to put it. "So, Feather, while you were thinking did you actually hear anything I just—"

"An angel always hears what a mortal says, when directly addressed," Feather replied, "no matter the distance."

"Yes," Teysa said, knocked off of her rhythm. "Right. So we're on the same page. That trick could come in handy if you end up within the verity circle. It will help keep our lines of communication open. But we'll get to that later."

"A verity circle will not be necessary," the angel replied, and Teysa didn't bother to tell her the truth-compelling magic would be there when Feather took the stand no matter what the accused thought necessary. "I will answer your questions," Feather continued. "First, Pivlic recommended you. Second, I do know what your services are worth. If you check your bank records, I believe there has already been a substantial sum transferred to your primary business account. That amount will be finalized when you accept my case."

"Where does an angel get zinos?"

"I was a wojek for twenty-two years, and the League insisted on normal wages, some kind of union rule, despite my . . . unusual status in the service. I never spent these wages but left them in the care of—"

"Pivlic?"

"Correct."

"It's always Pivlic."

"He invested the funds for me in various business ventures that met the strict legal standards I required and over the last twelve years has apparently—how did he put it—'grown my wealth' considerably. So you will accept my case." It was not a question.

Teysa scanned the angel's face, looking for a hint of jocularity or insincerity. She found neither. Pivlic. Her new second in command never failed to surprise and never seemed to open all of his books.

The imp made it his business to know everyone, which was one of the things that made him so useful. She made a mental note to draw up some contracts that would ensure his loyalty for the next hundred years. A well-connected lieutenant often wanted to become a well-connected boss.

"So how substantial is—?"

"Substantial," Feather said. "I ran the figure past Pivlic before I sent word to you, and he agreed it was generous."

"I will check on it, but let's say you're not lying. Since you're an angel. Don't lie to me, Fea—sorry, is it *Constable* Feather?"

"Most recently it was 'Legionary.' Before that 'Constable.' You may call me just Feather," Feather said. "And I do not speak falsely. Angels do not lie."

"Cannot or don't?"

"Angels do not lie."

"Feather," the baroness said, switching on number five: I'm the one looking out for you, so you can trust me. "Feather, everybody lies. But I'll give you the benefit of the doubt. Let's just say I think you're telling the truth. But before I take the case, I need to know a little about it first."

"I am accused on multiple violations. Desertion in a time of war. Striking a superior. Breaking oaths. Failure to attend to my duty as a wojek officer and as a Boros Legionary. I may well be guilty of guild-matricide as well."

¥ ¥ ¥ ¥ ¥

It took Feather half an hour to go over the charges in detail—angelic memory was famously precise and frighteningly accurate. Teysa suspected much of what the angel said was rote recitation from the formal accusation. As an advokist, she found herself aghast when the angel told her that much of the information within the charges was from Feather herself, who had actually *turned herself in.*

She wasn't just working for an angel, she was working for an angel who was either insane, or else had brought a warning that everyone in power on Ravnica needed to hear. When Feather was finished, the baroness knew she had her work cut out for her turning the tale into a worthy defense.

The mitigating circumstances were unbelievably compelling and would work to her advantage with the jurists. Those were her best hope since the angel insisted on testifying in her own defense. Within a few hours, her strategy became clear. Teysa actually had an honest client, and that was how she would win the case if she won at all. The truth, with a little assistance from her advokist, would set Feather free—or nothing would.

* * * * *

Crixizix shuddered as the Great Dragon Niv-Mizzet came into view over the horizon and momentarily blocked out the dim sun. Relief and dread fought for dominance in her heart. Relief that this disaster would almost certainly end or at least move into a welcome rescue-and-recovery phase, for she knew with the certainty of faith that nothing could stand before the unleashed might of the Izzet guildmaster. Dread that her short career as a master engineer was about to literally burn up.

The last time she called in to the sour dispatcher, Crixizix learned that the containment team was on maneuvers at the northwest pole and would be on their way as soon as contact could be reestablished—perhaps as long as thirty hours. The only other help to arrive, a small team of firefighting hydromancers who had teleported directly to the scene, unfortunately materialized on a spot that no longer had any ground beneath it. Crixizix watched helplessly, too far away to prevent them from plummeting into to the depths of Utvara's cold, dead undercity.

She aborted her first three landing attempts as more and more of Utvara fell under fists, feet, and other nephilim appendages. Crixizix then gave up on the idea of moving people out of the township one or two at a time in the cramped 'sphere when the terrified mob almost pulled the craft crashing to the ground.

The goblin finally settled on staying in the air, where she could do more good helping evacuees find paths they could not see with public-address enchantments. Angry and even more terrified than before, the people chased her more than obeyed her instructions, but the results were the same. Crixizix had gotten dozens to relative safety—she doubted the nephilim would be confined to Utvara for long, at this rate—but saw many more snapped up by the monsters, consumed, or casually flattened.

Had the dragon not agreed to handle the situation, Crixizix might have returned to the center and alerted the wojeks, the ledev, and the titans themselves. She did alert a minor Orzhov functionary, the highest level of attention she could get when the baroness could not be found on the leylines. She could not raise Pivlic, who at least would have been certain to have a way to contact Teysa Karlov. Regardless, the Izzet guildmaster had agreed to her first request, simply but with a great deal of underlying irritation. As promised, he arrived a short time later.

Crixizix had just gotten a shocked viashino family to the edge of the Husk when the dragon broke the long silence.

This is not acceptable, the Firemind said in her head.

The goblin did not respond but redirected the flame-pods and changed her vector to intercept and escort the guildmaster.

The dragon passed over the Cauldron ruins, abandoned hours ago by the nephilim in their press outward. He opened his reptilian jaws and without ceremony belched an inferno into what remained of Zomaj Hauc's legacy. The ruins were consumed in minutes, collapsing into drooping, molten shapes that soon merged completely with the volcanic caldera underneath. When the ruins were fully liquefied, Niv-Mizzet wheeled back over the surface and spread his great, leathery wings. He hovered, flapping mightily, and kicked up a tremendous dust devil centered directly over the volcanic scar. After another few minutes the winds had cooled the molten rock and metal before they dissipated into the open sky.

It took seven minutes, in total, for Niv-Mizzet to obliterate the Cauldron and cap an active geothermic vent. Crixizix hoped that wasn't the solution the guildmaster had in mind for the entire reclamation zone.

As if in reply to her anxious thought, the Firemind asked, *Why did you allow this to happen, Master Engineer? The remains of all my kin were to be incinerated.* All. *I resumed my meditations when you assured me that was taken care of.*

The mental image Niv-Mizzet projected—a perfect replica of his physical form—completely lacked the usual mental affectations others could not help. The goblin herself, for instance, could not get her mental knuckles off the mental floor when in his presence. She flinched when the projection cocked its head and mustered all the courage she had left.

Well? Niv-Mizzet pressed.

We were proceeding with that plan, great Niv-Mizzet, Crixizix thought back. *Had we the time, I would go over those plans in detail, but I assure you they—*

Your incompetence can wait, the dragon thought. *Do not fear for your life just yet, Master Engineer. This is ultimately Zomaj Hauc's doing. You are merely a goblin. Perhaps I asked too much of you.*

My lord, Crixizix thought, *I bow to your supreme judgment. Tell me what you will have me do.*

Stay out of my way, the Firemind replied then added, *it's been some time since I've had the opportunity to do something like this. I plan to enjoy it. If you wish to save that rabble, I suggest you do it now.*

I implore you, please take care to—

The mental slap knocked Crixizix's head back into her seat with an audible crack.

My wrath does not take care, the Firemind growled. *Once awakened, it will see blood. Enjoy the show.*

Crixizix kicked the flame-pods into a flash-burst to dodge the swooping dragon as he passed low over Utvara. She hovered overhead, doing as ordered and staying out of the way. As an afterthought, she activated the observosphere's recorders. When the Great Dragon promised you a show, it wasn't a bad idea to save it for history. Even if the show promised to be a disaster for Crixizix's newly adopted home.

But despite his words, the dragon did not—as the goblin had feared—immediately torch the entire place. It seemed Niv-Mizzet's wrath felt a bit more visceral today. He veered over the city with a roar that made all five of the rampaging creatures issue their own howled challenges in return.

From her new vantage point, Crixizix could see the battlefield Utvara had become. On the north end of town, devouring entire swaths of Golgari fields and Selesnyan veztrees, the four-legged beast that was all mouth and tail bellowed another challenge to the dragon. To the east, the tentacled brain-thing pulled down the walls of a low-rent hostelry. Just south of that, something that looked like a walking mountain topped with a statue's head dug cruel troughs in the ground, shaking another set of dwellings to their foundations and sending them tumbling over sideways. Due west, the snake-nephilim was crushing a Haazda watchtower in its constricting coils, surrounded by a ring of fleeing Haazda volunteers who ran smack into a wall of embryonic froglings headed in the opposite direction. The froglings' parent loomed over its brood and belched up a few more, and the hopping nephilim-spawn—each one half again the size of a man—pummeled every Haazda within reach.

Each of the original five nephilim Crixizix had spotted easily outweighed Niv-Mizzet after hours of uninterrupted growth. But the creatures still did not have the Firemind's ancient intelligence, power, and cunning. She felt a wave of roughly similar sentiment from the dragon himself. The Izzet guildmaster hurled a shot of flame at the tail-mouth, enveloping the nephilim in dragon fire. The eyeless monster wailed pitiably inside the blast, then hunched all four spindly limbs. It launched directly upward, on a collision course with Niv-Mizzet, dripping blazing chunks of oily, melting skin on the ruined buildings below.

Niv-Mizzet was not waiting around to be tackled, and looped around the burning creature. As it shot past, he raked it across the back, opening three grievous wounds and tearing out a good many spiked vertebrae that rained, clattering, to the ground. The flames had burned themselves out when it somehow landed on all four hand-feet in a crouch, charred, smoldering, and furious. The dragon extinguished that fury with another sustained blast of superheated pyromanic flames that reduced the facing half of the nephilim to white-hot cinders in seconds. The remaining half collapsed, twitching, against the last remaining part of Baroness Karlov's new mansion.

Crixizix's cheer died on her lips when she saw what Niv-Mizzet's quick first strike had caused. Sections of rubble were alight with uncontrolled—and likely uncontrollable—flames fed by the winds the dragon kicked up with every stroke of his wings. Worse, the other nephilim were all focused directly on Niv-Mizzet, the advantage of surprise was gone. The guildmaster looked distressingly . . . surrounded.

Nonsense, the Firemind said but did not elaborate. The goblin could feel the vast intelligence racing, ablaze with the immediacy of the fight, and decided to think more positively. Dragon fire was one of the few things that could melt the magically forged element mizzium, and Crixizix's observosphere would not likely survive a stray shot.

Niv-Mizzet flew low toward the brood-belching frog nephilim, strafing the open flats with fire. The encroaching horde of froglings popped and crackled in the flames, hundreds dying in the time it took the dragon to make a single pass overhead.

The horde's instincts kicked in, and several that had escaped only with burns managed to grab onto the dragon's tail. Without looking back Niv-Mizzet cracked that tail like a whip, sending dozens of the froglings to splatter against the stony ground.

The move was effective but was almost the dragon's undoing. The brood parent lashed out with a simian, sucker-tipped arm that wrapped around Niv-Mizzet's tail. The dragon flapped his wings furiously, blasting the landscape with scattered, unfocused mini-twisters but failing to free himself from the nephilim's iron grip. The nephilim set its remaining five limbs and wrenched Niv-Mizzet out of the sky. The dragon struck the flats with a crash that was heard, if not immediately recognized, for miles in every direction. Just before he struck, the dragon twisted enough to land on his belly without breaking a wing, but Niv-Mizzet's next roar was tinged with pain. The agony carried through the Firemind, and soon tears rimmed Crixizix's eyes as the pain, to a certain extent, became her own.

But Niv-Mizzet was not down yet, not by far. He recovered from the body slam within a few moments, pushed himself to all four feet and whipped his serpentine neck around to hurl a blast of flame directly into the frog-nephilim's open mouth. The creature's gullet inflated like a balloon, and hundreds more frogling spawn were immolated. Then even the nephilim's tough, ancient hide could withstand the pressure no more. The brood belcher exploded.

The blast sent pieces of brood parent and frog spawn in all directions, raining down over everything within the ring of the Husk for a full minute. The shock wave knocked Niv-Mizzet back past the observosphere. Crixizix had better luck, the 'sphere was built with such conditions in mind, and she managed to keep her vessel both stable and airborne. The hunks of nephilim that spattered over the observosphere forced her to feed a touch more pyromana to the flame-pods, but otherwise she appeared to be unharmed. She released the sphere-within-sphere cockpit clamps and swung around to follow the Izzet guildmaster's seemingly uncontrolled flight. The dragon appeared stunned, limp, perhaps injured. Halfway down the descending side of his arc, Niv-Mizzet's wings filled with air and he somersaulted out of freefall, coming to rest on all fours before the snake-nephilim. The monster's enormous eye gazed impassively at the dragon, but it unwrapped itself from the Haazda watchtower—the tower collapsed in a cloud of dust behind it—and rose like a cobra preparing to strike, a cobra with arms growing out of either side of its head.

With a threatening rumble, Niv-Mizzet mirrored the snake-thing's movement and arched his neck, mouth wide and showing twin rows of terrible, razor-sharp teeth. Smoke billowed from the dragon's throat and disappeared as he drew in a deep breath.

The breath was cut short by the impact of a bulbous mass of tissue against the side of Niv-Mizzet's head. The dragon recoiled, stunned, unable to pinpoint this second attacker before another projectile struck his left wing with frightening force. Crixizix and Niv-Mizzet spotted the fourth nephilim almost simultaneously. The tentacled beast tore loose another hunk of its own head—or more accurately one of the bulbous, eyelike spheres that covered it—and cast it with a snap. The dragon ducked, avoiding the projectile, and flapped mightily to regain the sky.

That, Niv-Mizzet thought, *was fun. But I grow weary of this.*

But my lord, Crix thought, *there are still three of them. You must—*

You presume to tell me what I must do? the dragon replied. *No. This was an enjoyable diversion—one that I am quickly losing interest with. Nothing more. I think I shall retire and watch the others try their might against the nephilim for a while.*

Crixizix was stunned.

You are leaving? The goblin asked in mental disbelief.

The Firemind did not reply. Niv-Mizzet wheeled one last time in the sky and veered off toward one of his many hidden aeries in the north. Crixizix noted that he did not go back in the same direction he had come. Niv-Mizzet was abandoning the City of Ravnica, it appeared.

Crixizix did not know what to do. Fear within the Firemind was inconceivable. As was the idea of the Guildmaster of the Izzet abandoning his people and his responsibility, allowing the Izzet to be destroyed by the rampaging nephilim. If she were to reveal this to the others—well, they'd probably use it as an excuse to drum her out of the guild. It wasn't as if she were popular—most magelords seemed to believe she had been promoted well above her station.

The goblin began to weep. Whether it was a result of disillusionment or shame, she wasn't sure.

As the three triumphant nephilim lumbered off, tearing a path through the Husk that exposed layers of civilization long since forgotten and likely never to be studied, Crixizix turned her gaze back to Utvara. She forced herself to calm down. So what if her mind felt like it had been torn in two. So what if the Firemind was, ultimately, a living thing that could be irresponsible, or afraid, or whatever had caused him to abandon the Izzet. These things happened. All things considered, the people down below had it far worse, and she was still in a position to do something for them.

She set the observosphere to land outside the Imp Wing—one of the only structures in Utvara that was more than fifty percent intact—and scrambled to collect every piece of medical and alchemical equipment she could find.

CHAPTER 4

*A ledev has no love but the open road and no family except
the Conclave—at least that's what the Conclave wants you to
believe.*

—Memoirs of a High Centuriad
Published anonymously, 9104 Z.C.
Banned by the Selesnya Conclave, 9105 Z.C.
Second printing, 9106 Z.C.

31 Cizarm 10012 Z.C.

The newly reopened Utvara highway narrowed considerably at
a point a couple hundred miles due east of Prahv. Fonn eyed the
half-empty buildings rising on either side of the road, which cut a
narrow cleft into the outlying regions of the central city. She had
traded in her dromad for a trusty wolf, and the part-time apo sat
tall in the saddle at the head of a small group of youthful scouts.
The half-elf had left behind her wojek armor for the time being
and returned to duty as a ledev guardian, one of the knights of
the road who protected the vital routes of travel and commerce
on Ravnica. And happily those duties also meant spending time
with her son. She, Myc, and the others were bound for Utvara, but
they were in no hurry. This sojourn to Utvara was not vacation.
The scouts were to learn the roads outside the City of Ravnica
in detail.

Fonn found the League gave her one form of fulfillment—
satisfying the desire to honor her father's memory in her own
way, since few others ever would. But she felt truly at home
on the road, and since Myc had begun training with the scouts
it felt less and less like duty. But duty it was, and necessary

training that Fonn was determined her son would have. Lately, it seemed to her, the ledev guard spent more time patrolling newly constructed temple outposts, defending Selesnyan interests, than serving the good of all by patrolling the roads. The ledev were, in Fonn's opinion, on their way to becoming nothing more than simple security guards. This did not sit well with the half-elf, and she knew she wasn't the only ledev to feel that way. But such was the legacy of the quietmen, who for thousands of years had acted as guards, servants, and even vessels for disembodied members of the guild's ruling collective. The quietmen had, unfortunately, been corrupted by dark forces at the Decamillennial and could no longer be trusted. The corpse fires had burned shamefully outside of Vitu Ghazi for weeks, and the Selesnya Conclave swore their faceless creations would never rise again.

She forced herself not to dwell on such things, though the road, for her, always brought long stretches of philosophical contemplation along with long stretches of cobblestone. Contemplation aside, it felt remarkably good to be alive. Traffic was light. Fonn nodded to a small merchant wagon that trundled past. She recognized the man as an Utvaran. He had been among the crowd that assembled at the memorial for Agrus Kos and all those who died in the dragon attack. She still felt guilty that in the last twelve years she'd cut Agrus Kos more or less out of her life, and his sudden and senseless death had left her feeling even more unsettled than usual. Not that Fonn thought she could have stopped the dragons herself, but she could have helped Kos, perhaps saved him from his needless fate.

Then again, Kos himself would probably have been the first to point out that *she* didn't make him retire and move to a reclamation zone. He did that on his own.

Fonn scratched her cytoplastic hand, a Simic replacement for the one she'd lost around the time she'd met Myc's father. The original could not be restored through conventional magic, thanks to some kind of curse left by the creature that had taken it. She hardly even noticed it anymore, but ever since she'd left the city, the hand had started to itch like a gobhobbler with fleas. Cytoplasty was a relatively new form of bioalchemy, the Simic had said, but one that was virtually foolproof, with a rejection rate of only a few hundredths of a percent. She'd worn it for twelve years without incident, and it was virtually indistinguishable from the original and completely functional.

Functional, but it could never be called attractive—pale and somewhat translucent, supported by a fibrous skeletal network of membranous blue and green tendrils that were clearly visible through the cytoplasm. The Selesnya Conclave did not approve of Simic cytoplastics on strict theological grounds, though there was technically no law against them.

Her wolf flicked his ears in alarm, and she scratched his neck. "Nothing to worry about. I smell it too," Fonn said in the wolf's ear. "That's Utvara. There's a geothermic vent there. Burning stone. That's all you smell."

Her eyes scanned the road, and she added, "Or maybe it's them."

A little more than a mile ahead, the road followed a broad tunnel that ran beneath a complex network of original and rebuilt architecture that was home to thousands of guildless Ravnicans and members of the savage fringe guilds, like the Gruul, Rakdos, and even Golgari. It was one of the reasons she like using this stretch of highway to break in new recruits. You never knew what you might run into around here, but it was also close enough to the city gates to provide an escape route if real trouble arose. Danger seemed unlikely today, with so much daily life going on all around them.

Even so, the band of travelers that had emerged from the shadows, clad in the familiar rags and leathers of Rakdos priests, caused a moment of alarm. It appeared to be a small prayer gang and not a raiding party, probably pilgrims headed to Krokt-only-knew-what sordid and bloody rituals. That was the thing about the roads of Ravnica—they were interconnected all over the world, a web of constantly moving people, commerce, and cultures, and just because you crossed paths with someone didn't mean they were leaving where you were going or going where you came from.

The Cult of Rakdos had a well-deserved reputation as one of the bloodiest-minded of the nine—no, ten, Fonn corrected—guilds. But that reputation had declined somewhat in recent years, tempered by the dispersal of the Rakdos rebels in an uprising several decades ago. These days those with the tattoos and scars of the Cult of Rakdos could be found working as bouncers, mercenaries, and laborers all over the city. Most lived in hivelike warrens where others rarely went and kept their sordid, bloody rituals to themselves. Supposedly, those warrens were huge carnivals of violence and mayhem, but no one knew for sure. The only Rakdos cultists who left the warrens for reasons other than work were priests observing the rituals and pilgrimages of their religion outside the range of the City Ordinances that did not allow things like the religious sacrifice of sentient beings, let alone killing for the express purpose of cannibalism. As Fonn understood it, that was the most sacred of all the Rakdos rituals.

But as long as their demon-god guildmaster, Rakdos himself, remained entertained in Rix Maadi, the Rakdos kept to their place in Ravnican society. But the demon-god would surely rise again, on his own schedule, as had happened dozens of times since the Guildpact was signed. Why the paruns had allowed a guild like the Cult of Rakdos to exist was something that scholars and philosophers debated to this very day, but Fonn's personal opinion was that it was simply to keep the near-immortal demon Rakdos in check by shackling him with a formal religion.

These priests, far from their kind, seemed almost comical at this distance. A few were strumming and blowing musical instruments in an atonal marching rhythm. Another lead a giant indrik pack-beast. Fonn could hear its flat, heavy feet thumping along at a leisurely pace that matched the music. It was slung with dozens of animal cages of various sizes, most empty, but they made the mammoth creature look like a walking zoo. Portions of its skeleton were exposed, a sure sign of the Rakdos' haphazard but effective necromancy.

Fonn grimaced. Well, this was what training was for. They'd just have to go on as planned. She'd chosen this road, after all. A fully trained ledev guardian wouldn't shirk from passing a small gang of Rakdos. She certainly wouldn't if she were alone. As long as they kept their wits about them it should just be a passing exchange of greetings.

And yet there was her son among the recruits, just eleven years old, even if that was only a few years short of adulthood for an elf. Myc was three-quarters elf so he was maturing even faster than Fonn had.

"Something wrong, Mom?" called a young voice from a few paces back.

"Probably nothing. I think Tharmoq just isn't used to geothermic vents," she replied quickly, fighting off a strange feeling of guilt. "But all of you, keep your eyes open. There's a mean looking bunch a few miles ahead of us, probably just pilgrims looking for stray beasts to sacrifice, but I want you all alert. It's not against the law for them to capture living creatures, as much as we may not like it."

"But Mat'selesnya is in all things," one of the recruits, not Myc, piped up. "The living must be free."

"Yes, and that's why we don't do what the Rakdos do. But they have their belief system, and we have ours. The Guildpact says that we must respect that, so we do," Fonn said. "Just because everyone doesn't respect the law doesn't mean we stoop to their level."

"But haven't we left those boundaries by leaving the city?" This from her son, who had some philosopher in him and a fascination with history.

"Technically, that may be true, except for the road itself," Fonn said. "The highway network encompasses all of Ravnica, from the northwest pole to the southeast pole, but it's all really one road to us, and those roads also run through the city."

"So the ordinances apply?" Myc said.

"Yes," Fonn replied, "and we enforce them. That's why you won't see these jokers trying to take, say, one of our dromads for their cages. And if they try, we prevent them from doing so." With a smirk that none of the scouts saw, she added, "And you'll address me as 'sir' when we're on duty, Scout."

Fonn heard a few snickers from the other trainees. Most of them had a few years on her son, who may have been as physically mature as the others for the most part but had still only had eleven years of real experience in the world. She momentarily regretted the public correction. Both of them were still getting accustomed to this. But Myc had wanted this more than anything, and he was of age, if just barely. Elves and those with elf blood had very long life spans, but they matured quite early, especially the Devkarin "dark elves" who spent most of their lives underground. Myc was half Devkarin and had grown up fast. She'd welcomed him into the guard as a scout recruit with a little apprehension but also a great deal of pride.

When they divorced, Fonn and Jarad agreed to let Myc follow his own path. Fonn had half-expected the boy to reject them both, but in the end he had shown more wisdom than she could have hoped, choosing to split his time between them as best he could.

The marriage had been an unlikely one and hadn't lasted beyond their son's sixth birthday. She must have been mad to ever think it would work out. In retrospect she chalked up the brief fling with matrimony to the exhilaration of survival the two of them had felt right after the Decamillennial. At least, for Myc's sake, they were still on relatively friendly terms. Fonn trained the boy in the ways of the ledev, and Jarad took him on hunts through Old Rav from time to time. It could have been worse.

Fonn had crammed a great deal of experience into a relatively short time as a ledev, and the Conclave had taken notice. She'd been made a member of the Order of Mat'selesnya, which came with the new title of centuriad, a permanent home in Vitu Ghazi, and responsibility for training recruits. The rank also made it easier to pursue her part-time work with the wojeks. It probably didn't hurt that her one-time wolf mount Biracazir had himself joined the Selesnya Conclave, the central ruling body of her guild. Even at this great distance, she only had to concentrate a moment to feel his reassuring presence in the song.

It wasn't the same song she remembered from the old days, but it was still strong. It connected all Selesnyans to one another, and with the world of living things. And it was different than it had been. In the last decade, the ledev guardians had cut back on global patrols, moving more and more troops back to the home territory in the Center of Ravnica. Vitu Ghazi had been fortified, and refortified, until it hardly resembled the living Unity Tree she remembered. It resembled, if anything, an organic version of the wojek citadel of Centerfort. A very, very tall version. It had always been visible from a great distance, and she knew that if she looked back she would see it clearing the top of the city gates, rising even above the towering sentinel titans. She would also see new spires and towers growing from it, landing platforms for griffin patrols, and watchtowers manned by sharp-shooting Silhana bowmen.

The protective mother in her wanted to turn back over one shoulder constantly to check on Myc, but she forced her eyes forward. She'd already embarrassed the boy once today. No need to make it worse. Boy or not—and to a mother, an eleven-year-old was still a boy even when he had a long sword slung over his shoulder and wore drab, green scout's chain mail cut in close proximity to the Devkarin style—he was committed to the life of the ledev, and he deserved a chance to prove he could do it. That meant letting him take his lumps.

Keeping one eye on the Rakdos cultists was proving difficult. A sudden shift in the wind had blown a smoky haze in from Utvara, which mingled with a bank of early morning fog. It reeked of sulfur and burning flesh. It perversely reminded her again of Kos's pyre.

Fonn wouldn't say she missed Kos exactly. She'd hardly seen her father's former partner in the last twelve years and had gotten used to his not being around to help her learn the ropes of 'jek work. She had been a bit hard on him over her father's death and still wasn't sure Kos wasn't at least partly responsible for Myczil Zunich's fall. But now that he was gone, Fonn missed the concept of Kos, the idea that here was one final living link to her son's namesake.

But Kos was no more. She'd seen the pyre, had stood shoulder to shoulder with Jarad when Kos's mortal remains had gone up into the heavens.

This was no pilgrimage. Utvara was just conveniently located for her purposes. It was a long ride but not tortuously so—a fairly busy road, not too crowded, not too empty, with the shanty tower throughway ahead that provided an opportunity for challenging but not necessarily deadly training. And the Husk always presented a challenge or two, in the form of Gruul outcasts, wild animals, and other strange creatures. The route she'd planned would actually take them around the Husk, not through Utvara proper. The ledev had been cordially uninvited to protect the road into the place. That job was handled now by the baroness's Utvar Gruul patrols. Fonn had met the Gruul's leader, a loutish but intelligent man named Golozar, and been impressed with his plans to protect the interior of Utvara and its booming population.

She heard whispering from the recruits. They thought they were speaking quietly enough that their dromads' hooves concealed it, but Fonn had the sharpest ears in the party and easily picked out the sound if not the content.

Ahead, the Rakdos cultists had become enshrouded in fog, though she could still hear their mad dirge of a marching song. Another mile, maybe. An irrational fear for Myc gripped her, and she quickly squelched it. This was exactly why she had chosen this route, to present the scouts with a challenge. So long as the kids didn't panic. She decided to ensure they wouldn't by maintaining normality until they reached the prayer-gang—or the prayer-gang reached them.

She reined the wolf to a halt and wheeled on them.

"Recruits, you're here to learn," Fonn said with all the authority she could muster, which, with the added emphasis of her raised hand, immediately silenced the chattering youths. "Now pretty soon it's going to get foggy, and you'll want to make sure you know where the others are, so we're going to get in a quick protocol lesson beforehand." She raised a hand again to silence the unsolicited groans and mutters that students on every plane involuntarily emit when told they're about to do something dull. "We're going to keep talking. One, because it's going to be hard to see. And two, because there's nothing more deadly than silence on a long journey. You want to sap your spirit and lose track of what you're supposed to be doing out here? Just ride along staring. Before you know it you'll be asleep at the reins." She turned her mount forward again, and resumed moving forward. "Therefore talking is encouraged."

The soft clops of the dromad's hooves were the only response.

"I'll start us off with an easy one then," Fonn said cheerfully, "a simple, random question: What's so funny?"

"Ma'am?" the oldest recruit, a young human girl with golden braids and a supreme overestimation of her importance in the world, blurted. Her name was Lilyeyama Tylver—"Lily," naturally—and her parents had wanted a son to carry on an aristocratic Tylver family tradition of theological politics. Lily had chosen the ledev guard instead, a decision Fonn respected even if the girl's reasons were more than a little fanciful. Lily wanted to be some sort of warrior-baroness. Fonn had overheard her tell the others. She was also the only recruit with a cape, and over more than two hundred miles of travel from the gates of Ravnica it had remained dust-free and spotless. It was black with green silk lining, and Fonn hadn't seen the girl so much as brush it. The half-elf had decided to allow the affectation. Customized uniforms were a ledev tradition. Myc had done much the same with the Devkarin-inspired chain mail.

None of that changed the fact that generally, in Fonn's experience dealing with groups of untrained rookies, the first person to say something—anything—was usually the one who knew precisely what was so funny.

"I said, what's so funny?"

"Nothing, ma'am," Tylver replied. She didn't stammer a bit.

"Anyone else hear anything?" Fonn pressed. "Maybe it's just these ears of mine, sometimes you pick up echoes in the canyons." She waved a hand at the towering walls that lined the road down to the underpass. Stark and flat, the smooth walls of the ancient public apartment complexes long since abandoned by the original tenants were also full of guildless squatters, Rakdos cultists, and varying forms of wildlife. "But maybe I heard voices in those buildings. We may need to investigate."

"Mo— Sir," Myczil piped up. Fonn sighed. She had hoped, for the boy's sake, he wouldn't be the next to speak up. He was the youngest if not the smallest of the recruits. The last thing he needed was a reputation as a snitch. But she also should have anticipated it.

Perhaps it was a mistake taking him out now. Perhaps she should have insisted he spend at least a few years in Old Rav with Jarad. He could be learning to track giant slugs with his father, and she wouldn't be fighting the need to keep an eye on him every waking second.

"Yes, Zunich?" she said with exaggerated dispassion in an attempt to hide her ill-concealed sigh.

"Sir, we're ready to investigate if you are," her son continued. "If you hear something, there must be something out there. We certainly weren't saying anything."

A little overdone, but Fonn was glad that her position at the head of the group kept the other recruits from seeing her smirk break into a full-blown smile of pride. Good boy. "Perhaps it was nothing after all," she said. "That still doesn't mean we can't all have a little conversation on the road. Does anyone know any traveling ballads?"

"Can we ask *you* questions?" another recruit said. Sounded like Aklechin, one of Tylver's sidekicks. He had the makings of an excellent swordsman but not, unfortunately, the makings of a scholar. He was a human, sixteen, and had a mildly polar accent, probably from the almost perpetually snowbound Monastery Territories in the far northwest. Alone among the recruits, he had dressed like he was heading to a desert. The others, even Myc, had brought along foul-weather gear—the central city was in the middle of another few weeks of the rainy season.

The ledev realized all of the scouts were waiting. She looked over at the Rakdos, still marching through the fog, ever closer. They'd pass them soon. Very well.

"You can ask me any question, any time. I won't always guarantee an answer, but never think you can't ask."

"Er, yes," Aklechin said. "Okay then. Will we get to fight?"

"Good question," Fonn replied. "Terrible timing." She called back to the fourth recruit and the only one who had yet to speak. "Orval, can you tell me why it was terrible timing before I give Mr. Aklechin his answer?"

"Yes, sir," the fourth recruit said. He was the only one not riding a dromad, since the four extra hooves would have been quite superfluous. "It was terrible timing, sir," Orval continued, "because it's a jinx. Any idiot knows that. Proven fact. Ancient centaur proverb. And it's particularly bad because it appears some deathmonger— beg your pardon, *Rakdos* deathmongers—are coming toward us. Sir. And there might be a fight *now,* even if there wasn't going to be before. Law of jinxes."

"More or less accurate," Fonn said, genuinely impressed. "Call it superstition if you will, or call it a challenge to fate. But only a fool begs for trouble. I don't think we need to worry about them, though. They're just travelers. Just make sure you know where your sword is. A ledev prepares for trouble so she doesn't—"

Tharmoq the wolf froze and dropped into a crouch, growling at the road ahead. Fonn also froze, in midsentence.

The fog was very dense indeed and rolling unnaturally down the road toward them. The marching dirge had quickened to a sound similar to an out-of-tune pipe organ played by a band of lunatics.

"Everyone, form up," Fonn said. "Stay close, and no matter how thick this gets, do your best to keep me in sight, or failing that one of your fellow scouts. And keep talking."

The trainees responded with a staggered chorus of "Yes, sirs," all of which sounded as nervous as she felt. The smoky cloud kept coming, completely blotting out the road ahead.

"Stay sharp, scouts. We're going to keep moving. We don't run from clouds." She half-expected more groans but welcomed the second prompt round of "Yes, sirs," this time in unison and a little stronger. "That's better. Let's go."

Unfortunately, Tharmoq refused to move.

"Come on, boy," she said, leaning down and whispering under her breath in the wolf's ear. "Not in front of the scouts." As she spoke the words, she felt a cold, clammy feeling wash over her, thick with the smell of sulfur.

The cloud swallowed Fonn and the scouts in seconds. The young recruits became a pack of shadowy shapes all around her, and they began to chatter, panicking. Only Myc's voice was clear, parroting what his mother called to the others: "Steady there," "Keep it together," "Stay calm," and so on.

Her son's voice was the last thing she heard before the sound of chaotic Rakdos music drowned him out. Fonn saw other shapes in the gray—tall, scarecrow bodies, and hulking things that were all shoulders and arms.

Her head grew dizzy, and she called out Myc's name. There was no reply. The wolf beneath her began to whimper loudly, turning in circles as panic seized his lupine mind. Fonn called for Myc again and got her sword halfway out of the sheath before a large, bony hand clamped an acrid-smelling rag over her mouth and nose. Fonn fought a losing battle to retain consciousness. Her hand slipped from the sword hilt and flailed lazily in the fog, striking nothing, before she finally lost balance, slumped over sideways, and hit the ground.

Darkness enveloped her mind as a gravelly voice whispered in her ear.

"You go to sleep now," it said. The voice became a rasping cough, then a cackle that rang in her consciousness until it, and her consciousness, slipped agonizingly away.

CHAPTER 5

Q: What did the zombie say to the neuromancer?
A: "You going to eat that?"

> —*101 More Zombie Jokes*
> (Dead Funny Press, 5410 Z.C.)

31 Cizarm 10012 Z.C.

Under Jarad's watchful eye, a hundred zombies made ready to put several acres of subterranean farmland to the torch. It had taken most of the morning for the farmhands to spread the necessary fuel to ensure an even burn throughout the fields. Golgari farms did not dry out well since they were invariably underground, and modern irrigation techniques tended to keep the atmosphere quite humid and damp. Merely applying open flame to the month-old remains of the season's harvest wasn't the answer, even after flammable molds were allowed to grow. Yet the fields had to burn. It was tradition. It was also good agriculture.

The seasonal burn was enough of an event for the Golgari that the guildmaster was expected to oversee the ignition personally, and this season was no different. And once again, the guildmaster had been late. Zombie farmhands and the Devkarin high priest anointed to bless the blaze had been left standing for an hour. Several had to go back for new torches.

Jarad arrived with several minor scrapes and wounds on his chest, arms, and face. He hadn't the time to pick up his ceremonial guildmaster's robes, but at least he'd managed to get some extra hunting in on the way back from handing off his son. For better or worse, the undercity was rife with gangs like the ones they'd destroyed the day before, and he had decided to work off some tension taking down a few more on the way home. The kill that he carried across his shoulders was just a lucky find he had come across in one of the wide sewerways he had taken to get back. Lately, if he didn't get out and kill something at least every couple of weeks, he found himself getting extremely irritable, a condition that seeing Fonn had exacerbated. When the guildmaster was irritable, his decision-making suffered. Jarad may not have wanted the job at first, but in memory of the noble creature his sister had once been and in defiance of the stereotypes of the Golgari that abounded in the world above, he was determined that he would do it well.

"Guildmaster," said the Devkarin high priest, "We honor your arrival and give you blessings of the god-zombie." The pale old elf was clad in traditional leathers and bones and he wore his hair—and beard—in long dreadlocks that hung past his waist. He leaned on a simple, twisted staff of ebony wood and scowled beneath his half-skull mask, a more stylized and affected version of the artifact that Jarad word over his own face. "Guildmaster, pray, what is it you wear across your shoulders?"

"What does it look like?"

"A gharial alligator?"

"There you go, then," the guildmaster said. Jarad did indeed carry a dead gharial alligator—a lucky find. Jarad shifted his weight and shrugged the big reptile's corpse heavily to the floor of the overlook. "Found this fellow trying to get into the ceremony through an irrigation pipe," he added. "I needed a new pair of boots anyway."

"And I thank you on behalf of the agricultural collective," said the foreman in charge of this stretch of farmland. The foreman was also a zombie, though he was dressed in finer clothes than the torch-bearing laborers who ringed the farmland spreading out below them. He extended his hand and Jarad shook it firmly.

"Foreman Ulkis," he said. "Good to see you. Is everything ready?"

"Yes," the priest cut in. "The prayers have been made. All that we await is your order." There was that impatience again. Jarad understood the man had been forced to wait, but his tone was unseemly for dealing with a guildmaster.

Jarad had never enjoyed negotiation, compromise, or profit margins. These days not an hour passed when he didn't have to consider at least one of the three in some capacity. Jarad had not wanted to leave his son to Fonn and the Selesnyans for long stretches of the boy's life. He had not wanted to watch his sister snapped like a twig. He had not coveted her power. But he was guildmaster, and he was damned well going to have the respect of the priests.

"Nillis," he said, "you seem to be in quite a rush. Have I kept you long?"

"No, Guildmaster," the priest said, predictably obsequious. "I only long to begin the cycle of renewal that will see the end of one harvest and the beginning of another. It is a holy time, and if I seem impatient it is only because of my eagerness to see it through, from start to finish."

"You sure?" Jarad said, walking past the bowing priest to stand at the edge of the overlook. The field was dotted with small, white packet bombs of incendiary substances, covered over with broken chunks of dead dindin stalks and the half-plowed stumps of rotting meatshrooms. The hundred torches awaiting his command cast dancing shadows on the walls, the huge sunfungus overhead was in the darkened nighttime phase. Even dimmed, the gigantic, spherical sporophore cast enough light to reveal a few things that should not have been out in the fields, large, brown, lumpy things that didn't match the detritus of the harvest or the bright, white sheen of the incendiaries.

Jarad whirled on one foot and marched back to the high priest, who raised his head hopefully, ready to receive the guildmaster's order. He received the guildmaster's fist across the jaw instead.

The Devkarin holy man's staff clattered to the floor next to him, and he groaned. "Guildmaster? What—?"

"You have placed sacrifices in the fields," Jarad said steadily, anger barely in check. "This practice is no longer allowed, Nillis. Why have you defied the decree of your guildmaster?"

"I— No, there is—"

"Don't lie to me, priest," Jarad said. "I don't want excuses, nor am I going to debate. You will personally retrieve every one of them and return them to their parents. The burn will have to wait until tomorrow." He turned to the foreman. "Ulkis, did you know anything about this?"

If the zombie foreman did, he was smart enough not to say it. He wasn't the most expressive being Jarad had ever met, regardless. He simply shook his head and looked at the priest sternly.

"Krokt," Jarad swore. He didn't have time for this. He was due to meet with the Simic guildmaster in just an hour. He didn't trust the priest either, but he wasn't going to have stolen human children burned alive no matter what the "god-zombie" wanted. The god-zombie was dead. His sister had seen to that. The god-zombie wasn't going to care either way, and whatever Nillis or the other priests thought about it, stealing kids and burning them in a field was not the way to gain respect for the guild. It was not the way that Jarad vod Savo ran things.

"All right," he said to the foreman, "You are going to watch Nillis here, and you're going to make absolutely certain he goes out there and personally frees every one of those children. Then we're going to meet here tomorrow and try this again. I've still got contacts with the 'jeks, and I will be checking with their missing children's bureau first thing in the morning. There had better be . . ." he counted quickly, "there had better be twelve success stories in their records by then."

"But Guildmaster," Nillis objected, "the calendar does not allow—"

"You should have thought of that before you defied my edict," Jarad said. "You're lucky I don't have Ulkis put *you* in a bag and leave you out to burn there in their stead. So don't push it. You've got work to do."

He nodded to the foreman and concentrated. When he spoke again, a slight echo tinged the edges of his voice, and the words he said would be impossible for the zombie to disobey. The Devkarin was not the necromancer his sister had been, but he knew a few tricks that he'd been able to practice to great effect in his new capacity as guildmaster. "Foreman, see that he does it. I'll see you both tomorrow, and I *will* know if you have not done as ordered. Both of you."

"Yes, Guildmaster," the defeated priest said.

The foreman nodded and agreed. "If he fails, I will break his arms, Guildmaster."

"No," Jarad said. "Save those for me. You can break a rib if you like. Just to let him know I'm serious."

"Guildmaster, really," the high priest sputtered, but by that time he was talking to Jarad's back.

Maybe that hadn't been fair. He had been late, after all. But that defiance of his personal policies had been too much. What was the point of being guildmaster if your minions wouldn't listen?

As it was, he was late to his next appointment too but not because of the gharial or the fight with the deadwalker raiders. As his huntress bodyguards stepped in behind him, he took the long way through the undercity, in no hurry to meet with the Simic. He stopped off at one of Old Rav's better tailors and picked up a new vest, a cape that was not too audacious, and took the opportunity to clean himself up. By the time he reached the receiving chamber in the labyrinth he had pulled back and knotted his dreadlocks, pinned the Golgari sigil to his breast, and once again affixed his Devkarin mask firmly to his face. His lieutenant met him at the door with the guildmaster's staff of office, an ornate piece of ebony topped with a simple, green stone into which the Golgari symbol was carved.

Jarad set his jaw and strode into the receiving hall with as much majesty as he could muster. Of all his duties as guildmaster, diplomacy was another one that he did not particularly enjoy. Like it or not, however, he did have to admit he had a knack for direct negotiation. It was not unlike the deceptions every hunter employed when dealing with tricky prey, even if this was more verbal and far less bloody, in most cases. And Jarad found that he was best at diplomacy when dealing with someone he did not like. It was just his luck that one such someone rose to his feet and approached Jarad as he walked into the receiving chamber. The Simic representative was a vedalken, one he had dealt with before and whom Jarad had only allowed to call again because the Simic guild seemed to have difficulty grasping his position. In fact, they were ignoring it.

"Dr. Otrovac," he said with an almost imperceptible bow. "Welcome. I trust we did not leave you waiting too long. We are between harvests, you understand. Much to do."

"I was not waiting long," the vedalken lied. Jarad felt something like a tingling in his scalp. No matter how many times he tried and failed, Dr. Otrovac always made a bold attempt to read the guildmaster's mind, every time the two met. It didn't work now, hadn't worked before, and wouldn't work in the future.

"Please don't be tiresome, Doctor. You know you can't get in there," Jarad said, tapping his forehead. "Guildmaster's privilege."

"I'm sure I don't know what you mean," the Simic said. "It is good to see you, Guildmaster. I bring a message from the great Progenitor Momir Vig, who sends his deepest respect and honorable greetings from the great greenhouse, along with respect from all of the elders of Novijen."

"And?"

"And?" the vedalken said, caught off guard. "And . . . and gifts, of course, with which we may open our negotiation."

"Are they the same gifts you brought last month?" Jarad said.

"Well, in part," the Simic admitted. "But I have also brought— I'm sorry, is there someplace we can speak more privately?"

"Of course," Jarad said. He led the Simic to an antechamber that he used for private meetings, ordering his bodyguards to stand watch at the door and keep an eye on the Simic's entourage.

"Please, have a seat," he said, gesturing at a chair in front of a simple desk that dominated the room. Jarad tapped on a few more glowspheres and sat down behind the desk. "Well?"

"You are direct, as always," the Simic said. "Since you have not seen fit to accept our previous offers, I have been authorized to 'sweeten the deal,' as the merchants say."

"I'm listening," Jarad said, placing his elbows on the desk, his hands together and his fingertips against his chin. The Simic soldiered on.

"In addition to what would be your first shipment of cytoplast enhancements, the great progenitor has released eight million zinos to a private account with the Karlov Bank, which I trust you realize is the most trusted name in financial circles. The account shall be released to you as soon as the contract has been signed. What you do with it is up to you."

"Zinos," Jarad said. "Impressive." His tone made it clear that the gold was anything but. "And?"

"And?" the Simic said. "I just told you that we set aside eight million—*million*—zinos, and you ask me 'and'?"

"We do not sell our harvest for free," Jarad said. "The slaughterhouses are not a charity. Well, we provide food *for* charities, but that's beside the point. The point is I *have* zinos. You're not offering me anything new, except what I already told you we don't want."

"Cytoplastic enhancement can increase the efficiency of your operations tenfold!" Dr. Otrovac said.

"Our operations are operating just fine without your enhancements," Jarad said. He might have married a woman who wore just such an enhancement, but he had never seen why the Simic pseudoflesh should be used for any reason other than replacing a lost limb. That made sense. Letting another guild affix god-zombie-only-knew-what things to the members of his own people was another matter entirely, and he viewed it as wholly unnecessary. "The answer is still no," he finished.

"All right, ten million."

"No."

"Fourteen million, and that is final," the Simic said.

"Are you deaf?" Jarad said. "No. In fact, the more zinos you offer, the less sense you make. This whole offer of yours stinks, Otrovac. You say you want to improve our efficiency. You want to give us these cytoplasts of yours as gifts, *and* you're offering me enough zinos to buy my own section of the Center of Ravnica."

"Our reasons are simple," the doctor said, "and I have explained them many times. We wish to achieve market penetration."

"You want to make us reliant on Simic bioengineering," Jarad countered. "What I don't understand, and the reason I brought you back here, is why."

"Why, good business, of course," the doctor said.

"You'd make a lousy Orzhov, Doctor," Jarad said. "I'll give you one more chance. Why?"

"There is no need to make idle threats," the Simic said, making to rise from his seat.

"I don't make *idle* threats," Jarad said. "You heard me."

"And you heard me," Dr. Otrovac said. "You have your answer."

"Then you have yours," the Devkarin replied. "Now get out of my labyrinth."

Jarad did not even open the door for the doctor. He simply sat at the desk and watched the vedalken leave. He pinched his chin between his thumb and forefinger and considered the meeting.

What was truly baffling was that the Simic were behaving so transparently. Their cytoplasts had been embraced by many industries on the place in the last decade. The Orzhov used them to justify raising the price of slaves. The Izzet appreciated the functionality. Others used them for more varied reasons, some illicit. The biomanalogical attachments affixed to tissue and augmented whatever body part they covered in ways understood only by the Simic themselves—formless transparent masses that wrapped around, say, a forearm and hand, then grew into a more functional, useful forearm and hand depending on the need.

At least, that's what the Simic had told him. And it was true, zombies enhanced with cytoplasts would probably work faster and more efficiently. But Jarad did not trust it at all and especially didn't like the idea of so much of his guild being changed in any way by the Simic.

Necromancy was one thing, and biomanalogical symbioses were another.

He pushed back from the desk and stood. Well, that had not been a complete waste of time. If the Simic didn't get the point now, he'd be more than ready to kick them out again, and again. If they kept it up, he'd start putting vedalken heads on pikes outside of Old Rav.

A part of him wished they would try again. When his son was born, he had sworn on Myczil's life that he would no longer harm anyone or anything that didn't deserve it, the closest thing to a vow of peaceful behavior that Fonn could wring out of him. The marriage vows might have been dissolved, but for Myc's sake he had kept this one.

It had been a long time since he'd found someone who deserved death quite as much as Otrovac. He just couldn't place exactly why.

* * * * *

Doctor Otrovac hurried from the Golgari labyrinth and into the streets of Old Rav with his small entourage and tugged at the collar of his tunic. He unfastened a couple of buttons and pulled the fabric aside to reveal his own small cytoplastic augmentation. He was not an unimportant vedalken, nor an unimportant Simic. He was a respected doctor, an even more respected negotiator, and if he'd been honest with the Devkarin he would have agreed with him. The Simic's offer didn't make that much sense. Otrovac figured his master knew what he was doing, but it was disconcerting to feel so ill-informed.

Perhaps his master could shed some light on this.

When he had placed it against his neck months ago, the cytoplast had been nothing but a formless amoeba of sorts, one large enough to fill his hand. It had immediately affixed to his pale, blue skin and conformed to fit the basic function he desired.

Since Otrovac was one of Momir Vig's personal ambassadors, that function had naturally also been what the progenitor desired. The cytoplast reshaped itself into the semblance of a single eye with a lipless mouth beneath it. Otrovac dropped his chin and spoke, softly. "You saw. He did not accept."

"He is a fool," the lipless mouth said with Momir Vig's voice. "But this was not unexpected."

"Honored Progenitor," the vedalken said, "perhaps it was not wise to offer the zinos. It appears . . ." Otrovac fought his instincts for obsequiousness. "It makes us appear desperate. I do not understand."

"You do not understand what?"

"Why have we not simply spread the cytoplasts regardless of his wishes?"

"That may yet happen," the voice said. "Though I suspect that the next time you make the offer, it will be accepted."

"Progenitor? What do you mean? He will kill me if I—"

"I suspect not," the Simic's guildmaster reasoned through the lipless mouth. "He has made a show of rejecting our offer twice, no doubt so that he will accept the third time with pride intact."

"I don't know, Honored One," the doctor said. "He seemed determined."

"Trust me," Momir Vig said. "Do not be concerned, Dr. Otrovac. I believe I have solved our Golgari problem."

"Yes, sir," the Simic ambassador said. "I look forward to hearing your solution."

"It is an intriguing one," his neck said with Momir Vig's voice. "Do not delay."

"Understood," Otrovac said, and pulled his collar back into place. He whistled to one of his attendants to fetch his carriage and puzzled over the progenitor's statement. How could you solve the 'Golgari problem' and still leave this Jarad in charge? The man was impossible to negotiate with, and that didn't seem about to change in Otrovac's informed and trained opinion.

He was still puzzling over the question when the carriage arrived, drawn by two cytoplastically enhanced dromads that boasted longer, more powerful legs and extra joints.

As his carriage pulled up the long, spiraling road leading to street-level Ravnica he hoped it involved some kind of torture. Otrovac did not like Jarad vod Savo. Otrovac did not like him at all.

CHAPTER 6

Ten years they have been gone. We must face facts, honored colleagues and lawkeepers. Whether they have abandoned us or somehow been destroyed, the angels are not here and we cannot find them. The Boros Legion must make permanent arrangements for the stewardship of our guild without angelic help. It will not be easy, but it is necessary.

—Wojek Commander-General Lannos Nodov,
Acting Guildmaster, Boros Legion
Address to the Azorius Senate, 19 Quaegar 10010 Z.C.

31 Cizarm 10012 Z.C.

Agrus Kos was dead. As far as he was concerned, fate should have been more than happy with that.

But no. That would have been too easy.

Over one century, and a quarter of another, he'd survived everything the old girl had thrown at him, until she finally turned on him. Kos knew this. He had died on the rocky ground of a dry place. He could not quite remember the name of the place, but there had been . . . wings. And a goblin, he thought. It was literally a lifetime ago.

But life, even for the dead, went on.

Especially if you'd signed certain documents at a wojek-recruitment desk that you could barely remember even when you were alive, since you'd lied about your age and joined the force when your voice was still changing. Especially if the possessors of those documents decided to hold you to them—like the one that bound one Agrus Kos, Lt. (retired), League of Wojek, Tenth Section, to a fifty-year stint in the Spectral Guard immediately following his death. He'd been at it for a few weeks or maybe a few years. He really had no idea. It wasn't his job to know. And spectral guards *were* their jobs.

"Good morning, minister," Kos said, nodding at the robed and hooded figure that shuffled up to him and smiled. "Good to see you looking well," he lied.

"Hello, Argus," the minister said. Kos thought he detected a hint of simpleton's glee at an obviously intentional mispronunciation of his first name. The first time it had happened, Kos had corrected him, only to find the minister of auguries simply repeated it again, louder the next time. Kos's sense of humor had been blunted by death, but he was fairly sure it wasn't particularly funny.

His own name was one of the things he could remember, as well as the names of Azorius functionaries, which always seemed to appear unbidden in his mind whenever he saw them. Other memories he had more trouble with. He could remember fleeting glimpses of people, strange people of every kind—elves, zombies, goblins, imps, and ghosts. He recalled feelings of anger, loss, happiness, disappointment and had no luck placing them to any complete events. He remembered being a wojek, a protector of the laws, and flashes of life on the job were the strongest memories of all.

But his past life might as well have been a book he read as a child and never picked up again. Not that he could remember much of his childhood.

They said ghosts had no sense of the passage of time, but no one ever asked a spectral guard bound by law to the Azorius Senate. Time did indeed pass for a ghost, and for Kos it passed very, very slowly. To his frustration, he had trouble tracking it accurately. He knew he was relatively new to the guard, but it already felt as if he'd been here for ages. He knew he had been a wojek for a very long time, much longer than this, but he also knew he'd enjoyed that a lot more. Perversely, from what Kos recalled of his tenure as a wojek—as a living, flesh-and-blood lawman of Ravnica, walking a stretch that only occasionally required him to draw steel—he'd always felt pity for spectrals and somehow knew that most 'jeks did. From the average officer's perspective, the spectral guard looked like a sad imitation, an illusion of a life that deserved to be honored, not extended by bond well into the afterlife.

The worst was being stuck in one spot. Shifts never ended for spectral guards. A spectral was a talking tombstone, unable to leave the shining white graveyard of Prahv. The temples of justice, the Azorius Senate, were home to thousands of flitting, industrious ghosts who had signed the wrong form or, worse, been such dull people in life that they'd requested this duty.

Kos knew intellectually that he would much rather have just been dead. He just couldn't get angry, annoyed, or otherwise vexed by it anymore. What he'd pieced together of the man he used to be indicated that this was the last thing he would have wanted, back when he was alive. Yet here he stood, in a manner of speaking. He was solid, so long as he didn't stray from Azorius territory. If he tried, he would dissipate. He did not try.

"Good morning, Tribune," he said to another late arrival. The Azorius Senate would be in session in just a few minutes, but Tribune Naruscov showed no signs of hurry. Or of hearing the ghost's cheerful greeting. Kos gave a phantasmal shrug to his opposite, a spectral called Castell. Castell, as usual, shrugged back, and they both turned to see who would pass next. Kos had tried to make conversation with Castell once and regretted it. Castell had a tin ear for small talk. Which, of course, only added to Kos's interminable boredom.

The four hours of quasi-nonexistence wasn't the only way the Azorius ensured the sanity of spectral guards—the loss of memory was by design, to prevent spectrals from developing too much of their former personality, personality that could disrupt the time-honored formality of the Azorius Senate and courts.

Sometimes on long, dark nights he saw imps and their ilk traversing the lower towers, traveling to and from Old Rav on all sorts of errands. He had known an imp. Pavel? Pilkin?

The Azorius had kept all of Kos that they needed. He remembered every law he had ever learned and had a suspicion that there were many more he had been taught by Azorius ectomages.

So it was with great surprise and all the shock a ghost could muster that Kos realized he clearly recognized the woman coming next up the steps. "Woman" was a misnomer, in fact. She was female, of that there could be little doubt, but she was far from human. She stood a full foot above the paladins who flanked her, and a pair of golden wings sparkled in the morning sunlight. He saw her and immediately knew her name. At the same time, he knew it was not truly her name but a nickname. A nickname he'd given her. Hadn't he?

There was only one way to find out.

"Feather," Kos said. "Is that you?"

The angel's eyes opened wide when she heard his voice. The pair of large, silver plated paladins guiding her up the stairs jerked her along forcefully as they passed Kos. Feather opened her mouth to speak, but no sound emerged. That was when Kos saw that the angel not only had her wrists bound together with lockrings, she also wore the familiar wing clamps she'd carried when serving in the League of Wojek.

She'd been a frequent partner of his. At least, he was pretty sure.

He was also sure he'd spent a long, long time looking for her when he was alive. She was the last thing he'd seen before his death. The wings. He'd seen her flying toward him.

The paladins leading Feather into Prahv jerked her head forward and gave the angel a shove that almost knocked her over, and she stumbled up the steps. Kos tried to turn and follow her but felt a palpable wall of force that kept him in place. One of the paladins eyed him suspiciously and barked, "Mind your place, spectral."

The late Agrus Kos was compelled to obey. But that didn't mean he couldn't watch as the paladins pulled and prodded the angel to go with them through the great archway of Prahv.

"Good morning, Guardsman," a gravelly voiced wheezed beside him. Compelled by the greeting to respond, he turned and nodded.

"Minister Bulwic," he said automatically. "Good morning."

Kos and Castell returned their attention to the steps and the slow procession of ministers and other officials making their ways to the halls of law and justice.

The vision of an angel danced around the corners of his mind. The passage of the bound and shackled being had already fled. A roc passed before the sun, a disk obscured by thickening cloud cover that promised more rain.

"Good morning, Minister," Kos repeated, received a nod from another arriving senator, and nodded in return. Kos heard shouting and catcalls at the top of the steps but kept his attention on the arrivals.

Agrus Kos was dead, but his spirit lived on. The spirit wasn't particularly happy about it, but you would never know it from asking him.

* * * * *

The skyjek patrol was not the first to see the Parhelion return to Ravnica. But Air Marshal Shokol Wenslauv was the first to go in for closer look.

The flying headquarters of the Boros angels, absent since the Decamillennial, reappeared directly over Utvara several hours earlier, behind clouds that rippled with holy thunder and unnaturally scarlet bolts of lightning. What remained of the Utvaran populace hardly noticed, understandably preoccupied with survival as the nephilim continued to plow their township into rubble.

At first Wenslauv, a veteran roc-rider familiar with a great many types of mental conditions that exhaustion and thin air could trigger after several hours of open-air flight, had thought it must be some kind of mirage. The patrol had been on their way back to the nest, there to check in for an eight-hour rest period before she set back out on another fourteen-hour shift—four on the ground with paperwork, ten in the air.

It was, she soon ascertained, no mirage. One second, the sky was empty except for the usual dawn traffic—riding birds, passenger bats, small personal zeppelids and their much larger freight-moving cousins, and a few Ravnican citizens capable of flight on their own flitting here and there between messenger falcons. Storms looked to be in the offing to the east, not common this time of year but not unheard of.

The next second, there was a golden castle under heavy sail emerging from the clouds at ten o'clock. It was as solid and real as one could hope. At one time, it had formed the upper half of Sunhome, and it still docked there upon occasion.

"Krokt," Wenslauv swore under her breath and immediately added a short prayer of penance for dishonoring the angelic host with casual blasphemy. The air marshal hand-signaled her wing-mate to pull close enough for a shouted exchange.

"Lieutenant," Wenslauv shouted over the high-altitude winds that screamed through the city's tower tops around the wings of her flight helm, "report this to Centerfort. I'm going to hail the—" The air marshal paused and peered at the Parhelion. It was still somewhat distant, but she was heading toward them—and by extension, the Center—with all sails unfurled. Most of them, anyway. There was something very odd about the familiar but long-absent aerial headquarters of the angels of Boros, and not just its silent reappearance high over the City of Ravnica. Many masts hung empty or had been reduced to broken stumps. One of the six massive belly-mounted floatspheres that kept the fortress aloft was blackened and caved in, trailing a thin stream of oily smoke. Several of the spires that should have risen to form a peaked arch in the center of the Parhelion were broken off, smoldering and sputtering with magical energy.

"Sir?"

"One second."

Open flames flickered in several shattered windows, and what looked like impact craters spotted the Parhelion's surface. Wenslauv was something of an expert on what happened to objects dropped from a great height, and she was also a fine shot with the goblin bam-sticks all skyjeks carried as standard issue these days. The holes that peppered the great vessel reminded her of both. The Parhelion looked as if it had been through a war. But the strangest thing wasn't what Wenslauv saw but what she didn't see. When Razia had patrolled the skies of Ravnica from the Parhelion's command deck, century upon century, a wing guard of at least a dozen angels led the way, always led the way, their pure voices raised in an ever-changing hymn that helped to guide the flying fortress on its course through the skies.

Though the Parhelion was back, the angels were nowhere to be seen. With no wing guard to navigate, the Parhelion seemed to be at the beginning of a slow, descending arc that ended some distance behind the air marshal, in the Center of Ravnica. If there were living angels aboard, there was no way they would be sailing on that vector, listing lazily to starboard at such an angle. They would certainly not have flame-pods burning at what the skyjek swore must be at least one-half power, driving the Parhelion onward. This was all wrong.

She tore her eyes away from the Parhelion long enough to scan the skies around her—as expected, she and her wingmate were the only law enforcement within hailing distance. And it was starting to rain again, as it had off and on for the last three days.

"Sir?" the lieutenant, a gifted goblin roc-rider named Flang, cried back. "That's the— I mean, the angels! They're back!"

"Belay my previous order," Wenslauv hollered. "That thing's heading right for Prahv. Skip Centerfort and head straight to the Senate. Use my authority and get that place evacuated, now!"

"But sir," squeaked Flang, "The brass must be notified!"

"Fine," Wenslauv said. "You're right. But fly quickly, and to hell with the speed limits. Get the reserve patrol from Centerfort and take them with you, and a strajck team if there's one already on station. I don't think the Parhelion is going to stop, and Prahv is right in its path."

"Are you sure, sir?" Flang asked.

Wenslauv took one brief glance at the vessel, tested the wind with her thumb, and nodded. "Dead sure. Get those people out of there, Lieutenant. At this rate you should have a few hours."

"That's a lot of—"

"Lieutenant, if anyone in Prahv gives you trouble, you're going to arrest them. That's what your backup is for. I hope you won't need it and the evacuation turns out to be an overreaction. I'll find out when I get there," Wenslauv said, pointing at the new arrival. "It might not be too late to stop it."

"Sir, what can you do?"

"There must be some way to keep it airborne, if I can get onboard. That's what I'm going to do. Good luck, Flang," Wenslauv said and tossed him a final salute.

"Yes, sir!" The goblin saluted then wheeled his roc Centerward.

"Me?" Wenslauv said aloud to no one within earshot. "Oh, I'm just going to go keep half of Sunhome in the air all by myself. No problem."

She spurred her roc forward and made a beeline for the Parhelion. The younger skyjeks might swear by the tireless pegasus, but for Wenslauv's zinos nothing flew like a roc.

* * * * *

"Rakdos?" Capobar said incredulously for what felt like the hundredth time as they left Old Rav by way of a little-used gate. "Why the Rakdos? Don't you know how bad uprisings are for business? You're going to ruin me. Us. Ruin us. The business." Silence. He mentally kicked himself for never learning the shades' true names. At least he'd have someone to curse when they got him killed.

The previous ninety-nine times Capobar had launched into this rant, the shadewalkers had said nothing, though they still gave occasional, invisible shoves to remind him they were close. Capobar was feeling ever more obstinate and emboldened as they moved at a brisk pace through an unending series of blind alleys. The thief had to admit he was lost, and was beginning to suspect that the situation was driving him a little mad. And so he asked again.

"You sold some of it to the *Rakdos?* It's mad. You don't spend enough time in the visible world, you. This is a bad, bad idea. Izolda will not let us live. They'll find me easily enough, but they'll find you too. That was a bad deal, and you had no right to—okay, maybe you did, but it's still crazy."

Capobar, he told himself, you're just talking to hear yourself talk, and that, old boy, is an early sign of hysteria. He forced himself to shut up by repeating his portion of the numbered account holding the zinos the blood witch had just paid them. The shadewalkers had the other two thirds. But he could not bring himself to trust the deal. Izolda of the Rakdos was not a guildmaster, exactly, but she might as well be. The demon-god officially held the title, but his was a remote form of leadership. For hundreds of years Izolda had been the real power behind the thrill-killers.

Marching down cramped throughways in the darkness—the alleys and less significant streets of Ravnica only enjoyed the sunlight around the noon hour due to the towering architecture around them—he calculated the odds that the shadewalkers really did know what they were doing versus the blood witch's reputation for ruthlessness in all of her dealings. Scattered, blinking glowspheres illuminated the damp cobblestones under his feet, throwing his calculations off. Capobar was developing a wicked headache.

Then, to add a little random terror to the adventure, one of the shadewalkers chose that moment to break the long silent treatment.

"You talk very much," a voice said. The sudden sound made Capobar yelp involuntarily. "Why do you talk so very much?" He felt a cold, invisible blade tap ever so lightly against his chest in warning.

"Fine," the master thief muttered. "But no good will come of ripping off a g— a client. I made a deal for the entire amount. I didn't promise to get the client half, or two thirds, or a share. And *my* client doesn't strike me as the kind of person who likes sharing. You went over my head. You'll never work a respectable job again. And you're going to bring ruin to Capobar and Associates. I can't accept that, you know."

"What, I wonder, is respectable?" The shadewalker seemed amused.

Another voice came from the air to Capobar's right. "This is the place."

"It is?" Capobar said nervously. "The place for what?" The press of a blade tip against his chest was the only reply. He held up his hands, palms out. "All right, all right."

Capobar felt his upper arm clamped by a hand that exerted just enough pressure to tell him that the arm would be broken if he struggled. "Will you continue to sputter like this or must I cut out your tongue?" The master thief, feeling less masterful by the second, opened his mouth to reply, felt the blade still south of his throat, and thought better of it. He nodded, carefully.

"Good," the first voice said with glassy satisfaction. Then, to the other shadewalker: "Sketch the seal."

Capobar saw a chalk line begin to form on the ground to his left. It curved around in front of him and kept going to describe a full circle around him, six paces across. Then smaller marks appeared, some kind of magical letters, Capobar thought, from the look of them, were scratched in a smaller circle, inside the original. Finally, a third circle was drawn, this one inside the lettering. The entire process took about ten minutes, and every time Capobar tried to so much as scratch, he felt the blade at his chest. As the third circle closed, the master thief felt a second hand clamp on his opposite arm.

The disembodied voices began a brief, whispered chant in a dialect that had a lot in common with High Vedalken, but Capobar couldn't make out the stylized, complicated words. He recognized the last two, however: the name of his client.

Then there was a flash, and the next moment he was standing between two very visible shadewalkers in an identical circle somewhere muggy and green. At first, focusing on distant objects only watered Capobar's eyes. All he could make out were vibrant colors, something like a chandelier a few dozen paces away, and the smell of damp earth. There was a familiar smell, but at the moment his senses were too scrambled to place it. But he could get a good look at his employees—soon to be former employees, one way or the other.

He was surprised to see how small the shadewalkers were—each one came up to about his shoulder, with wiry bodies. They were wrapped loosely in blue, gauzy bandages, like the mummies of ancient Grand Arbiters resting on the great mall of Prahv. A pair of glowing eyes peeked out through the face wrappings, and their arms were longer than was quite right, simian and oddly double-jointed. The two primary arms, Capobar corrected. Each shadewalker also had a smaller vestigial arm tipped with a clawed hand growing from his torso. The third arm was bare, revealing pale, almost-transparent skin filigreed with black and blue veins. Around their necks each shadewalker wore some kind of silver collar with three blue gemstones set in a triangle at the throat. Capobar wondered if the collars were the secret to shadewalker invisibility, then a more relevant question popped to his teleportation-addled mind.

"Why can I see you?" he blurted.

"All is seen in this chamber." A distinct, cytoplastically enhanced voice slithered from the tangled green mass of life directly before him. The neuroboretum, the extended intelligence of the Simic guildmaster, Progenitor Momir Vig. The client. *His* client.

The shadewalkers might be keeping their word after all. Whether the two could successfully make the transaction without Vig's discovering that the prize had been shared was still open to conjecture, but he could still cling to the hope.

Capobar should have recognized the greenhouse just from the humidity, but he'd been discombobulated. The greenhouse was a constantly changing living structure atop the Simic guildhall, Novijen. Novijen itself had, by all accounts, been grown rather than built, but it was the greenhouse that the progenitor seemed to use as an ongoing experiment in biomanalogical architecture.

Momir Vig was there, standing upon a flattened platform that resembled a giant, silver lily pad amid the tangle of tubes, vines, strange fungal plants, and indescribable organic growths that formed his neuroboretum. Sunlight filtered into the chamber, feeding the thriving life inside the greenhouse. Momir Vig rarely left the greenhouse, and with good reason. Capobar could feel the tingle of mana infusing the humid atmosphere and knew that Vig was said to thrive on it.

The guildmaster of the Simic was not alone. To the right of the neuroboretum stood a figure who had once been a female Devkarin elf but had obviously been heavily altered by necromancy. Her skin—and there was a disturbing amount on hideous display—was charred and wrinkled like tree bark. Her sallow, sunken face sat atop a neck that bent at an unnatural angle beneath tangled mats of wiry, black hair. Capobar could make out a vertebra jutting through gray skin. She wore tattered, scant robes that looked religious in nature, perhaps some kind of zombie priestess. She could have used a hood, if only to keep Capobar's stomach from turning somersaults.

The figure to the thief's left was harder to make out. He seemed not just to lurk in shadow but also to be a *part* of the shadow. He was tall, thin, in a black cloak, and had a pair of glowing eyes that were the only clear things in the darkness.

Capobar looked up again at the membranous windows overhead, then back at the shadowy stranger. Whatever the stranger was, he seemed to be creating the shadows on his own, bending the yellowed sunlight around him. Nice trick.

He glanced at the shadewalkers and noted that they were staring at the shadow man. Their third arms coiled apprehensively, but they said nothing.

The awkward silence lasted until Capobar cleared his throat and decided to go for broke. "Hail, Guildmaster," he said. "We have retrieved the objective. My associates should be able to take care of everything from here. And since that's the case, I think I will try to get back to the office and catch up with some paperwork. It's been a pleasure."

His body wouldn't move. Should have expected that, he told himself.

"Welcome, master thieves," the Simic guildmaster said. "We're all quite pleased to see you. All of you."

"Right," Capobar said. "And as I said, I believe we've completed our end of the deal. My apologies to your honored guests. I do not wish to be rude. But a successful thievery doesn't run itself."

"No need to apologize," the progenitor said. "Since you're not going anywhere."

Finally one of the shadewalkers spoke up. "Progenitor, we did as you ordered. The death cultists were allowed to share in the prize."

"Well done," the Simic said.

"You ordered?" Capobar said, a question that hung unanswered in the humid, magical atmosphere.

"With plenty left over for your project," the second shadewalker said. "So we will leave the prize to you now. We trust that all proper payments have been arranged, as per our contract." The shadewalker pulled the giant syringe from under his bandages and set it on the spongy floor, then pushed it with its foot. The blunted tube rolled to a stop before the Simic guildmaster.

The undead elf cackled. "Oh yes," the broken-necked priestess hissed. "I do hope you brought enough of that stuff to go around. Big plans, you know."

"God-zombie," the shadow said, and the undead Devkarin creature's laughter stopped abruptly. Her lopsided grin didn't.

Capobar heard a whispered curse from the shadewalker to his left and almost had to laugh. It was plain as day that the shadewalkers were as surprised to see the others as he was and that their plans had also been thrown off the path and sent barreling into a ditch. He suspected their sudden visibility was distressing them almost as much. The shadewalkers shifted from foot to foot, visibly anxious, unused to concealing their body language at all.

Desperate, he took a shot in the dark. "But what about those other creatures?"

The progenitor's eyes flashed. "Other creatures?"

"Yes," Capobar said. "The creatures that, er, ate what was left of the dragon. The nephilim of Utvara. They were growing at an amazing rate when we left. I know, sir, that you have an interest in such things. Unusual forms of life." The last he tried to say with a friendly grin, but he feared it probably looked more like lunatic desperation. Which wouldn't have been far off.

Momir Vig turned to the Capobar and eyed him like a spider sizing up a juicy bloodbug. "How many?"

"Er," the thief said, "five. And they're huge. Getting huger by the minute, I don't doubt."

The bald, pale face turned back to Capobar. Vig had once been an elf—some of the few remaining original parts left on the progenitor's head were distinctively pointed ears that gave him a demonic look in the misty light. Vig's race of elves had long since died out, their name long forgotten, killed in tribal wars with the pre-Guildpact armies of the ancient Silhana and Devkarin. The two surviving elf races agreed on very little, but they both agreed that Vig's kind had been an especially cruel and ruthless strain of the species, and their passing was mourned by no one, not even the progenitor himself. "Thank you for telling me of this, master thief."

The first shadewalker, still a step behind, said, "We had assumed you knew, Progenitor. We will gladly return to Utvara and bring you—"

"No, I don't think so," the Simic said. Without warning, glistening, ropy blue cytoplastic vines sprang from the floor and snaked up the shadewalkers' legs and around their torsos, growing and spreading until the shadewalkers' wiry bodies were fully encased in translucent fibers. It happened so quickly that the shadewalkers didn't have time to make a sound, and after another few seconds their blue eyes went dark.

Capobar felt his muscles relax slightly, and he experimentally flexed one hand. He could move again.

"My agreement was with you," the progenitor said in response to Capobar's incredulous look. "The agreement is fulfilled. And you have done me an additional service, as well. I have long wished to have my own shadewalkers upon which to experiment. These two, I think, will do nicely."

Capobar, bewildered, said, "So I'm—I'm free to go?"

"Of course," Momir Vig said. "When I have need of your services, I shall contact you again. Go, enjoy what remains of your life."

Ten minutes later, as he walked across the pavilion in a daze, breathing in clean, cold air that smelled of impending rainstorms and no magic whatsoever, Capobar was still trying to figure out whether "what remains of your life" had been simply a figure of speech.

A mental picture formed of what the Simic progenitor might be able to do with the giant nephilim—which, Capobar realized, with an uncharacteristically guilty conscience, he had told the guildmaster about—and started walking a little faster.

He wasn't a drinking man, but he had the urge to crawl into a barrel of bumbat and never crawl back out.

* * * * *

Wenslauv's steed gave a keening call that mingled with the whistling wind. She was pushing the bird to its limits, aiming for the open landing deck closest to the Parhelion's command floor.

They were still outside the city. There was still time. Time for

Flang to clear out Prahv, a little less to try to regain control of the slowly descending angelic vessel.

She still hadn't seen any sign that anyone, angelic or otherwise, was aboard the Parhelion, but if she could get to command in time, Wenslauv might be able to keep the thing in the air until help arrived. Otherwise Prahv, and a lot of the rest of the Center, might well be doomed.

Her mount's wings flapped furiously to maintain the speed and bearing Wenslauv desired as they entered the flying castle's lee and the wind disappeared along with the sun, both completely blocked out by the shape of the mammoth vessel. The artificial eclipse revealed that the landing deck was dark and seemingly empty. The platform should have been brightly lit by glowspheres. A legionary of the watch should have stood at the edge of that platform, directing traffic.

Wenslauv brought the roc down at the outer edge, where she could clearly see where she was landing, and dismounted. So much for what *should* have been. What *was* shook her to her very core.

The roc squawked over her shoulder as she peered into the gloom. The glowspheres had apparently been smashed. The remains were scattered over the floor before her. She turned back to the big bird and patted her on the neck. "Go back to the nest, Jayn," she said softly. The air marshal wanted to tell the roc to wait with all her heart, but the odds were she would either pull this off or die in the attempt—there was no point in the loyal bird's dying with her. With luck, Wenslauv would stop the Parhelion's descent in time, and she would leave when help arrived. And if not, she wouldn't be leaving. The five remaining floatspheres on the underside of the vessel would never withstand a collision at this velocity, even if the flame-pods burned out before impact. At best they would break, leaking toxic fuel into the Parhelion and the surrounding crash site. At worst, the floatspheres would explode, taking out the angelic sky fortress and a great deal of whatever happened to be near it—or inside it—at the time.

The roc looked at Wenslauv with familiar avian intelligence and cocked her head.

"Good bye," Wenslauv said. "Be sure to get clear. Go on, now." She slapped the roc's neck to emphasize the command. "Go!"

Jayn the roc shuffled around and stuck her beak into the rush of air outside the slow-moving Parhelion. Her talons clacked against the mizzium floor twice, as if to give Wenslauv one last chance to change her mind. The air marshal just shook her head. With a mournful cry, the roc launched into the sky carrying an empty saddle and veered toward the Center, loyally keeping her distance but refusing to leave her master completely behind. Wenslauv smiled grimly and turned back to the darkness. With a practiced motion she drew a short silver baton and almost dropped it when the deck shifted a few degrees as the wind picked up. She twisted the hilt of the distinctive wojek weapon and the pendrek hummed to life. She wished it threw off light as well, but wishing wouldn't make it so. Wenslauv's eyes had adjusted enough to the darkness to make out what had to be the exit to the rest of the Parhelion.

Focused on the dim doorway, faintly outlined by some distant illumination deep inside the vessel, she didn't see the obstacles on the floor until one sent her sprawling. The skyjek managed to keep her balance and stay on her feet by dumb luck, which saw the deck shift again in precisely the right direction to keep her upright.

Wenslauv really needed to get some light in here. She found an open panel on a wall next to the vague outline of the exit and felt for the button that would send mana to the glowspheres. If they were *all* smashed, this would be worse than pointless, but if any remained intact. . . .

The landing deck flashed into existence all around her as at least a dozen remaining glowspheres flickered to full power. A painful jolt struck her hand, still on the switch, and she jumped back in alarm. She tripped over the same object on the floor and this time couldn't catch herself before she went over backward. To her dismay, exactly what had tripped her up was exactly what she had feared most.

The dead angel had been partially dismembered. Only one wing remained affixed, twisted under the corpse, splayed like a flattened bough. The other wing lay crumpled into a feathery heap a short distance away. One arm was completely missing. Only a ragged black and red stump pierced by a sharp piece of jagged white bone remained. Wenslauv had tripped over the angel's legs, which were facing the wrong way—a vicious red seam showed where something with incredible strength had twisted the angel at the waist, sending innards spilling out onto the floor. There should have been blood all over the place, and there was, but the mana-powered lighting revealed the corpse had definitely been here for some time. The pools of blood had dried and even flaked away in a cloud when a gust of wind found its way onto the exposed landing deck.

The angel's face was one of the only things left intact, more or less—her eyes were open, staring, and shriveled. Her jaw was hanging slack, stuck, it appeared, to the floor. A silver sword lay in three pieces, two on the floor and one, the tip, stuck squarely between the angel's eyes.

The angel's dried, open mouth writhed with tiny white shapes.

Wenslauv choked back bile and fought to keep her stomach where it belonged. The air marshal was not of a weak constitution, but the worms were the straw that broke the dromad's back. Only the fact that she had skipped rations that day kept her from adding to the already vile scene involuntarily.

The corpse was at least a week old. If whatever did this was still aboard, she had even less hope than she thought. But she had to try. Wenslauv stepped over the body gingerly one last time and headed into the gangway, turning in what she hoped was the right direction.

* * * * *

A few seconds after Wenslauv's departure, a fistful of worms poured deliberately out of the dead angel's mouth, rolled themselves into a cylinder, and gradually took on the physical form of a snake. More seconds passed, and details grew distinct. It was an Utvaran leaping viper, with the characteristic red stripes lining its spine.

The viper slithered quietly after the skyjek, careful to keep its distance.

CHAPTER 7

The Boros Legion shall be the enforcer of the law. The Selesnya Conclave shall be the living spirit of the law. The Orzhov Syndicate shall be a check on the law's reach and protect the rights of citizens to challenge any charge in a court of Ravnican law. The Azorius Senate shall be the ultimate interpreter of the law and sit in judgment on all court proceedings.

—Guildpact Article I, Section 2

31 Cizarm 10012 Z.C.

Golden sunlight cast a beatific light on the unusual tribunal that was called to order. The Azorius Senate chambers of Prahv rang with the clanging of a gigantic brass bell that hung suspended in a managravitic field under the silver keystone of the Senate dome.

The sound only slightly disrupted Teysa's mental calculations. She'd heard it before, many times, though only rarely while sitting directly beneath it.

The cavernous Senate chambers of Prahv were largely empty, though the ghostly shapes of the soulsworn flitted to and fro over the largely empty benches ringing the amphitheater.

Teysa had entered a motion to hold the trial here, and she had successfully invoked the high tribunal statute. It was an obscure rule left over from the earliest days of the Guildpact, when the guilds of Ravnica had more frequently and fervently opposed each other. She got away with it because if Feather really was the last angel, as some of the crowds outside were chanting and she herself claimed, there was a good chance that she would be the Boros guildmaster by default. The angel had told Teysa she had no interest in becoming guildmaster, but the baroness had reminded her who was the advokist here, and she had dropped her objections, at least for purposes of the hearing. The topic of Boros succession had not been satisfactorily addressed in all the statutes, articles, amendments, and ordinances, Azorius scholars agreed. But to ensure complete fairness and accordance with the Guildpact, Feather would be treated as if she were the guildmaster, even though the current acting Boros guildmaster was in the chambers with them.

The tribunal system had many advantages, chief among them the diversity of opinion and viewpoints afforded by its very nature. It wasn't much of an advantage—indeed, it might prove to be no advantage at all—but she'd still take this situation over a standard trial before a blind adjudicator and a jury of vedalken mind readers. Instead of a purely Azorius court, the accused would face three sages of three high guilds: Azorius, Selesnya, and Boros.

The current Selesnyan Living Saint of the Conclave, a loxodon named Kel, represented the Conclave. He entered with little fanfare except the bailiff's formal announcement and walked heavily to his seat. From the other side, another of the tribunal judges did much the same but with a more deliberate step, a warier eye, and salutes from the bailiffs. The commander-general of the wojeks and acting Boros guildmaster was a lantern-jawed man with a dark, weathered complexion that testified to his decades of service in the roc-riding skyjeks. He wore a gleaming ceremonial breastplate of office adorned with the Boros sigil. He strode purposefully to the judges' dais and stood at attention beside his chair, returning the bailiffs' salute and waiting at attention for the tribunal leader's entrance.

Grand Arbiter Augustin IV descended into the chambers on a shaft of light and several thousand pounds of polished stone. The Grand Arbiter's torso ended upon a throne of white marble lined with silver and borne upon four small floatspheres that he controlled with the palm of one pale hand. He touched down at the center of the dais without effort or even an adjustment in posture.

Despite the diversity of the tribunal, Teysa was still concerned about the Grand Arbiter. She did not know him as well as she might have wished, Augustin had only been in his position for a few decades, replacing the wise and respected Lucian III after the latter succumbed to a long battle with Goff's disease. The others had a say, but ultimately the Grand Arbiter would pronounce sentence on Teysa's client. There was to be no jury at all, unless you counted the soulsworn. The rest of the Senate chambers were filled out with a few senior ministers and lords of both houses of the legislature—sworn to maintain silence—the bailiffs, the accused, a single clerk to transcribe for the archives, and of course the accused's advokist. There would be no prosecutorial lawmage. For this unusual proceeding, the judges both would ask the questions and make the charges. Teysa's job would be to respond as best she could. Fortunately, the baroness had reason to believe in her own ability to improvise.

She stood in her most conservative advokist's robes behind a long table, standing and facing the tribunal at Feather's side. The bailiffs had released the angel from leg irons, but Feather's wrists hung bound before her, and the heavy suppression rings around her wings still sapped much of her strength and power. Fortunately for her advokist, this also meant she was less likely to fly off the handle, literally or figuratively, while on the stand. Angels had famously fiery tempers. At Teysa's right were Elbeph and Phleeb, two of the Grugg brothers who had long served as her assistants in the courtroom and in her everyday business dealings.

The Grand Arbiter sat silently, his chin slumped to his chest and his eyeless face giving nothing away as he breathed slowly and steadily. He looked like a pale blue grandfather sleeping off a heavy afternoon meal. After almost a minute, he turned his sightless face to the angel. The Grand Arbiter considered her for another full minute.

Teysa's leg ached, but she kept her face set in a firm number six: I have deep respect for you, honored elder.

Finally, when even the wojek commander-general was beginning to shift in his seat and the Living Saint Kel had given in to his instincts and flapped one ear at a persistent greenbite fly, the Grand Arbiter nodded to the chief bailiff, a pudgy man in silver dress armor. The bailiff huffed his way to the third step before the dais and slammed his ceremonial spear against the stone. His two lieutenants each followed suit.

"This special tribunal is assembled!" the pudgy man boomed. He turned on his heel, set the spear to lean against his shoulder, and marched deliberately down the Senate steps with a great deal of pomp. When he reached the bottom, he snapped to attention and stayed there.

"Be seated," Augustin IV said. Teysa and Feather both took seats behind the table while the thrulls crouched. The Grand Arbiter's voice was rich and gentle, in sharp contrast to his bloody reputation for ruthless sentences. He had come to power during the last Rakdos uprising and had ordered more executions because of that one event than any previous Grand Arbiter in guild history. Teysa had had the honor of arguing two cases before him in her career. Both times she had found him fair but difficult to predict and almost impossible to deceive.

She was counting on that. For once, her strategy involved not even the formalized deceptions of her legal trade. Even Augustin would not be able to deny the truth from the mouth of an angel.

"This hearing," the Grand Arbiter continued, "is met and formally called to order. The senatorial stenographer will mark for the record that this tribunal has assembled in full accordance with the Guildpact and all related statutes and articles. Mark also for the record that Pierakor Az Vinrenn D'rav, angel of the Boros Legion, also known as Constable Feather of the League of Wojek, does stand accused of the following crimes. Bailiff, you will read the charges."

What followed was an almost note-for-note version of the charges that Teysa had already gotten from Feather in the interview cell. The chief bailiff finished the recitation of charges, rolled up two copies, handed one to the judges—the loxodon snapped it up and began to pore over it with a nearsighted squint—and one to Feather's advokist. Teysa unfurled her copy and set it on the table before her.

"Pierakor Az Vinrenn D'rav, angel of the Boros Legion," the Grand Arbiter said, "you stand so accused. You will step into the verity circle to testify to your actions at this time, unless you refuse to do so. Do you refuse? This is your right but will be taken as an automatic confession of guilt."

The question was asked of Feather, but as protocol dictated Teysa replied first. "We do not refuse the offer to testify, your honor," she said.

"And do you wish to call additional witnesses to testify in this case? Now is the time to name them," Augustin said.

"No, your honor," Teysa replied. "My client is the only available witness to the events that have resulted in these charges and therefore waives the right to witnesses now but does not forfeit that right should witnesses be required at a later time. I cite the case of—"

"Yes, agreed," the Grand Arbiter said. "No need for that. Legionary Pierakor, take a seat in the circle, if you please." Feather walked into the circle, which had been placed between Teysa's seat and the chief bailiff, and sat down on a simple stool. Her wings would have made a normal chair difficult. "Legionary, the crimes of which you stand accused are numerous and grave. You have chosen to act as your own witness, which presumes you are ultimately claiming innocence by way of circumstance. Once you choose to do so, you will give up the right to refuse to answer the questions of this tribunal or your own advokist. Do you understand?"

"Yes, your honor, we understand," Teysa said, and Feather nodded.

"I understand," she said.

"Good," the wojek commander-general said. "Your honor, I would request the honor of the first inquiry."

"That is your right," the Grand Arbiter said. "She is of your guild. As yet."

Nodov pushed himself up from his seat and leaned forward on the lectern. "My first question pertains to the charges, Legionary," he said, "and what the charges do and do not spell out for us. Where, in particular, did these events take place? Give us all some context." He pointed a finger at Feather and demanded, "Where did the angels go?"

For a long time, the only sound in the cavernous Senate chamber came from the spirits of the Azorius soulsworn, whispering in voices just out of the range of clarity. Even they fell silent when Feather began to speak.

"With one exception, your honor," she said, "it is my belief that the angels are all dead."

* * * * *

Fonn heard the song right before she woke up, just as she always did. The song was always the first thing to hit her conscious mind, before she was even aware she was conscious. Usually she found it a reassuring way to enter the waking world each day, like knowing immediately that you're safe at home, even when you're sleeping next to a wolf and a rained-out campfire on a road on the other side of the world.

Strangely enough, that wasn't too far off. Fonn blinked her eyes open against the afternoon sun. She sat in the middle of the road, slumped against a roadside milepost. With a start, she jumped unsteadily to her feet.

They were gone. The Rakdos. Her wolf. The dromads. The scouts. Her son. Gone.

Fonn took an unsteady step to keep her balance as panic gripped her, the world spinning around her head, and she almost slipped on a pool of blood. She turned around slowly. Don't let it be his, she prayed. Please.

It was neither Myc's blood nor any of her other scouts'. But wherever her missing charges were, they were not riding dromads. The beasts had been slaughtered out of hand and scattered malevolently across the road. After she got over the initial sickening wave of nausea, she made out pieces of indisputable lupine body parts among the carnage and finally lost the battle and doubled over, sick and shaking with deep sobs. The Rakdos had torn Tharmoq to pieces as well. The only thing that kept Fonn from a complete nervous collapse was the equally indisputable lack of any human, elf, or centaur remains.

Her son was gone and needed her help. Nothing could bring Tharmoq or the dromads back, but Myc and the others might still be saved.

She spun around in the bloody street, looking for any sign of the scouts or the Rakdos who had taken them. It was then that Fonn noticed the small crowd that had gathered around her. Some looked at her with horror, others with fear, but none apparently had possessed the fortitude or courage to come near her. Her person was still intact, her gear still in place, and her weapons—both hidden and apparent—remained.

Fonn charged to the nearest shocked bystander, a plump woman she recognized from a fruit stall they'd passed not long before the smoke closed in and took her recruits.

"You!" she shouted to the merchant woman. Fonn wobbled on unsteady legs, and the woman drew back. "What did you see? Where did they take them?"

The woman stammered for a moment before her mouth formed actual words. "You're alive," the merchant finally gasped. "You're not a— You're so— You're not a zombie, are you?"

"What?" Fonn said and looked down at her clothes. They were soaked in blood, and her arms were similarly encrusted. She grimaced and felt dried gore flake off of her cheek. "Oh. Yes, I'm alive. I'm an officer of— No, I mean I'm a ledev guardian. Order of Mat'selesnya. They took my— They took my recruits. They're just kids. Tell me you saw, which way they went. There were Rakdos. Thrill-killers."

"I just— I only saw a cloud, ma'am," the woman finally managed. "Sir. Fog. It rolled in thick, then it moved in on you and all—all *this*—was all that was left." She swallowed hard.

"Look, I'm not going to hurt you. The cloud. The fog. Which way?"

"It *were* Rakdos," said another bystander, a large man wearing an eye patch and a blacksmith's apron. "Bellavna, you're too worked up to know what the Krokt you saw. Me, I remember it, centuriad. I've seen that fog before, so I have. Saw it the night all the kids went missing out near Chaurn. It's a demon fog, they say. Only the Rakdos can call it."

"So none of you saw *anything*?" Fonn almost shrieked.

A younger woman in a shopkeeper's apron stepped forward. "I saw— I don't know if this is important or not, but I saw rats. Lots of them. And my cat's been missing for days."

"That's true," another bystander said, and several others chimed in agreement. Several pets were missing, and rats were showing up everywhere, the crowd agreed. An interesting connection to the case she had left in Lieutenant Pijha's capable hands but not particularly relevant to her current crisis.

Or was it? Rakdos was known by many other names. The Defiler. The Enslaver. The Demon-God. And, in more obscure histories, the Rat-King. Fonn filed that away for further consideration after she'd picked up the cultists' trail.

She forced herself to breathe steadily and regain some semblance of calm. The last thing Myc needed was for her to become hysterical. She focused instead on the song. Ever since he had been born, Fonn found she was able to effortlessly pick out that one strand of the eternal chord, that single note, which was the sound of her son's living soul. And she heard it even now, lower in pitch. He was already some distance away.

Somewhere, her son was alive. Fonn's heart leaped as she latched onto that hope like a drowning man clutching a line.

"Sorry, lady," the blacksmith grumbled, "Just trying to help. You reckon you're going to want all this meat? I only ask because—"

Fonn had her sword in her hand and the blade at the man's throat before he finished the "because."

"That isn't meat," she snarled.

"Er, none of it?" the merchant woman asked. "The wolf, I imagine he's pretty gamey, you know, but that dromad will feed my family for two weeks. Just one of 'em. If you don't want 'em—"

"Yeah," said another, as the crowd began to see that she was just a lone woman and not some revenant come to devour them all. "Wolf meat is good for all kinds of conditions, you know, and it's healthy besides. And the skull alone is worth . . ."

The ledev dropped the point of her sword and stepped back unsteadily. They couldn't help themselves. Like so many that lived in regions like this, they were practical about such things. But the thought of anyone, let alone these strangers, further desecrating the remains of Tharmoq or loyal dromads made her instantly furious. Almost murderously so. This was no good.

Fonn shut out the sounds of the babbling bystanders, who were already closing in on the corpses and poking them with sticks, looking to take what they could. Scavengers.

Scavengers were part of life. Even sentient scavengers. These people may not have been at the bottom of the social ladder, but they couldn't have been more than a rung or two up. Fonn could not bring the wolf back, or the dromads, but somewhere out there her son was alive. Let these deaths serve some purpose, even if there was no way these strangers could appreciate the sacrifice.

She closed her eyes and shut out everything except the song, and latched onto Myc's single note. Slowly, she turned herself around in a circle, and as she did the note altered its pitch. When she turned to the north or south it sounded pretty much the same. When she faced east, toward Utvara, it was lowest. Facing west, the pitch was highest.

West, the way they had come. The Rakdos were taking the scouts—Myc, at least, and she had to assume the others were with him since their bodies weren't scattered about with the dromads—right back to the city.

More than two hundred miles, with no mount. There was no telling how quickly the Rakdos could really move. It was clear that their leisurely caravan had been at least in part a ruse. She scanned the babbling crowd again but saw nothing more than a gaunt pair of oxen and a swaybacked dromad surrounded by a cloud of black flies.

She could run for it, and if she picked up the trail, she might even catch up. But if transportation could meet her on the way *there*. . . .

Fonn had no one else left she could turn to. It would only cost her some pride. He could meet her on the way there, and together they'd get Myc and the others back. He wouldn't be able to refuse.

She patted her chest, just below her chin, and felt the pendant still there. Fonn pulled it from her tunic and looked at the green and blue speechstone. Jarad had one much like it. They had exchanged them on the day Myczil Savo Zunich was born. They were incredibly expensive, and neither had used them since the divorce, but she still wore hers and knew Jarad still wore his, a direct line they agreed they would use only in an emergency, due to their limited duration. This certainly qualified.

She pulled the blood-soaked glove from her remaining original hand and tapped the blue-green stone three times. On the final tap she added, "Jarad. It's an emergency. I need your help. I'm at the Bargond shanty tower, east of the city. The big one, with the tunnel. My wolf is dead, Myc's been taken."

The stone glowed bright green, and the Devkarin's deep voice emerged tinny and remote from within. "I told you he was not ready to—"

"Later, for Krokt's sake!" Fonn snapped. "Rakdos took him."

"Why didn't you say—"

"Shut *up*. I'm getting to it! Rakdos took him, but he's alive. I can hear him. They're headed back to the Center, but I'm pretty sure they're still on the road. We need to catch up to them, but I'm on foot. How soon can you meet me?"

"I— Soon," Jarad replied. "Just give me enough time to grab my sword. The guild can run itself for— How long do you think this will take?"

"No telling. And we have to move fast," Fonn said. "I'll need my own ride. We can't afford to weigh down one of yours. Find me on the road. I'm going to get as far as I can on foot before you arrive."

* * * * *

"Pivlic!" the goblin shouted. "Are you in there?"

The imp heard the voice and recognized it, but it took a moment to place a name to it. Crix. No, the Izzet had a new name now. She'd already called ahead to tell the imp the good news via leylines. That had been a few hours and a lifetime and a half of pain ago.

Crix . . . Crixi . . . Crixizix. That was it. Pivlic had scheduled a meeting with her to go over her initial blueprints for the rebuilt Cauldron at—well, some point today. And it was day, his blurred vision told him, because torchlight wasn't that bright.

At the moment, he felt none too bright himself. Pivlic blinked blood out of his eyes and struggled to bring the room into focus. This proved difficult, as there was no longer a room as such.

"Pivlic!" the goblin repeated, more urgently. "It's Crixizix!" Yes, Crixizix. Good to know the old total recall was coming back intact, that ability was the butter on his bread. "Pivlic, talk to me!" Crixizix added. "Are you alive?"

"Yes?" the imp tried to call, but his own voice sounded faint. It battled inside his ears with the distant sounds of monstrous roars and heavy footsteps that were still close enough to shake dust from the fallen pillar directly over his head every time they made landfall. The voice also had the imp's heartbeat to contend with, which was pounding in his ears. "Yes!" he tried again, louder this time. "Here!"

Pivlic found it was agonizingly hard to breathe, and it took the imp another second to figure out why. The pillar over his head had toppled toward him, he remembered that much, when the nephilim—"nephilim" the Gruul called them, yes, nephilim but enormous, gigantic nephilim—had turned on the township. Or maybe the dragon, another Krokt-forsaken dragon, had sent the pillar over with his tempest-spawning wings. Pivlic had been trying to retrieve the baroness's most important documents before heading to his private zeppelid when the architecture had given way. The base of the pillar pinned his legs to the floor and compressed his lower abdomen in what should have been an incredibly painful way.

Or would have been, he guessed, if he could actually feel anything below roughly the center of his chest.

"We're going to get you out of there," Crixizix called, "but it's going to take some time. The town's a mess, and the ogres are doing all they can to keep what's still standing. The Izzet are sending help too." The goblin's voice sounded hoarse and raspy, like someone screaming at a funeral. "More help, I mean," she added quietly.

"We're paying Kavudoz to handle construction, not freelance ogres—" Pivlic objected automatically. His business sense was never far from the surface.

"Kavudoz is dead. Can you hold on?"

"I think so," Pivlic called back but wasn't at all certain he did think so. This kind of injury—he'd seen it before, after a panicked lokopede had picked up the *kuga* plague and gone berserk, rearing up in the middle of a busy street. The lokopede had crushed seven bystanders, one of them in much the same way Pivlic was injured. The man had seemed fine—conscious, even joking—but when the lokopede was taken away and the man pulled from the wreck, his ruined body fell apart. He'd died instantly, no time for teardrops or healers.

The imp suspected that he, too, was living on borrowed time. He tried to call to the goblin again, but his throat was too dry to make much more than a croak.

"Hurry," he rasped.

* * * * *

Myc Zunich had always been in a hurry growing up. Like other kids, he'd had a hundred different things he wanted to be when he became an adult. But unlike many other kids, Myc had done something about it. He'd studied and he had trained, from a very early age. He knew far more about swordplay than even his mother realized. His father had been giving him advanced lessons in the blade since Myc had been able to hold a sword. In truth he hadn't found the tests for scouthood to be all that challenging, though he'd politely refrained from telling his mother. They'd pitted him against other students, who weren't anywhere near as far along as he was, and he had beaten all of them. He knew they resented him somewhat for that, especially since he was so much younger than most of his fellow students.

Myc didn't blame them for it, but he understood it. Their occasional mocking didn't bother him in the slightest, because he had priorities. He was going to become a ledev guard by the time he reached legal adulthood at sixteen. If the worst injuries that happened to him in the process were to his pride, he'd be lucky.

He also knew that most of them didn't really mean it. He had been helping each of them with certain aspects of their training individually. But in a group, kids—Myc never thought of *himself* as a kid, of course—could change in funny ways.

These subconscious thoughts gave way to a wakefulness as Myc felt his body bounce with sharp, jarring pain. Fear returned. His hands were bound behind his back. He was in a cage.

A ledev would not be scared. A ledev, when captured, would first find a way to escape and free his fellow guards.

The latch was so primitive it could not be picked, only opened with brute force. No luck there. Myc winced as another jolt of pain shot up his forearms. The bindings were just tight enough that if he tried to lie on his side as still as he could, the ache in his shoulders and knees subsided to a dull throb. But any attempt to move just met with pain, no doubt by design.

Myc was hardly more than a decade old, but he'd been a ravenous reader of histories since he was three. His father had caught him rattling off the preamble of some contract or other Jarad had left out on the table, skipping the bigger words but, Myc would hear later, speaking with remarkable clarity. He didn't really remember it. Myc couldn't recall a time when he had not been able to read. Over his short life he had taken every opportunity to immerse himself in stories of the great guilds, the great heroes, and the infamous villains of Ravnican history. Naturally he had a special fascination for the Golgari and Selesnya Conclave guilds, especially since he wasn't sure which guild he belonged to. His father was guildmaster of the Golgari, but his mother was a heroic ledev guardian of the Selesnya Conclave.

They didn't like each other much anymore. That was something Myc tried not to analyze because whenever he did he came to the conclusion that somehow it was his fault.

The Golgari, the guild of monsters, did not frighten him. His father's guild fascinated Myc. And he'd never stopped reading the histories of the guilds. The noble Boros and their fiery angels. The shady Orzhov, guild of lawyers, ghosts, and zinos. The high-minded sages of law in the Azorius Senate, the brilliant doctors of the Simic Combine, the methodical and power-hungry Izzet, and the wild and savage Gruul. Not to mention—in fact, his mother had slapped him once for doing so—the Unseen, House Dimir, the tenth guild, the guild that wasn't. It hadn't been easy finding those stories, but Myc knew the libraries of central Ravnica well. And, of course, there were the Rakdos death cultists, the guild no one seemed to want him to know about. He didn't see why. A road guardian had to expect to run into just about anybody, and like many a boy his age he found the dangerous Cult of Rakdos fascinating. Not that he wanted to be like them. No, Myc had pictured himself fighting the Rakdos uprisings, going toe-to-toe with hideous slavers and freeing the just and innocent with his daring sword and mighty wolf.

Now that he saw and smelled the Rakdos up close, every

thumping step the massive indrik took jolting his joints, he didn't feel very daring and didn't even feel much like helping the innocent, except himself. And the others, if they were in the same situation.

The boy kept his focus on his new anger, lest his fear overpower him. Anger could be directed and could help him think straight. He blinked his bleary world into sharper relief just as a nearby cultist chose to jump at the cage with a snarl, laughing like a mossdog. Myc yelped and tried to push himself away but could get no purchase on the cage's grated floor. The cultist's face was horribly scarred, especially around the mouth. It looked like the man had cut away his lips and cheeks, leaving his jaws and yellow teeth exposed. The thrill-killer's eyelids were also gone, and his red eyeballs rolled madly within their sockets as he snapped his teeth at the young scout and giggled with vile glee. Self-mutilation (and self-cannibalization) was a Rakdos tradition.

"Z'reddok, down," a priest hissed. Which priest Myc could not tell. His efforts to back away from the door of the cage had only succeeded only in turning his face around toward the indrik's gray, wrinkled hide. It smelled of sour sweat and swarmed with biting flies, which were frequently sampling Ledev scout whenever the opportunity arose. "They are not for you, these ones. One of 'em's for Izolda."

Z'reddok, the cackling one, babbled something in a guttural tongue Myc didn't recognize. He had a good ear for languages, and could speak ancient Devkari and the Silhana dialect of Elvish fluently. He could place most other languages in at least their broad family group, but this one eluded him. Myc was glad. It didn't sound like what Z'reddok was saying was anything he wanted to hear.

So his chance of escape, at least at this time, was not good. But he could still try to check on his comrades, assuming some of them were with him. The priest's statement about "one of 'em" convinced Myc he wasn't alone on the indrik. He had half-hoped he was the only one here. The others might not be up to the plan that was forming in his mind. But then again they had passed the same tests he had, so they had the training, if they could master their fear.

One thing he knew, his mother was not here. He could hear her note in the song, but it was several miles behind them.

The others were not blood, and he could tell nothing about their proximity. He'd have to risk calling out. Maybe if they could talk they could figure something out together. From what the priest had said, they were going to leave them alone for some undefined period of time, because at least one of them was intended for something—or somebody—else. Had he really said "Izolda"? Myc recognized her name from the newssheets. He didn't want to imagine what such a creature wanted with him or the other scouts.

"Ledev scouts," he called in the Silhana dialect. All scouts had to show some fluency in the elf language, and few outside the Selesnya Conclave understood it, making it a convenient code language if Myc kept things simple. He, of course, had learned it at his mother's knee. "Are you here?"

The Rakdos didn't react to his call, at least not that Myc could see. But he didn't get an immediate response in the Silhana dialect either. He tried again, and still no one called back. He thought he heard a few Rakdos hiss and spit something about "foul elf noise" before another one of the priests shouted them down.

Finally, Myc heard a soft voice call back. One of the other scouts. Female. "I think we are all here," the voice said in an adequate attempt at the Silhana dialect that she spoke with a thick, central-Ravi accent Myc found he liked for some reason.

"Lily?" Myc called in reply. "Where are you?"

"In a cage," the older scout said. "You?"

"Same," Myc said. "Below you, I think."

"Myc?" That sounded like Aklechin. "Lily? I'm tied up."

"Me too," Lily said.

"Quiet!" hissed one of the priests and smacked Myc's cage with a gnarled wooden club. "No more elf talk!"

Myc waited a few minutes, and the priests and other cultists spread out along the road again. When he felt he had a little breathing room, he resumed, whispering this time. "Lily? Have you heard Orval?"

"No, but there's someone in the cage to the right of me. You can tell by the way it's bouncing. I think I can see a hoof," Lily replied in kind. "They wouldn't put him in a cage if he were—if he were dead, right?"

"I hope not," Myc said quietly. "And no one saw what happened to my mother?"

"She vanished in the smoke," Aklechin whined. "She must be—"

"No," Myc snarled, "she's not. But they're taking us away from her. I can tell. Believe that."

"I believe it," Lily said.

"I said no elf talk!" the priest barked. "We get hungry, maybe we eat the one that talks the most. Z'reddok's hungry, aren't you, Z'reddok?"

Myc clamped his mouth shut. He wouldn't be the cause of harm to the others. Instead he tried to see recognizable architecture through the grated cage, without much luck. The sun was behind the towers, throwing any identifying features in dark shadow from Myc's angle. He suspected they were still on the main road but couldn't be sure. Without any other point of reference, like the time of day, the position of the sun didn't really help him tell what direction they traveled in either.

Z'reddok, for his part, confirmed that he was indeed hungry and unfortunately went on to describe some of his favorite foods, to no one in particular, with nauseating zeal.

CHAPTER 8

Don't say I've got the voice of an angel,
Don't tell me that you think I'm true.
Don't say I've got the voice of an angel,
'Cause an angel would never lie to you.

—*Face of an Angel*, by Shonya Bayle,
the Balladrix of Tin Street

31 Cizarm 10012 Z.C.

An angel, perhaps. Failing that, a ghost. A simple, run-of-the-mill ghost. Wenslauv would have loved to see a ghost. It would have somehow made the carnage she slogged through on her way to the Parhelion command floor a bit more familiar. She had seen death, but death was always accompanied by spiritual residue. When this many things—this many people died, there were always a few who lingered. Spirits, sometimes vengeful, often simply lost, but almost always useful for a clue or two. Here, there was nothing.

Only dead angels.

Wenslauv had been raised to believe that angels were immortal and indestructible. Ravnica would always be safe, her people always at peace, because the angels of Boros sailed the sky in a golden, flying fortress called the Parhelion. No one could *kill* an angel, and an angel never grew old or sick. Angels were magic and justice and vengeance given form and the perpetual, invincible heroes of the cheap adventure books she'd grown up on. As a very young girl she'd believed for a while—led on by her sister—that if your heart was pure and true, you could grow a pair of wings and become an angel yourself. Then she'd discovered that Jirni had made the whole thing up, which had led to a fight that left young Shokol with a fat lip and Jirni with a black eye. Wenslauv would never had admitted it to a soul, but she had joined the skyjeks because, quite simply, they flew with the angels.

She wasn't flying now, and neither were the angels. Not anytime soon.

The bodies had been infrequent at first. She'd gone pretty far down the hall before she found the second, broken and twisted like the fallen angel on the landing deck. Broken sword, broken bones, signs of decomposition. Also about a week old, from the look of it. After a few more, she'd stopped looking them over too closely.

She spotted the snake as she doubled back from a passage that ended in a collapsed bulkhead. A flash of black slid from the corner of her eye, and it was gone. Wenslauv padded back to the T-junction and saw a scaly tail slip beneath one of the corpses. This particular body was faceup had been left all of her limbs, but most of her the neck was gone. The lifeless head was turned grotesquely but mercifully facedown.

The snake did not emerge from the other side of the body after a few seconds. The serpent's very presence was improbable, but mages and druidic types were known to use them as servants. Perhaps it was watching her every move, or perhaps it was just lost. Either way she couldn't just leave it slithering around, That species was poisonous, for one thing, and she had work to do. The air marshal reached down with one foot, silently prayed the angels would forgive her, and pushed the corpse aside with the sole of her boot. It slumped over, revealing an eyeless mug.

The floor beneath the angel was empty. Wenslauv pushed the corpse a little further to the side without looking into the empty pits in the angel's face and still found nothing. The snake must have slipped through a broken seam in the walls. There were enough of them in this floating disaster. That didn't explain what it was doing here.

Whatever the case, she was wasting time. She had a crash to avert.

Wenslauv held a hand over her nose against the smell as she headed down the gangway and followed what signage remained. The passages were cavernous, as befit a crew consisting of flyers, but the lingering odor of death hung heavy and turned them into a network of airy tombs. The air marshal felt smaller and smaller the more bodies she passed, the closer she got to command. The listing deck told her she was headed in the right direction.

Wenslauv had an hour, maybe two, if she were lucky. The shattered floatsphere might overheat one of its counterparts and trigger a massive explosion at any time. Whatever had killed the angels could jump out from around the next corner and tear her limb from limb. Apparently, she might even die of snakebite if she wasn't careful. Something was very wrong about that.

Lost in thought, she almost walked past it without noticing, but the glint of silver in the orange glowspheres caught Wenslauv's eye, and she stopped with a start. She looked at the baton in her hand then turned back to gaze in stupefied wonder at a wall lined with bam-sticks, pikes, swords, explosives, and a surprising assortment of axes and long knives.

An hour. Maybe two. But she had to live that long. If she had to fight, best to be loaded for drekavac. Wenslauv shrugged and ducked into the armory.

* * * * *

"Agyrem?" Nodov blurted. "That's— That's a story," he finished lamely.

"It is a very real place," Feather said. "I am in the verity circle.

You may step inside if you wish to confirm I speak the truth."

"The accused shall not issue challenges of any kind," the Grand Arbiter said.

"Will you confirm the verity circle is working properly?" Saint Kel said. "If so, this is—well, 'blasphemy' is probably too strong a word—"

"It's just another word for—for heaven, though," Nodov said, "the place you go when you die. It's like saying the Parhelion flew off to another plane of existence."

"Not another plane," Feather said. "Not exactly. More of a . . . pocket of existence."

"What do you mean?" the Grand Arbiter asked. When Teysa arched an eyebrow, he added, "For the record."

Blind, my eye, Teysa thought.

"We—the angels—have long known, as have you, my lord, that Ravnica is sealed off from certain . . . eventualities," Feather said, "other places and worlds and states of being. Long ago, when even the angels were young, there were those who came to this world from these other places—these worlds like this one but not like this one—with their own angels and demons, their own people and gods. Most of the newcomers did not even realize they had not always been here. A few of the visitors, powerful beings indeed, left again, for those other worlds. Sometimes they would return, with tales of these places."

"We know this, do we?" Nodov said.

"Objection. Badgering the—"

"Continue, Legionary," the Grand Arbiter said. "I suppose this is inevitable."

"What is inevitable?" the loxodon asked.

"This was long before the Guildpact," Feather said. "After a while, we noticed the visitors had stopped coming as frequently, and the visits stopped completely. Only a few remembered that there had been such visitors at all. The first Azor knew and passed it down to his successors, did he not, your honor?"

"The accused will not pose further inquiries," Augustin IV said. "But for the sake of speeding things along . . . yes, he did."

"What other secrets are you keeping from us, I wonder?" the loxodon said with a suspicious curl of his trunk.

"This is not the time, Holiness," the Grand Arbiter said.

"When the visitors stopped coming to Ravnica, a few angels decided to try to find them."

"Were you among them?" the Selesnyan judge asked.

"I was one," the angel agreed. "We did not understand how they traveled to these other places, nor do we to this day. But we built the Parhelion anyway, with scraps of what magic and artifacts the visitors left behind. We took the sky fortress to the ends of the heavens, trying to follow the strangers to their other worlds."

"This is remarkable," the wojek commander-general said softly. "What did you find?"

"We learned that there is a great . . . nothingness out there," Feather said. "At a certain distance, existence ends. The universe that we know simply stops."

"This is nothing new. This is common natural philosophy," Saint Kel said. "What does this have to do with this so-called ghost city?"

"Much, Holiness," Feather said.

"But all of this happened before the Guildpact," Nodov said, "didn't it?"

"Yes," the angel replied. "The preface is necessary to explain what Razia believed Agyrem was. What it is, in fact. Razia believed that the sky—that existence itself—stops out there because this world is isolated. Contained. No energy or matter ever leaves or arrives. A closed system. If not for this phenomenon, the Guildpact's magic would not have been able to establish relative peace for so long. But the seal isn't perfect. It overlaps and folds in on itself, like a blister on the skin. Agyrem is, to put it less than delicately, that blister. Souls can't escape Ravnica, you see. There is no beyond for them to reach. That is why the dead linger, and when they depart the realm that humans occupy they are caught in the fold of Agyrem like fish in a net." The angel turned to the Grand Arbiter. "As you know, your honor," she added, "Razia did not figure this out until after the Parhelion had run aground, so to speak, in Agyrem."

Teysa had to suppress a grin. The other two didn't trust Augustin now and weren't even thinking about how to punish her client. They were too awestruck at the implications of what Feather described.

She knew she risked the Grand Arbiter's wrath for revealing a secret that the Boros angels and the Azorius judiciary had apparently shared for millennia. It was worth it.

There really was a place you went when you died. Assuming ectomancy, necromancy, a Boros grounder, or the Selesnyan "song" didn't bind you to the physical world of Ravnica, you would eventually turn up in Agyrem. And that was a fact that carried the potential to confirm or change a lot of belief systems around the entire world.

"Let the record show that I, Augustin IV, do confirm reliable theories pertaining to the existence of a place like the one described," the Grand Arbiter said. "But I admit my own curiosity gets the better of me, Legionary," he added. "How did you—did you say 'run aground'?"

"Yes," Feather said. "Are you all familiar with the phenomenon over the Utvara reclamation zone known as the Schism?"

"I am," Teysa murmured.

The others, too, knew of it.

"The Schism, it seems, twisted the fabric of Agyrem," Feather said, "knotted it up, so to speak." .

"How so?" Saint Kel asked. "I have heard of the phenomenon, but I thought it was just a trick of the light, residue from some Izzet magic."

"It is more than that," the Grand Arbiter cut in. "It was an unnatural experiment, created with Orzhov magic and zinos, if I'm not mistaken, Counselor."

Teysa grimaced. The Grand Arbiter, not surprisingly, had very good sources of information. "I'm sure I don't know what you mean, your honor," she said. Advokists were under no obligations to the verity circle. "However, I question the relevance—"

"Relax, Counselor. The Orzhov fulfill their part of the Guild-pact, just as we all do," Augustin replied. "You're not on trial."

When a few moments of silence had passed, Teysa nodded. "Go ahead, Legionary."

"Agyrem became—'snagged' is the best word—on the Schism."

"You're saying Agyrem floats around in the sky?" Nodov asked incredulously. "Just a big, invisible ghost city, plying the heavens like a leaf on the wind, mocking our great religions?"

"I do not say that the city of ghosts mocks anyone's great religions, or which religions might qualify as such," Feather said calmly. "I am a sworn protector of justice, vengeance, and the law. Those are not gods. They are ideals. Nor do I claim to understand how the fabric of existence behaves in relation to our realm. I know only what my guildmaster told me, and I believe it is the truth."

"You must or you would not be able to say it," the Grand Arbiter said. "Legionary, how did the Parhelion find its way into this 'fold in existence.' I admit I can not quite fathom it myself."

"My lord, the Parhelion was built to find the ends of our—of our reality," Feather said. "The mana that powers her does so by bend-ing our reality ever so slightly, as I understand it. It stays aloft not because of the floatspheres, not entirely, but also because a small part of it is in a slightly different place and stays there. Forgive the clumsiness of this explanation. I am no engineer. This small part of the Parhelion, this reality engine, is what allowed the vessel to slip into Agyrem after it snagged on the Schism," Feather explained. "The Parhelion punctured the veil and went through to the other side. Razia was not immediately sure how to return. And after a short time, she chose to stay long enough to explore the place."

"A noble sentiment," the Grand Arbiter said. "The quest for knowledge. Not very angelic. Nor was abandoning her responsibility to protect Ravnica."

"That is difficult to dispute," Feather said, "except to point out that the guildmaster was anything but a typical angel. She chose to investigate a possible threat on the chance that this world could get by without angels for a time. Nor do I dispute the fact that in retrospect, I believe it was the wrong decision to make." For the first time since her testimony had begun, emotion—sadness, deep sadness—crept into the angel's voice. "The Parhelion had only been in Agyrem a short while when I found them. I admit I don't remember much of my own journey except that it was not easy."

"Yet you crossed this veil you speak of on your own?" Augustin IV asked. Teysa wasn't sure she liked the intrigued look in his eye.

"I did but only with the help of my kin on the other side," Feather said. "They guided me there."

"What is it— What is this place like?" Nodov said. "What does the great hereafter look like?"

"Everything," Feather said. "Agyrem is every place that ever was, all at once. Unfortunately, I had little time to explore it."

"Why?" the Grand Arbiter asked.

"Because the ghosts of Agyrem had gone to war with the angels."

* * * * *

Wenslauv decided to load up on everything she could. No point in going out without a fight. From the position of a few different corpses she surmised that the angels had tried to get to the weapons but had not made it in time. Wenslauv stepped quietly from the armory, a pair of loaded bam-sticks slung over her back, a third loaded and held in her right hand, a pair of short swords, and a net slung on her drooping weapons belt—you never knew when a net might come in handy. Twin bandoliers of the small, orange spheres goblins called bangpops crisscrossed her breastplate.

Air Marshal Wenslauv flicked the safety catch off of the bam-stick's firing stud, clutched the weapon before her like a shield, and marched on to the command floor.

The tilting floor forced Wenslauv to keep one hand on the wall to avoid slipping. Adorned as she was with explosives and weaponry, one misstep and a fall at the wrong angle would have left pieces of air marshal all over the bulkheads.

A few minutes later, she emerged on the command floor, and her heart sank. It was completely empty. No corpses, though bloodstains covered the floor. No apparent foes, but the place was a shambles, and all of the other entrances and exits appeared closed. The great wheel was off its post, broken into four pieces. The various control stations were in no better shape: Two were still burning with low, green flame that looked both magical and electrical. Only the front-facing invizomizzium windscreen of the Parhelion remained intact and largely unharmed.

Someone behind her coughed. She spun around, her bam-stick charged and her thumb on the release.

Wenslauv had been wrong. There was still one angel here. The angel was alive and didn't look like she'd be that way for long.

Dissension

* * * * *

Lieutenant Flang was not the only goblin skyjek in the League, but he was the only one assigned to the elite Centerfort squadron. He also had a well-deserved reputation for bad luck amongst his skyjek squad mates, bad luck that Flang hoped had changed when he transferred to a flight group that called wojek headquarters home base.

Flang's luck had to turn around sometime, the goblin was certain of it. Three out of the five fortune-tellers he'd consulted had told him so. Flang was a great believer in luck, and three to five was a winning percentage.

The transfer turned out to be just another visit from Krokt, the goblin god of misfortune for Flang. Flang the Unlucky was his nickname. He coined it himself, which was unfortunate.

Who always seemed to be the last one back to the landing platform and therefore responsible for getting the platform swabbed clean? Flang. Who showed up just a few minutes too late to sit in at the card table? Flang. Who sometimes got to the card table and lost a month's wages in the first five minutes? It had to be Flang.

Who, while flying as fast as ever he could for home base with a message of the utmost importance became so distracted thinking about Flang's bad luck that he veered too close to the underside of an aerial walkway, was knocked clear from the saddle, and dropped like a stone before coming to an abrupt and deadly stop on the roof of—as misfortune would have it—Flang's favorite goblin restaurant?

Flang.

CHAPTER 9

Look, I don't have any idea where they went. I don't know what they did with the vampire, either. Yes, I know the wolf. I'm sure he's going to do fine. On second thought, why don't you make all of that 'No comment.'

—Lieutenant Agrus Kos, quoted in the *Ravnican Guildpact-Journal*, 2 Seleszni 10000 Z.C.

22 SELESZNI 10002 Z.C.

Feather—she had long ago stopped thinking of herself as Pierakor Az Vinrenn D'rav—emerged into the city of ghosts with a chill that cut to her bones. During her tenure with the wojeks, she'd been bound to the surface of the world. After two years of searching Ravnica, pursuing lead after lead about the Parhelion's disappearance, she had grown completely accustomed once more to the palpable feeling of wind flowing over and under her wings. The gusts, the updrafts, the clouds, the palpable embrace of the air.

Here there was no wind, no air. Feather did not need to breathe unless she wanted to speak, and she sailed through open space, but it was not true flight. It felt more like willing herself forward into a cluttered nothing.

Things worked differently here. They certainly looked different. She had lived for a very, very long time and had never seen anything like Agyrem.

The world of Ravnica had disappeared. Feather floated low over a haphazard, patchwork town that might have been contrived by mad gods with a terrible sense of humor and a worse sense of aesthetics. Something like an inverted Rakdos warren sat atop a bulbous, deformed Selesnyan outpost tree. Roads left the surface and curved along impossible arcs with no respect for logic or gravity. Translucent denizens were everywhere, moving to and fro, a ghostly population that made the world shimmer and change as they passed.

Of greater interest was the vessel that had called her here. The Parhelion floated with its great sails sullenly limp and no wind to fill them.

She had found her missing kin at last. Had she been able to take her eyes off this glorious sight, she might have noticed that the Parhelion wasn't all she had found. A swarm of glowing, white shapes was moving up from the patchwork city to meet the flying fortress, flickering in her peripheral vision. She ignored them.

The host. She had missed them.

The angel had been able to hear them calling out in every magical fiber of her being, their absence an ache that beckoned to her from a great distance. The golden parapets of the Parhelion gleamed in a sunless sky, white sails flashing in greeting, all flight decks open, floatspheres glowing like fire.

The shapes left her peripheral vision and entered her direct line of sight. The angels were under attack.

The host emerged from the landing decks, rising to meet the chaotic swarm of flitting, ghostly shapes that rose from Agyrem in an unending river of ectoplasmic energy. Trios of angelic wing guards cut through them like spears, scattering the spectral energies forever in little white flashes of energy, but the enemy had the angels horribly outnumbered. Feather could tell that the angels' maneuvers were being improvised and hastily coordinated on the wing. A thousand angels, give or take, had dwelt in the Parhelion, but even as Feather watched, one of those thousand fell from the strange and distorted sky under a swarm of screaming, amorphous shapes. The doomed angel disappeared into what looked like a lake of oil, part of the ever-shifting landscape of this strange place.

There was no turning back now, not after what she'd gone through to get here. Feather did the only thing she could do—she drew her sword and charged into the fray.

A pack of wailing ghosts rose to meet her. The ghosts called to her, called her full angelic name. Feather felt fear. No, not just fear. Terror. She realized why the ghosts looked familiar.

The quietmen.

She tucked her wings and dived. If she could break clear of the pack of ghosts of the quietmen she could get to Razia, perhaps lead the Parhelion back to the world that needed it. At least, that was the plan. But the ghosts followed at the speed of thought and reappeared in front of her before she realized they'd even moved. The leader of the specters glowed and became opaque. By the time the ghostly quietman's fist drove into Feather's jaw, it felt quite solid. She almost dropped her sword in surprise but managed to hold on as she tumbled backward in midairless void. She regained enough control to make a furious slash at the bold phantom that cut the shape neatly in two as if it were a mere puff of smoke.

The ghost of the quietman vanished in a flash of white light.

Could a ghost die? Feather was no philosopher, but she guessed they could be destroyed, at the very least, and that was perhaps what made Agyrem truly different. There was no lingering, just a flash, a pop, and nothingness. Before she could consider the question further, another blow, this one from behind, knocked her helm from her head. Then a fist slammed into her gut. Dizzy, the angel let herself drop. She slashed wildly behind her with her sword, hoping to get under her persistent foes and reach the Parhelion.

She saw more white flashes, then the welcome site of Anezka, first lieutenant of Razia.

"Pierakor?" Anezka asked. The other angel's face displayed a mix of shock and happy recognition. That allayed Feather's immediate concern about the voluntary end she'd called to her wojek service. "Pierakor! You heard us! Come quickly. We need every able sword that we can—" Another ghost flew in on a suicide run. The Boros lieutenant flicked her sword and sliced through its translucent face. Another flash, another ghostly quietman gone.

"What is happening?" Feather asked. "How can I serve?"

"Razia will explain," Anezka said. "We have to get to the Parhelion."

* * * * *

It had been decades since Feather strode the decks of the Parhelion or soared unfettered through its cavernous gangways. But she could not relish her homecoming. As soon as she and Anezka broke through the swarm of ghosts—not all of them spectral quietmen, to Feather's dismay, which implied that the danger to the vessel was even greater than she'd initially thought—two stoic members of the guildmaster's personal guard were there to meet them. They saluted Anezka and greeted Feather with a nod and "Greetings, Legionary." They turned and marched the new arrivals directly to the command floor.

Feather had not seen the guildmaster since Razia had cast judgment on Pierakor Az Vinrenn D'rav and sent her to work with the mortals as her sentence. The crime was not one that the mortals would probably have understood, and Feather had never found a proper way to explain it to her wojek colleagues, though naturally they were curious and had always found new ways to ask about it. Fortunately, mortals expected taciturnity from an angel, and few had ever pressed it. Of those, only Kos had ever come close to finding out, and he'd taken his best guess to his grave.

Feather wondered if he was here.

After decades among mortals, Feather felt a strange sensation of . . . shame? . . . as she stood before that holiest of beings, the parun and guildmaster of the Boros Legion. That which each of her kind longed to be. The burning flame of Boros. The guildmaster of justice. Vengeance incarnate.

Feather dropped to one knee and lowered her head.

"They tell me the mortals have given you a pet name," Razia said without preamble. "Do you prefer it to your proper one?"

"Sir?" Feather said, looking up in surprise at the abrupt question. The guildmaster beckoned her to stand, and she did.

"Your name, Constable," Razia said. "Names have power, and you forsook your own for one from a human. Do you prefer to be called 'Feather'?"

Of all the things Feather had expected the guildmaster to say first, this was not one of them. "I answer to that name," she said, compelled to reply. "I answer to my holy one as well. 'They will know you by deed, not by name.' "

"Feather, you're quoting a book I wrote," Razia said. She made the moniker sound both ridiculous and utterly demeaning, "Why do you stand on my command floor? We have engaged in a holy war against an enemy who may well be impossible to defeat. This is a job for angels, not the fallen host."

"Holiest One," Feather said, "circumstances, at the time, decreed that I act as I did. As you say, I was assigned to serve the League of Wojek—"

"And to set an example, you, an angel, violated the direct command of your guildmaster," Razia said. "What are the mortals to make of that?"

"If I may speak freely, sir—"

"You may."

"I was given few outstanding orders," Feather said, "and the Guildpact itself was threatened."

"Don't you understand, Constable?" Razia said, whirling on

one foot, eyes blazing. "You helped *break* the Guildpact. You and that fool Agrus Kos."

"Guildmaster," Feather said, probably with a bit more challenge in her voice than was wise. "Agrus Kos stopped House Dimir. The vampire was going to destroy Mat'selesnya and had corrupted the Selesnya Conclave. Kos's solution was simple. He arrested him."

"Exactly," Razia said. "Constable, the Guildpact is—was—a powerful magic, certainly the most powerful this world has ever seen. Without it, that world we protect would have descended into chaos and petty wars thousands of years ago, destroying itself over and over again. Look out that window. What you see is the result of a peaceful history. Can you imagine what it will look like when the Guildpact fades? What kind of power you've handed Szadek?"

"I don't understand," Feather said.

"This war!" Razia shouted. "No angel shies from a just battle. This current fight is no such thing, yet here we sit, trapped and under siege. We are destroying souls, Pierakor! These beings who live and die, they go on, don't you see? And what is left is something irreplaceable. These abominable acts are your doing!"

"How—" Feather began, but a blur of motion outside the invizomizzium windscreen cut her short.

A tidal wave of ghosts barreled toward them. At the head of the massive spectral army, a familiar shape, more shadow than substance but topped by a pale face with black eyes, flew like a monstrous Golgari bat. The Dimir guildmaster's silver teeth glittered in the weird phantasmal light.

Razia saw the look of shock on Feather's face and turned to face the coming onslaught just as Szadek and his ghostly army made contact with the Parhelion's hull. The vampire moved through the hull as if it weren't there, and his soldiers followed.

* * * * *

If there was one thing an angel was always ready for, it was a fight. Even during her tenure as a wojek constable, Feather had never shied from combat, though the opportunity did not present itself often for a peacekeeper. It was one of the reasons she had enjoyed helping Agrus Kos; her old friend had never been one to shy from a fight, either. He also had a knack for getting into the fights of others.

Despite the battle readiness that was practically an angel's natural state, none of them had expected the Parhelion's confines to be breached so easily. Feather would later reflect with great humility in the Azorius Senate that the angel's arrogant assumptions concerning their fortress's supposed impregnability were ultimately their undoing.

The first to fall—that Feather saw, at least—was Anezka, who had placed herself between the guildmaster and the spectral Dimir vampire. Feather didn't have time to wonder how Szadek had gotten free, let alone how he had found his way to the city of ghosts. All she knew was that the Dimir guildmaster was here, and his apparently still-potent power to manipulate the spirits of the dead made him probably the most powerful being in this place.

Anezka met the charging shadow with a holy blade. Before it could find home, a pair of ghosts, moving so quickly they were little more than amorphous blobs of white light, slipped into what should have been harm's way and wrapped ectoplasmic tendrils around the weapon's blade. The Boros lieutenant froze in midstrike, eyes flashing with frustration, but the ghosts would not let go. With a crack, the tendrils snapped Anezka's sword in two.

The spirits then parted, allowing their vampiric master to step forward. He reached out, grabbed Anezka by the throat, and tossed her like a doll against the bulkhead. The angel's skull shattered on impact, and the first lieutenant of Boros slumped to the floor beneath a rosette of gray and red.

Angels, like the nephilim, did not age. They were invulnerable to many forms of magic and were the most skilled warriors on the plane. Only certain weapons and metals could pierce their skin. Their bones were almost impossible to break.

At least, that was how it worked on Ravnica.

But Feather wasn't on Ravnica anymore, and it appeared that in the strange pocket world of Agyrem, angels were only just *so* immortal.

Razia might have been entertaining similar thoughts, but if she did the guildmaster did not show it. Instead, the sight of her lieutenant's dashed brains on the bulkhead sent Razia into a rage. She drew holy steel, and Feather stepped to her side, her own sword in hand.

Feather had missed much of the drama at the Decamillennial, and by the time she had actually seen Szadek, the vampire had been in a truly sorry state—half-consumed by his own shapeshifting servant, Lupul, and bound by wojek lockrings. Here in Agyrem, Szadek had, apparently, recovered. This new incarnation of the House Dimir guildmaster was half-solid, half-shadow, terrible and pale, with eyes that burned with blue flame. Szadek spread his arms, and the wailing ghosts parted to go after the rest of the angels. They left a clear circle on the Parhelion command floor containing the vampire, Razia, and Feather.

"Razia, it's been ages, hasn't it?" the vampire said with a silvery smile. "I am so glad that you found this place. I was beginning to think that I had not made the trail obvious enough even for you."

"What have you done, vampire?" Razia roared. "The Guildpact —"

"For someone as old as you are, your memory is a trifle spotty," the vampire replied. His casual, almost conversational tone was unsettling, and Feather began to wonder if that unfamiliar feeling—uncertainty—was the vampire's work. "I'm doing exactly what your Guildpact dictates."

"Silence!" Razia cried and swung her sword directly at the vampire's neck. This time, no ghosts appeared to block the strike. Szadek did it himself with his open hand.

"No, I don't think so," the vampire said, the wicked smile widening. "I allowed myself to become vulnerable once and with good reason, but you will find I have regained a measure of my old self." Szadek grasped the blade and yanked it free of Razia's hand.

It was the opening Feather had hoped for, and she unleashed her own strike just as Szadek moved. The vampire's arms were a blur, and with a clang the angel found her sword met with Razia's own. Szadek whispered a word and a whip of purple energy lashed out and caught Razia in the belly, sending her flying backward across the deck. On the other side he blocked Feather's strike with the pommel of the guildmaster's sword and shoved the angel away with an elbow to the chin. The vampire was unbelievably strong, and Feather had to fight to keep her balance.

Szadek tossed Razia's sword in the air in a spin and caught it by the hilt. He appraised it like a collector and extended it to point toward Feather.

"A simple weapon?" Szadek said. "You seek to harm *me* with a sword? You're going to have to do better than that. I mastered the blade long before you were incarnated."

Feather saw that Razia was still dazed and regained her footing as best she could before Razia made another lunge. Szadek met this one as before, knocked the guildmaster to the deck once more, and turned to Feather. As the wailing ghosts rushed through the Parhelion all around them, their screams mixing with the shouts of the angels who fought them, Szadek and Feather engaged in a one-sided duel. The vampire hardly even considered the angel as one hand fended off every blow, every strike, and covered every opening. All the while, Szadek took step after inexorable step toward Razia, smiling. No matter how she maneuvered, Feather could not place herself between the enemy and her fallen, stunned guildmaster.

This was not going to work, Feather realized. And so she did something no angel found it easy to do. She broke off from the attack. With a leap, she soared the few feet to the stricken Razia, slung the guildmaster over her shoulder, and bolted for the exit.

Szadek's laughter followed her down the poorly lit gangway. So, she saw when she risked a look back, did Szadek himself.

* * * * *

"Pierakor," Razia said, her voice straining through what sounded like a great deal of pain, "put me down. We are not going to win, not today. It is my destiny to fall at their side."

Feather ducked a screaming, ghostly shape and leaped to avoid the body of another fallen angel. The host was being slaughtered left and right.

"I disagree," Feather said, "We must live to fight another day." She hauled the weakened guildmaster deep into the bowels of the Parhelion, where the powerful reality engine drove the floating fortress through the sky. If they could escape from the hatches that opened from there onto the vessel's underbelly, together the angels might be able to get back to Ravnica to warn the Legion that the fugitive Szadek had been found. There was still hope, Feather was sure.

The fugitive's laughter echoed down the hall behind them.

After almost an hour of constant running through the labyrinthine passageways, the laughter, to her surprise, faded away. "I think we might make it, Holiest," Feather said. If they had to flee, escape hatches were directly beneath them.

She set Razia down gingerly at the junction of two of the biggest generators after checking back to ensure Szadek no longer followed. She saw no one—the angels who could sometimes be found down here tending to the engines had obviously charged into the fray, and the distant sounds of fighting between specter and holy warrior were all she could make out.

The guildmaster was weak. The vampire had caved in her ribs, right through her breastplate. Blood covered Razia's cracked and dented armor. Feather put a hand to her own shoulder. It came away damp and red. Whether it was her own or Razia's she wasn't sure, but Feather didn't think she herself had been struck.

"He's not going to stop," Razia said. "He will kill me first. That's what he's after."

"Why now? Why this way?" Feather asked. "Ten thousand years he had to launch an assault. Why lure you—lure us—into this?"

"Is it not obvious?" Razia said. "This place is a playground for him. The ghosts dance like his puppets, and there is no Boros Legion or Guildpact to stop him."

"I can't leave you here, Holiest."

"You can and will," Razia said. "Help me stand."

Feather offered the guildmaster her hand, and pain wracked Razia's face as she pulled herself to her feet. She pushed Feather back and pressed the other hand to her crushed chest. "He has your sword," Feather said. "Take mine."

"Thank you," Razia said. "But you must go. Go back and warn them. The Grand Arbiter must be told and the other guild leaders. You are our last emissary."

"Holiest?" Feather said. "I stand with you. The angels of Boros—"

"The angels of Boros won't survive if you don't do as I say," Razia gasped. "I see that you are not to blame. Forgive my anger. This was Szadek's doing, Legionary. I will fight the Dimir, and

I will likely die. You have your orders. You can prepare them for what's coming, but you have to go. Now."

A loud clang of metal on stone resounded throughout the engine decks, and Feather heard a mizzium door clatter against the mizzium floor, the hinges and locking assembly twisted and smoking. Feather took flight, weaponless, and whirled in midair to instinctively protect her guildmaster.

"This one is persistent, Razia," Szadek sneered. "You should be proud. When you began shaping these offspring of yours, I was certain they would prove mere shadows of the original. This one is almost as tenacious as you."

"Legionary!" Razia called, and screamed as she pulled herself into open space beside Feather. "Go!" The guildmaster slammed into Feather's shoulder just as Szadek leaped forward, sword extended, sailing down from the upper tier on swirling, tangible shadows. Feather lost control and tumbled back to the deck. The latch of an exit hatch set into the flooring appeared directly in her line of sight just as the angel's head collided painfully with the mizzium.

She rolled onto one shoulder and looked up just in time to gape in horror as Szadek impaled the guildmaster upon her own fiery sword.

The blade of Boros burst into flame as it made contact with Razia's flesh, driving through her heart and out the other side. A lance of blazing plasma emerged from the guildmaster's back, sputtered, died out. The sword Feather had given her dropped from her hand.

Feather flung open the hatch and dropped from the belly of the Parhelion into the phantasmal, blue skies of Agyrem.

* * * * *

The next ten years played out as an eternity for the last angel. In fact, Feather told the tribunal, she had assumed it had taken her much longer to return—perhaps a century. Years of constant flight through the nightmarish landscape of Agyrem, hiding here, carrying out a few risky counterattacks there, always forced back on the run, again and again. Years that she was hunted through the twisting, ever-changing streets of the city of ghosts every waking minute. If she had actually required sleep, she never would have made it back.

It was blind luck, she told the tribunal, that she was near the fracture point when the Schism opened a passage between Agyrem and Ravnica. When she'd spotted the open, blessedly solid and *normal* ground of the real world below, the angel had wept. Then she heard Kos calling her name and bolted to the unfamiliar Utvara reclamation zone. She should have known, Feather said, that the old man would find a way to help guide his old friend back to the world. An angel always heard those that called to her.

But Kos, it turned out, had been calling to Feather as he lay dying. After a few days of mourning, Feather decided to return to Agyrem one more time before turning herself in to the Boros. If the Schism had let her though, it might let other things through, things like Szadek. She had to know for sure that the ghosts were going to stay in their own realm.

That had been a mistake. The forces of Szadek's ghost army, flanked by what looked like the possessed shapes of Feather's fallen kin, hounded her as soon as she emerged in the ghostly realm. But she did learn that the specters feared the Schism itself for some reason. Feather could think of no other explanation for why the army had not followed her.

And so, battered and injured, she had returned to the city and turned herself in to the authorities. She had reasoned it was the simplest way to get the warning to the leaders of Ravnica, and helped elaborate many of the specific charges herself in an effort to ensure that her hearing would be before Augustin IV himself, as Razia had wished.

And that, Feather told the tribunal, was where the angels had gone and why she stood before them.

CHAPTER 10

Our world is one, ultimately, of diametrically opposed forces in balance with one another. And you may say, 'Does this not mean perpetual conflict?' And I would reply, 'It means perpetual peace.' To diminish one's opposite diminishes one's self.
—Grand Arbiter Konstantin II, *Commentaries On the Guildpact*, 3209 Z.C.

31 Cizarm 10012 Z.C.

Agrus Kos returned to the world in a rush of memory, emotion, and the raw stuff of life. One moment he was a ghostly, mentally neutered spectral guard with a mind like Golgari cheese, full of holes though curiously complete on the subject of laws, and the next moment it was all there, more than 125 years of pain, loss, joy, wonder, heartbreak, and physical experience.

Kos's next thought was typical street-'jek suspicion. Kos had been indentured to the Azorius for fifty years. But he'd served, he realized with surprise now that his mind was complete again, only a few weeks. It felt like so much more.

And here he stood, alive, his entire mind in one piece. Whatever had just happened, Kos suspected it was going to cost him. How, he wasn't sure, but it would have to. This could not have happened for free.

Kos could remember now that his body—his body had been burned on a pyre in the town square of Utvara. The body he was in now, a living, breathing body, felt . . . off, somehow. He took a breath and felt his lungs fill with air. He looked down and saw hands and feet. His hands were pale, and he was wearing loose-fitting blue robes. He was human.

Otherwise, the body below him did not look remotely familiar and was in stark contrast to the flood of memories that fought for attention inside his head. He knew who he was, and this wasn't it.

The hands were pale and pink. His body had a substantial paunch. Kos patted down his own arms, learning quickly that they were somewhat flabby, definitely not the original issue. Kos had died an old man, but he'd been in wiry good shape to the end. Busting heads was a good workout.

"Krokt," Kos said. Was he possessing someone? Could he do that? Kos had never had anything in the way of real magical talent, hadn't wanted it and hadn't trusted it. He'd seen and fought against the Orzhov's taj, but they inhabited corpses, something like and unlike zombies in their way. Maybe it wasn't something you figured out. Maybe it was something you had done to you—far more likely, with his luck.

So if he wasn't a zombie and he wasn't himself—whose head was he in?

It's our head now, a voice not unlike the one that Kos had just spoken with murmured in the back of his mind. *And you try staying in shape with my schedule,* it added defensively. Before Kos could puzzle that one out, the anger set in as one particular memory—his death—came into sharp focus. Kos's own demise had been a hazy factual recollection out at the Prahv gate, his scattered ghost mind unable to fully focus on the images and memories that now formed into sharp relief.

"Krokt," Kos repeated in that odd, nasal voice and this time added, "what a way to go."

Kos remembered the desperation that had spurred him into that contraption with the goblin. He recalled how the two had fought a dragon and come out on the short end of the fight. Along the way, something had exploded inside the observosphere, and he'd been impaled on a hunk of wreckage. Two or three times, he couldn't remember. He'd risked his last teardrop to heal the grievous injury, and a goblin named . . . Crix. Yes, Crix, the Izzet messenger with the rocket-feet. She had gotten him out of the conveyance and carried him to the ground.

Kos had gambled and lost. He'd been warned. So many times he'd been warned that one more teardrop might kill him. But what else could he have done?

Kos supposed he should be grateful. Most people probably didn't get the chance to realize how foolish their deaths were. Fate's sense of humor was once again kicking Agrus Kos in the head. The joy of life had settled to a dull roar as the *fact* of it sunk in to his mind.

"Kos," a familiar musical voice said, "are you in there?"

Kos blinked and finally remembered that he wasn't just alive— he was in a body that was *somewhere*. He straightened up his paunchy new body and took in the rest of his surroundings. It was somewhere less familiar than the voice but familiar nonetheless. He'd testified for the prosecution here half a dozen times over the years. The Azorius Senate chambers, a cavernous amphitheater littered with ghostly soulsworn and a trio of officious-looking judicial types from . . . Azorius, Selesnya, and Boros, if his eyes weren't lying. Bleary-eyed, Kos eventually pinpointed the source of the voice on the central floor.

He'd hardly dared hope that he was right about the speaker's identity, and his (borrowed?) face split into a wide grin. "Feather?" he said.

At last it dawns, that odd voice said in his mind.

Who are you? Kos thought back. *What's your problem?*

Your anchor, the voice replied, making Kos wonder if he wasn't just dead but going crazy as well. *My name is Obez Murzeddi. That's my body you're wearing. Don't get too comfortable, I'll want it back.* The voice added bitterly, *I came* this *close to taking today off.*

* * * * *

"So I'm— I'm what, again?" Kos repeated. Every time he spoke, the voice changed a bit more to sound like his old one but would never be perfectly identical. His spirit, or whatever you called it, was trying to force this new body to sound like the one it remembered, with only partial success.

The blind Azorius judge sighed in exasperation, but Kos didn't care. None of this made any sense in his newly resurrected mind, and if it took a longer explanation than "Welcome back, Kos," then by Razia's breastplate he was going to get it.

"I have made you an avatar of Azorius," the Grand Arbiter said. "You currently reside in the body of the lawmage Obez Murzeddi, a trained ectomancer and one of the most able and trusted members of my staff. He has volunteered to be your physical anchor while you continue your service at our behest."

"And why did you do that?" Kos asked. "Wasn't a hundred-odd years of service enough? Haven't I earned the right to retire?"

"You are still a spectral guard, and you therefore serve the Azorius," Augustin said. "You will find that the contract is quite firm and does not change just because your specific assignment has been adjusted. A contract is a contract, and this one should give you more than enough time for this task."

"You can't force me to do anything," Kos said.

"Not true," the Grand Arbiter said. "This is quite compulsory."

"Then this is it," Kos insisted. "I do this task for you, and you let me just go to Agyrem or wherever. This job is worth a few decades of service, I think."

"Agreed," Augustin IV said. "In all honesty, it does not matter.

This is the job you were preserved to perform."

"Me," Kos said, "and the Guildpact. Why me?"

Feather spoke up. "Kos, the Guildpact is broken. And you—we—are responsible."

"How so?" Kos snapped impatiently.

Easy, the voice in his head said. *We're all on the same side here.*

Quiet, Kos told the voice. *Leave me alone.*

I would be happy to, but I'm a servant of Azorius. As you are. We do the bidding of the Grand Arbiter.

Suck-up, Kos thought.

Yes, that *will certainly help. Insult me. Why don't you find out what's going on before you begin name-calling?*

The voice had a point, but Kos struggled not to think it in as many words. He didn't like having a clever, sarcastic voice in his head that wasn't his own clever, sarcastic voice.

"How are we responsible, Feather?" Kos demanded. "Baroness, what do you have to do with this?"

Teysa Karlov shrugged. "I'm just the advokist," she said and jerked a thumb over one shoulder at the figure on the floating marble seat. "Tell it to the judge."

"She has played her part," the Grand Arbiter said without elaboration. "You, unfortunately, played Szadek's part for him twelve years ago. I will make this as clear as possible, and you will do as ordered," the Grand Arbiter said imperiously. "In your previous existence, Agrus Kos, you involved yourself in matters of great import to the Guildpact. You were duped by a being who is deception incarnate, but still, you were a dupe."

"What are you talking about?" Kos said. "Who 'duped' me? I may have been overcharged at the Backwater a few times, but—"

"You arrested the Dimir guildmaster. In so doing, you broke the Guildpact."

"That was Szadek trying to destroy the Guildpact, your honor," Kos objected. "I stopped him. And I never saw him again. He was taken away by the *Azorius* guard, I believe. And now, you," he pointed at the members of the tribunal with Obez Murzeddi's hand, "you managed to lose him?"

"How the Dimir vampire escaped is immaterial," Augustin replied, "though I doubt it would have been possible if the Guildpact had not already suffered mortal injury through your other erroneous actions." The Grand Arbiter leaned forward. "Szadek let you get close enough to do it. Your crime is ultimately ignorance, with complications."

"If I'm so ignorant," Kos said, "why not spell it out for me? Sir?"

The judge scowled beneath his silver blindfold. "The Dimir exist to oppose the Guildpact, to strengthen its power by the force of that opposition. It is why House Dimir was welcomed into the accord. Rakdos and his foul ilk, too. The Guildpact could not have lasted as long, or been as powerful, without that equal and opposing malevolence. But you arrested Szadek for crimes against the Guildpact. You created a paradox in that his actions were the very essence of his purpose within the Guildpact."

"You mean he was supposed to destroy the Guildpact, and the only way to save the Guildpact would have been to let him go ahead and do it? That doesn't make any sense."

"That is why it is a paradox," Augustin IV said.

"So what's the real story then?" Kos said. "Shouldn't someone be out there trying to fix this?" As the last words left his borrowed mouth Kos regretted them.

"Yes," Augustin said.

"Krokt. It's me, isn't it?"

"Yes, it is you."

"Of course. Because . . ."

"You were the agent of the Guildpact's collapse, though it was not your intent. Yet that gives us a chance, with luck and perseverance, to seal the breach and restore the holy document of law. We high guildmasters were not the only ones to suffer from arrogance and hubris," the judge said. "Szadek had to drop his defenses to let you succeed and used his lurker servants to convince you he was beaten. For that trick to work, however, he had to truly allow you be a danger to him."

"How did he know I wouldn't kill him?" Kos asked.

"Another gamble but a correct one," the Azorius guildmaster said. "You behaved as he predicted, as an honest lawman would. By creating the paradox, you achieved what he could not, even if you didn't know it. But once the vampire allowed you past his protections, he could not raise them against you again."

"Why not?" Kos asked.

"His power is based on secrecy, deception," the judge said, "and his protections are based on a similar principle. He did not break his own magic. He simply made *you* a chink in his armor, and not even he can take that back from you once granted."

"How do you know?" Kos asked. "Seems to me I never heard about this Dimir paradox until now."

"I know," the Azorius said. "He is my opposite number."

"So what, you can read his mind?" Kos said.

"I can read his plans, through centuries of study and thousands of years of gathered data."

"Didn't seem to help you when he showed up to eat the Selesnya Conclave," Kos retorted.

"No," the judge replied, "It did not. He used—certain methods to elude detection that I had not anticipated. It is an imperfect world."

"So you brought me back from an afterlife of interminable boredom to carry out a hit," Kos finished. "Like a common thug."

"You object?" the Grand Arbiter asked.

"Actually, no," Kos said after some consideration. "I'll do it."

"You can destroy him, but first you must find him."

"Now wait a minute," Kos said, the thing that had been bothering him about the Grand Arbiter's reasoning finally rising to the surface. "You mentioned his 'lurker servants.' Well, I'm not the only one who can hurt him. The lurkers did a nice job on him for a while there."

"That did occur to me," the Grand Arbiter said. "I have hypotheses. Perhaps the vampire did not believe he needed any kind of protection from the lurker. Perhaps the lurker has his own ways of piercing defenses that works counter to Szadek's own. Regardless, the lurker has been vanquished."

"How do you know that?" Kos demanded. "He—it—can look like anyone."

"A decade-long effort conducted by my own agents, at great risk and in total, necessary secrecy," the Azorius replied. "The lurker is destroyed."

"I was just making a point. So . . . this will fix the Guildpact?" Kos said. "And then that's it? You release me, and the world goes back to normal?"

"It is possible," the loxodon, Saint Kel, said, "but only just. The Guildpact magic is still there in the song. It may yet be healed. This wound may not have to be mortal."

"My honored colleague is more optimistic than I," Augustin IV said. "But if you can destroy him, he will be unable to drive this world further into darkness and conflict, conflict on which he thrives. His machinations are many, and I sense his hand in a great many troubles in Ravnica."

"Seems to me that the best time to eliminate the problem would have been not to let him in ten thousand years ago," Kos said. "Not that I'm any judge. In any respect."

"Hindsight is always clearer than foresight," the judge agreed.

"Yet ten thousand years of peace are nothing to scoff at. The Dimir must be stopped, but without Szadek and the House Dimir there would have been no Guildpact at all. We made law and magic into one, and magic respects certain numbers."

"Ten, in this case," Teysa volunteered.

"So what do I do?" Kos said.

"As an avatar of Azorius, you have been granted a fraction of my power," the Grand Arbiter said. "Your ghostly form is anchored, as I said, to lawmage Murzeddi. But you may leave it for a time and move—temporarily—to other bodies, over a considerable distance, as needed. Whatever body you possess, you will still be *you*. You will still be Kos. And so you will be able to harm him."

"Just 'harm him'?" Kos said. "Just like that? How do I jump out of this body?"

"You will, of course, need to suit your tactics to the situation," the judge said. "Lawmage Murzeddi will aid you."

Kos considered. His immediate anger at being drafted against his will—and after his actual death, at that—was cooling. He had served the Guildpact, served Ravnica, for most of his life. Strange as the circumstances were, was this really any different?

No, of course not, the voice of Obez Murzeddi said, but Kos ignored it. He needed no more convincing.

"I guess I'd better get started," Kos said. "But I'm going to need help."

"You can count on me," Feather said and turned to the judge, "assuming, my lord, that this means the charges—"

"The charges are dropped, of course," the Grand Arbiter said. "But as the last remaining angel, you are the new Boros guild-master. You have duties."

Feather indicated the wojek commander-general with one hand. "Acting guildmaster Nodov shall serve in my stead. You are the one who pointed out my own responsibility in this, your honor. You cannot deny me the chance to help Kos set things right."

The judge considered this for a moment and nodded.

"All right, Feather. You're with me," Kos said gratefully. In this body, Kos would be lucky to be able to hold a sword, let alone use it. The skills would be there, the muscles to use them might not. He didn't want to count on finding a convenient trained athlete to possess, assuming he could even pull of that little trick. Feather would fill that gap and then some.

"Before you begin," the Grand Arbiter said, "my personal intelligence network may have discovered Szadek's true hiding place."

"But you all just explained he's in some city of ghosts," Kos said.

"Despite what the legionary believed, I suspect that Szadek did not need the Schism to travel back and forth between Agyrem and Ravnica," Augustin said. "It is my belief he is already here. He waited until all of the angels were in Agyrem to attack the Parhelion, when he apparently could have done so whenever he wanted. I believe he is making a similar feint again, holding his forces back until he has all of the pieces where he wants them. Fortunately, we have something Szadek is not known for providing—a living, breathing, witness." The judge turned and said, "Bailiff, bring in Evern Capobar."

A older man walked into the Senate chambers from an anteroom. He looked sullen and angry. He bore a nasty wound over one eye.

"Evern Capobar," the Chief Bailiff announced then returned to his post.

"He's wanted on several counts of—"

"Not now, Nodov," the loxodon said.

"He was found in the Center," Augustin said. "He is the one we seek."

Kos and the small assembly listened with rapt attention to

the master thief's drunken story. The shadowy figure Capobar described fit Szadek's description perfectly. Kos was perhaps most disturbed to hear that the Dimir guildmaster had not just allied with the Simic progenitor but also, apparently, had a Devkarin woman with him he called "god-zombie." Kos didn't like the sound of that at all. He'd heard about the god-zombie from that other Devkarin, Jarad the bounty hunter. Svogthir was supposed to be dead, but it seemed no one was staying properly dead these days. And he could only think of one Devkarin woman who fit Capobar's description.

Kos involuntarily shuddered at the memory. *I really wish you hadn't just thought of that,* Obez's voice echoed.

Then don't go looking, Kos replied.

You fill up my whole brain with a graphic memory of snapped necks and worm-monsters and I'm not supposed to look?

He wondered if he could refuse to act until the Azorius could get him a new "anchor," but it was obvious that wasn't going to happen. He turned his attention back to the thief's testimony.

The Simic progenitor's involvement was harder to figure out. The Simic were the guild of medicine, the bioengineers of Ravnica. They created cures for an entire world of diseases. Over the years they'd saved the population from plagues, produced ton after countless ton of magical salves and healing teardrops. If he knew the Guildpact was broken, it stood to reason that the progenitor was eager to try creating things that might not be so beneficial. Momir Vig had a reputation as a genius, and even though the Simic functioned as the doctors of Ravnica, they had an equally well-deserved reputation for experimentation. The *kuga* plague, Kos had always suspected, reeked of such experiments. Then there were the virusoids that the Utvaran Simic, Dr. Nebun, had used to tend his laboratory back in the reclamation zone. The wojek-turned-bouncer-turned-spectral-turned-avatar didn't require much imagination to see how that could be taken to extremes if the Guildpact was not holding the Simic back anymore. Especially if the master of the Simic knew the Guildpact was in trouble.

It all made sense, but Kos couldn't escape the feeling that he was stepping into another trap.

* * * * *

It had taken hours, but Crixizix had finally managed to dig a small tunnel down to Pivlic. The imp wasn't sure how he had lasted even that long except for his absolute determination not to die.

The goblin crawled forward slowly, with exaggerated caution, determined not to bring down the remains of the Imp Wing Hotel and Tavern on Pivlic. The imp appreciated the caution but would have appreciated speed a little more.

"Hello," Pivlic croaked. His throat was dry as sandpaper. "What brings you to the Imp Wing? Can I interest you in our special of the day, my friend? Imp pâté. Real bargain."

"Glad you're still with us," Crixizix said. "Don't waste your energy. I'm going to get you out of here. I have teardrops, and there's a pair of ogres ready to pull this column off of you at my signal."

"But the town—"

"The town is lost," the goblin said sadly. "Many are dead, but most of the townsfolk were able to flee. They didn't seem too concerned with us. Too small, I think." Something else even worse than the destruction of the township obviously troubled the goblin.

"Who wasn't too concerned?" Pivlic said. "Have the stone titans set upon us? Have the dragons returned?"

"You'll probably remember soon. If not, I'll fill you in as soon as you're free."

The goblin wriggled beneath the pillar, pulling a length of strong rope behind her. Crixizix reached around the imp to pass the rope under the column, blocking Pivlic's line of sight with her tattooed forearm.

"This won't work," Pivlic said, recalling the lokopede accident. " 'Drops can't change the fact that I'm crushed. If you pull off the column, I will die."

"I said don't talk," Crixizix said with gently chiding humor. The goblin was one of the more unusual members of the species Pivlic had ever met, possessed of a great deal of intelligence and a charming demeanor. The imp suspected she could make some Orzhov a fantastic agent if Crixizix ever chose to leave the Izzet. "So I suppose you're a doctor now too?" Crixizix continued. "Baron-regent wasn't enough for you? I told you I'm getting you out of here. Don't you worry about a thing."

"Is that what you told Kos?" Pivlic croaked. Pivlic hadn't called many people friend in both word and thought, but Kos had been one of them.

Crixizix's gentle grin took on a sterner cast, but she said nothing.

"Sorry," the imp said. "Go ahead." Crixizix nodded, and the grin returned.

The goblin released the rope and leaned back, allowing Pivlic to see the thick cord run past overhead, seemingly of its own volition. Crixizix leaned in close to Pivlic's ear. "You're right. Your lower body is crushed, and in normal circumstances I'd say it looks bad."

"You shouldn't go into nursing," Pivlic rasped.

"Maybe not," the goblin laughed hollowly, sounding less confident to the imp than she was putting on. Well, better false confidence than none at all, Pivlic reasoned. The imp saw the glint of reddish light from out of the corner of his eye, and heard the telltale clinking of teardrops.

"Won't work," Pivlic said.

"Sure they will," Crixizix said, "as long as I apply them fast enough. And I'll have you know I'm faster than I look." She turned over her shoulder and without any warning at all shouted, "Pull!"

With a pair of mighty grunts, two unseen ogres hauled on the rope. The column started to rise, slowly at first, then faster as the weight shifted in the ogres' favor. In another few seconds, feeling returned to Pivlic's lower body, and he tried to scream. The blood welling up in his throat prevented any sound but a pathetic gurgle.

Crixizix's hands moved in a blur. The goblin slapped opened teardrops, two at a time, into the imp's lower abdomen and legs. The pain continued, burning as nerve endings grew back in the time it took to blink. The agony reached a feverish crescendo as he felt and heard shattered bone slip back into place, grinding as it did so. The torture finally subsided just as Crixizix pressed the last two 'drops she had left into Pivlic's side.

The imp made a habit of avoiding bodily injury, especially to his own person. It was part of a sound business strategy, staying whole and alive. Therefore, he'd rarely had need for this kind of first aid. It was over before he knew it.

Pivlic blinked. He wriggled his toes. "Better," he managed.

"Good," Crixizix said. "Can you still fly?"

Pivlic flexed his wings and sat up to take a good look at his lower body. Aside from some cosmetic scarring, he appeared whole. "I think so," he said.

"Hurry!" a growling voice called from overhead.

"Right," Pivlic said. "The column. But I can't carry you."

"No need," Crixizix said, rocking back onto her heels. "In fact, this will go more quickly if— For now, just hold onto my shoulders, tight."

"Er," Pivlic said, "all right."

A few seconds later, the imp heard the goblin clack her heels together, then together they blasted up from the crater that was the center of Pivlic's most recent—and most recently destroyed—place of business. Orange flames blasted from the bottom of Crixizix's feet, carrying them high into the air. Below them, Pivlic could make out the ogres, one of which growled, "Them out! Let go!"

With a crash, the stone pillar dropped back into the hole that was all that remained of the Imp Wing. It almost hurt as much—no, more—than the pain of being crushed from the waist down, he decided. Pivlic released the goblin's shoulders and flapped his wings, hovering. Crixizix did the same, ratcheting down the output from her feet enough to float effortlessly alongside the imp.

The ruins included not just a successful establishment of which the imp had been justifiably proud. The Imp Wing had also held all of the records in the baroness's temporary offices—Pivlic could take comfort in the fact that the records would have been no safer in the baroness's new mansion—along with a great number of his own zinos, and some rare illicit art that would cost Pivlic a fortune to replace.

With a final, resounding crunch, the hole collapsed inward swallowing the expensive column completely, one final insult.

"Krokt," Pivlic said. "Was that really necessary, my friend? True, I live, but the deductible on my assurance contracts—"

"The damage was done," Crixizix said. "I doubt any contract you've got covers this, though. You want to blame something, blame those."

Pivlic followed Crixizix's pointing finger to the nephilim. Having flattened Utvara, the enormous creatures had set out to explore the rest of the world that they had once called their own. The three of them had turned to the west, crashing through the Husk and onto the wide road that led back to the City of Ravnica. Their unimpeded physical growth had apparently ceased, but even at this distance the trio looked gigantic: the snakelike creature with its unsettling humanoid arms and that damnable eye, the stomping crustacean mountain, and the tentacled beast covered in bulbous growths that seemed to float over the stony ground on the sucker tips of its writhing appendages.

"They're leaving, at least," Pivlic said.

"And heading right to the city," Crixizix said.

Pivlic, as was his wont, immediately started to dwell on what this bizarre turn of events meant for Pivlic. The baroness had only left him in charge for a couple of days, and in that time the entire town had been flattened. From his new vantage point, Pivlic could see a great many toppled mining towers too. The Cauldron was completely destroyed and looked disturbingly paved while fires raged on the edge of the Selesnyan territory and across the Golgari fields.

He might have taken this opportunity to warn the Utvar Gruul, but Vor Golozar's tribe was quite far from his mind. His first responsibility was to his baroness, and she was back in the city. No, Pivlic corrected, his first responsibility was to himself, as always. But warning the baroness qualified as protecting Pivlic's interests, he reasoned. It made the decision easier to think of it that way. And since the baroness was currently directly in the path, as luck would have it, of three of the five monsters that had just ruined her finances in only a couple of hours, he'd be one sorry Orzhov if he didn't figure out a way to make that a win in the Pivlic column.

Crixizix shook her head. "I don't know what to do," she said. "It's all gone. Even if the containment teams arrive now, this place—and there's something else I have to tell you. Niv-Mizzet was here."

"The dragon?" Pivlic said. "Right! I remember seeing a dragon. He was— He was a *good* dragon of sorts, yes, my friend? Where did he go?"

Crixizix pointed to the horizon.

"Gone."

"Dead?"

"No. But I . . . I do not know if he will return any time soon," Crixizix said. "I will have to go on without his guidance, it seems. At least for now."

"You think *you've* got problems," Pivlic said, falling on his old standby, cheerful ignorance. "I've got to go tell the baroness about all of this. You, on the other hand—who's to know *where* Niv-Mizzet is? You understand me, friend? You say he's left you all, but maybe—maybe he's left you in charge, yes? Who can say otherwise?"

For a moment, Crixizix looked as if she might tear the imp's wings off with her teeth. Then she began to giggle, a little madly, but to Pivlic's relief it settled into a release of obviously pent-up tension.

They settled upon a stable portion of the ruined transguild courier's office. Two of the golem messengers lay smashed and motionless in the rubble, but the building's marble floor was solid and intact.

They found some food in an unbroken storage cooler and feasted on cold flatbread and dried fruit for a while, the only conversation meaningless small talk that helped the shock wear off.

At last the goblin's face grew somber once more. "Thank you, Pivlic, for your perspective. Are you sure you will go back to the city?" Crixizix asked.

"After a jolt like that," Pivlic said, "I could probably fly to the other end of the world. But I've got to get to the baroness, yes. What will you do, my friend?"

"The ogres have sort of, er, made me their chief," Crixizix said, a strange but proud grin spreading across her features despite the devastation. "They said that in a crisis like this, the ogres needed one, and one of them saw this little trick," she pointed to her feet, "and decided I was perfect. Very practical, ogres. And somebody needs to try and help the injured. Most of the people got out, I think, but there are still people trapped down there. Until I hear otherwise, I'm going to help. That containment team has to get here sometime, and I'm going to put them to work."

"What about—"

"The dragon?" Crixizix said. "I will tell them . . . something. I am not sure yet. Great Niv-Mizzet, in truth, was never a very hands-on manager when it came to the guild."

* * * * *

"Holiest," Wenslauv said. She instinctively reached for one of the teardrops on her belt, but before she could snap off the tip and apply it to the worst of Razia's wounds—a gaping hole in the angel's chest that exposed heart and rib—the guildmaster held up a hand.

"No, I can't— Don't use those," she managed. "Save that for yourself."

The angel Razia was in even worse shape than the rest of the Parhelion's command floor. The Boros guildmaster sat in a sheltered alcove to the rear of the command deck. Her right arm ended in a charred, twisted appendage that was more claw than hand. Her holy sword was gone. Scorched, pitted holes and grievous wounds showed through gaps in her ornate, once-pristine armor.

"You're hurt," Wenslauv protested.

"And those won't help," the angel said, looking over the newcomer. The angel must have recognized the tri-wing pin on Wenslauv's chest because she added, "Report, Air Marshal."

"The other angels— The others are dead," Wenslauv said after considering what, exactly, her report should name first. "I've seen no sign of hostiles. I believe you are the only one left, Holiest. Forgive my protocol, but what happened here? Who did this, sir?"

"If you are here . . ." the angel coughed, "if you are here, we must be back in Ravnica."

"Over it, sir," Wenslauv said and, taking advantage of the opening, added, "We're on a collision course with the Center, Holiest. From the look of it the helm is in pieces. I—I'm not sure what to do. I need your help. Can you stand?"

"Yes," the angel said but made no effort to do so yet. "The helm. And the rest—all dead. I remember. There was an attack. We have been in a war. There were boarders."

"Sir?" Wenslauv said. "I saw no boarders, though I have not been able to perform anything like a thorough search. The Parhelion is— We need to find a way to keep it in the air. I am a roc-rider, I am no stranger to flight, but this— Sir, I am not sure where to begin."

The angel extended her good hand. "I can stand. I will guide you."

Wenslauv pulled the angel to her feet. Standing, even hunched with pain, the guildmaster towered over the skyjek. The angel wobbled after a few steps, and she pressed her burned hand to her forehead.

"Are you all right, Holiest?" the air marshal said.

"I have been better," the angel replied. "Help me to that station," she said, pointing at one of the few panels on the wide array of command consoles that was still even remotely intact. "You will have to be my hands," she said.

"Of course," Wenslauv said. Out of the corner of her eye, she saw that they'd broken through the cloud cover during the time she'd been helping the angel to her feet. The white towers of Prahv were clearly visible through the invizomizzium screen.

Air Marshal Wenslauv was, as she said, not qualified to pilot the Parhelion, but she had extensive experience estimating flight speed without magical instruments or multicolored switches and levers. She guessed they had, at best, three minutes, but only if their course held steady. With an unbalanced and still-burning propulsion system, there was no such guarantee.

The panel was plain and didn't look particularly important. In fact, it resembled nothing more than a rectangular mizzium plate with a single red gemstone off center. "What do I do?" Wenslauv said.

"Press the gemstone three times. On the third press, you must speak the code phrase."

"What's that, Holiest?"

" 'Pin dancer.' "

" 'Pin dancer'?"

"And mortals think we don't have a sense of humor," the angel replied. "We don't have much time, Air Marshal."

Wenslauv nodded, suppressed her opinion of the "joke," and pressed her thumb against the red gemstone. One, two, three: "Pin dancer," she said.

The mizzium panel slid aside with a slow, wheezing grind. Beneath it sat a pair of levers with red handgrips. "I'm afraid this usually calls for angelic strength," Razia said, "and I will not, unfortunately, be of any assistance."

"I'll do my best, Holiest," Wenslauv said and took hold of the red levers.

"The one on the right controls our pitch, the left, our yaw," the angel said. "Simple and only for emergencies."

"Yaw won't help. People are going to die no matter which way we turn," Wenslauv said. "Our problem is lift. We need to stay in the air."

"Agreed."

The air marshal released the left lever and took hold of the right with both hands in an iron grip. She placed the sole of one boot against the console and pulled with all her might.

The lever would not budge. The towers of Prahv drew ever closer, and to Wenslauv's surprise no skyjek patrols had risen to meet them. She tried again. No change.

She scanned the command floor for some tool, anything, that would give her leverage. Nothing was close enough.

A small gull collided violently with the windscreen. The impact helped Wenslauv estimate that speed somewhere around one hundred miles per hour. When the mess cleared away, the skyjek no longer saw sky.

The towers of Prahv filled the windscreen, the translucent Senate dome dead ahead. If the Parhelion had been an arrow, it would have been headed directly for the bull's-eye. At this distance, she could see a fleeing crowd. A few seconds later, she was close enough to make out faces.

"Krokt," she swore and turned back to the angel. "Holiest, it won't—"

A few seconds earlier than Wenslauv estimated, the Parhelion collided with the dome of the Senate. The crash was heard from the depths of Old Rav to the skirt districts beyond the city gates and even made the nephilim pause in their tracks.

CHAPTER 11

Are you as hungry as a demon? 'Demon-size' your order for only a few zinos—ask your server how!

—Sign over the entrance to Pivlic's Old
Ravi Cabaret and Eatery
(Destroyed by unexplained fire, 9963 Z.C.)

31 Cizarm 10012 Z.C.

Myc Savod Zunich had a fair amount of faith in the Selesnyan belief system, but with a Devkarin father who had a knack for necromancy to provide a counterinfluence to his half-Silhana mother, he had never considered himself devout. He wasn't even sure what "devout" entailed. He wanted to be a ledev. There was appeal in the open road, a new adventure always coming down the path ahead. He also wanted to be a hunter, if not a guildmaster. They were two sides of the same coin, much like Myc himself. Though many Golgari worshiped the god-zombie, even now his father didn't, so he didn't particularly feel attached to that belief system either.

One thing he did know—the Cult of Rakdos was certainly not any kind of religion he wanted anything to do with. It was the kind of religion that could put you off of religion for the rest of your life.

He and his fellow scouts had been jostled, carried, hauled, and eventually dragged (when the indrik could not fit through the last stretch of subterranean tunnel) into a sweltering underground hall. Judging from what Myc could hear of the song, they were quite close to the Unity Tree, and it was somewhere overhead. That meant they had to be near the Center.

Myc knew exactly what was underneath the Center because it rose like a burning sore in the middle of the Golgari domain of Old Rav. His father had always taken pains to point out Rix Maadi, the guildhall of the Rakdos. Rix Maadi was a beehivelike structure, so shaped because the Cult of Rakdos was constantly adding to it by piling on more junk. Jagged, spiky chimneys dotted the outer surface and leaked thin streams of black smoke. Rix Maadi was part of the undercity but in truth a separate Rakdos world that, it was said, had levels that went far deeper into the ground than any one stretch of the Golgari domain—deeper even than Grigor's Canyon. There the Rakdos mined the metals that made them a major power in the world despite their distinctly antisocial bent. Jarad had made the boy promise he would never go near it without his father. Naturally, Myc had broken that promise the first chance he had gotten, but the closest he came to infiltrating the den of Rakdos iniquity was lurking around the perimeter with a couple of friends. Many challenges were issued, and the first kid to venture up to the Rakdos guards would have won the respect of them all. That respect had, to date, gone unclaimed. Myc would have done it, he always said, if it weren't for the trouble it would cause his guildmaster father.

Now that Myc was presumably in the heart of Rix Maadi, he could not fathom why he'd ever wanted to get inside. The place reeked of sulfur and rot, and was filled with smoke from hundreds of braziers burning Krokt-only-knew-what oily materials and foul-smelling incense. Rats crawled over every surface he could see, small, large, some the size of mossdogs and three times as vicious-looking—more rats than Myc even knew existed on Ravnica and all swarming like pets awaiting meal time.

And the heat. The cavern was huge, and the open, glowing lava pit in the center turned the place into a heat chamber. A twisted honeycomb of ramps and pathways wound up the inner surface of the hive, and far overhead there was a way out that he couldn't reach without a pair of wings—several of the familiar ventilation tubes that were a common sight everywhere in the undercity. There was a substantial network of chimneys and vents built into the structure's walls and ceiling, but they didn't seem to be doing a very good job. What ventilation there was had to compete with an open, glowing, viscous pool that bubbled ominously, like thick soup left to boil. Rix Maadi was a stinking oven the size of a small town.

Amid it all, a chaotic carnival of sorts was in full swing. Morbid entertainments, lewd dancing that Myc's mother would probably not have appreciated in the slightest, and clusters of growling singers adding to a dull roar of unending noise. Everywhere he looked, Rakdos were drinking, dancing, or brutally fighting their fellow cultists. The air was thick with smoke, stench, and cruel, cackling laughter.

He and the other scouts were all still in their cages but had been lined up in a row for inspection. At last Myc could see that, for the moment at least, the other three were all right. He also noted that his instincts had been correct: His mother was not among them.

Myc suspected he wouldn't enjoy this inspection; especially once he got a good look at the inspector. The cultists called her Izolda, which Myc thought meant something close to "blood witch" in Old Ravi. Her pale shape was wrapped in thin chains and slick, blackened hides. Her hands ended in long, black, bladelike claws that dripped thick, red fluid onto the stone floor as she approached the captives. Her wholly white eyes had scars that ran through them, from eyebrow to cheekbone, but she seemed to have little trouble navigating the boisterous and bloody crowd.

Maybe—and the idea was almost too terrifying to Myc to consider—Izolda was some kind of vampire.

Whatever Izolda was beneath the scant clothing, rough-hewn chains, and ivory skin, the young scout was positive he didn't want to know why she was called a "blood witch." He was also relatively certain he was going to learn soon, whether he wanted to or not.

Izolda considered Myc with her empty eyes, her steady, calm breathing a snakelike hiss. She cocked her head and sniffed the air, nodding. Then she turned on one heel and turned her attention to the end of the line. The blood witch hunched over the first prisoner, the centaur Orval, and reached a clawed hand into the cage. She extended a single talon and swiped it across the centaur's forehead. The move elicited a stifled yelp from Orval and drew a few tiny droplets of blood. Izolda retreated from the iron cage and moved with a determined but measured stride through the celebrants to the large brazier mounted in the center of the deathmonger's temple floor.

Yes, it was a temple, not a cavern or hall, Myc realized. This was a place for high worship of low deeds. The congregation was a madhouse.

The Rakdos blood witch held the talon over the glowing coals for a few seconds. Her empty eyes peered at it all the while, watched it begin to glow orange. Then she snatched the hand back with a sensual purr that drew out into another hiss.

Izolda was really giving Myc the creeps.

"Not that one," the blood witch hissed to her cackling lackeys. "Next."

Izolda repeated the process twice more. Aklechin was sniffling before the claw got to him and stifled a sob immediately afterward. Lily, to Myc's surprise, didn't make a peep. And he saw her moving, so he figured there was an eighty, eighty-five percent chance she was alive. His Devkarin heritage never let him forget about the fifteen to twenty percent of people who moved and did not necessarily live, but he didn't see any telltale signs of necromancy on her. She was just being obstinate and brave.

Myc found that combination impressive and compelling. So when the blood witch hooked a claw toward Lily's cage and two lumbering, masked zombies shuffled forward to tear the cage open, Myc shouted angry epithets at them, words he wasn't entirely sure where he'd learned but that poured forth as the cultist slaves pulled the blonde girl from the cage by the arms. They held her in the air, her feet dangling, as Lily joined in the screaming and cursing.

"Take her to my abattoir," the witch said. "She amuses me."

"Leave her alone!" Myc shouted.

"Yes!" Lily screamed, "Leave me *alone*!"

The blood witch laughed, a cold sound that cut through the oppressive heat. "Wait your turn, boy," she snarled and waved at the zombies, who dragged Lily off through the crowd, still shouting threats at the Rakdos as loudly as she could.

Myc felt his knees wobble as Lily disappeared from view, and Izolda slinked toward his cage. "And now for you," she said. "The girl will make a fine servant, but you, I think, have another fate awaiting you. Does that frighten you?"

Myc didn't respond, but with heroic effort and by biting almost all the way through his bottom lip he kept himself from crying. "No," he finally spat.

"It should," the blood witch said and reached inside the cage. Myc tried to press his body into the corner, out of reach, and waved his head back and forth, but she still easily swiped the tip of her talon across his forehead with a casual flick.

"Yes," Izolda hissed. "It is this one." She nodded to a second pair of simian lackeys. They pulled him kicking and screaming from his cage, but to his surprise and dismay they did not drag him in the same direction they had taken Lily. Instead they hauled him toward a twisted, rusted effigy of a Selesnyan veztree bolted into the floor before the lava pit. His exposed skin burned at the proximity.

"This one what? The one *what*?!" Myc demanded as the zombies pushed him onto the lowest "limb" of the iron effigy and tied his wrists to the branches with rough, painful ropes. More zombies closed in around him, called forth with vicious glee by the blood witch, who bid them all gather round for the main event of the charnel-house carnival. Once his legs were bound together and affixed with the same rough rope to the trunk of the effigy tree, they all pressed closer, but none of them touched him. It seemed they were saving him for their mistress.

As terrified as he was, Myc was even more frightened for Lily. There was no telling where they had taken her or what might happen to the girl. He held on to that hateful, angry emotion as a shield against his fear.

Myc hauled with all his might on the rough ropes. He had a tiny amount of slack but could not fit his hands through the knotted fibers. Perhaps, if he could wriggle the rope back and forth, the edge of the metal "tree branch" could wear through it. . . .

Izolda raised her clawed hands into the air and began to chant in a barking, guttural tongue. The cultists took up the chant, of which Myc only understood a single word. A name. Rakdos. The Defiler.

He felt blood trickling down his wrists, but Myc tugged on the ropes harder than ever.

* * * * *

Fonn had expected Jarad to move quickly. They had their differences. Different expectations, different interests, goals, and callings. Differences that had, after a few years, grown insurmountable, at least when it was so easy to hit the road or the Leaguehall rather than deal with them. Whatever they thought of each other these days, she had never known him to hesitate when their son was involved. Even so she hadn't expected the Golgari guildmaster to muster such a search party in so short a time.

Hippogriffs, dusky bats, manticores, and a few giant ravens flanked the Devkarin as he swooped down from the sky over the wide expanse of the Utvara highway. Jarad sat astride his personal mount, the great bat Vexosh, and he led another bat of equal size by a long tether.

"Don't waste time landing," Fonn called to him. "Just fly low."

The Devkarin nodded and waved. "Be ready," he called. Jarad aimed his bat straight for the ledev centuriad, hauling on the spare mount's lead, and, just before it was too late to pull up, released the tether. The riderless bat kept heading straight for Fonn, and at the last second she leaped into the air, over its head, and caught the reins. She spun in the middle of her somersault and came to a jarring rest upon the saddle. Fonn hauled mightily on the reins and pulled the bat through a tight turn that brought her alongside Jarad's wing.

"What's happened?" he called, not shouting but using what Fonn had come to think of as his "guildmaster voice." It cut through the noise without sounding too desperate or emotional. He used it when negotiating on behalf of the Golgari. It was also handy for communicating when you were speeding through the air as fast as a bat could fly. The ancient subspecies that the Golgari had bred for thousands of years could achieve a good deal of velocity—not observosphere speed, or even roc speed, but more than fast enough for the undercity, where the ability to maneuver was much more important for a flyer.

Fonn closed her eyes for a moment, listening. "Underground. He's underground. We've got to go back to the undercity. Toward the center. Probably—"

"Rix Maadi. The damned warren," Jarad said, adding a few choice Devkarin curses. "I should have torched that place when I took over the guild. There's no need for—"

"Just get us there as fast as you can," Fonn said. "Once Myc and the others are out of harm's way I'll help you start the fire."

Jarad nodded. "This way. We'll go back the way I came."

As she followed Jarad into an access tunnel that led to Old Rav she explained the details of their son's abduction. A chorus of animal cries trailed behind them, and she occasionally had to shout over the noise of the teratogens bringing up the rear. Fonn suspected they hadn't been this worked up since Savra sent them to attack Centerfort.

Jarad, for his part, surprised her by—for once—not going out of his way to start an argument. He didn't blame her again for the situation, as she'd half-expected. If anything, he seemed to have some idea why the Rakdos had been interested in kidnapping.

Being master of the guild that controlled much of Old Rav, one heard many rumors. Jarad had the extra advantage of his insect minions, with which he had a special mental bond that made learning the secrets of his allies and enemies, or potential allies and enemies, relatively easy. When they'd met, he'd used them to keep her prisoner. Their courtship had been unusual in many respects.

This time Jarad told her he didn't need insects to learn that the Cult of Rakdos was up to something. There were rats everywhere, he said. Over the last week he'd heard dozens of reports of whole undead colonies being consumed by hungry rodents, to say nothing of the rats' collective impact on the insect population at large. Rats were the harbingers of the demon-god Rakdos, parun and nominal guildmaster of the cult. The cycle of violence continued, and this spoke was rounding the wheel with malicious timing.

When Jarad explained his suspicions, including a very specific—and terrifying—reason that the scouts might have been kidnapped, a surge of panic made her dig her heels into the bat's side so hard the creature squeaked a high-pitched objection.

They'd covered more than half the distance to Rix Maadi

when they both heard a tremendous crash overhead that made the teratogens roar and squawk in alarm.

They did not stop. Whatever it was, it had nothing to do with Myc. Fonn could still hear him in the song, directly ahead. This new disaster would have to get in line.

*   *   *   *   *

The crash did not have anything to do with Myc, not directly, and when Myc heard it, the sound was just part of the hooting, clanging nightmare his life had become.

Once, when he was five, his father had taken Myc on one of many hunting forays through the wilds of the undercity, his first time venturing out in the cold, underground winter. During the first night of this particular foray into the wilds, the boy had fallen asleep too close to the campfire. Myc had woken up a half hour later feeling like his face was ablaze. It wasn't, but he'd gotten a nasty burn just from the proximity of the flames.

The heat of the lava pit behind him was far, far worse, and it wasn't letting up. If anything it just kept getting hotter. The rational part of his mind that fought to keep in charge argued that he was just getting cooked, and it wasn't getting hotter at all. It just felt like it.

Myc Zunich had packed a lot of learning and growing up in eleven short years. But he *was* eleven years old, and a quarter of the blood in his veins was human. Before long, his brave façade washed away in a wave of pain, heat, and fear. He had given up on the ropes. One seemed to be fraying, but the other didn't show any signs of wear—besides, he simply had no strength left. He'd cried out at his captors for the first few minutes then just cried. Now his throat was so dry and hoarse, the heat growing so intense, that he focused all of his attention on drawing breath.

It wasn't easy. The smell and the dense, smoky air did not get easier to take with time, like the killing floors of the slaughter-houses. The walls were covered in a thick carpet of rats, and every so often one lost its grip in the heat and dropped into the lava to burst with a puff of smoke and a wet pop.

Myc coughed miserably.

The chant degenerated into a general cacophony when the crowd parted beneath the spiked bludgeons of the blood witch's personal thug squad. Izolda strode purposefully toward the effigy tree. She had retracted her claws—or maybe removed them—and in one hand she held a small, wide, silver bowl containing a viscous fluid that scattered the firelight and glowed with some inner magic. The other hand clutched a jagged, inscribed knife as long as Myc's arm. Her scarred mouth was spread in a skeletal grin. Somewhere between the time she'd started the chant and the time Myc saw her approach, she had wrapped her skull and arms in bloodstained razor wire.

The blood witch raised the bowl and the blade high over her head, as if offering them to Myc. Izolda resumed her rhythmic, guttural chant, which was picked up again by the surrounding cultists, their many calls and bloody songs merging into one. The blood witch held that position for almost a minute, soaking up the collective bloodlust of every creature in the room.

Finally, with a sound that was half howl and half scream, the pale witch lowered her hands, slowly, with great concentration, as the chants continued on their own, self-perpetuating through the bloodthirsty priests. As her hands drooped, her feet left the floor, buoyed by the crowd and floating on a cloud of dark, swirling energy. Izolda floated toward him, howling her terrible wail, and her empty white eyes bored into Myc's heat-addled spirit.

He had to think straight, but the blazing pit beneath him was cooking him alive—not a very conducive circumstance for quick thinking. He couldn't move away from the heat. Izolda was closing on him, and everywhere else a variety of claws, fingers, and jagged, bone weapons swiped at him. The ropes were too strong. He was just a kid.

He was, he realized, going to die.

Myc's voice was gone. He could no longer cry out. Aklechin and Orval were still in their cages, but even if he could call to them, what could they do? Nothing. What could Myc do? Nothing.

What was Izolda going to do? Nothing good.

* * * * *

"This isn't good," Pivlic said. "This isn't good at all."

The imp's aching wings carried him over the Utvara highway at what for him was an admirable velocity. But imps were not made for soaring, sustained flight, and the strain was getting to him. They were better at quick jumps and maneuvering in cramped spaces. He had at least succeeded in getting ahead of the nephilim. The dense, blocky towers of the city outskirts had slowed the three remaining monsters' initial progress considerably, and Pivlic had leaped ahead. They seemed to be in no rush, though they never veered from their course.

Pivlic did not consider himself particularly empathetic, but even so he was horrified at the carnage he saw as he passed over the giant nephilim—a microcosm of what they might do if they reached the city and an extension of their carnivorous rampage through the reclamation zone. Hundreds of bodies, partly consumed or smashed flat by one of the three, lay strewn across the road below. Hundreds more had been eaten whole by the ravenous monsters. Ghosts were everywhere, woundseekers, most of them, but unable to do anything to the monsters that had killed them. Fortunately for Pivlic, the woundseekers—vengeful, mad ghosts who could cause great harm to the living if they chose to try—lingered on the ground, screeching pointlessly at the titanic nephilim. Unfortunately for the survivors of the carnage, the ghosts only added to the panic, and most fled toward the city—and that wouldn't help them at all if the nephilim continued on course.

* * * * *

The jagged, silver knife did not slice neatly through the skin of Myc's palm. It cut painfully. It dug in and tore the skin aside, forcing blood to well up around the blade as the young scout tried to yell, but found his dry, swollen throat allowed no more than a scratchy croak.

The blood witch of the Rakdos pinned him in place with a white-eyed gaze that pierced his soul like a spear. The fibrous ropes cut deeper into his skin as he tried to pull away from that cruel, ghastly visage, and he felt like he was made of stone. But the pain in his hand was excruciating, and what little water his body had left leaked from the corners of his eyes. Izolda lost not a drop of Myc's blood as she held the silver bowl beneath his dripping hand. The scarlet liquid plopped into the weird fluid already inside and swirled atop it like water on oil. For a full minute the Rakdos held the bowl there collecting Myc's blood, until she was apparently satisfied with the amount. Then she pressed the glowing, hot, flat side of the knife blade against his bleeding palm without warning. Myc managed a sound between a squeak and a croak.

The wound cauterized, Izolda pulled the blade away. Myc smelled his own flesh cooking and would have retched if he had anything left inside him.

The priest started another growling chant, and the crowd joined in again. Myc had never seen anything quite like the Rakdos gathering, which seemed to be growing more populous by the second, even though death screams were frequent, and at any given time it seemed one cultist might turn on any other on the merest whim. Their vile laughter rang inside Rix Maadi, interrupting the rhythm of the chant, moving through the gathering on the heels of . . . clowns?

At least, Myc guessed that they were clowns. That was the closest word he could think of for them, though they were not the kind of clowns any kid ever wanted to see. They were fat, deformed, scarred creatures, human but only just. They wore tattered parodies of Ravnican formal wear—waistcoats with white buttons and shredded sleeves, cylindrical hats caved in on one side, fingerless white gloves, striped pantaloons atop huge, red shoes with ridiculously oversized buckles. Those affectations alone were not that frightening.

But the buckles were apparently made with broken pieces of human skull. The waistcoats were sewn together from pale, barely cured leather soaked with black, spattered stains. The hides had not come from any animal Myc had ever seen. Their coats and pantaloons were also stained with dried blood, and their buttons and cufflinks were clearly knucklebones. The hats remained atop their heads thanks to a single nail driven through the edge of the brim and some ways into the skull, from the look of it. They juggled flaming, irregularly shaped objects—what they were at this distance Myc couldn't tell and didn't want to know—and made attempts at barking banter that was mostly ignored by the rest of the crowd.

The hideous clowns weren't the only things that gave a carnival atmosphere to the tortuous affair. Several food sellers wandered among the pilgrims, shouting the names of their wares, and everywhere were fights, brawls, stabbings, happy murder, and gleeful bloodshed amid the musicians, dancers, priests, and thugs.

The blood witch's latest chant grew into a low, steady song that pulled his attention back to her. Izolda's song threatened to lull Myc to sleep despite everything around him, despite the agonizing heat and perhaps aided by the loss of so much blood. He doubted he contained a lot more.

His blood. It was still in the "mixing bowl," but the blood witch had tucked the unholy dagger into her belt and held the bowl aloft as she hovered. She floated in a smooth orbit around the effigy tree, all the while gazing at him with her white orbs.

He realized with a somewhat nauseated feeling that he understood many of the words of Izolda's new dirge. They were not in some demonic tongue, as he'd first guessed, but heavily accented and stylized Ravi, quite archaic in its construction:

> *"Enslaver, the world to take, the world to enslave,*
> *Defiler, devourer of lives, rise,*
> *Master of all demons, consume this discord,*
> *Feast upon the blood of innocents,*
> *Let your harbingers mark the time."*

That was just one verse. It went on like that, every pass a new variation on the theme of Rakdos awakening, Rakdos defiling, Rakdos in general and all that the demon-god was and would be. It wasn't pleasant.

Izolda extended her empty hand, and her talons slipped from the tips of her fingers with a snap. She dipped her claw tips in the bowl, stirred it three times, then scattered drops of the mixed of blood and mystery liquid over the glowing lava below. The droplets sizzled and hissed as they struck the roiling surfacc.

Myc knew exactly who the Defiler was, had been dreading him since he realized they were in Rix Maadi.

Rakdos the demon-god was in many ways the least attentive of the guildmasters, beings who, if his father's experience was any indication, spent almost as much time with politics as they did with leadership. But when he paid attention to the events outside his domain, Rakdos and his cult of thrill-killers tended to make up for lost time. The last of their "festivals" that had bled onto the streets of Ravnica, long before Myc was born, cost the city hundreds of wojeks and destroyed entire city blocks before the forces of order quelled the rebellion.

Myc did not understand why the Guildpact would allow one of the guilds to live for violence and death, but when he'd heard the stories his mother reminded him that violence and death were as much a part of life as friendship, honor, and love. Rakdos miners provided the raw materials from which the world was built. Rakdos mercenaries served their purposes as well.

Not that her mother was fond of the Rakdos. They were killers, but, as Fonn had told her son, there were plenty of people who thought of his father as little better than a "saprophytic zombie master" who "thrived on death" as one particular newssheet had called him even before Myc's parents split up. There were even people who hated the noble Selesnya Conclave (and by no small coincidence, many of them were Rakdos cultists). At the time, the intuitive, young Myc had seen the logic and made sense of how the Guildpact brought balance to the world.

Myc was a smart kid and had a smart kid's pride in being right, especially since it happened so often. This time, however, being right was cold comfort.

As Izolda's shrieking hymn reached a fever pitch, the demon-god Rakdos emerged from the pit.

CHAPTER 12

The Gruul call them "nephilim," the prey that will not die. They are the gods' proof that the Gruul must never give up the hunt. And they're just one of the amazing sights you'll see from the safety and comfort of a luxury lokopede when you choose Husk Adventure Tours. Our Gruul are the only guides backed by an ironclad Orzhov guarantee. Don't take a chance with your life or the lives of your family when you visit wild and mysterious Utvara! More information available at the Imp Wing Hotel and Tavern, Thoroughfare Utvarazi, No. 8. Bring this advertisement to receive 10% off all expenses.

—Advertising flyer for Husk Adventure Tours, 100012 Z.C.

31 CIZARM 10012 Z.C.

Pivlic plummeted. Pivlic dropped. Pivlic fell and kept on falling. Pivlic came very close to passing out. In a corner of his conscious mind, it occurred to him that he'd probably flown higher than he ever had before, which somehow didn't make him feel better. Altitude had probably sapped his strength and deprived him of air at least as much as exhaustion.

Then, the dropping sensation ended with a jolt, replaced by more of an upward, eastward feeling. Pivlic discovered with a mix of alarm and relief that his abrupt halt was not due to the usual reason a fall ended. This was different. For one thing, he was still alive. Better yet, he was moving through the air again.

Rocs did not have the capacity for speech of the usual kind, and in the imp's experience they did not think as imps, elves, or even humans did. They were birds, big birds. They thought birdy things. But rocs were very smart for birds, and the well-trained rocs of the skyjeks were perhaps the best trained of all. This one was certainly smart enough to catch Pivlic on her back, but that didn't explain why the imp had landed on an empty saddle.

The roc, for her part, was simply trying to get her rider back and had spotted Pivlic falling from the sky. The bird figured the falling imp was about Flang-sized. Smart for a bird, but still just a bird. Pivlic didn't know this, nor would he have cared, but the roc was relieved in her avian way.

Landing on the saddle was not the same as being in the saddle, and Pivlic, on his belly, exhausted, and surprised to be alive, realized he was already starting to slide off. He dug into the leather with both hands, his tiny claws catching just enough of a grip to keep him in place. With what remained of his strength, he pulled himself into the seat, careful not to let his own wings catch the wind and carry him free, and grabbed the flapping reins as he sat upright.

The roc cried out, a sound that battered his sensitive, unprepared ears, and he almost lost his grip again. He could not quite reach the stirrups, so he just clamped on with his legs as best he could. Those muscles, at least, were still fresh.

Pivlic was a flyer, but he usually flew under his own power. Still, he figured mounted flight, human-style, couldn't be that complicated. Humiliating, certainly, but needs must when the demon drives, as the saying went.

Two reins, one on the right of the bird's head, the other on the left. Just like riding a dromad, which he'd seen close up. He'd been a passenger, but he'd seen it done. Simple.

"Hello, my new friend," Pivlic said in what was left of his comforting, welcoming innkeeper's voice. "I will need your help for a while longer. I am going to try these reins now. Please do not throw me off." He doubted the bird could understand his words, but the imp's silky-smooth voice had soothed worse than a roc.

And, he admitted privately, talking helped stave off panic.

He gave a short, experimental tug on one of the leather straps, and the roc pulled its head to the right, making no effort to throw the imp. So far, so good. It wheeled in midair, turned from the outskirts and back toward the three gigantic nephilim currently tearing their way toward the city gates. The rocky one he'd dubbed Stomper was in the process of toppling a water tower. As Pivlic watched in morbid fascination, the tower reached the tipping point. A torrent of water sloshed over the side before the nephilim knocked the last support away and the whole thing came crashing down onto the rooftops. There were fewer bodies here, though ·bodies there were amid the flash flood, and he chalked that up to the crowds of fleeing people streaming through the outer streets of the skirt districts.

Slither, the snake-thing, was a bit further ahead of Pivlic, coiled around the base of another tower that was beginning to crumble and crack, plucking terrified occupants from the windows with its clawed hands and thrusting them into the grinding, metallic mouth below its baleful eye. The tentacled "Brain" was the closest to the city, roiling along on its mass of tentacles, now and then tearing off another bulb from its central head and flinging it into a nearby building to irreparable effect. The buildings' occupants ran head-long into the remains of the mob fleeing in the other direction, and chaos reigned. Here and there he could see desperate wojeks attempting to coordinate the efforts, without much luck.

The roc settled down as it acclimatized to Pivlic's weight, and he grew more comfortable with the slow, lazy flapping of her broad golden wings. The roc *was* made for sustained flight, and Pivlic admired her effortless movement.

The respite gave him time to think and time to scan the skyline of the central metropolis for the giant sentinel titans. The nine towering statues would surely make short work of the marauding monsters. Pivlic had hoped to warn them, but surely the 'jeks and the Boros were aware of the danger by now.

The nine remaining titans—the tenth, Zobor, had fallen in the Decamillennial battle—stood where they had for thousands of years. They had not moved at all.

The imp did spy the tiny shapes of his "fellow" skyjeks, however. Several wing formations were headed out from the center, tiny spots against the disc of the setting sun. He wondered what they could do about the nephilim but saw that the roc-riders were not heading this way—they were headed for the great golden shape of . . . the Parhelion? Yes, it was the Parhelion. It plummeted toward the white towers of Prahv. Pivlic saw with mounting horror that the riders were not going to make it to the descending fortress before it struck Prahv. Even if they had, what could they have done?

With a resounding crash the imp heard over the roaring nephilim and the toppling architecture, the flying fortress made landfall. Or more precisely, domefall. The just-visible roof of the Azorius Senate crumpled and collapsed. Along the way, the Parhelion took out three of the six towers of justice. They fell over like massive, stone trees and clouds of glittering dust rose in their stead. An enormous roiling mass of smoke and rubble erupted in slow motion around the crash.

Pivlic instinctively dug his heels into the roc's side and aimed his mount for the crash site. He'd headed this way to warn Teysa of the nephilim and now had a rescue on his hands, from the look of it.

There was still a chance his baroness had survived, and if she hadn't he was going to need proof for the Obzedat. Already the cloud spread out from the ruined Azorius demesnes, swallowing up the tiny roc-riders flitting around it like flies but revealing the state of Prahv. The Parhelion had come to rest on its face, and what remained of the Senate and the towers appeared to support its weight, at least for now. Pivlic doubted it could stay in that precarious position for long, but its speed had not been enough, it seemed, to completely flatten the structure beneath. There could still be survivors staring up at the front end of the flying fortress. The baroness could well be among them.

All the while, the sentinel titans remained motionless, their towering stone bodies frozen in time. All the while, the nephilim drew closer to the city. "Why aren't they *doing* something?" Pivlic asked the roc.

If the roc knew, she didn't say.

* * * * *

From her view post atop the wojek headquarters of Centerfort, Section Commander Migellic, commanding the League of Wojek in Nodov's absence, wondered much the same thing.

"Why are the titans motionless?" she bellowed at the trio of Boros mages who stood around the activation shrine that supposedly brought the sentinel titans to life.

The leader of the Boros guildmages, a bald, tattooed man of advancing age named Morr, wore an apologetic look as he held his hands palms up with a shrug. "There is nothing we can do, Commander," the mage said. "The great guardians do not respond. It has been many decades since they have been called into action."

"Zobor fought the Golgari horde twelve years ago," Migellic snapped. "Don't give me excuses."

"The tenth titan hardly had a chance to move," Morr said calmly, refusing to be drawn into the flames of the commander's rising temper. "The magic that created the titans is thousands of years old, and we— Well, much of that knowledge has been lost over the years. Sir, I must admit that we do not entirely understand how it works anymore. Not completely. It may be that the loss of Zobor caused the others to go into something like a coma. Perhaps it destroyed the magic entirely. It is more likely, in my opinion, that the cause is the Parhelion."

"The Parhelion that just crashed into Prahv *on my watch,* with the commander of the entire legion sitting in the Senate chamber," Migellic almost screamed. "What does that have to do with it?"

"The ancient records indicate that the angels themselves gave of their own power to make the titans the ultimate guardians of Ravnica," the mage explained, doing his best to sound parochial and succeeding, in Migellic's opinion, far too well. "It would appear the angels are no longer aboard the Parhelion, since we can assume they would not have just driven it into the dome of the Senate. Therefore, it is logical to assume that the power they gave the titans is also gone."

"So they're—" Migellic had lived her entire life in Ravnica's central city, like most wojeks. The titans were a constant reminder that theirs was a world of laws, and every child of Ravnica grew up with the unbreakable belief that should disaster ever strike, the titans were there to defend the people. That quite shaken belief was still so strong that it made it difficult for Migellic to finish her sentence. At last, she said, "So they're just . . . statues?"

"At the moment," Morr replied, "I fear that is a completely accurate statement."

Migellic cursed and pounded the central table, jarring the scale model of the central city and toppling three of the miniature towers of Prahv.

"All right," she said deliberately, "then we don't have the titans to fall back on. Time to call up all of our other reserves." She beckoned a lieutenant and gave the order to mobilize the wojeks of Ravnica into an army of last resort. "Tell them to open the armory," Migellic said. "Siege weapons and crowd control. Break them into teams. And hurry."

* * * * *

As Fonn and Jarad approached the outside of the hivelike shape of Rix Maadi, the ledev saw why the Devkarin had gone to the trouble of assembling this small teratogen horde. They were the diversion that would let the two bat-riders get inside with the least amount of wasted time. Negotiation with the Rakdos always devolved into fighting anyway. Jarad had decided to skip right to it.

The teratogens soon had the Rakdos guards tied up in small clusters of violence, and Fonn had to admit that the creatures— which she'd always considered the ugly stepchildren of her ex-husband's none-too-pretty guild—acquitted themselves nicely against their equally savage and bloodthirsty opponents. The Rakdos had few among their number who could fly but made up for it with pure ferocity. Before she and Jarad had reached the open portcullis leading into the bowels of the hive, she saw a hippogriff brought low by a hurled boulder, and chattering goblins swarmed over the fallen creature brandishing jagged blades and blazing torches. In seconds it had disappeared, and so had its cries of terror and pain.

Elsewhere, other teratogens were having better luck. A pair of giant ravens were fighting over pieces of an armored troll, having already pecked out the creature's beady eyes and torn apart its throat. One of the manticores had landed, but its thrashing tail kept a swarm of chattering Rakdos goblins from getting too close while it swiped at berserkers and ogres with its leonine claws. The lower half of an ogre hung from the manticore's jaws and disappeared down its gullet in a single gulp.

"Follow me," she called to Jarad as they passed over the huge but misshapen outer gate. A few seconds later they found themselves swallowed by the thick, sulfurous atmosphere of the Rakdos domain. The hive appeared to be built in rings. This was just the outer one. They'd still have to get into the structure itself.

"Do you really know where you're going?" Jarad called.

"Toward my son. Keep moving. Don't stop to fight."

"Right behind you," Jarad called. "It looks like we're heading for their carnarium. It's a kind of death temple in the middle of this whole thing."

"How do you know that?"

"I *am* a guildmaster. I have been here before." Fonn heard Jarad draw steel, and she automatically did the same. The Rakdos cultists who flashed past them below were as yet too surprised by their sudden appearance to strike back in any organized fashion, but it was only a matter of time.

With one eye on the screaming cultists, one hand on the reins, and every remaining bit of her attention on the rising pitch of her son's lonely note in the song, she guided them into a small vent tube that led into what, if Jarad was correct, was the middle of the hive. The bat landed at the edge of the passage instinctively. Its wings would never fit inside the tube. Fonn dismounted without waiting to see if Jarad was following and was gratified to hear his feet hit the ground. The tube had looked small from the back of the bat, but inside it was roomy enough to allow them both to stand erect, if only just.

"Do we have a plan?" he asked.

"Sure," Fonn replied. "We follow this tube into the temple, kill all the Rakdos inside, and get Myc back."

"Good plan," Jarad said. "I always said you would have made an excellent huntress."

"Now's not the time," Fonn said, but a tiny part of her appreciated what, from Jarad, was high praise indeed. Maybe, she thought guiltily, their marriage had needed danger to survive.

* * * * *

Myc wanted many things. Cold air to breathe. His freedom and the freedom of his fellow scouts. He wanted to know where the deathmongers had taken poor Lily. A glass of water would have been nice.

More than anything, he wanted to be home at Vitu Ghazi or in the labyrinth with his father. Or anywhere else, so long as it wasn't here. Yet he could not keep himself from craning his neck to watch the demon Rakdos return to the world.

The demon's horns emerged from the lava first. They glowed dull orange in the smoky air, fading to a glossy black as they rapidly cooled. Then came the top of the demon's head, revealing a bony, exposed crest, a heavy brow that kept his eyes out of view, and a long, caprine snout. Then the shoulders emerged, supporting a pair of black batwings dripping with molten rock. The demon was lined with bulging veins that glowed with inner fire.

The blood witch continued her wailing chant as the demon roared, pulling himself to his full twenty-five-foot height and spreading his dire wings. The demon's face was only a few feet from the scout's own, and he found himself unable to look away.

The arrival of the demon-god had finally torn Izolda's concentration away from Myc. She floated before him, raising the bowl with its mixture of blood and that strange, quicksilver liquid over her head, calling to Rakdos. Slowly, she raised the edge of the bowl to her lips—

With a clang, a distinctive Devkarin arrow knocked the bowl from her hands. The arrow continued on to strike the rope holding Myc's left hand, and he pulled it free with a painful jerk that reopened the jagged cut across his palm.

Izolda screamed in fury. The bowl tumbled into the air, scattering its remaining contents over the head of the demon, over

Myc, and into the roiling lava below. The silver bowl disappeared into the pit.

A second arrow followed a fraction of a second later, severing the ropes that bound his legs together. He grabbed on to the remaining ropes with both hands and let himself swing around to the side of the effigy tree opposite the floating blood witch. He found himself staring up at the chin of Rakdos and felt his skin blistering anew in proximity to the demon.

The boy did not see what happened to the blood witch next because the moment the contents of the bowl struck his face, his world changed.

Myczil Savod Zunich fell into the grip of something like madness. His entire being was seized with primal, animal rage, rage he knew was not his own.

He did not feel imprisoned. He felt free. He felt . . . gigantic. A tiny section of Myc's mind told him he felt, more than anything, like Rakdos looked.

He was a demon-god. Blinded by rage and lust, Myc did not see the demon reach down with a wickedly clawed hand. Rakdos chuckled, a deep, deliriously exhilarating sound to the addled ledev scout, and plucked Myc from the effigy tree like a piece of fruit. He lay there, on his back, in the demon's open palm, looking up at that terrible face. He found that he was no longer afraid, and that his sadistic cravings were giving way to something like . . . curiosity?

Could a demon-god be curious? Or was this Myc's own feeling? He could not tell.

The demon looked him over. Without taking its huge, black eyes off of the young ledev, the demon reached out with his other hand and knocked the blood witch out of the air with a casual swipe. She shrieked in surprise, flew into the revelers, and was swallowed up by the crowd. That triggered at last the tiniest bit of self-preservation instinct, and the deathmongers drew back from the resurgent demon-god with awe. Izolda's chant had faded, though the assembled cultists and performers of the unholy carnival screamed their own chants more loudly than ever at the sight.

Myc felt an alien wave of satisfaction wash over him. Neither this nor the lust for blood and flesh were his own. As the thought passed through his mind, he could hear another consciousness, vast and ancient, cunning and evil.

I hunger, the mind said. *What are you, I wonder? A morsel?*

I am not food, Myc thought back. *Put me down.*

Food, the demon-mind said. *Yes, I must feed. I will destroy them all, drive them before me, hear the lamentations—*

I get it, Myc cut in. Then he grimaced. Now he was hungry too.

Yes, it is time to feed, the demon-god said inside their shared mind.

Feed, Myc told him, *on those clowns first.*

Yes, the demon-mind agreed, and Myc saw the demon taking in the crowd in his mind's eye. *I hate clowns.*

So overpowering was Myc's inexplicable connection to the demon-god, he could not hear his own mother screaming his name.

* * * * *

"We're too late," Jarad whispered, notching another arrow but unable to see what he should be shooting at.

"Myc!" Fonn called from the edge of the vent tube that opened inside the cavernous Rakdos temple. "Myc! Can you hear me?"

The boy sat in the open palm of the demon-god Rakdos. He was not dead—from the look of it he was struggling within his bonds—but he did not reply either.

"We've got to get down there," Jarad said and reached to his belt. He produced a long, thin line with a collapsible hook, like those the wojeks sometimes carried. He scanned the ceiling of the hive, searching for something that might hold the grapple he swung in a small loop at the end of his hand.

"Myc!" Fonn called again. No response, but she hadn't really expected one. Some of the freakish cultists down below heard her, however, and a few pointed and shouted. Tinier figures that had to be goblins scrambled toward them and began to climb the sheer wall under their perch.

"Jarad, we've been spotted," Fonn said. "What's going on?"

"There," the Devkarin said and let slip the grappling hook. It lanced out and wrapped around a coil of heavy chain not far overhead. Without ceremony he stepped to Fonn's side and put his arm around her waist. "Hold on," he added. Fonn did as she was told.

"Is that sturdy enough?" she asked.

"I hope so," Jarad said.

"Wait!" Fonn shouted. "Holy mother of— Look!" She pointed at the demon as Rakdos placed her son almost delicately upon his shoulder. Myc, bloody but otherwise intact from the look of him, clambered from the demon's shoulder to a great chain Rakdos wore around his neck. Her son took a seat on the links.

Myc smiled viciously at the mob and said something Fonn could not hear. He paid no heed to either her or Jarad.

"What is he doing?" Jarad asked.

"I have no idea," Fonn said. She listened for Myc's note, and found it easily—but it had changed. It was still her son, but there was a deep, abiding, ancient rage there as well. A sour note, out of tune.

The Iedev's concentration shattered when the first goblin made it over the lip of the tunnel in which she and Jarad stood. The chattering creature, snarling, was preceded by a coterie of red-eyed rats that they kicked away frantically. The goblin met Jarad's booted foot squarely between the eyes, and the creature flew out into open space, landing with a sizzle and a scream in the lava pit. Another almost immediately replaced it, and another. Fonn got in a few good kicks, but they couldn't last this way forever.

Fonn drove her sword through a goblin's eye and kicked his lifeless form over the edge. "I see more cages," she said, pointing. "That must be the other kids." Please, she added silently, be the other kids. I can't take much more of this.

"But Myc is over there."

"They're all my responsibility," Fonn replied, though her heart screamed to take flight and head straight for the demon, which had already lifted a massive hoofed foot from the pit and would soon be completely clear of the lava. "Get us down there, and I'll go for the scouts while you see what you can do about that demon."

"On three," Jarad said at last, once again taking her by the waist. "One. Two." He planted a foot in the face of another goblin, and it went over backward with a scream.

"Three," Fonn said.

CHAPTER 13

Civilian air traffic within the City of Ravnica shall adhere to regulated flight paths at all times. This regulation does not apply to authorized law-enforcement officers.

—City Ordinances of Ravnica

31 Cizarm 10012 Z.C.

Kos was probably the first inside the Senate chamber to notice the shadow of the Parhelion float across the tinted glass of the Senate dome. He cried out a warning that interrupted the hasty planning he, Feather, and Teysa were engaged in, and a second later the broad prow of the floating fortress collided with the skylight. The thick, colored glass shattered with a clamor of cracks, pops, and whining, twisting metal. Then the golden vessel struck a pair of support beams, and the entire roof of the cavernous hall crumpled with a successive series of booms.

To say the sound was deafening was like saying an angel had wings. It was a tremendous, bone-shattering noise, and Kos's borrowed bones didn't enjoy the feeling one bit. Then, to his surprise, he dived under a table as Obez Murzeddi's survival instincts overwhelmed the stunned and momentarily awestruck wojek ghost.

He was not alone. Both the thief Capobar and the baroness had the same idea, and the three—four?—of them winced and covered their heads as the noisy destruction continued above them. Any second, Kos expected a hunk of roof or the Parhelion itself to come crashing down on the heavy, metal table, crushing them all flatter than a roundcake.

Like you had a better idea, Obez mentally challenged.

Don't do that again. I'm either in charge here or I'm not.

Who said you were in charge?

But the crush, the collapse, never came. After a few minutes, the noises faded, and the Senate chamber was filled with eerie silence.

"Is everyone okay?" Kos whispered.

"Who said that?" a woman's voice, Teysa's, replied.

"Me, Kos," he said. "Sort of."

"Will you people be quiet? I'm trying to hear what's going on out there." This from Capobar, who sounded like his drunken haze had fled in a hurry, leaving behind someone as terrified as he was grumpy. Kos knew the feeling.

The silence continued for another few seconds, then Kos heard a cough, and another, outside their makeshift shelter. "I've got to see what happened," he said. "I'm going out."

He wriggled Obez's plump body from under the half-collapsed table. Several large chunks of stone had dented the top, but it could have been far worse. He could have been the acting Boros guild-master, for example. One of the support struts of the glass dome had fallen free and dropped into the seats of the Senate, where it had stuck, quivering like a spear. The spear almost completely obliterated wojek Commander-General Nodov—only a single leg remained.

The Grand Arbiter had been behind the 'jek, and Augustin's throne must have been thrown over onto its side by the impact. The Grand Arbiter, looking very like a helpless old man, lay on the cracked steps amid shards of glass but resolutely pushed his legless body into a sitting position. Feather had been nearest the loxodon, and Saint Kel owed his life to the angel, who, it appeared, had tackled him before a chunk of stone as big as a dromad crushed the Selesnyan's seat.

Missing completely were the three bailiffs and the poor ste-nographer, but one look at the rubble, the wreck, and the blood left little question as to their fate. The soulsworn were still flitting about uselessly, unable to aid their Azorius master and unable to serve their usual purpose—to agree with Augustin IV in every argument.

The Parhelion itself, the agent of all this destruction, stared Kos in the eye, mute and unrepentant. The invizomizzium windscreen hung overhead but was scorched dark; he could not make out anything inside. The entire flying fortress had become wedged into the Senate chamber, the square peg in a round hole taken to ridiculous extremes. The two floatspheres on the vessel's belly—the only two Kos could see from this angle—were dark, charred orbs. The great reality engine was silent.

There was not an angel in sight.

"Feather," Kos said, "you all right?" He called to the others, telling them it was safe to emerge, and clambered over the steadiest-looking rubble to reach the fallen judge.

"I am intact," Feather said. "I regret that, shackled as I am, I could not reach the commander-general in time."

"The shackles will be removed," Augustin said softly but with a judge's resonance as Kos helped the sage guildmaster back to his floating throne. As the Azorius spoke, the silver rings clattered into the shards of broken glass, and Feather's eyes blazed.

"Thank you," was all she said as she helped the loxodon to his feet.

"Feather," Kos said, "get help. We need to—"

"You need to go to Novijen," the Grand Arbiter said, and it was not an observation. It was clearly an order. "You will enter the greenhouse. Momir Vig has been harboring the Dimir, according to my intelligence network. You have work to do, Guardsman."

Kos ground his teeth, but he felt inexplicably compelled to obey. "Feather, as soon as you get me to the greenhouse, you have to send help back here."

"The guildmaster is not going anywhere," the Grand Arbiter said.

Feather looked apologetic but nodded slowly in agreement. "The Grand Arbiter is correct, Kos. This duty falls to me now. I must explore the Parhelion. You must find Szadek."

"But I was counting on you to get me there," Kos said. "Feather, if I run into—"

A shadow passed over his head, making him jump. The shadow resolved into a huge, golden bird with an improbable rider that settled onto the upper Senate steps.

"Trouble," Pivlic, out of breath, gasped as he slid wearily off of the roc's back. "Trouble is on the way."

"Pivlic?" Kos and Teysa said simultaneously.

"Who else would it be?" the imp said, then did a double take. "Excuse me, who are you? How do you know my name?"

"Pivlic, I don't have time for this," Kos snapped. "What trouble? I mean, other than that?" He jerked a thumb at the fallen Parhelion.

"Kos?" Pivlic said, recognition dawning as the familiar tone, cadence, and half-voice sunk in. "How is this possible, my friend? How is this possible? You—"

"Later," Kos said. "Trouble. Tell me about the trouble."

"Right," Pivlic agreed. He did not appear completely convinced, but he had been a part of the Orzhov guild long enough not to be too surprised at this turn of events. "Do you remember the nephilim of Utvara?"

"Those 'immortal monsters' the Gruul swore were gods?" Teysa, obviously feeling a sudden stake in this conversation, interjected. "Golozar mentioned them."

"I fear Golozar may be dead. I have not seen him since the attack."

"Attack?" Teysa said sharply.

"The nephilim, baroness," the imp said. "Something's happened to them. They're bigger. And— Baroness, I am sorry. Very sorry." He gulped and bowed his head. "As your appointed representative, your friend, and most importantly your assurance agent, I regret to inform you that the township of Utvara may well prove a total write-off. The property damage outweighs the loss of life, I believe, but—"

The rest of whatever Pivlic had been about to say was drowned out in an unholy roar. The nephilim had arrived in the big city.

* * * * *

Crixizix felt the last of her pyromana charge give out just as she came to rest at the edge of her makeshift "field hospital" with the proprietor of Giburinga's Hardware draped over her shoulders. The hospital was an open space on the flats near one of the only remaining mines. There Dr. Nebun did what he could for the injured with the help of the mine's owner, a friendly ogre named Garulsz who had once run a bar in the City of Ravnica and therefore had plenty of experience treating bruises and abrasions. Crixizix had carried the woman from the wreckage of her devastated shop, and the goblin set her down as gently as she was able. Giburinga was unconscious, but Crixizix had found no broken bones and suspected from the laceration across the hardware seller's brow that she was simply concussed. The master engineer was getting pretty good at that particular diagnosis.

It was both gratifying and frightening to find so few dead among the wreckage. Utvara's scattered, decentralized architecture was the one reason, Crixizix theorized, ever the thoughtful mage. There had been plenty of room to flee, and the initial appearance of the nephilim had given more than enough warning. The population was already easy to spook, thanks to the dragon attacks a few weeks ago. That probably saved many of them.

Or so she told herself to avoid sinking into despair. There was no way for her to account for the number the ravenous nephilim had consumed. Bits and pieces of them littered the streets, a reminder that there was very little good to be found in any of this.

The mining station was one piece of good. It miraculously gave the only Simic doctor in town a place to work that miraculously still possessed running water and exterior glowspheres to fight the encroaching night. A few hundred people of various species lay in somewhat orderly lines on the open ground, for the most part, though the worst cases had been placed on crates or still lay on homemade stretchers.

Nebun's laboratory was almost entirely gone, though a few of his living specimens had escaped. The frog aberration Uvulung hopped along beside the doctor as the Simic greeted Crixizix and launched into a quick summary of the butcher's bill.

"Concussion," Dr. Nebun agreed as he examined the unconscious woman. "She will be fine. There is room here yet. She may stay until she recovers." The Simic produced a small blob of a translucent, jellylike substance.

"Cytoplasts?" Crixizix said. "She doesn't need a new limb. She got knocked in the head. What will that do?"

"Please, goblin," Nebun said.

"Crixizix, if you please," Crixizix said.

"Certainly, *Crixizix*," Nebun said with no venom, just the tired tone of an arithmancer explaining basic mathematics to a child for the umpteenth time. "This is a new type of cytoplast designed as a less drastic form of healing—something that might replace the commonly used teardrops someday."

"You're experimenting on them?" Crixizix said. "Doctor, when I found *you* in the wreckage, I brought you here to help these people, not see what you can learn about cytoplasty. Hardly seems the time, does it?"

"Every moment is a chance to learn," Nebun said parochially. "And I find it curious that you, of all beings, would object. But no, this is not an experiment. It's simply a lucky coincidence that my supply was not destroyed. She will come to no harm. Assuming the nephilim are through with us, that is." With that, he slipped the small amoebalike shape onto Giburinga's forehead, and it flattened, smoothed, and soon formed a sort of helmet that glowed a soft, bluish green. Crixizix put her ear to the woman's chest. She was breathing steadily.

"Very well," Crixizix said. "I need to get back out there." She sighed. This part was starting to hurt. She trundled over to the pyrogenerator she'd retrieved from the Cauldron, attached the jury-rigged pyromanic tubing to the slots in her heels, and charged up for another flight.

As she did so, she closed her eyes and searched for the Firemind on instinct. But the Great Dragon was still gone, leaving Crixizix with his secret. The dragon had been afraid, afraid for his own life. That or he did not care for the Izzet one bit. Either way, the knowledge of the Great Dragon's actions could destroy the very foundations of the Izzet belief system. No, Pivlic's idea was an elegant solution—at least until the dragon returned.

* * * * *

"What the hell is that?" Kos said.

"I think it's Stomper," Pivlic said.

"Stomper?" Teysa asked.

"He stomps," the imp said, "looks like a cross between a mountain and a crab, with a statue's head floating on its— Look, it will make more sense when you see it, friends. And there are at least two more headed this way." Once he had explained the monikers Slither and Brain, Kos grew even more concerned.

Teysa, on the other hand, was not sure whether to be furious at Pivlic for allowing her barony to be flattened or grateful that the imp had been loyal enough to find her and bring her the news. She admitted to herself that she was surprised Pivlic had made the journey. She hadn't thought the imp had that much sand.

The roar sounded again, more distant. "Sounds like he's not heading toward us," the imp said. "Just passing through."

"Kos," the Grand Arbiter interrupted. "This is immaterial. You have your orders. Pierakor, you must stay here with us, and together we will find a way to deal with the nephilim threat."

"I'm going to help with that, I think," Teysa said. "If you don't mind, your honor."

"Your input would be welcome," the judge said.

"I'm not sure I can do this alone," Kos said, not to Teysa but to Pivlic.

"What do they want from Pivlic?" Pivlic muttered under his breath. "I bring a roc, I bring the news. 'Thank you, friend Pivlic.' "

"Kos," Feather said, "I have the utmost faith that you can do this. You must be strong."

"I'm not doubting myself. I just mean, no offense to Obez, here, but he's no fighter. I doubt he's a roc-rider. If I'm going to take this bird all the way to the greenhouse—and get in the way we planned—someone will need to wait with the bird." Kos looked at Capobar for a moment, but the old thief held up both hands, palms out.

"No way," Capobar growled. "I was here as a witness, and I'm going to go home while it's still standing."

"Where did you live?" Pivlic asked.

"What?"

"Where did you live, my friend?" the imp repeated.

"Eighth Section, the Parshan block. Why?"

"It's not. Still standing."

"Look, I don't care!" the thief said, panic taking over as he stumbled backward over his own feet. "This isn't my fault! I told you where to find that shadow thing. Now just leave me alone. I've got a—a ruined life to get back to. Think it's about time I got around to drinking myself into the grave." A few seconds later he had turned, scrambled over the wreckage with surprising spryness, and disappeared through a gap in the far wall, one of many, before anyone present could catch him.

"Well," Teysa said, "it appears you've volunteered, Pivlic." She permitted herself a smirk before she locked him with smile number fifty-three, a special and rarely used Orzhov expression: No good deed goes unpunished.

"Come on, Pivlic," Kos said, slapping the imp on the back. "Just like old times."

"In old times, my friend, Pivlic would be home behind the bar," the imp said. "I am not an imp of action, despite my admittedly heroic efforts this day and many days before. Besides, Kos, how do I know that is really you?"

"It is him," Teysa said. "Trust me. Now get going, we're going to try and— What are we going to do?"

"Rally the city," Feather said. "Evacuate as necessary." As if to punctuate the urgency, another, different, roar echoed down the urban canyons to the ruins of Prahv and the ears within.

"But first," Teysa said to the judge, who had remained ominously silent for almost a full minute, "we need a plan."

The judge finally raised his head to watch the roc and riders leave the Senate hall through the most obvious exit—the missing roof. Teysa followed his gaze. The bird wobbled a bit, but then the imp regained control and they wheeled out of sight.

"Yes," the Azorius said, "a plan."

* * * * *

Capobar emerged from the remains of Prahv sweaty and cold, like something was grabbing at his soul. This was ridiculous, the wiser part of his mind said.

"There's no one after me," he muttered aloud, challenging fate to contradict him. Indeed there did not appear to be anyone in pursuit. Yet his statement was more of a declaration to stave off the inevitable than a real belief.

Thing was, he'd felt someone following him since he'd fled the Senate chambers, but every time the thief whirled around to see who it was, there was nothing there. There were people, and ghostly Azorius guardsmen, making their way into the rubble, but no one going his way or really paying him the least heed. And why should they? An unassuming old man in a cape, yes sir, that's all he was. Big disaster? Back that way. Me, I'm out of here.

If something invisible was following him, he didn't want to think about it. But he did spare a moment to mourn his lost mana-goggs.

Where *was* he going to go that the shadewalker—if it was a shadewalker—couldn't find him? If the imp was right, he was now homeless. In fact, he was probably also completely broke, at least until the Orzhov assurors checked out his home and central office. And the payments could take weeks, probably much more than that, all things considered. Assuming he was covered. Assuming Ravnican civilization survived to see another dawn.

It was a testament to Capobar's addled state of mind that he then ran headlong into a stone wall. He jumped back in surprise. Not a wall—another toppled column, with rough, haphazard brickwork laid out in a curious pattern that resembled an armored—

"Oh, Krokt," Capobar whispered as he gazed down the length of the "wall," followed it up the smooth, almost graceful curve that grew into a distinctive, crustacean leg. The floating statue's head that topped the mountainous nephilim—the one the imp called Stomper—swiveled on its floating axis and stared down at him with blank malevolence.

He turned and bolted and was met with another living wall, scaly and coiled around the based of a crumbling apartment tower. Bodies lay everywhere, and as he took in this second nephilim a screaming man came to an abrupt, messy stop on the cobblestones not far away. That would no doubt be Slither. Capobar wished he'd thought of naming the bloody things, he might have been able to turn a profit on *that* somehow.

Capobar backed away from the second nephilim's coils. Then it paused, as if listening for something. A second later, a distant roar split the darkening sky.

The thief heard it too. A roar, not from any of the nephilim but from somewhere far below them. It carried through the stone and shook the street under his feet just as another wave of screaming people careened past him. Could there possibly be yet more of these things, ones he had not yet seen?

Capobar was fed up. It had started out as such a *simple* job. Then he'd been betrayed at every turn by employees and employers, and even been forced to testify. To *testify*. His license to steal was doomed. The union would revoke it out of hand just for the confession, no matter the duress or circumstances.

The thief's mind snapped, and he turned his face to the sky.

"All right!" Capobar cried. "You want me? Is this it, damn you? Here I am, right out in the open! If you're going to destroy me, destroy me already!"

The impact left a crater the size and shape of a small amphitheater. What remained of Capobar would have fit in a good-sized syringe.

* * * * *

"Kos, if that is really you, what is my favorite drink?" Pivlic asked.

"Your favorite drink is ten-year dindiwine, served in a bumbat glass with three cloves of crushed garlic and half a pickled cibuli onion. The onion's cut across the middle, not top to bottom," Kos said. "And it's disgusting, in case you were curious."

"Convincing," Pivlic said. "But an imposter might know that. When did we meet and under what circumstances?"

"We met when I arrested your bartender at the old canyonside place for selling spare parts to the zombies. You were the one who helpfully pointed out that it was proof they had sold the spare parts to the zombies without paying the proper shipping dues, which was why the bartender went to jail and you didn't. You said it was principle, even if it meant the extra cost of hiring a new bartender. I appreciated that. You might have let him go free."

"I do not suffer fools in my employ," Pivlic said. "Yet a lurker could have been there at the time, my friend. You just don't know. You could be a lurker *now*."

"Pivlic, it's me," Kos snapped. "Either accept it or don't. You're right, an imposter might know all of this. But an imposter would have eaten you by now."

The imp burst into laughter that Kos estimated was at least seventy percent nervousness. Still, he appreciated it. "All right, my friend, of course it is you. Certainly. You just look so strangely different."

"Well, dying, having your corpse burned on a pyre, and jumping into the body of a fat lawyer will change your looks a bit," Kos said.

Lawmage, the voice in his head said. *And ectomancer, thank you. Please, no mere lawyer would be able to master the mystical energies necessary to—*

All right, Kos told Obez. *Point made.*

I'm not fat.

Point. Made.

"But you—died—just a few weeks ago," Pivlic said. "You could show a little sympathy. I lost a good friend. For a while. This wound cannot be healed by your reincarnation—"

"I was never completely unincarnated. I didn't go to the afterlife. I went to Prahv. You might have tried looking there. Don't get metaphysical on me."

"You don't get metaphysical on *me*," the imp said.

"I tell you what, Pivlic," Kos sighed, "next time I sign a contract of any kind, I'm having you read it top to bottom." He tapped the imp's shoulder and pointed at a rising silhouette blocking out the setting sun. "Is that what I think it is?"

"It is Novijen. That large structure atop it is the greenhouse," Pivlic confirmed.

"Can you take me in fairly close?" Kos said.

"I believe so, my friend," the imp said, "but I cannot vouch for much else. I think the roc may be getting hungry."

"You didn't feed her?"

"How was I supposed to know how to do that?" Pivlic said. "I assumed that they ate on the wing."

"Poetic, but no," Kos said. He had never served as a full-time skyjek, but he'd taken the training every other recruit had. "After this, we feed her. You can't just run a trained mount like this into the ground."

"That is not my intention."

"Very well. Then I guess I won't be but a minute," Kos said. "At least, if this works the way Obez says it will. Just get up there."

You know, I could just go to the front door and knock, he told the lawmage.

There is no time, the voice of his anchor replied, *and there is no guarantee you would ever see the progenitor.*

I guess you're right, Kos told the voice, *but I'll be honest with you, Obez. This scares the hell out of me.*

Just remember, you have to wait at least half an hour before jumping again.

What? Just remember? I can't remember what you never told me.

I'm sure I mentioned it, the voice sniffed.

Whatever. Why? Kos asked.

Magic, Obez said. *Just how it works.*

Kos passed this information on to Pivlic. "Damned inconvenient," he added.

"You mean I circle around out here for half an hour or more and wait for you to wake up?" the imp said. "What will the fat lawyer be doing?

"He'll be . . ." Kos paused. "He said he may be in and out, and please don't let him fall off of the bird."

So really, what happens if you fall off? Kos thought. *What happens if I get stranded?*

You will become stuck where you are, unless you can make a blind jump into another host. And then the host must match your spectral and spiritual frequencies in such a way that you are not violently rejected, Obez replied. *Without contact with a trained— trained, I say—ectomancer, your personality will eventually merge with the one in the person or creature—*

Person or creature? Kos interjected.

Perhaps both, Obez said. *You have been given a great gift, wojek, a true afterlife of sorts. And you treat it like a burden. You could be more cooperative.*

"Kos, we're almost there," Pivlic said, "as close as I would like to get if you want a guarantee we will still be here when you return."

"Almost ready, Pivlic," Kos said. "I'm still trying to— Hold on."

So how do I find the right person to—what, possess? Take over? Kos asked Obez.

'Possess' is appropriate, the voice replied. *And please be patient. I'm finding your new temporary home now.*

Can I help?

Yes, you can let me concentrate, Obez retorted. *Please.*

Kos tried not to focus on anything and let his host do the work. He felt his attention wander, and without thinking about it he felt his feet start moving in a steady rhythm. He walked free of the ectomage's body, picked up his pace, and leaped. Kos, disembodied, sailed over the city. Novijen rose up to meet him with impossible speed, then the greenhouse that sat atop its organic spires filled his mind.

His mind wasn't wandering. It was going along for the ride. In Murzeddi's spectral eye, the living Simic inside the greenhouse went about their business with an unreal air—they looked more like blue-green light given a vaguely human shape—that he could see even before he passed effortlessly through its outer walls.

The interior of the greenhouse appeared equally unreal, and quite alive. A steady glow of magic and intelligence shone from the distorted cluster that was the neuroboretum, overhead and still somewhat far away.

Kos and Obez wandered down passages, stopped occasionally at one shape or another. It reminded the wojek of a dog tracking a scent. Finally, Obez found one he liked, a shape with a vaguely a duller color of life than the rest.

Clear your mind. I am going to place you in the target.

"If I'm not back in half an hour," Kos said aloud to Pivlic, splitting his attention between the here and the now, "wait another half hour, would you?"

Please, clear your mind.

"This is taking advantage of my famous generosity," Pivlic said, "but all right. After that," he said, pointing out the just-visible head of Slither coiling up another tower that crumbled under its weight, "I don't think we have any guarantee of a city to bother saving."

Clear your mind! Obez commanded.

All right, all right. Clearing, Kos thought, *clearing.*

No, you are not, Obez's voice replied. *You are thinking of—*

I'm trying, Kos thought.

Listen, I'm going to count down from ten. Just listen. Ten. Nine. Eight . . .

Kos kept the count with him but lost it in a rush as his ghostly form was wrenched from Obez's body and slammed into his new home.

The first thing he noticed was that his hand, which gripped a wicked-looking pike, appeared an unpleasant shade of green. The second was that he was not even remotely human, nor elf, vedalken, loxodon, even. Not an imp, not an ogre. Not a zombie, thank fortune's small favors. He was alive, at least. Or rather, the body he was in was alive.

The third thing he noticed was that his new body smelled like an infirmary during a plague outbreak.

CHAPTER 14

And so the happy little dromad, the mother dromad, and the father dromad ate the farmer and his family, went home to their pasture by the bubbling, blue brook, and lived long and contented lives. The farmer had learned a valuable lesson, and his ghost would wander the wilds of the undercity until the end of the world, telling all who would listen: 'Never get between a happy little dromad and his parents.'

—*The Happy Little Dromad,* by Evkala Belott
(Matka Children's Press, 7290 Z.C.)

31 CIZARM 10012 Z.C.

"I was wrong," Fonn said. "We're not under attack from *all* sides. Just the two."

"Yes," Jarad said. "I take back what I said about you taking up huntressing."

"We were spotted up there," Fonn said.

"Yes, but now you're getting us *more spotted,*" the Devkarin corrected.

"You kicked the first goblin."

"The cages are at two o'clock. Get there. I'll keep them off of us."

"We'll both keep them off of us," Fonn replied and drew her silver long sword. She considered removing her glove, but even after all this time she didn't completely trust the grip of the cytoplastic hand. And it still itched. Jarad matched her movement, drawing his kindjal long knife. He had left his bow behind when they made their way down here as it was too awkward to bring along.

"They'll be uncoordinated," Jarad said. "Take advantage of their—"

"I have done this before, you know," Fonn snapped. She followed that with a yell as she met the first charging cultist with a nonlethal boot to the kneecaps. Nonlethal but intended to cause at least a few compound fractures with the force Fonn put behind it. The tattooed human blocked the boot with the flat side of a blunt bone axe and grinned, showing all four of his filed, pointed teeth. Fonn turned her foot, pinning the axe head to the floor, then followed with a second kick that knocked out the four teeth.

The deathmonger moved more quickly than Fonn expected and grabbed her ankle with both hands, shoved upward, and flipped Fonn onto her back. She rolled over into a crouch and neatly hamstrung the Rakdos, who collapsed with a shriek. Without finesse she drove the point of her blade through the top of his head, killing him instantly.

Jarad took out two more cultists in the time she'd taken to kill her first. A pair of trolls carrying stone clubs and wearing little more than the chains of human skulls around their necks charged the Devkarin from either side. When Fonn looked back, the kindjal was in one troll's eye and the second troll's nose had been crushed with own club. Shards of thick troll brow turned the creature's forebrain to jelly, and it collapsed over the corpse of the first. Jarad retrieved the kindjal with a wet sound that left no doubt as to the fate of that first troll.

A trio of babbling goblins, horribly scarred little beasts wielding blood-encrusted pieces of slag pounded into savage approximations of swords, closed on Fonn from her blind side, the rear quarter neither she nor Jarad could cover completely. She risked a long, wide sweep with her blade, which put her off balance for a moment but forced all three back at once. All except the third, who tripped in midcharge and caught the tip of Fonn's sword across the throat.

The other two found this hilarious and, in their glee, hopped about, swinging their hunks of slag, until with uncanny timing the goblins cut each other down with simultaneous blows to the forehead.

Fonn heard another roar and risked a look up at the giant demon that had taken her son. Myc looked alive, even alert, perched in the demon's chain collar like a kid on a swing. The demon-god Rakdos was growing taller still. Now his horns came close to the ceiling overhead.

Howling, a pair of viashino fire jugglers attempted to batter Fonn with burning projectiles. She sliced them neatly out of the air. The jugglers proved to be acrobats besides, and when she attempted to follow through with the killing blow, the target somersaulted out of the way in one direction while his viashino mate did the same in the opposite direction. They moved so fast she wasn't sure which one lashed out with a curved dagger and bisected the leather uniform pauldron on her right shoulder, taking a bit of the shoulder underneath as well. First blood drawn by the cultists drew enthusiastic hoots from the gathering crowd.

The shouts and grisly cheers did not keep her sharp ears from tracking the hopping jugglers behind her. She waited for them to predictably cross in front of her again and got around one's guard and took one arm off. The viashino shrieked, and her mate stopped capering and joined in. His mouth foamed red as he sunk his own teeth into his thin reptilian lips in a blood frenzy. The lack of control made him easier to dispatch than the other, who had already gone pale and silent, the ground slick with cold blood. The male juggler lunged at exactly the wrong moment, falling for the ledev's feint, and she spun around as he whipped past her to skewer him neatly through the heart. She missed, but the viashino's capers ended on the tip of Jarad's kindjal.

And so it went, all the while Fonn's son sitting overhead, ever closer, like the trophy at the end of some grotesque, cruel tournament.

Which, the half-elf supposed, wasn't far from the truth.

The fighting went in fits and starts, but steadily they began to attract more attention. No matter how much progress toward the scouts or their son Jarad and Fonn made, they stood back-to-back at the center of a moving mob. Against all sense and strategic reason the Rakdos cultists continued to attack alone, in pairs, or at best small groups. It *was* a competition to them, she realized, and while they could have just swarmed Fonn and Jarad, they were taking their time, confident that the desperate parents would be worn down before too long, but not without providing some excellent entertainment.

"Jarad!" Fonn called as she decapitated a skeletal zombie dressed in most of a wojek uniform that looked at least three hundred years old. "We have to get out of this! That demon is going to take Myc!"

"I lost the grapple!" Jarad called back. "It's in the chains. I can't fly and I can't even get to the Krokt-forsaken demon's feet! How *can* we get to him?"

We can't, Fonn thought, but couldn't bring herself to say it.

Rakdos drew himself up to his full height, his black horns drawing sparks as they scraped against the inner roof of the Rakdos temple. He roared again, and Fonn screamed with rage. She charged like a thrill-killer into the mob, sword flashing, blood and cultist body parts flying.

The gigantic demon, if he noticed her at all, paid no heed. Myc appeared to watch her, but when Fonn called his name, there was no reply. Not even a nod.

She was perhaps fifty feet from the edge of the pit, in real danger of being trampled by the demon, but then so was everyone else—including the scouts she could see in the cages along the caldera's rim and could now hear calling her name.

What Fonn had taken for a wall, the wall facing the way she and

Jarad had come in, began to rise. She spotted half a dozen ogres on either side of the huge, wooden door, and the burly creatures heaved on mammoth chains hidden in a long shadowed alcove. The demon-god Rakdos turned to face the rising portcullis, and Myc left her line of sight.

Then Jarad was at her side again, and together they furiously drove through the Rakdos mob. The cultists finally seemed to be giving up on the competitive, mano-a-mano approach and did eventually try to attack en masse, but by then the ledev and the Devkarin were working with brutal efficiency and coordination, and the cultists never had a chance. The mob was just, well, a mob, and only so many of them could get close to the life churcher or the guildmaster as long as the two stuck together.

Twenty feet. They were on a path to the cages, but to get to the demon they would have to go around the lava pit or across it somehow.

By the time they broke through to the first cage, Rakdos was through the archway and disappearing into the shadows.

"Centuriad Fonn!" Orval called, and the others took up the same call. "Help us! Centuriad Fonn!"

A gigantic demon—*the* gigantic demon—was getting away with her boy, but she could help these scouts. And they were her responsibility. They were someone's kids too.

A roar pierced the darkness, and a glow as something erupted into flame, but she couldn't see what.

"I can still catch up to him," Jarad said. "I brought beetles."

"*Beetles?*"

"They will help me track him," the Devkarin said. "Fonn, even if we can get to him, we have to get him down." He paused to impale a goblin and kick its body into the lava.

"Jarad, I am not going to abandon my son!" Fonn was more furious than ever. To consider it on her own was one thing. To hear Jarad suggest it enraged her—illogically, but it enraged her all the same.

"He will be safe," Jarad said, "for now."

"Safe?" Fonn shouted. "How will he—"

"He's rigged himself some kind of harness," Jarad said, as reassuring as he could be in the middle of the still furious, though less enthusiastic, melee. "Look. The demon's jaw protects its own neck quite well. Myc will be protected as well. At least long enough to free your charges and for us all to follow him."

Fonn considered Jarad carefully before she replied. He surprised her. It had been a long time since the Devkarin had reminded her of why she'd married him in the first place.

"You're right," she said, and placed a hand on his shoulder. "Send your spies. I'll get to work on the first cage." Jarad nodded inscrutably and turned to his task.

The first Fonn managed to free was Orval. The centaur appeared healthy and immediately took up a pike dropped by a dead troll. He then used it to transfix the guard nearest his cage with a ferocious centaur battle yell. Jarad freed young Aklechin and handed the young scout a cutlass.

"Sir," Aklechin stammered, "the witch. She took Lily away. And— and Myc."

"I know, Aklechin," Fonn said. "We're going to find them all. I promise. But now we have to fight. Stay close, and remember what your instructors have taught you."

The young man set his jaw and summoned all of his remaining courage to raise his cutlass and answer Orval's battle cry with one of his own.

Armed and furious, the small band hacked their way around the pit and toward the mammoth archway. The door was already falling back into place, the gears lining its slots, grinding and shrieking above the din.

Charging, they cleared the bottom of the door with room to spare. The cultists just behind them weren't so lucky. More than one thrill-killer's skull or torso burst messily as the door clanged shut.

"All right," Aklechin said nervously, "what now?"

"Scared of the dark?" Orval asked.

"No more than you," the young man snapped back.

"Quiet, both of you," Fonn said. "I'm listening for Myc."

"Holy mother, heart of life, you are our charge and we are yours. Holy mother, heart of life, you are our charge and we are yours," Aklechin whispered.

"Scout," Fonn said.

"Yes sir," Aklechin said.

"I admire your devotion, but I need you here right now."

"I think I see a faint glow perhaps a half mile distant," Jarad said. "He is making good time. The beetles are having a tough time keeping up. I'm calling in some greenbites."

"After you, huntmaster," Fonn said.

"Guildmaster," Jarad corrected absently. He pulled a brass cylinder from his waist and twisted it with a snap of his wrist. The brass shimmered and took on a bright green glow that extended just far enough for them to keep track of each other but little else.

They had reached the bend in the tunnel when the shriek of the door mechanism started to reverberate off the walls, joined by the shrieks of the cultists forcing it open.

* * * * *

Myc knew he shouldn't be enjoying himself, but it was hard not to.

He didn't remember rigging his belt into a harness, but he must have. It only made sense. His immediate past wasn't sticking around.

Myc found he didn't care all that much.

The scout closed his eyes and found himself once again looking through the demon's instead. He, *they,* strode down a small—to Rakdos—tunnel, and he could see perfectly well although Myc's own eyes found little illumination.

Another, isolated part of his mind, an original Myc, remained hidden, watching and waiting for the time to try and rectify this turn of events. This original mind nudged the conscious one as best he could.

"Rakdos," Myc said with his eyes closed—that, and speaking aloud, seemed to help him communicate with the demon-god without being overwhelmed by its vast, ancient mind—"where are we going?"

The demon spoke, a slow barrage of snorts and guttural syllables Myc's own mouth would not have been able to imitate but which he understood perfectly.

"My children have grown restless," Rakdos said, "and it is the season of dissension. We go to lead them."

"What are we going to do when we get there?" Myc wasn't sure he wanted to know.

"We will go to Old Rav," the demon said. "From there, I believe I will carve out a way to the surface. It has been too long since I last enjoyed the pleasures the City has to offer. I think I will start by laying low the towers of insipid justice. Then I will move on to burn that damned life churcher tree. Perhaps afterward, I will crush the Boros lawkeepers and their toy titans."

"That's a good idea," Myc said, and for a second he meant it. Then he reconsidered. He had a lot of friends in some of the places the demon-god had just mentioned. He was pretty sure someone— his mother?—fell into at least two of those categories.

For some reason, he didn't want to destroy his friends, or his mother, or father. Rakdos assured him he did. The original mind nudged back with the opposite assurance.

The demon-god continued another few long steps, then extended a clawed hand. Myc closed his eyes and saw the demon's talons grasp a lever as tall as his father.

Father. He could clearly remember his father in his mind's eye, though the shape of Ja— Ja-something soon melted away and took on the look of a demon with glowing, orange eyes.

The rational part of his mind worked feverishly. The rest of his mind was oblivious.

Myc and Rakdos slammed the lever down. Another door, this one solid, rough-hewn rock, slid to one side. Myc looked down through the demon-god's eyes and saw dozens of stunned citizens gape at the sudden appearance of the winged monster. Myc bellowed, sending already quite harried and exhausted crowds stumbling over each other in flight.

"Why did you shout?" the demon demanded. "I am not a plaything. I do not understand why we share a mind, but until I learn how to extract you and destroy you without permanent harm to myself, *I* will decide when I shout."

"You were going to step on them," Myc said.

"Yes."

"First, you make them scared," Myc said, maneuvering frantically as the original mind took over his mouth, "then you have them cornered. It just seemed like more fun."

"I disagree," the demon said. "But these insects are little sport. My pets await above. They herald my return."

"The rats?"

"The rats," Rakdos agreed. "They wait at the elves' tree. I think we shall begin there and move out when I have consumed my fill."

Myc suppressed a chill at the thought of what Rakdos envisioned. Vitu Ghazi, the heart of the Selesnya Conclave. More than that abstract danger, he felt immediate concern for a family friend who was part of the Conclave itself, an old wolf by the name of Biracazir. He had spent many a day communing with Bir, who taught him in simple thoughts and images methods that helped the youth pick out strands of life in the song.

At least he had diverted the demon from striking directly at Old Rav, his second home. But if he couldn't figure out a way to halt the demon before he reached the surface, what then? He didn't dare try to get away. That would leave Rakdos completely unchecked. And their minds were still linked. He wasn't sure simply leaving would change that.

It wasn't easy being smart, eleven, tied to a demon bent on killing, and, worst of all, saddled with an overgrown sense of responsibility.

* * * * *

"The way out!" Orval called. "Look!"

The light hardly brightened the cavernous tunnel, but Fonn gazed in the direction the centaur pointed and saw that there was indeed an indisputable sliver of orange, fading daylight painted on the wall atop a long, iron ladder.

"We can get to the surface and warn them," Aklechin said. "Centuriad, respectfully—"

"Don't bother, Scout," Fonn sighed bitterly. "You're right. I've got to get you kids out of here."

"Fonn," Jarad said, "I will follow him. I will get him back, and—" he pointed to the green stone around his neck, "I will call you and tell you as soon as he is safe."

"There's another scout, too," Fonn said. "A girl, Lily. If you find her—"

"I will try," the Devkarin said.

Before she realized what she was doing, Fonn kissed him lightly on the mouth then pushed back with a start. She hadn't planned to do that, and any reaction was impossible to read on Jarad's face in the dim, greenish light.

"Good luck," Fonn said. Jarad smirked, the Devkarin equivalent of a wide, open smile.

"Fonn, when I return," Jarad said, "I—"

"We need to talk," Fonn said.

"Right," Jarad said. "I will— I will see you both soon."

The Devkarin turned and dashed ahead without another word. She lost sight of him a few seconds later as the green glow of the lightstick faded into the blackness.

"Ew," Orval said. "You *kissed* him."

Fonn ignored the comment, glad the darkness hid the redness she felt in her face. "Orval, can you get up the ladder?"

"Why wouldn't I be able to get up the ladder?" the centaur asked.

"Because you— Never mind," Fonn said. "Just get going. Then you, Al."

"My name is Aklechin," the young scout said, adding a hasty "sir."

"I like 'Al,'" Fonn said. "I'll bring up the rear."

"I really have to follow *him*?" Aklechin asked incredulously.

"Why wouldn't you want to follow me?" the centaur asked, one hoof already on the bottom rung and two strong arms several rungs up.

"Get moving, Scout," Fonn said. "That's an order."

She closed her eyes and focused on the song as the scouts hustled up the creaking ladder. The din of the pursuing mob was growling. They couldn't be more than a minute or two behind them. The only reason they were that far back was that, from the sound of it, the Rakdos cultists were fighting each other to be in front.

There was Myc, still in the grip of that angry sound, a sound that had to be the demon-god. The Devkarin would have no trouble catching the demon if he kept up his speed, and Jarad could run at a steady pace for miles at a time without breaking much of a sweat.

She hunted for Jarad's note and found it humming away into the darkness, but Aklechin's whisper broke in on her remaining concentration.

"Sir? I think I see torches. They're coming after us!"

Fonn's concentration left entirely as Rakdos poured into the tunnel in the darkness behind them. She hauled herself up the ladder with all the strength she had left. Rung after rung, well over two hundred feet up, half of which hung down into the cavernous tunnel, the other half through a narrow tube that pierced another hundred feet of undercity to emerge, she hoped, at street level. The light they had seen was already gone, but there was still a general glow at the top from the dull corona ringing the top of the passage.

The scouts took to it remarkably well, especially the centaur. It had never occurred to her to wonder what centaurs did when faced with ladders, and the answer was that centaurs had incredibly strong upper bodies and surprisingly deft control of their forward hooves. Orval moved up the ladder quickly, despite the awkward bulk of half his lower body. Al was a bit slower, but considering the conditions both scouts had been held in for the last several hours he still made good speed. Fonn herself was breathing hard by the time the clanging thumps of someone climbing onto the ladder far below rang into her palms and feet. She risked a look down and coughed as a puff of black smoke struck her in the face. After so long in the tunnel, the Rakdos torches were almost blinding, but it looked like the entire carnarium had given chase. Already a pair of enterprising goblins were scrambling up the ladder, and a couple of humans were below them.

"Move!" Fonn called. "Faster!"

"They're following us, aren't they?" Aklechin called.

"Yes," Fonn said, "but I'm more worried about the strain their weight is going to put on the— -"

A low creak of bending metal groaned from the ladder and efficiently made Fonn's point.

Orval reached the top of the passage just as the first goblin took a swipe at Fonn's boots. The goblin didn't get another chance. Fonn planted a foot in the creature's face and shoved. The goblin lost its grip and, flailing, caught its kinsman below with all four claws in the back of the neck. The second goblin screamed and lost its own hold on the ladder, and the pair screeched curses and tore at each other until they struck with a wet thud amid the milling, snarling crowd of cultists.

The nearest remaining cultist on the ladder was a human but one who only just qualified as such. His cheeks were sliced clean through, a mutilation that left him with a permanent skeleton's grin. His bare, bony crown bore hundreds of overlapping scars. He held a dagger in his silver-capped teeth, and he winked at Fonn as he started to climb again, the goblins forgotten.

Fonn continued her own efforts and checked on the scouts. Orval was through the exit with a clang, shoving the lid aside, and the dusky sky that appeared overhead was one of the most beautiful things she had ever seen. Aklechin managed to hook both hands on the edge when the ladder creaked again, more ominously this time, and Fonn felt the iron beneath her ping with the sound of snapping bolts. Just another few feet . . .

The iron ladder broke free and dropped.

Fonn started a shout that ended as abruptly as the fall did. If not for the strength of her artificial cytoplast hand, she might have joined the Rakdos who found the jarring stop too much and slipped from the ladder, bouncing painfully off of the now-inclined rungs before dropping into open space.

Fonn almost laughed. The ladder had dropped the last couple

of feet to the ground but was still held upright by the passage in the ceiling. She was home free.

Or would have been, she added silently, if she were eight feet tall. Even from the top rung, there was no way she could reach the edge of the exit hole now, even if she jumped. The passage was too narrow to allow her to bend her knees much at all.

She started to explain this to the pair of anxious faces watching her from above.

"You're going to have to leave me," she began. "Orval, you're in—"

"No sir," Aklechin said. "Orval, grab my ankles."

"Al, get out of here," Fonn ordered. The ladder groaned again as more and more cultists climbed aboard.

"No sir," Orval parroted, taking hold of Al's ankles. Before Fonn could raise another objection, Aklechin dangled upside down, his extended arms just within reach if she stretched.

She caught hold of the young scout's wrists on the first try, and Al shouted, "Heave!"

The scouts pulled their centuriad commander up with a collective yell, and the three of them collapsed in a heap in the middle of a street that Fonn would probably have recognized if she hadn't been staring at the dark gray sky peppered with sparse stars.

Another loud groan of twisting metal and Fonn heard the ladder finally give way and fold up. The shouts of the plummeting cultists disappeared among the shouts of their fellow deathmongers enjoying an unexpected feast. The ledev crawled to the edge of the hole and looked down.

An unhinged smile greeted her, and she blinked. The Rakdos cultist's fist connected with her jaw and knocked her over onto her side. The man was through in a heartbeat, hauling himself up with both arms. He dropped into a crouch and snarled, drawing a jagged, rusty blade.

Had Fonn, or any of the other scouts, been just a few feet one way or the other, they too would have been flattened by the nephilim's step.

The foot lifted slowly and came down again a few feet behind them. Another one was on its way down to replace it, but by then they were scrambling for cover.

"Are they following us, sir?" Orval asked as they watched the giant, rocky thing rumble past down the broad street.

"I don't know, Scout," Fonn said. "If they are, they missed us. But it looks like they're headed in the same direction as that demon, the demon that just kept getting bigger and bigger. . . ." She lapsed into thought. Whatever had gotten to the nephilim, was it the cult's doing? And what had the stuff done to Myc?

"Change of plan," Fonn said. "You two are not going with me."

"Sir?" Aklechin said, confused.

"I've already gotten you almost killed on three separate occasions," Fonn said. "I'm going to get my son or I'm going to die trying, and I don't need to be worried about you two as well."

"Sir, we are ledev scouts, sir!" Orval said. "Unless you are dismissing us from the ledev guard, sir, we will stand at our commander's side."

"Sir," Al added. "We want to get Myc back too. And Lily. Wherever she is."

Fonn was unable to muster a good counterargument. Besides, where could Orval or Aklechin go that was safe? The nephilim were between them and Vitu Ghazi. In fact, the thought occurred to her that the nephilim might not be headed for Rakdos at all. They might be going for the tree, or anywhere in the Center of Ravnica, for that matter.

The problem with arguing with yourself, Fonn mused, was that you sometimes won. She nodded and tapped a knuckle over her heart. The scouts returned the salute.

"All right, Scouts," Fonn said, "Follow that monster."

* * * * *

Myc's original mind was fairly sure it had won control of his actions but still kept itself hidden. As the demon drew closer and closer to the top of Rix Maadi and the point where it made contact with the surface, Myc began to wonder how he could get the demon-god to stop before Rakdos reached the top and punched right on through the central pavilion. Worse, if Myc's judgment was correct, the improvised exit would see Rakdos enter the city very near the base of Vitu Ghazi, the Unity Tree that Myc, raw scout though he might be, had sworn an oath to defend.

The young ledev was still going over the possibilities when he felt and heard the first jarring thud of the demon's huge fist as it made contact with the stone.

"They thought they had uprisings before." The demon laughed.

That gave Myc pause. Rakdos was right. There had been uprisings before. For ten thousand years, the demon-god had vanished for long spells of whatever sadistic pleasures took his fancy, returned, whipped the cultists into a murderous frenzy, and watched them cavort into the City of Ravnica to stir up chaos. Unpredictable in the specifics, over the long haul the uprisings were spaced over roughly similar intervals corresponding to the demon's attention span.

But in all those ten thousand years, there was no record of something like this, the demon, grown to titanic stature through some spell or another, attacking the city personally. Myc winced at the thunderous sound of another punch and a corresponding shower of rubble that plummeted past his perch. Perhaps it had just never occurred to the demon-god to just drive up through the streets and attack the city himself.

Something was wrong. Perhaps the song was not faint because

of interference from Rakdos's mind. Perhaps it was weakening. Perhaps Rakdos's very proximity to Vitu Ghazi was causing the change.

Despite the furnacelike heat the demon gave off, the young scout felt an unearthly chill.

CHAPTER 15

Three cheers for the Simic Progenitor. Momir Vig has only been in place as guildmaster for a few weeks, and already more than a dozen new clinics with free medical treatment have sprung up where they're needed most. We say those who object to signing a simple waiver in exchange for good health are rude, ungrateful, and untrusting. Three cheers for Momir Vig.

—"Three Cheers," *Ravnican Guildpact-Journal* (11 Tevnember, 9211 Z.C.)

31 Cizarm 10012 Z.C.

Kos was a virus. A six-foot, green, lightly armored, fully ambulatory virus armed with a peculiar pike. The blade was some kind of polished, sharpened, metallic bracket fungus, and the haft of the weapon appeared to be one long, narrow femur from some thin-boned giant. The virus was barefoot, but Kos couldn't imagine those stumplike feet fitting into any traditional footwear he had seen. As Kos stared at his new stumps, he noticed the floor was also disturbingly organic. It glowed faintly from within, and hazy networks of something like blood vessels pulsed under a leathery surface.

The Kos virus stood alone in an empty hall, but he heard squishy footsteps not far away. On this floor, he couldn't imagine footsteps that would not be squishy, so the peculiar sound gave no clue as to who might be approaching.

So I'm a virus, he thought at Obez.

Virusoid, said an alien voice that was as unlike Obez's as Kos could imagine.

Of course, he was no longer with Obez. Or was he?

Yes. A virusoid, Obez's familiar ring came in but obscured by something Kos could only describe as mental static.

I can hear you.

Of course you can, I'm your anchor.

Right. Why am I a virus?

Virusoid, the virusoid repeated.

I mean, why am I a virusoid?

Tough, very hard to eradicate, and liable to be ignored by the progenitor, Obez's replied. *It also had the right frequency. So long as there's just a piece of your virusoid friend there still alive, you will also be intact. Not much in the way of a mind, so Vig uses them as muscle. You'll be able to get into his main lab, find clues, and do your wojek thing.*

Almost immediately the unfamiliar, alien virusoid body grew more familiar and comfortable. It appeared that occupying a weak-minded person—virus—*being*—made acclimation take less time. He wasn't sure that was something he wanted, but since when did Agrus Kos get what he really wanted? Peace and quiet in a well-deserved retirement? Sorry Kos, need to hatch a few dragon eggs. The silent embrace of death? Shouldn't have signed those papers, old man. A second chance? Forget that, you're an avatar and will follow orders.

At least following orders was something he understood. And on the bright side, his memories, though not all happy ones and indeed occasionally quite unhappy, were his again.

If you're quite through, Obez said.

Sorry, Kos replied. *Got to thinking. So which way to the laboratory?*

Follow your nose.

My what? Kos said.

Follow its *nose,* Obez said. *The virusoid knows which way to go.*

Virusoid, the virusoid interjected.

Virusoid, Kos agreed.

* * * * *

Teysa could hardly believe her ears.

"You're calling the Senate to order?" she said incredulously.

"You object?" Augustin IV said, and dull amusement tinged his rumbling voice.

"A building just crashed into Prahv," Teysa said.

"As—as guildmaster," Feather said, seeming to have a little trouble getting her mouth around the word, "I must say, your honor, that this seems imprudent. Surely our first concern should be for the safety of the city. I would be surprised if you could even round up enough members to do much of anything. Do not two thirds of the upper and lower houses need to be present?"

"I am calling the Senate to order," the Grand Arbiter repeated. "Under emergency powers granted to me by the Guildpact."

"Well you can call whatever you wish to order," Saint Kel said. "*I* am returning to Vitu Ghazi, if it's still standing."

"That is your right," the Grand Arbiter said. "Do be careful."

"Your honor," Feather said, "I believe the Living Saint—"

"What you believe, Guildmaster," the Grand Arbiter said, "is immaterial here. By Hesperia's wings, I *will* call my Senate to order. We have business to discuss."

" 'Your Senate'? " Teysa said. "You're in a ruin, your honor, and with all due respect now is not the time. Feather— Guildmaster Pierakor is right. I implore you."

"Without due process, we fall into chaos," Augustin said distantly. He didn't seem to speak to anyone in the room. "The senators, ministers, and others will join us."

"Join us," the soulsworn ghosts repeated, their voices soft and unearthly but ringing with agreement. "Join us. They will join us."

"No thanks," the loxodon said and stomped down the steps to follow the path the thief Capobar had taken. "Lost your mind," the Living Saint grumbled under his breath as he went.

There was a long, uncomfortable silence when the loxodon had gone. Finally, Feather said, "Your honor, you must do what you must do. But I must as well." The angel indicated the hulking wreck that occupied half of the ruined Senate chamber. "I intend to board the Parhelion and recover Razia's body."

Teysa was probably more surprised than Feather when she said, "And I'm going with her." She wasn't sure what motivated her to say that—the unease she now felt coming from the Grand Arbiter and his ghostly coterie or the intense curiosity she felt about what might be on board the Parhelion. The third possibility, that she was growing frightened and didn't want to stand there alone without the angel at her side, was the most likely, she decided.

"Yes," the angel said, and Teysa released a breath she hadn't realized she was holding. "That will help."

As advokist and angel found a path through the rubble to the only open landing deck that was visible—its surface tilted precariously to the side—the Grand Arbiter said nothing. Once the unlikely pair cleared the lip of the deck, he spoke, but not to them.

"All of you, come home," he said. "The Senate is called to order. The senators shall attend, immediately."

Feather helped Teysa up onto the deck, and with the help of her cane—still in her hand, against all odds—she stood leaning on the tilted surface.

It wasn't until the sound of thunder erupted behind them and she saw a new mountain of rubble pile up outside the deck that it sunk in. Another section of the Senate dome had collapsed, whether by accident or design it was impossible to say.

Either way, she and Feather had just been sealed inside a ghost ship. Minus the ghosts, with any luck.

* * * * *

It didn't take Kos long to learn that something stunk inside the greenhouse. The virusoid's mind was simple, but it could take direction very well. And the virusoid had standing orders to "Stop intruders" and "Prepare for the next step." Kos had more trouble retrieving any idea of what the "next step" was from the slow-witted creature's consciousness.

No doubt I'll find out, he told himself. There wasn't anyone else in his mind worth telling.

The squishy steps had, it turned out, been just another virusoid. The encounter gave Kos a good chance to see what he looked like these days. If his own borrowed guard looked anything like this fellow, he had only the merest suggestion of a face—a mouth like a wide slit, no nose, bright patches of shinier green where the eyes should have been. No, they were true eyes, Kos realized, or *I wouldn't be able to see the other virusoid.* Just simple ones.

Kos wasn't sure if he should nod when the other virusoid walked by, but he did it anyway, automatically. This brought the second guard to a halt, for a moment, but Kos kept moving, hoping the creature's basic thought processes would soon take over.

For a few seconds, he thought he was going to get away with it, but then the wet footsteps behind him stopped, then turned and started to follow, not hurrying, but definitely not getting any more distant.

I think I'm being followed, Kos thought.

Stay calm, Obez thought back. *And try not to acknowledge anything unless someone's giving you an order. Whatever you do, do not speak. The virusoid has the tools for it, but they are not given the ability to do so. Your nature would be revealed instantly.*

Fine, no talking. What do I do when I get to the lab? Kos asked.

You'll have to improvise, came the reply. *If you see the vampire, I would say kill him. If you don't, get back here as soon as the half hour is up.*

How much time do I have?

You've only been there three minutes. So stop nodding at people like you're a 'jek on the stretch, all right?

Right.

The steps that followed kept pace with him but did not draw any closer after the first few seconds. Kos wasn't even sure the other guard was really following him after a while. It might just have been a coincidence. And if he meant to learn anything in here, he'd have to assume it was a coincidence. He was gratified to hear the steps peel off as they passed an asymmetrical, membranous door that resembled the entrance to a giant intestine—and smelled like one too.

Kos knew he was headed in the direction of the lab because his borrowed body told him so. It was a strange feeling, your consciousness not just in your head but distributed throughout your entire form. He could not be sure, but it felt like he didn't even have a skeleton, let alone any of the usual organs like brain, heart, and so on. But the strange body knew right where it was going when he nudged it with a simple mental command: *Find the progenitor.* So Kos followed his feet.

He passed more Simic along the way, not just mute, hulking guards like the one whose body he wore but vedalken, humans, even a goblin and viashino here and there. All of them wore some kind of cytoplast enhancement. Kos had seen the like out at Nebun's place in Utvara, freakish deviations from the simple artificial limbs like the one Fonn wore. A vedalken with a translucent crustacean claw half again as long as its other arm brushed him. It took all of his control not to jump in panic and keep on shuffling. Two goblins walked silently past, waving their arms frantically, their lips moving but no words passing between them. The virusoid shared in wordless thought that the bulbous cytoplastic helmets each wore made them short-range telepaths at the cost of their speech centers. A woman in silver robes who appeared relatively normal from the waist up, though her skin was unnaturally blue and pale, scuttled by. Her legs split in four places just below the hips, and she walked on eight insectoid limbs that punctured tiny holes in the leathery floor that seeped reddish sap. She was almost half again as tall as Kos, and a row of unblinking eyes lined either arm.

After the silver widow had passed, Kos caught himself looking at the wounds the crab-woman's claws had left in the floor. The sap congealed over the tiny holes in seconds. The greenhouse was self-healing, to a certain extent. And for a giant mushroom its sap looked remarkably similar to blood. He didn't dawdle any longer, but he could have sworn that the sap was already starting to flake as it passed out of sight.

Odd that more Simic didn't go into construction. Indestructible homes could make a fortune. That reminded him.

Obez, he sent. *You and Pivlic doing all right?*

So far, we have been ignored. But there is much activity.

What kind of activity? Kos demanded.

Just concentrate on getting into that lab and going after the vampire.

How can you be sure he's even there? Kos thought, fighting the urge to salute as a pair of virusoids passed wordlessly, one after the other, in a plodding march.

We can't, Obez said. *But even if he's not there, Vig is your best witness.*

The virusoid's instincts told Kos he was nearing the entrance to the progenitor's chambers—or at least the entrance to the entrance. The instincts were vague on that point. He saw why when he reached it.

The door was flanked by two silent, immobile virusoids. The door itself was another shade of green, and, as he approached, a small opening appeared in the center and widened as the membrane split open of its own volition. His borrowed feet continued on through, stepping high to clear the lip of the retracted door, and Kos found himself at the bottom of a spiral staircase of sorts. Three other membrane doors lined the spongy, glowing walls, which provided diffuse sunlight without glare. The steps of the staircase were hard, flat bracket fungi growing on a single—not tree trunk, exactly, but it was about as big as a good-sized Silhana oak and had a barky exterior. The stairs that coiled around the trunk went through a floor some fifty feet overhead, probably to another exit. He hoped.

Kos virusoid mounted the stairs to the laboratory, wondering with mild concern at the absence of anyone—or anything   else going the same way.

* * * * *

Pivlic fought the urge to elbow the fat lawmage in the ribs. He would have had to release the reins to do so, and that would be even more trouble than the human's irritating way of pointing out and explaining everything that went past them in the sky or thundered through the city below. It wasn't the information—Pivlic always had use for information—but rather the unsettling sensation, bizarre as it might sound, that someone in the greenhouse would overhear them speaking. Someone who wasn't Kos.

Kos. Pivlic wished he'd had the presence of mind to place a

bet on how long it took the old 'jek to find a way back to the world of the living.

So far, the skyjeks had not accosted them, despite the quite clear golden sigil on the roc's breast that Pivlic had not bothered to remove. Of course, the skyjeks had their hands full. What their hands were full of was still in question. Pivlic suspected that it was not success.

The three nephilim had split up after passing through the gates, though all of them seemed intent on clearing through the clustered towers of Ravnica's most densely populated metropolis—knocking the towers over as needed—and reaching the Center. Pivlic supposed the monsters might just be passing through, but there was something that told the imp otherwise. The Center was the Center for a reason. Events that had shaped the history of Ravnica, from the formation of the Guildpact ten millennia earlier to its near-end twelve years ago, were always, well, centered there. It could not just be that the nephilim saw something they really wanted on the other side. Pivlic was sure of it. He just wasn't sure which of the great guildhalls might be their goal.

"There, you see?" Obez said, and again Pivlic had to flick his left wing to free it from the lawmage's fist. "The creatures have yet to attack each other. They have a definite goal."

"What I see—the waist, if you please, my friend, my wings are quite delicate appendages—What I see are the best parts of the central city getting knocked to pieces."

"But it proves what I was saying," Obez insisted. "This is not random. They're going somewhere, communicating somehow, cooperating."

"Should this make me happy?" Pivlic said, banking the roc to the left for another arc of the lazy circle they flew around the greenhouse.

"It means there's more to this than monsters eating a dead

dragon," Obez said. "No matter what the thief would have had us believe."

"Perhaps," Pivlic said, "and perhaps they are simply hungry, and the Center is in their path." But even as he said it, he didn't believe it.

The imp struggled briefly with his balance when an updraft caught one wing of their feathered mount. The roc was steering . . . oddly. Its weight didn't seem to shift quite right. Of course, the imp's experience with roc-riding was limited enough that he couldn't be sure of the hunch, but his experience with his own hunches was such that he felt uneasy.

A trio of roc-riding skyjeks streaked past them, tearing around the greenhouse like their tails were on fire. Pivlic's borrowed bird called out as they went past, but otherwise they were ignored.

Pivlic followed the skyjeks as they set a vector that took them straight for Stomper's head, the spherical, statuary head floating over the nephilim's mountainous back. From this angle it appeared to float on a cushion of golden energy that seeped from the monster's back, some kind of magic, to be sure, but it appeared to be natural to the nephilim. With a shout, the lead skyjek ordered her squad to take aim, and on the wing leader's command, three bamshots—they sounded like popping corks at this distance—erupted from the ends of their raised bam-sticks.

The orange pellets bounced harmlessly off of the nephilim's stony back but must have stung at least. Stomper roared a challenge at the skyjeks and reared up on its spiny stone legs, and then opened its segmented crab-mouth. Before the skyjeks could veer off to make another pass, the nephilim's maw erupted with a blast of fire—not pure flame like Pivlic had seen so recently belched from a dragon, but more a reddish-orange fluid that ignited on contact with the air and enveloped the roc-riders in an inferno worthy of Niv-Mizzet himself.

Pivlic urged his roc to dive below the leading edge of Stomper's blast. "Didn't know he could do that," Pivlic managed when he was sure they'd made it clear. "Remind me not to shoot at him."

"Remarkable," Obez said. Pivlic wasn't sure he liked the awe in his voice.

"They're not pets," Pivlic said. "They are killing people, my friend. Without even taking out a contract, for that matter."

"But still remarkable," Obez repeated.

"Why aren't the stone titans stopping this?" Pivlic asked, not really expecting an answer.

"If they haven't acted yet, I'm beginning to think they won't," Obez said. "Look there."

Slither, a half mile away, was doing his level best to dismantle Centerfort. The snake-thing's claws lashed at the buttresses of the wojek headquarters, smashing new and old architecture alike in the recently rebuilt structure, which had suffered greatly during the Decamillennial. What had made Obez point was what had already toppled—the central tower, where the brass had their command center in times of crisis.

"How is destroying Szadek going to stop them?" Pivlic said. "How will it save those people?"

"I'm not sure it can," Obez said sadly. "But Ravnica is more than just this city, and we will rebuild, with a strong Guildpact renewed. I have to believe that."

"I don't," Pivlic said, "but I will, just because the alternative is too depress—"

A shadow fell across the imp and the lawmage, casting the roc into brief darkness beneath a gigantic round shape that blocked out the sun. Pivlic spurred the mount as hard as he could, and the roc bolted forward to avoid a random projectile that Brain hurled in their general direction. The roc didn't quite clear the nephilim's shot in time. The ball of nephilim flesh did not strike their mount, but Pivlic felt a jarring lurch as the bird tumbled in the cyclone of displaced air.

Despite his best efforts, Pivlic felt his legs lose their hold on the saddle. The roc struggled to right itself and he tumbled over the bird's head, still clutching the reins. Obez, of course, was still clutching his wing and went along with him.

By the time the roc did right itself, the bird found itself riderless again but carrying much the same burden as before, imp and lawmage hanging precariously from the reins around its ruffled neck. The confused bird mistook the tugs as Pivlic struggled to maintain his grip for a command to turn, and by lucky coincidence—and as far as luck went Pivlic's wasn't doing so great—the roc wheeled back around toward the greenhouse. But Pivlic wasn't sure how long his luck would last, hanging from a confused giant bird, a rampaging Stomper directly underneath, and a screaming lawmage holding on by the end of the imp's painfully twisted wing.

A panicked shout caught in Pivlic's throat when he heard a thumping sound coming from the pavilion, a sound even louder than the stomping nephilim beneath him. A radial crack appeared in the empty square, almost entirely devoid of fleeing citizens, most of whom had long since cleared away from the open space and taken shelter. There was another thump, a crash, and then a small eruption of stone and brick as a huge, horned fist the color of midnight drove through from below.

"What's *that*?" Obez shouted, all clerical and clinical reserve gone.

"I think it's a demon," Pivlic said. "And please be careful of that wing. If my grip slips, it's the only thing that's going to keep us from becoming a pair of stains on the street."

Pivlic stifled a yelp as the plump human shifted his weight and caught one hand on the imp's belt, taking some weight off of his wing but making it distinctly difficult to breathe.

"Hurry up, Kos," Pivlic gasped.

The roc cried out, wobbled a bit, but miraculously stayed more or less on course.

* * * * *

The top of the stairs did indeed open into a sort of vestibule. Here there were guards, two more pairs of virusoids flanking only two of the membrane-doors.

Which one do I take? Kos thought.

There was no reply.

Obez? Kos tried.

Virusoid, the virusoid replied.

Never mind, Kos thought.

Perfect, he thought. Up a fungus stairwell without a guide. Well, the virusoid's instincts had worked before. He concentrated on instinct, on making the virusoid understand where he wanted to go.

Kos felt his borrowed feet march toward one of the two doors. He forced the virusoid to let him take over the locomotion along the way, and as the membrane door popped open with a release of humid, sickly sweet air, he stepped over the threshold and into Momir Vig's laboratory under his own power.

Sorry, Obez's voice finally came. Oddly, though it was only a sound in Kos's borrowed consciousness, the lawmage sounded out of breath.

Too late, Kos thought. *I'm here now.*

Look around, Obez said. *Tell me what you're— Excuse me.*

Obez? The lawmage was gone again, and Kos felt a distant touch of the lawmage's panic. He could not tell what it was, however. The link didn't seem to work the same way for Kos as it did for Obez. The lawmage could see through Kos's eyes, but Kos could only get feelings and impressions in the other direction.

Still, he knew what he had to do. Find Szadek or, failing that, find where Szadek went by interrogating those that knew. Those who, assuming the verity circle worked and the thief's word could be trusted, had seen the vampire, and conspired with him just yesterday. The Grand Arbiter, the man who was the ultimate authority on the law, believed it, and Kos, like it or not, had become Augustin's creature, something he'd been trying not to dwell on but which was inescapable.

If he found Szadek, he was to do everything he could to destroy him, up to and including the loss of the life he was borrowing—in this case a dim virusoid—and, if necessary, anything or anyone that tried to stop him. The judge had been less helpful in how to actually tackle the vampire, but since he was susceptible to Kos and not some specific kind of weapon, it had been decided Kos should improvise.

If he did not find Szadek, Kos would *really* have to improvise.

Instincts—his own from decades of walking his stretch in the Tenth, not the borrowed instinct of the virusoid—made Kos suspect that the latter was most likely. Verity circle or no, the thief struck him as sketchy.

The laboratory reminded Kos of Nebun's place, and he wondered if all Simic designed from the same basic floor plan. The floor Kos emerged onto was of the same translucent, leathery, veined stuff as the rest of the place, but its glow was dimmed in many more places by activity. Long tables covered in glass jars and burning beakers, each one attended by a young vedalken student and a half dozen (that Kos could immediately count) older-looking educators who strolled up and down the place, correcting here, praising there. Beyond the experimentation section of the floor, bigger experiments in bigger versions of the beakers and jars nearby were interrupted by the occasional cloud of greenish dust spores or a jet of sterilizing torch-flame. To Kos's relief, there were also virusoids, most of them standing stock-still, others helping in whatever experiment needed a live subject. To his dismay, a few were in the process of regrowing appendages from charred stumps as a result.

Kos strode through the experiments with a slow but steady purpose, trusting the virusoid's feet a little more than he would have liked, but it did keep anyone from accosting him for several minutes.

He heard a pop overhead and to his right, then saw one of the membrane-doors open to admit a swarm of large insects, or perhaps small birds. Without a sound, the door reformed into a solid, drumlike sheet. There was a way out, if he needed one.

Kos spotted Momir Vig as he passed what he guessed was about a quarter of the way around the central axis of the greenhouse. The Simic progenitor hung suspended in an operating harness that grew into the neuroboretum cluster, which overshadowed the entire lab like a bizarre bush made of brain tissue and nerve endings. Vig prodded and poked at a prone virusoid lying on a flat metal table set at a slight incline. One silver, bone-thin arm, more like an insect's than an elf's, held a small translucent cylinder topped with what looked like a small blade of pure cryomana. The mana scalpel was halfway through the middle of the virusoid's arm, carving it like a roast. Momir Vig's other hand was busy with a new cytoplast, which the Simic held casually but expectantly, like a cook preparing to toss a piece of meat on the grill as soon as the temperature was right.

The cytoplast looked disturbingly like a piece of the neuro-boretum cluster. Or perhaps the neuroboretum itself was made of the stuff.

There was no sign of Szadek, or of the "zombie priestess" who Kos feared he might encounter and worse, might recognize. The operating area was lit with bright, normal glowspheres of the type that lined the walls of the wojek infirmary. Only the guildmaster, his patient, a vedalken researcher preoccupied with glass tubes and open flames, and three other virusoids standing in a ring around Vig's operation occupied the space. These other three virusoids and the vedalken all wore cytoplastic limbs, headgear, and other augmentation artifacts. Kos had seen such artifacts before, enhancements like the cytoplasts but of metal and magic, worn by the goblin Crixizix. Izzet manufacture, or so he had thought.

As Vig completed his smooth cut through the virusoid's arm, Kos felt a hand on his.

"Virusoid, stop, I need you," the vedalken attached to the hand said, a blue female with silver eyes and the lilting accent of high education.

Kos allowed the Simic to lead him to the end of one of the long tables but couldn't keep himself from stealing a glance over his shoulder. The vedalken placed a bowl of noxious, acrid fluid in his virusoid hands.

"Virusoid, you will hold this bowl over this open flame until it begins to boil. Then you will drink it," the vedalken said.

"I'll *what?*" Kos said. The voice, as before, sounded like him to his own borrowed ears, in part, but more of the sound was a rumbling, raspy groan that must have been the original owner's. That didn't change the fact that, unlike every other virusoid he had seen so far, he had just—

You just—

I know, Kos thought.

"Did that virusoid just speak?" Momir Vig said, looking up abruptly from his work.

* * * * *

Saint Kel shouldered through crowded streets that had gone insane. Rubble was everywhere, bodies and parts of bodies, screaming people of every species, and a few desperate wojeks who no longer knew who was their enemy and lashed out at anyone they could. At first the Living Saint had stopped to help the most desparate, but the sheer number of dead and the brutality and carelessness of the destruction eventually overwhelmed even his spirits. Now he simply wanted to be at Vitu Ghazi, to commune with the Conclave and find out what, if anything, he could do to stop this.

And if not, the Living Saint would make someone pay—these monsters, the Dimir, the Simic, *some*one.

If the Conclave chose to be complacent, it was time to take bolder action. The wolf, at least, would support the decision, and the wolf had great influence on the relatively young collective.

All Selesnyans that accepted the song heard it for the rest of their lives. Most of the common members of the church were not able to play upon its strings and find specific people but just heard the song and knew they were a part. On the opposite end of that spectrum were the members of the Conclave, who could not only hear the song but find each and every distinct note and conduct the spiritual chorus like a bandleader. It was a method of spiritual healing and, for the Selesnya Conclave, a method of leadership that made the Conclave *collective* guildmasters.

As the name implied, the Living Saint was the most spiritually mature member of the Selesnya Conclave, the one who generally roved the farthest from Vitu Ghazi and represented their collective public face, the most independent yet also the most in tune with the song.

And so it was that although Saint Kel told himself he was calmly returning home to form a plan, his quite broken mind—a mind that had finally fractured to the chorus of snapping strings that ripped the song to pieces—plotted a way to do it that was just as mad as the devastated streets through which he stomped.

The titans stood lifeless. The song screamed. Wojeks and ledev died left and right, along with civilians. The city was falling in on itself and the song shrieked with thousands of tiny agonies. He had failed them too. So Saint Kel was going to make things right.

It was time for Selesnyan justice to take back what the others couldn't.

* * * * *

"Virusoid," Kos rasped as stupidly as he could manage.

"I think not," Vig said, his weird pipe organ voice echoing in the greenhouse's muggy confines with irritation. Then he called over his shoulder toward a corridor that led out to another section of the greenhouse. "Svogthir, come here. I think you might enjoy this."

The wojek cursed his luck and the fact that he had not fully inspected every corner of the lab before he was discovered.

This god-zombie looked nothing like the old one but was still intimately familiar to Kos. The reanimated corpse of the dead Golgari priestess Savra shuffled into the lab to stand at Vig's side. Her twisted neck and lopsided head could not hide the wicked smile that cut across her sagging features. Nor could a state of suspended decomposition hide the fact that Savra's eyes blazed with supernatural energy. But when she spoke, it was not with the Devkarin priestess's voice, a sound that was burned into Kos's memory. No, this voice was much older, masculine, and sounded as if it emerged from the bowels of death itself.

"What is it, Vig?" the god-zombie rumbled. "I was enjoying a snack." She—he—tore a thumb off of a bluish severed hand, swallowed it, and tossed the rest aside.

"We have a visitor," Momir Vig said, "an Azorius servant."

"Really?" the god-zombie said and sniffed the air. "Doesn't

smell Azorius. Smells like Boros to me. A wojek if I don't miss my guess." The Savra-thing chuckled. "A *familiar* wojek. By the depths, I do believe that this Azorius servant is that same wojek who ruined the priestess's plan so long ago. His spirit is quite familiar. Kos, I think the name was. How . . . delicious."

"Interesting," Vig agreed as if the two were discussing the weather. "Perhaps we can learn more. Udom, tear off his arm."

Kos released a very unvirusoidlike scream through his wide virusoid mouth, but it caught in his throat. The virusoid's nervous system appeared to shut down once the simple message of the pain—"Hey, you just lost an arm here"—had been sent. It was efficient and alien, but Kos realized his little yelp had only made the progenitor more determined.

Obez, there's nothing here, he thought. *I'm caught. And I'm recognized, on top of that. The zombie priestess is still here, and I think she's a—but never mind that. How long before I can come back?*

He heard no response.

"Why are you here?" the Simic progenitor repeated. "You are obviously an Azorius agent, Mr. Kos. Augustin can't keep his mind on his own business. But this is just clumsy. Answer me, please."

"Virusoid?" Kos said.

His plan had fallen apart the moment he'd spoken. There was no Szadek here, just this cold, analytical creature and a corpse possessed by (if his guess was correct) one of the most powerful necromancers Ravnica had ever seen, the god-zombie Svogthir, whose head had last been seen atop Savra's staff. Turnabout revenge was grisly in the reclamation guild.

He considered his options. Obez seemed to have abandoned him, but the lawmage had said Kos might be able to get back to the anchor on his own. If his half hour had passed. If his ghost could find the lawmage again. And if Svogthir didn't stop him somehow. Kos had heard plenty about Golgari necromancy and how its practitioners used the ghosts of the dead to reanimate their own corpses. He certainly didn't appear to be any closer to finding Szadek. And what if Vig then just killed him outright? Would he die again? End up in that ghost city, Agyrem?

"A leg I think this time, Udom," the progenitor said. "Azorius spy, do not be under the mistaken impression I am torturing you." In fact, Kos only felt a twinge this time as the second limb came off. "I am dismantling you. You can stay in there as long as you wish. Eventually, you will be in pieces. Tell me why you are here."

"I would do as he says," the Golgari god-zombie rumbled, and it dawned on Kos that the two were playing one of the oldest interrogation games in existence: good 'jek/bad 'jek.

Obez, for Krokt's sake, talk to me.

Silence. He tried to force himself out of the virusoid's body by imagining it staying in place while he flew free. One, two, three. Push.

Nothing. "Another leg," Vig said, and a few seconds later a tear, a twinge, and cool air where it shouldn't have been told Kos that it was done.

"Krokt," Kos swore.

"What was that?" Vig said.

"I said 'Krokt,' " Kos said, "as in 'Krokt Almighty, that hurt.' All right, you got me. I'm an Azorius spy. I—*we* know everything." The combination of his own voice and the strange and simple virusoid mouth made it sound like "Ee no e'ry'ing," but Vig seemed to have no trouble understanding.

"I knew it!" Vig said, and he actually sounded . . . happy? Less irritated, at least. "So you have come to stop me, eh?"

"What?" Kos managed.

"You've uncovered my plans. You have learned why I wanted dragon cerebral fluid," Vig said, the smile only slightly curling downward, but it did show concern. The god-zombie looked strangely at the progenitor when the augmented elf said 'dragon cerebral fluid,' but Kos didn't understand the look. Then Vig's smile turned back up, and the progenitor said, "Aha! I can see by your expression that I have surprised you. Your Azorius masters didn't know it was *dragon* cerebral fluid, did they?"

"No," Kos said with complete honesty. Then, he added some falsehood icing. "We knew it was some kind of cerebral fluid, but we had no idea it was *dragon.*" Keep the suspect talking.

"So you have uncovered Project Kraj," Momir Vig said but didn't seem particularly disappointed. "Dragon cerebral fluid is so hard to come by now that the dragons have been hunted nearly to extinction, and so long did I work to keep the spread of cytoplasts from becoming too obvious. Months and months of slow refinement of the process, awaiting the delivery of that precious substance, the one that courses through this neuroboretum cluster even as we speak, giving life, granting true consciousness, to my most magnificent creation. The creation that will show the puny normals of this city who their true master is." As if to emphasize the point, Vig freed himself from the harness and stepped toward Kos, pacing as he spoke. "With the dragon cerebral fluid imbuing Project Kraj, every cytoplast on this world will return to the nest, crippling thousands and augmenting Kraj. Kraj and its master shall be invincible!"

"I agree, you've thought of everything," Kos lied as fast as he could. "But you must admit it's dangerous to bring the Dimir into this, what with everything that happened at the Decamillennial and all."

"Dimir?" Vig said, and all at once burst into laughter. "Oh yes. The Dimir. You Azorius are just obsessed with the Dimir, aren't you? An unproven, impossible 'other' to oppose their laws. The only laws that are unopposable are the laws of nature, avatar."

Time to go for broke. "We know he was here, just yesterday, when you accepted the delivery. Like I said, risky and dangerous. You can't trust him."

"Of course," the Simic said. "The Dimir. You've said too much, my foolish spy. Tell your master he'll have to try harder next time. If he survives. Throw him out, Udom. Unless you have any objection, Svogthir?"

"None at all," the god-zombie said through Savra's withered lips. "Good bye, Kos. It was amusing to see you one last time."

"Wait!" Kos said. "He'll betray you too. It's what he does. Ask the god-zombie there how much you can trust Szadek." He did the best he could to struggle in the grip of the Simic's augmented henchmen, without much luck, as they hauled him up a spiral ramp to the large membrane-door Kos had seen open to admit the swarm earlier. Cool air rushed into the greenhouse against his bare, virusoid back. "Just tell me where he went and you can do whatever you want with the cytoplasts! We didn't even know about the cytoplasts! I'm just supposed to find this damned vampire and kill him!"

"Just tell you where he went?" Vig snarled. "*Szadek?* You mean that Augustin did not—" The progenitor's mirth overcame him, and he broke into terrifying alien laughter. He may have still been an elf on the outside, but whatever was inside made some very unusual sounds.

"Please," Kos said, playing his last card. "You're a guildmaster. The Guildpact is dying. Can't you help me save it?"

"Oh yes," the god-zombie hissed. "We must protect the Guildpact, Vig. Why, imagine the chaos that might result. You are a fool, Kos. An old, dead fool."

"But noble," the Simic replied with venom, "In his way. In case you hadn't noticed, Mr. Kos, I don't give two zibs for the Guildpact. It's high time the Simic Combine ruled this world as it should be ruled."

"Whenever that may take place," Svogthir said, warning lacing his voice.

"Of course," Vig said, nodding, but it was clear to Kos these two "allies" were both up to something that didn't involve the survival of the other.

The seed of a really bad idea took root in Kos's mind. If his anchor wasn't available, he would have to jump *some*where. . . .

"So, no then?" Kos said. *Obez,* he tried one last time. *Obez, if you're ever going to respond . . .*

"Toss him," Vig said.

Kos closed his eyes and concentrated as hard as he could. Again he pictured himself stepping out of this body, leaping through the humid air, and landing. . . .

To the wojek's surprise, it worked. He opened a new albeit long-dead set of eyes and watched with detached fascination as Udom the virusoid tossed Kos's former host through the hatch.

Kos! came Obez's inner voice at last. *Are you—*

I'm fine, Kos thought. *Isn't that right, Svogthir?*

This is a revolting development, the god-zombie thought. *You will not last long in here, wojek.*

Maybe not, Kos thought, *but as long as I am here, let's talk about your deal with Momir Vig.*

CHAPTER 16

Golgari Acres Insect Patties are made from only the finest ingredients and the choicest meat-beetles harvested by skilled laborers. Just because you've passed onto the postmortem stage of your life doesn't mean you have to eat like a zombie. If you've got a hunger that could wake the undead, ask for Golgari Acres Insect Patties by name.

—Handbill promoting the Golgari Acres
Insectivorium (10007 Z.C.)

31 Cizarm 10012 Z.C.

Jarad's eyes were closed, but he saw much more than two eyes could ever have shown him. He split his attention between two groups of insects, the greenbite cloud and a few dozen assorted beetles, as they plumbed the depths of Rix Maadi. Through their tiny minds he sought Izolda.

He had stretched the truth with Fonn, again. And Jarad was sorry he had to do it. But if he had told her what his bugs had shown him and that he planned to deal with the blood witch personally, she might have stayed behind. The ledev scouts and Myc needed to get home, and he had complete faith that Fonn could save the boy, if only Jarad could figure out how the witch had latched his son to the demon in the first place.

Jarad had seen her batted aside by the demon, but then she disappeared. A being that was the Rakdos guildmaster in everything but name, running the day-to-day operations of the cult, would not give up so easily. Izolda marched down the tunnel toward him, just around the corner. The Rakdos cultists behind him were wrapping up with their fallen comrades by ripping their bodies to shreds. The cultists consumed them while they still screamed, screams that didn't last long and soon died out entirely. Soon, the atonal musical chant kicked up again, and the mob set out toward the last of their prey, Jarad.

They didn't move fast. Most had twisted legs that had been broken at least once and left to heal without being set. They also fought among themselves for position, each wanting to be the first to sample fresh Devkarin. Jarad could afford to keep them to his back for a few moments. He had to. The two groups of insects let him triangulate Izolda's location. She would soon round the corner and be on top of him.

Jarad cut himself off from the insects as the blood witch rounded the corner and the Golgari guildmaster could see her with his own two eyes. She had not brought an army, but she was not alone. Trailing behind the blood witch were two thugs, shuffling and snapping their bony knuckles against the stones. The Rakdos witch was a ghostly, white shape robed in black, backlit by torches her simian zombie thugs carried. A flash of flame illuminated Izolda's white-eyed face when the lackeys took near-simultaneous swings at each other.

It was the smallest of the four—a girl three or four years older than Myc from the look of it, but obscured by a ragged cloak and hood—who made even Jarad's blood run cold. Hair the color of moldy straw hung wet and matted from the figure's skull and both her eyes and lips were crudely sewn shut. The wounds the crude black thread left were fresh, but did not bleed. The girl was dead but hadn't been for long. Dead or not, the blood witch had not allowed her to rest.

Jarad did not look forward to telling Fonn what had happened to her missing scout. But he planned to soften the blow with swift revenge on the scout's tormentor.

"Guildmaster," Izolda hissed, drawing out the "s" in "guildmaster" long enough to sound like one of the gorgon sisters, "how nice of you to stay behind."

"You tried to kill my son," Jarad said. "Nice is not what I had in mind." He drew his kindjal even as he heard the mob of cultists closing in. He risked opening a line to a few beetles, just to watch his back.

"Yes, your son," Izolda said. "I have already spoken of him with his old friend. I enjoyed the sound of her voice so much—her terrified wailing was especially savory, you only had to look at her to set her going—that I wanted to be the last one to hear it. She is now mine. You child will be mine. I would say it's nothing personal, Guildmaster, but it really is."

Jarad was running out of time. He had to try something. He had far too few greenbites at hand to do anything more than annoy the blood witch, and the beetles on hand were a relatively harmless variety that would not be much help either. So he stalled. At the very least, if Izolda was preoccupied with him, she would not be above, threatening his son's or Fonn's life.

"I'm sure I did something to you," Jarad said, "but I can't for the life of me imagine what."

"Oh, it's not at all what you did. It's what you are," Izolda said. "Do you have any idea how long it has been since a guildmaster had offspring?"

Three of the beetles died as the cultists walked over the Devkarin's line of no return.

Jarad sent in the greenbites. The small swarm descended on the mob, which had gotten smaller as more and more cultists turned on each other to engage in sacramental and deadly violence. At first the mob bat at the glittering bugs, irritated. Then there were slaps and yelps as the greenbites settled onto any exposed patch of skin or, if it was available, open wounds. Upon landing, the greenbites bit. The bites carried a mild poison that would cause a small patch of skin to rot away within a day, sometimes two. More importantly, this particular swarm carried a necrobiotic infection Jarad had discovered in the deep canyon cliffsides. Greenbite rot consumed the victim from the inside out, starting in the bloodstream and quickly moving on to organs and bone. Upon the victim's inevitable death, the deceased returned as semi-intelligent deadwalkers. Here, it was especially useful to Jarad, since the disease also affected intelligent zombies, and there were a few within the cultist mob. Zombies infected with the rot literally fell apart. In the living, the disease killed without fail within two hours. Zombies rotted within minutes.

One by one, the cultists slapped and snarled as the bugs set upon them. The thugs, too. Jarad kept them from the girl, though he had little hope of her recovery. The zombies would be down soon, but the rest would be a threat for half an hour or so, when the symptoms kicked in hard. While the body was still living, the spread of undead bone and tissue caused excruciating pain. Whatever the ultimate result, the greenbites had for now given him the only other thing he'd asked for—a sudden diversion.

Jarad had no escape route, in a conventional sense. But as long as he had walls, a Devkarin hunter had a way to get a leg up. He crouched against the middle of the tunnel and vaulted against the wall with what, to anyone obeying the usual laws of gravity, looked like a wild, flying kick. At the same time Jarad mentally triggered a silent enchantment that he had learned as a small child. He bolted up the wall, using three limbs for stability, fast enough to get above and then behind Izolda. The Golgari guildmaster gripped the kindjal in both hands and swung the blade around for a sharp, pile-driver blow, then dropped.

The dead girl caught his leg on the way down with a sickle he had not seen concealed beneath her cloak. She hooked the curved blade around his shin and pulled, tearing a gash in what felt like a fairly important artery. Worse, the girl threw him off course enough that the tip of the kindjal slammed against the stone, and Jarad struck soon after.

Izolda brought a black leather boot across his jaw with the strength of an ogre. Jarad tried to roll with the kick but couldn't get enough leverage to avoid taking most of its power. The tunnel spun like a windmill overhead, and he spat out a tooth.

"Do that again," he said.

The blood witch merely smiled her cold smile and hooked a finger at the dead girl in the cloak. "Go ahead, little ragamuffyn." Without taking her eyes off of her new plaything Izolda drove the toe of her boot into Jarad's ribs. It was a different boot, and this one bore a long iron spike on the steel toe. He bit almost all the way through his lower lip when the spike separated two of his ribs and punctured something he was sure he wanted to keep in one piece—a lung, from the feel of it. Jarad didn't make a sound, but grabbed on to the witch's ankle with one hand and did not let go. He yanked the spike out of his side and turned the foot 180 degrees. That move should have crippled Izolda for life, if not torn her foot completely off, boot or not boot.

Instead, Izolda spun her entire body around with it, almost horizontally. She drove a heel into Jarad's chin and flipped backward, ending up standing, fearless, beside the dead girl.

"I'm going to kill you," Jarad said. "What do you want with my offspring?"

"Oh, we would have been happy with you, had we known you would stay here to be taken—and alive at that, Guildmaster," she replied. "I doubt you're going to kill me. I assure you it would be quite redundant. It's just that guildmasters have certain protections that even I respect. Makes a child so much easier to take, and use."

"Use for what?" Jarad coughed. "What have you—"

The dead girl sliced off the top half of Jarad's left ear with her sickle. He snarled and lashed out with a leg but found he barely had the strength to move it.

"Do not fear yet, or too much, Guildmaster," Izolda said as the dead girl fascinated, toyed with the triangle of pale flesh that had until recently been attached to the side of Jarad's head. The world was no longer just spinning, it was swimming. The open artery in his leg had taken its toll quickly, and Jarad's hand slipped in a pool of his own blood when he tried to push himself onto all fours. He settled for a roll onto his side.

"I'm bleeding to death," he said, smiling. "Guess you won't be getting any of this after all."

"Nonsense," Izolda said. "Stay back," she ordered the green-bitten cultists. She crouched over him and hissed an incantation. Rough black threads sprouted from the skin around Jarad's wounds and then drove sharp points into the other side. Within seconds his injuries had been bound in what he was fairly sure was the most painful way imaginable. "And as for your bugs," she added, "I've been putting a vaccine into their blood swill for decades. I've been following you for a while now, you know. You, I think, will take the boy's place. His blood was lost. The exchange was incomplete. I do despise an incomplete act of bloodshed."

"Why should I believe anything you say?" Jarad said.

"You have no choice," Izolda said. "If you think the demon will release the boy of his own free will, you are a fool. But if you serve my purpose, the demon will have no choice but to do so. I'm afraid it will mean the end of your life, naturally. You are quickly running out of both room and options, I think. What is your answer, Guildmaster?"

* * * * *

Why do you think I'm here? Svogthir thought. *Because that wretched Devkarin has taken my rightful mantle. He has stolen my guild. And I want it back.*

Good luck with that, Kos replied. *I mean why are you in this body?*

I have been ever since you foiled this one's plans. It was child's play to take it for my own. After a lifetime of necromancy, she was half dead anyway. I do miss my old skull, but the move was necessary. But, the god-zombie thought with mild surprise, *I have not allowed you in.*

Maybe that's the point, Kos thought. *It's not your place to allow it. We're both squatters in the corpse of a dead woman near as I see it. Now tell me what the progenitor is up to.*

Kos, you have a mission to—Obez broke in.

Quiet, Kos said. *We have company you don't want to be talking around.*

Svogthir's long-borrowed form—the body that had once belonged to the Devkarin Matka Savra—was a very uncomfortable place to be, as far as bodies went. And Kos had already been in several, so he could think that with authority. What he had not been sure of was whether the Azorius power the Grand Arbiter had given him would be enough to take control of this body from one who had, in effect, already stolen it.

And to Kos's surprise, he could. Easily. It must have been the stabilizing aid of his anchor, for he had driven the great god-zombie into one corner of the undead Devkarin's mind with ease.

"God-zombie, the time is close at hand. The demon bellows in the night, and the beasts of old are tearing the lifeless stone world apart. We will be their saviors. We will remake it all. Do you wish to say a few words before we bring Project Kraj to fruition?"

Now Kos merely had to interrogate Svogthir without letting

Vig know what had happened. It was almost like being back at the Tenth.

"Just get on with it," Kos snapped, guessing that the god-zombie, a being who claimed to be the oldest on Ravnica, would not be patient with a grandiloquent biomancer.

"You are as much the parent of this magnificent creation as I," Vig said, "for death we will bring, as much as life."

What the hell is going on here? Kos demanded.

Did you want him to sketch it out on the floor for you in bright white chalk, wojek? Look around you, Svogthir said. *Look at that enormous intelligence in the center of it all. Now picture this place from the outside.*

Why?

Because we, you pathetic pustule of a spirit, are inside the head of Project Kraj, Svogthir said. *That fool is going to unleash it on the city and with it wipe out the nephilim and the demon. He thinks.*

You don't? Kos asked.

"Svogthir," Vig said, "you appear distracted."

"The gravity of the moment," Kos replied. "It is indeed awe-inspiring what we will accomplish."

"You will have your undercity back, and I shall have this entire surface to cultivate," Vig offered. "Project Kraj will deal with the demon and the old beasts, and the survivors will be ours to lead. Survival breeds change, the essence of new life."

Nice plan, Kos thought. *You are a real piece of work.*

It's a good plan, Svogthir replied. *You weren't part of it.*

Too bad. I am now.

"Perhaps we should begin," Kos said through Savra's cracked mouth.

"You are anxious, aren't you?" Vig said. "I would have thought someone as old as you would have learned patience by now."

"Never forget who is in this body you speak to so dismissively, pustule of—" Kos, who had only let his mental guard down for a moment, cut off Svogthir's outburst with a forced cough. *Don't try that one again. I* will *find a way to kill myself in this body if you try it again.*

I doubt you would, Svogthir replied. *You don't strike me as the type.*

"I forget nothing," Vig said. "And you are right—the time is nigh. Look." The Simic guildmaster waved to a virusoid, who walked to one of the translucent membranes and brushed a bump on the spongy wall next to it. The membrane shimmered to display the demon Rakdos facing off against the serpent-thing. The nephilim stood half again as tall as the demon, and sat upon a roll of coils at least twice as long as that. The demon, on the other hand, carried a chunk of mizzium ripped from some ancient piece of architecture—perhaps Sunhome itself—that he wielded as a sharp cudgel. As Kos watched, the demon spread his wings and took to the air.

It is a pleasure to see him fight again, I must admit, Svogthir said. *He is a magnificent killer.*

It did not take long. The snake-nephilim was fast, especially for its size, but the constrictor was built for an enemy on the ground. Rakdos, though not quick to maneuver, could build up a tremendous head of steam on a dive, and the demon drew first blood when one of his horns tore a chunk from the serpent's abdomen-face. The nephilim grabbed at him as he flew past, but the blow had knocked off the snake-thing's equilibrium so badly that its strike missed completely. A second dive, and Rakdos drove the chunk of jagged mizzium—a piece of virtually indestructible metal the length of a zeppelid yacht—through the enormous yellow eye on the beast's "chest." The demon left the weapon there but on the way back up snagged one of the nephilim's flailing arms in his opposite hand. Heaving his wings, Rakdos hauled it into the sky.

The nephilim flexed its coils and whipped its body at the demon in a desperate attempt to grasp onto and choke the life from the unholy guildmaster. Rakdos brought up a hoof and drove the mizzium spear out of the snake-thing's back, drove the second hoof against the round metallic mouth, and caved that in on one side. Finally, Rakdos dived again. The nephilim's momentum carried its serpentine body into the air while the demon plummeted in the opposite direction, headed straight for Vitu Ghazi. The snake-thing's entire body whipped around to follow, still writhing pitiably, until it struck the side of the tree and was impaled on a row of spiky branches. They were part of the increasingly insular Conclave's new defensive tactics, and in this bizarre case, at least, Kos thought they worked like charms.

The snake-nephilim twitched for a few seconds as its blood drained away down the side of the Unity Tree then its body drooped against the mammoth trunk just as a small army of ledev guardians swarmed toward it.

"Udom," Vig said, and the virusoid struck the growth switch again. The filmy membrane was once again a mere window, allowing warmth inside. He turned to Svogthir. "Yes, it is time. The demon is the only thing that stands between us and mastery of this wild, new natural world we shall create. Life and death, two sides of the same world."

"Yes," Kos ventured.

"It is time to begin," Vig repeated. After a moment, Kos realized the elf biomancer was frowning.

"Yes," Kos repeated.

What is he waiting for? Kos demanded.

I hardly have to tell you that, Svogthir replied.

Listen to this joker, Kos thought. *You really think he's planning to share? You may be ancient, but I'd swear you were born yesterday. I can read him like a newssheet.*

Who said I planned to share? Svogthir retorted.

"God-zombie, again I say," Vig said, noticeably irritated, "It is *time*."

What am I supposed to do? Kos said.

All right, Svogthir said. *This could be interesting. He's looking for the glass tubes—three of them—on your belt. He's got the other three. All six will bring the project to life, and then there will be one more giant monster walking around out there. But this one is going to be something a little different.*

Kos patted Savra's belt as casually as he could, and found the tubes.

"Yes," Kos said, "it is time."

You need to slot the tubes in one by one, you and him, simultaneously. And after the third one . . . hold on.

* * * * *

Myc roared to the heavens, and Rakdos joined in. Now, for the life churchers.

The demon-god turned on Vitu Ghazi, seething. "Selesnya Conclave," he bellowed, "your time has come to an end." As he spoke, rats swarmed the streets, slipping through every grating and crack. They encircled the base of Vitu Ghazi, chattering so loudly Myc could hear them with his actual ears, even from his seat under Rakdos's chin. The ledev had already take positions there along a low wall that had been built only a few years earlier.

Rakdos drove a hoof through the wall before Myc could stop him, and the rats poured into holy Conclave territory.

High in the Unity Tree, a Living Saint did everything he could to ensure they didn't stay there long.

* * * * *

"Jarad," Fonn said. Her voice was distant, tiny, as if heard through a network of pipes. "Jarad, where are you?"

Jarad blinked and was instantly gratified to find he could. He'd half-expected to awake, if he awoke at all, with his eyes sewn shut.

"Jarad, for the holy mother's sake," the voice echoed, and the Devkarin felt the sound not just in his ears—one of which was caked with blood—but on his chest. He reached for the speech-stone but found his arms would not move. That was when he took in the rest of his surroundings.

Jarad hung tied, with both rope and rusty chains, to the effigy tree. There were fewer cultists here this time and little hope of rescue. If what Izolda said was true, however, Jarad was not sure he even wanted to be rescued. Was it worth his son's promised freedom (a hope that required him to believe Fonn could save Myc if the boy's bond to Rakdos was broken) to unleash Rakdos under the sway of a creature like the blood witch?

For that was the ceremony she had been trying to complete. Each guild had its own unique ways and distinct styles when it came to magic, but in many places those powers and ways overlapped. Izolda was performing some kind of domination rite: magic with the purpose of controlling another being. When he realized that, it was only a short step to the obvious fact that his arrow shot had stopped the first rite and caused Myc's connection with the demon by freak accident.

"How do you expect this to work when your guildmaster is out there ripping up the Center?" Jarad asked.

"So he puts the pieces together," Izolda said. "I had hoped you would not disappoint me. But do not concern yourself with that, my dear. It will work. The blood of a guildmaster—your son's—has mixed with the burning blood in the pit and with the blood of the demon himself. With it I have blended the essence of a dragon."

"But now you've just got blood," he sneered. "Good luck."

"Waste not, want not," the blood witch replied, as she retracted her black claws with a slurping sound, and snapped her fingers. One of the simian thugs shuffled forward with a small bottle. Izolda produced the silver bowl and carefully poured in half of the bottle's contents. This close, Jarad's nose told him exactly what the substance was. Krokt, he thought, she could really do it. And if she did, Myc, Fonn, and the entire world would have to deal with it. The sacrifice would not mean much.

Silently, betraying no hint of emotion or the plan he furiously composed, Jarad reached out to find the common Ravnican acid-fly. He found four within easy reach and steered them at their top speed to the chains on his hands.

Izolda raised the bowl in one hand and handed the bottle of dragon cerebral fluid back to the thug. She kept the hand extended and called, "Child, the knife."

The dead girl emerged from behind Jarad, where she'd been hiding in plain sight. She carried the jagged blade that had cut Myc's hand open, still black with his blood. She held the knife up like a prayer offering, and Izolda gripped the handle, taking it with a nod. The girl retreated back to her corner. Along the way, she hummed a happy, broken tune that sounded like a twisting of a common Selesnyan hymn.

The acidflies alit upon the chains and ropes binding Jarad's arms. The insects immediately spit the substance for which they were named, a potent corrosive that could, if the Devkarin wasn't careful, burn all the way through the chains, ropes, and his wrists if he didn't pull them out in time.

The blood witch sniffed the air, and her white eyes widened in surprise a second too late.

Jarad jerked one hand free, then another, and let himself drop forward at the waist. He pulled the chains around his ankles free easily—they were not locked, just wrapped in long coils that he easily loosened—and then dived into a roll that brought him into a crouch at Izolda's feet. Instead of kicking him, the blood witch stepped carefully back, cradling the silver bowl to her chest.

"What are you fools waiting for?" she demanded. "Grab him! Hold him down!"

Old habits die hard, and to the Rakdos individual combat was a natural way of living. They could barely form any kind of short-term alliances. Their broad guild bond was the closest they came to such behavior—and that was more of a common belief system tying them together, than true camaraderie. So, fortunately, Jarad only had to take on two at once. Fortunate, because he had no feeling but a dull tingle in his lower legs.

He rolled aside from the first simian zombie, pulling his legs up with his arms in a mad attempt to get his blood pumping. It worked. Now instead of a numb tingle he had the overpowering sensation of all feeling returning to his legs at once. Jarad still couldn't stand, so he rolled back the other way when the second thug attempted to grab hold of his arms. He didn't roll far and managed to catch the zombie's wrist on the follow-through. He hauled downward, swinging the thug skull-first into the stone floor, and caving its head in with a wet splat and a spray of gray matter—dry, useless-looking gray matter.

The maneuver cost him, however, giving the blood witch a chance to shout another order. "*All* of you get him!" she bellowed. "*Now!*"

Jarad was hopelessly outnumbered, barely able to stand, and completely unarmed, and the crowd was literally after his blood. Yet he forced himself to his shaky feet, whirling dizzily to take in the foes that surrounded him on all sides and closed in relentlessly.

The dead girl had not moved but just stood there, not far from the blood witch, humming her happy melody. Jarad could not take his mind off of the sound. It grew louder in his ears, pouring into his brain. It shattered his focus. The acidflies were lost, along with any other contact he tried to establish. His balance was next to go, and he stumbled over his own feet as he tried to back away.

The mob was on him as soon as he hit the floor. Bony, knotted fists gripped his arms, and a heavy club shattered his right kneecap. The cultists hauled the beaten guildmaster before the blood witch.

"Entertaining," Izolda said, "but now I need that blood, Guildmaster."

"Jarad, Myc's still up there. He's still alive. Are you going to get to him or what?" Fonn's voice rang over the speechstone.

It took every ounce of remaining strength in his body, but Jarad wrenched one arm free of the Rakdos's grip long enough to tap the stone and shout, "Get him down! I'll set him free. *Don't wait for me—*"

Izolda hooked her knife under the leather strap that held the stone in place and cut it. The stone dropped to the floor, and the dead girl scampered forward to pick it up, apparently fascinated.

"Jarad?" Fonn called. "What do you mean don't wait for you? Talk to me!"

"Child," Izolda said calmly, "throw that in the pit, would you?"

The girl turned and without a sound—or eyes, apparently—tossed the speechstone into the open, searing crater from which the demon-god had emerged.

Then the blood witch plunged the knife into his heart. Jarad watched his lifeblood flood the silver bowl. He held on long enough to see Izolda raise the bowl to her lips and drink deeply of the mixture.

At least my son is free, Jarad thought just before his life drained completely away.

* * * * *

Myc's mind felt split in two. He could not hear Rakdos anymore, though he could certainly hear the monster bellowing threats at the Selesnyans as he led his derranged followers against the Unity Tree.

He was no longer connected to the demon, but he still had a demon's rage. And as Myc realized that he could no longer hear his father in the song, that rage exploded. He screamed, he cursed, he called down every evil he could conceive on Rakdos, on the blood witch, on anyone that had ever tried to harm him or his family.

No one could hear him but the Defiler.

"Shut up, boy," the demon said. Then he reached up with a clawed hand and plucked the ledev scout from his neck. Rakdos held the relatively tiny Myc up to one eye. "You," the demon growled, "were in my head. That was a bad idea, insect. I am Rakdos, the Defiler. You do not touch my mind without— *Arrrgh!*"

Rakdos the Defiler clutched his bony temple in one hand. The other hand flung open in shock, dropping young Myc Zunich from a terrible height.

* * * * *

Kos slid the last glass receptacle into place, feeding the third dose of dragon cerebral fluid—so this is what the stuff looked like—into the neuroboretum cluster that formed the central intelligence of Project Kraj. Momir Vig turned to him and smiled.

"And now, we change the world," the progenitor said. Without another action from the Simic guildmaster, Kos could feel the Kraj intelligence spring into being all around him.

I wonder what will happen now? Svogthir thought.

This, Kos thought. Then he seized Savra's staff and plunged the sharp end into Momir Vig's beady, black eye.

I am not a monster.

> —*I, Loxodon* (Act V, Scene 5, line 102)
> by Montagon Trevis (6037 Z.C.)

31 CIZARM 10012 Z.C.

"Kos has lost his mind," Obez shouted. "He's *inside* the god-zombie. And he just— I mean, do you have any idea how dangerous— Imp, have you ever heard of something called 'Project Kraj'?"

"The god-zombie?" Pivlic gasped, straining. "Project what, now? What are you talking about?" The roc had long since returned to join its flock—in this case, a passing wing of skyjeks—and now all that was keeping imp and lawmage in the air were his tired, tired wings.

"The god-zombie," Obez repeated. "That 'zombie priestess' the thief told us about—it's Svogthir. He's back. Again."

"Sure, why not?" the imp said.

"Can you get us back to the Senate?" Obez said. "The Simic are up to something. Look."

"I can't. In case you hadn't noticed, my friend, I'm carrying four hundred pounds of lawmage."

"That's a lie, I'm— Look, that doesn't matter. Something is happening to Novijen."

"What?" Pivlic gasped.

"It's standing up."

"*What?*"

"Kos, what are you doing?" Obez said.

"What does he say?" Pivlic asked.

"To trust him," Obez spat. "This is ridiculous."

"I would," Pivlic offered. "You must have fa—faith. You must try to . . ." Gasp. "You must try to lose some weight. Pivlic is not a mule. Besides, should we not stay close? Catch Kos when he leaves this 'god-zombie' of yours?"

"Azorius must be told," Obez said. "The return of one as powerful as Svogthir can only mean that the Guildpact is failing even faster than he anticipated. Szadek and Svogthir together, why—"

A bellowing roar from Stomper made the fat lawmage break off. Waiting to meet the roar with one of his own, at the edge of a fresh crater that had reduced a quarter of the central pavilion to nothing, stood the demon Rakdos—leathery hands clenched into fists, eyes ablaze, terrible wings spread wide, and flames curling up from his glowing, orange veins.

There was someone on the chain around his neck, but from here Pivlic could not see who—more likely it was a skeleton. Then the demon-god passed behind one of the remaining towers, and the imp focused again on staying in the air.

He might still be able to get them to the ground alive. Though he was starting to wonder if there would even be a Ravnica left by the time this day was done.

"Pivlic, we're dropping," Obez observed. "That rock-monster is getting closer."

"You ask too much of Pivlic," the imp said, his lapse into third person a sure sign of exhaustion. "Too much of this today. Too much flying. Just . . ." The imp trailed off, but his wings remained spread, filled with a warm updraft from below. Even unconscious, Pivlic acted as a glider, allowing the lawmage to steer the two of them to the closest surface. Which was, as it happened, Stomper's back.

* * * * *

"I'm going to get kicked out of the guard," Fonn muttered.

"Why's that, sir?" Orval asked.

"If you have to ask, Orval . . ." Aklechin said.

"Oh, right," the centaur said. "This."

The three of them stood astride the wide, flat back of the three-legged rocky nephilim that had almost stomped them flat not long before. With a carefully timed set of jumps and a few friction-increasing climbing spells, the small group had found it relatively easy to ascend the beast. It had been an impulsive move. Fonn's plan consisted of little more than "Stop this thing before it gets to my son," and she felt stymied. Her brief contact with Jarad hadn't helped—she was frankly worried sick. She could no longer hear him in the song, and though she told herself that Jarad could hide himself from the song if he wished—he had done so in the past—this time felt different. It would be a while before she could try to speechstone again, so until she learned Jarad's fate she would just have to do her best for the scouts she had left.

Between the three of them, they'd stabbed, hacked, and shouted at the Stomper until they were blue in the face. It had no more effect on the creature than flies on a dromad. They were close enough to the demon that Fonn could see Myc clearly, sitting under the demon's chin in a trance. He had to be in a trance. The song would have sounded a sour note immediately if he was— if he had not survived.

Then, before her horrified eyes, the demon plucked Myc from his perch, eyed him, then lurched and tossed her son like he was a burning cinder. The boy flailed in midair and caught hold of the wiry hairs covering Rakdos's left leg.

"Good job, Son," she whispered and hoped Myc could feel her concern through the song.

"Hold on. It's moving!" cried Orval, who for obvious reasons was especially sensitive to shifts in balance. "Rearing up!"

Aklechin needed little warning. He was already on all fours, hands digging into the unforgiving hide. Orval took his stolen pike and jammed it into the nephilim's stony back. The blade didn't enter far enough to even draw blood, but it kept the centaur stable as their ride raised its forelegs off of the stone and opened its segmented mouth wide.

"Get down," she said, and they both followed Aklechin's lead.

"Sir, what's it doing?" the scout said.

"I don't know," Fonn said. "Maybe it's going to bite him?"

It was a logical guess but turned out to be completely wrong. The nephilim instead drew a deep breath into massive lungs. At the same time, Fonn heard a series of whistles that slowly fell together into a solid musical chord, like someone tuning a pipe organ. The sound came from the nephilim beneath them, and Fonn saw six membranous nostrils that lined the monster's back in two rows flex open. They reminded her of the blowholes the brachiosaurs of the southeast pole used to breathe the cold, thin, polar air, but much larger.

"It's singing while it breathes," she said.

"What?" Orval asked. "I mean, what, sir?"

"It's breathing," Fonn clarified, pointing down the line of the monster's back. "Through those. It must not breathe often. I hadn't even noticed before. That's—"

"Fascinating?" offered Orval.

"No— Well, yes, but that's not my point. It means we have a chance here to keep it from drawing a breath," she said.

"The mouth is glowing," Aklechin interjected, shouting over the rising pitch of the "pipe organ" note.

"Myc," Fonn said, willing the boy to hurry up. Truthfully she was amazed that he had even managed to hold on this long but could not imagine the alternative.

Then she returned, momentarily, to the beast beneath them, and Fonn realized that Myc was in even more danger than she thought. The glow, the long indrawn breath, Rakdos standing there like a bellowing peacock. She knew exactly what would happen when the inhalation finished.

"Scouts, listen up," she said clearly and calmly. Panic could send one or more of them tumbling off of the unsteady back of the nephilim. "We've got to block all six of those blowholes, now. Ideas?"

"We stand in them," Orval said immediately.

"Impractical," Fonn said. "We might suffocate, and there's only the three of us. Six holes."

"Sir?" Aklechin said and opened his jacket. Slung across his tunic was a double-bandolier of bampops, the small pyromanic grenades that were technically outlawed for everyone but the Boros and the Izzet but were a favorite of cultists, especially at carnarium time.

"Where did you get that?" Fonn said.

"I pulled it off of a dead Rakdos," he replied.

"Brilliant, Scout," she said with a grin. "Now if we can bind them together or maybe drop them in clusters, we could—"

"Sir!" Orval cried.

"Yes?" Fonn said.

"The sound stopped."

So it had. The loud pipe-organ chord was only an echo in the remaining towers.

For some reason Fonn shouted, "Hold on!" even though the three of them already held on with everything they had. She caught a last glimpse of Myc as the boy let himself drop to the rubble below. He disappeared behind a toppled column, so Myc's mother could not see whether or not he survived.

The stone nephilim exhaled.

* * * * *

Myc flung his arms in front of his face and hunched himself into the smallest ball he possibly could as the blinding beam of fire and light struck overhead. Of all things, Myc had miraculously landed in the wreckage of a hostelry, on a pile of furniture that had bruised him considerably but certainly saved his life.

As the furious blast engulfed Rakdos, the demon spread his wings and arms to embrace it. The demon seemed to absorb the hellish energy directly into his skin, and his eyes blazed even wilder then before when it was done.

Myc ignored the heat to concentrate on his parents in the song. His father was still unsettlingly lost in the general noise, but he pinpointed Fonn easily enough. She was only a few hundred yards away. As quickly as he dared, Myc scrambled through the perilous ruins of central Ravnica to reach her before some new disaster struck.

* * * * *

"Myc!" Fonn hollered into the darkening sky. The glow of the energy blast had faded, leaving a smoldering and very angry-looking demon. From her vantage point, it was impossible to tell if Myc had survived the fall.

You'll find him in the rubble, she thought. Right. He's not on the demon any more. He's safe. And Jarad— Well, she pushed Jarad out of her mind for the time being. She needed all her concentration to time this. Aklechin had handed her a way to kill—or at least seriously wound—the mountain-monster.

Ledev often used explosive charges to clear blocked roads, and the typical ledev guardian knew quite a bit about placing explosives. Fonn knew far more than most. She credited her father's influence, and her recent foray into the League of Wojek, with the knowledge. The Leaguehall kept stores of explosives, and old Myczil Zunich had been one of the few wojeks who could be considered expert in their use.

She quickly sketched out her plan for the two scouts, stealing glances up at the demon, which was still seething and hadn't yet responded. The nephilim seemed winded, and as the thought passed through her head she heard the organ notes start again.

"We've got maybe twenty seconds," Fonn said. "Each of you take two of these," Fonn said, turning the dial atop each bampop ten clicks as she handed them out, doing the same with the six left on the bandolier. Then she spoke the activation words. "Bang-boom-bam."

Ten. "Let's go. They're clicking," she said and charged ahead along the rocking surface of the monster. Eight. She reached the front two blowholes and hurled two bampops down the left one. Six. Two more at once, right. Five. She spun on one foot and slammed two more into the second one back on the right just as Orval did the same with the third. Aklechin backed away on all fours. Three. "Go, Orval!" She shouted and the two of them bolted after the other scout. One.

Fonn spun at the last second and turned to watch the fireworks. "Boom," she said.

The bampops echoed her words but in a much louder manner. Six geysers of orange liquid and reddish-gray tissue blasted from the nephilim's stony back—it may have looked like a walking mountain on the outside, but inside it was definitely flesh and blood. Fonn and the scouts held on for dear life as the explosions were followed by wave after wave of spasms and shudders that resembled an earthquake. Orval finally gave up on his spear when it snapped off in the monster's back and folded his legs beneath his body, holding on only with his powerful arms.

The nephilim's "head" just about killed them. The stone face, heretofore suspended by some magic field over the creature's back, collapsed atop the nephilim and rolled straight for them. Fonn cleared her charges out of the way just in time, and the head rolled over the edge of the nephilim's stony shell.

A few seconds after the head crashed into the ground with a monstrous thud, the spasms stopped all at once. The nephilim went rigid for a moment, then with a sigh that expelled only a blast of warm, putrid air and a cloud of bloody foam, it collapsed, all three legs splayed. The monster's sudden drop knocked the wind out of Fonn and almost cost her a scout when Al bounced at the bottom of the fall. He would have tumbled over the side had Orval not caught him by the ankle. Al smiled up at Orval, dirt and scrapes decorating his face.

"Guess they're not *entirely* immortal," Fonn said as she helped the centaur haul the young man back up.

"Is it dead?" Aklechin asked, a question echoed by Orval.

"I think so," Fonn said. "I think those went right to whatever it's got for a brain, and the constriction and shape of the—" The scouts were staring, still terrified but hiding it under all the bravery they could muster. "Yes, it's dead," she finished. She stood carefully and peered at the demon, which had taken an abrupt step back when she and the scouts had stolen his thunder. He turned to the sky and roared. There was still no sign of Myc, but a sound—a scream, rapidly increasing in pitch and volume, intruded on her thoughts.

The sound came to an abrupt halt when a fat man and an unconscious imp fell on Fonn's head.

* * * * *

When Fonn came to, she was looking up into Myc's tearstained eleven-year-old face. "Mom?" he said. "Are you—"

"Myc!" She clutched her son to her fiercely. "I think so," she said. After a few seconds and a cough from her son, she let Myc help her to her feet. "How long was I out?"

"Just a few seconds," Orval volunteered, and Fonn realized she still stood on the back of the dead nephilim. And a strange, pudgy man in the blue robes of an Azorius lawmage stood before her.

"Who's the fat man, Myc?" Fonn asked.

"I don't know. All he seems to do is think really hard," Myc said. "But the imp says his name is Pivlic. The imp's name, I mean. Is Pivlic."

"Pivlic?" Fonn said. "How did you get here?"

"I wish I knew," the imp replied. "It is good to see you again, my friend, but it has been a rough day." With that, he fainted.

Before she could get answers about where Pivlic had come from, who the fat man was, and why they were here, Fonn's hand tore itself from its stump and flew away.

* * * * *

Kos, Obez sent. *Kos, what is going on? What's happening up there? Great Hesperia, you just—*

Killed a lunatic, Kos finished. *But there's still one in this body with me.*

Kos, Novijen—it's come to life, Obez thought. *Most of it.*

Don't worry, Kos sent. *The pilot of this beast is out of the picture. I don't think Rakdos is going to leave it in one piece. I think it's time you brought me back, don't you?*

What about me? Svogthir demanded. *This thing has no master now! The cytoplasts will return with no intelligence to bond to. The entire thing will fall apart!*

Guess you should have thought of that a while ago, Kos replied. *Obez, get me out of here.*

My pleasure, Obez said.

* * * * *

"Are we safe here?" Pivlic asked when he came to again. "Aren't those a little clo— Krokt almighty, that's the demon Rakdos!"

"Fill you in later, Pivlic," Kos said. He turned back to Fonn. "And that's why I look like this." He spread Obez's arms wide and gave an experimental turn, like someone displaying a new suit.

"It's really him, Pivlic?" Fonn said, skeptical but not unconvinced from the sound of it.

"Him? You mean Kos? The fat human here?" Pivlic said. "Oh yes, my friend, that is him. Well, was. Kos, you are in there, yes?"

"Yes, Pivlic," Kos said. "Your favorite drink is—"

"All right, all right," Pivlic said and genuinely smiled. "It is good to see you back, my friend." After several introductions and reintroductions, the impromptu meeting was, as Pivlic had predicted, interrupted by the clashing demon Rakdos—cast free of the influence of the eleven-year-old Myczil Zunich, something that was definitely going to warrant more explanation later—sometime when Kos hadn't been lied to, sent on a fool's errand, and put in the path of a raging demon and the out-of-control Simic project.

It hadn't really sunk in until now that Kos had killed a guildmaster. He wondered what that would do to Augustin's delicate balance of power and how he was supposed to find Szadek now. Or whether Szadek was even the real threat.

Enormous mass of fibrous tissues and fungal growths that had been Novijen and was now the thing called Kraj, Kos supposed, shrieked, a sound the demon apparently took as a challenge. The air was filled with cytoplasts, clouds of them, all flying toward this new monster and adding to its bulk and bizarre shape. Kos wondered what it would have looked like had Momir Vig lived to see it through to its completion. He also wondered whether he should have left the god-zombie in there. He hadn't mentioned that part to Fonn yet and wasn't sure exactly how he would.

Rakdos roared back at the ecological nightmare that was Project Kraj. Without further challenge, the demon drew back a knotty fist and threw what Kos thought was a respectable roundhouse punch that connected and kept on going. Soon Rakdos's arm was encased in slimy cytoplastic material and the spiky botanical monstrosity that made up the rest of Kraj. The demon roared again, this time definitely in pain, and tore its arm free with a jerk. Much of the flesh on his forearms was gone, exposing pulsating muscles that glowed with fire and crackling bones that were charred from within.

The demon-god was not a fool. He backed away and spread his wings, preparing to take to the air. He cleared perhaps fifty feet before the shambling bulk of Kraj reached him. It extended a slimy pseudopod that reminded Kos disturbingly of lurkers and wrapped it around the demon's leg. It pulled Rakdos easily back to earth, but the demon did not hit the ground. Kraj, or whatever intelligence it still possessed with Vig gone, slammed Rakdos into its own body, engulfing the unholy guildmaster in a roiling mass of translucent cytoplasts, shattered growth, and—Kos was certain—a wide variety of deceased Simic who had aided their guildmaster's plan.

After a few minutes of writhing and kicking, with muffled roars from within the body of Project Kraj, the demon's legs stopped moving and finally fell still. Kos wasn't willing to bet Rakdos was dead. This was an original parun who slept in lava pits. But Rakdos wasn't tearing up the city, for now. Kraj, facing no threat but without any apparent guiding intelligence, remained where it was, pulsating. After a few minutes, it, too, stopped moving. Perhaps swallowing a pill as bitter as the demon-god ruined your insides no matter what you were made of.

"Shouldn't we do something about them?" one of Fonn's scouts, a centaur who had introduced himself as Orval, asked expectantly. "Sir?"

"They're awfully close to Vitu Ghazi," the other said. "What if they wake up?"

"I don't think so," Fonn said, pointing.

"Are those—?" Kos asked.

"Quietmen," Fonn said darkly.

The familiar white shapes swarmed into the sky from the direction of Vitu Ghazi. They looked like tall, thin humans, but were covered from head to toe in white silk robes that also hid their faces—if they had faces—completely from view. Many had already sullied the glistening silk with fresh blood.

The quietmen did not carry weapons. They were weapons, holy living weapons sent forth by the Selesnya Conclave by a deranged Living Saint. The quietmen were anything but insane, however. They coordinated their attacks silently, flying in tight formations that tore through their enemies with deadly precision.

"But they're all supposed to be dead, aren't they?" Kos said.

"So were you," Fonn said. "Looks like the Conclave decided to keep a few around for emergencies."

"Fair enough," Kos said. "But what happens if they win?"

"I'm counting on Biracazir to keep them in line," Fonn said. "I've got faith."

"At least one of us does," Kos replied.

For the first time in a while, Obez's voice burst into Kos's— well, technically Obez's—head. *This is all immaterial,* he said churlishly. *You must find Szadek. Do you know how much time you have wasted?*

I'd say it's been time well spent. A threat to the city has been eliminated.

Along with another guildmaster! Obez shouted in his mind.

You're an avatar of the Azorius, and you have your orders. We'll both be executed for this.

I'm not sure, Kos replied.

What does that mean? Obez replied, growing frantic.

It means I'm not sure, Kos thought. *That felt like a wild gob-hobbler chase. And I'll stand by my decision to kill Vig no matter what.*

And now you delay us further with this ledev and her brood, Obez thought back nastily. *We are wasting time with your attempts at heroism. You were not returned to life in order to chat with old friends. We* must *track down Szadek.*

Will you listen to yourself? Kos said. *Szadek is not out here. I have an idea where he is, though.*

Where?

Back where we started, Kos said.

"Kos?" Fonn said. "You still in there?" It wasn't until then that Kos noticed her artificial hand—no, *cytoplast* hand—was gone. Fonn's original hand had not been cut or even bitten off—it had been torn from her. The stump was grown over but had never been a pretty scar. She seemed to be rolling with the loss for now, however, with all of her attention on her son and her friends.

Watching the quietmen tear Project Kraj apart piece by piece, revealing a comatose Rakdos beneath, it occurred to Kos that perhaps everyone would be missing cytoplasts. And he felt pity for those who, unlike Fonn, had put their bodies through ridiculous physical changes to accommodate the Simic augmentation.

Wasting. Time.

Hold your dromads, Kos snapped.

"Kos," Fonn said.

"What?" Kos said. "Right. Sorry, still here. Having a talk with the landlord."

Kos refocused on the real world and let Obez's shouts demanding his attention go unheeded. It wasn't easy, but Kos had been both a bouncer and a lawman. Getting yelled at by lawyers was nothing new. "What were you saying? Oh."

The quietmen were attacking both Rakdos and the Simic monster, using their own aerodynamic bodies as projectiles. The demon was wounded in a few places—the blood glowed orange like lava beneath the shimmering cytoplast surface.

"That actually works to my advantage," Kos thought aloud. "They might just have this under control, especially if the skyjeks can mount another offensive. I don't know why the titans aren't doing anything—"

"No one is," Fonn interjected.

"But if the quietmen can keep them penned in," Kos finished, "I can get back to— Feather?"

The angel's shadow fell over them all, blocking out the just-risen full moon.

"Kos," Feather said, "we need you back at the Senate."

"See?" Kos said to the rest of them. "Now this is someone who knows how I think."

* * * * *

Far below Kos, the quietmen, Rakdos, and Vitu Ghazi, Izolda the blood witch collapsed in a heap under the weight of the wounds she willingly shared with her demon-god. She drew shallow breaths, but the mob surrounding her barely took notice.

One had fallen. One who falls—*any* one that falls—became prey.

And prey was best devoured alive.

Without a sound from their former mistress, the Rakdos cultists consumed an unholy feast like none they had ever consumed. By the time they sat in a circle, cracking open Izolda's bones, each one snarled with the soul of a demon. A soul that was split into hundreds of pieces.

From that day forward, the old Rakdos proverb, "There is a demon inside each of us, screaming to get out," took on a quite literal meaning.

* * * * *

Somewhere in a night that seemed very far away, the bells began to toll midnight throughout Ravnica. Or they tried. Not many clock towers were still standing, from the sound of the distant, ghostly clangs.

From the command deck of the wrecked Parhelion, the sounds were distant indeed. Teysa suspected she would probably never hear them again, and the thought of missing that joyous midnight cacophony made her sadder than the thought of impending death. She had accepted she was going to die, accepted that it might happen soon, but that didn't mean she couldn't hope to avoid it if the opportunity to do so arose.

She still didn't entirely remember following all of the passages that led to this tilted, ruined command center of the angel's flying fortress. There had been that compulsion, that dreadful compulsion to step inside, then the same compulsion—the unmistakable touch of Azorius magic—had led both Teysa and Feather to the deck.

Then, the sight of the wounded angel. And not just any angel. Razia, the guildmaster of the Boros, wounded but alive, had risen to greet them both.

The surprise was so great—especially on the part of the joyful Feather—that it took a fateful few seconds to put together the implications of the compulsion magic, the sight of the Boros guildmaster, and the dead—no, unconscious, she was breathing faintly—skyjek slumped in the corner.

Teysa managed to say, "Feather, that's not—" before Razia exploded.

That was the only way she had to describe it. One second a wounded but stoic angel had stood there greeting them, and then Razia's arms erupted into writhing pseudopods. Others sprang from her torso and knees, and three at once slammed into Feather and sent her flying into a bulkhead. Teysa had managed to dodge the pseudopods lobbed her way but lost her cane in the process.

Then the thing that was not Razia pulled the pseudopods back into her body and spoke. "That was a demonstration," it said. "You cannot move fast enough to avoid me. And I will kill you if you try to get up."

That had been a half hour ago. Teysa had expected Feather to defy the shapeshifter but had caught a look of concern the angel shot her way that made it clear Feather wasn't going to risk getting Teysa killed. If she'd been able to risk speaking to the angel—the real angel, not this imposter—she would have told Feather to try it anyway, but when she'd tried that a few minutes earlier it had gotten her a pseudopod slap.

Finally, Teysa decided to risk asking a question of their captor herself. Itself. "Why?" she ventured.

"Why what?" the phony Razia said.

"Why are you holding us here? Why not kill us?"

"Auguries," the imposter sneered. "You are to ensure they come true. The angels must become extinct. But not until the proper moment."

CHAPTER 18

Don't say I've got the wings of an angel,
Don't tell me that you want to fly,
Don't tell me 'bout the wings of an angel,
When you've never even seen blue sky.
—*Face of an Angel,* by Shonya Bayle,
the Balladrix of Tin Street

1 Tevnember 10012 Z.C.

Frej Ralinu, minister of tax collection, Seventh District, was also a full member of the Azorius Senate and entitled to call himself "Senator." Ralinu was also a member of the higher house of that august body, which entitled him to use the loftiest entrance into the great Senate dome of Prahv. And as a human being, not a vedalken, he often spoke out on behalf of his much-maligned and populous species. Part of being on the biggest team, Ralinu liked to say, was that all the smaller teams—elves, goblins, vedalken, and the like—tended to go after you. Frej Ralinu possessed a wealth of experience when it came to the dangers of politics.

Yet even though he had entered the ruined chambers through the less prestigious lower-house entrance, that slight hardly entered his mind. What occupied his thoughts most earnestly was why the Grand Arbiter had issued the order to convene now, of all times. He said as much to Nitt Vinloskarga, the vedalken minister of budgetary management, Sixth District, as they stepped cautiously through the rubble-strewn floor of the hall leading into the chambers.

"He's the Grand Arbiter," the vedalken said. "He has sent the call, and we must answer. It is our duty to the Guildpact." It was clear she thought that was the only answer necessary, but Ralinu pressed the issue.

"Look at this place!" he objected. "It's hardly standing. We're risking our lives coming here."

"It is the Senate," the vedalken said. "Where else should we convene?"

"Why do we convene?" he repeated. "To what end? What's the point? Our city is being destroyed. It's only a matter of time before those quietmen start picking fights with the 'jeks and then the rest of us. You remember the Decamillennial."

"That was before my election," the vedalken said. "I heard the stories and read the newssheets."

"So you know what I'm talking about," Ralinu said triumphantly. "This is not a time to call the Senate to order. We should be locked safely in our homes while the angels—"

"As you said," the vedalken replied, "look at this place. The angels do not appear to be present, and their fortress appears to be wrecked. I would not put your faith in the angels. Put your faith in the Grand Arbiter."

Of course that was the answer, and every fiber of Ralinu's being wanted to agree, but a stubborn, human part of him objected to that pat response. "It's just—irregular," he managed lamely.

"It is the Senate," the vedalken said. "I for one am looking forward to seeing how many of us are left." They walked on in silence, and it was with that grim thought in mind that Ralinu and his fellow minister emerged into the rubble under what had been the most magnificent dome in the city.

The answer to the vedalken's question came with a quick look around the chamber. The ruined Parhelion dominated the view, lying nose down, right where it had crashed. With all of the other disasters erupting across the city, it almost looked peaceful. The chamber itself was barely there, a broken and crumpled eggshell of a structure. Roughly a quarter of the steps where senators usually sat remained intact, though small hunks of stone and brick lay scattered across them. On the seats sat no more than a dozen senators. Below them, atop his floating throne, Augustin IV steepled his fingers, his blind visage scowling.

"At last, the stragglers have arrived," he said, nodding to Ralinu and Vinloskarga. "Please, ministers, have a seat."

"Your honor," Ralinu began but found he could not continue. He looked at the Grand Arbiter incredulously, but no words would form on his tongue.

"A seat, ministers," the Grand Arbiter repeated.

"Come, Frej," the vedalken said, and together they climbed the seats and settled next to the greatly reduced body of the Senate. Ralinu saw Borbin, the minister of tax collection for the Eighth, a colleague, a good friend, and one of the only other humans in the Senate. There were Illindivossk, Yindervac, and Pollotorus, the three vedalken ministers of the Senate treasury (it was a big treasury). Others he only knew by name. Hovering amid them all were the soulsworn, whispering praise to the Grand Arbiter and, as usual, making the hair on the back of Ralinu's neck stand on end.

"Very good," Augustin IV said. "We are met. I hereby declare this a convocation of the full Senate, pending a check against surviving records. Do I hear any objections?"

Ralinu was completely unsurprised to hear that there were none.

"Excellent," the Grand Arbiter said and shot a hand into the sky. Overhead, the bell of the Senate—still hanging by the lone remaining rib of the dome, the dome having fallen away in pieces—began to toll.

When the sound had faded away, the Grand Arbiter gestured again, and a living image sprang to life in the air before them.

It was a common way to present facts or testimony in court or in the assembly when a witness was not available. The images moved in a swirling mass of blue haze, but their edges were sharp enough. This first one depicted the monsters that had torn into the city.

"Assembled senators, honored ministers, Azorius, Ravnicans," the Grand Arbiter said, "it is my sad duty to inform you that after ten thousand years, our Guildpact—indeed, all of Ravnican civilization—is on the verge of erupting into total war."

What followed would have dropped Ralinu's jaw on his chest if he'd been able to move it. He had seen the wreckage, the rubble, the destruction; but even so had assumed this was a local problem, insofar as the City of Ravnica was "local." It was also sprawling, and the nephilim of Utvara were not the only signs that the power of the Guildpact was slipping away.

"The quietmen, banned by Guildpact amendment, flying free through the skies," the judge said. The image flickered. "The Simic greenhouse—indeed, most of Novijen—taking on a life of its own and tearing through the streets." The image changed again.

The Rakdos uprising. Rakdos himself daring to set foot on the surface of Ravnica for the first time in millennia. The flying fortress of the Boros angels, lying like an enormous broken toy. And the ghostly Szadek, vampire guildmaster of House Dimir, impaling Razia of the Boros with her own sword. Gasps erupted in the small flock of ministers. After a short but interminable pause during which the image replayed over and over, one of the ministers—it sounded like Borbin—bellowed, "Enough!" and stood.

"Yes?" the Grand Arbiter said expectantly.

"Your honor, it is clear to me, as it should be clear to all in this—" he coughed, "in this august body. You are right. The Guildpact is crumbling, and I for one say the time for action is now."

"Go on," Augustin IV said. Ralinu had a feeling he knew right where Borbin was going. He wasn't sure he agreed, but they had to do *some*thing. They were the Senate.

"Your honor," Borbin said, "we must declare the Guildpact a failure and establish martial law, without Boros or wojek assistance. They are a failed institution without a living guildmaster. But we, I can only hope, can fill that void. I move that you, honored judge and wisest of the Azorius, immediately assume the full responsibilities of judicial dictator for the indefinite future. I further move that we immediately issue a compulsory draft of the population, as well as a compulsory draft of the ghosts of Agyrem, to form an army of Azorius that shall be the enforcers of the law. And finally, I move that we make this vote without delay."

The Grand Arbiter nodded thoughtfully.

"That," he said, "is a bold step. Many bold steps. Enthusiasm noted, Senator. Will anyone second the first part of this motion?"

"I second the first part," said Illindivossk.

"I will second part two of my honored colleague's motion," piped Yindervac.

"Point of order, your honor," called a voice from overhead. Ralinu looked over and saw an angel and a ragtag group of people standing in doorway. The unwelcome speaker was a fat man in the tattered blue robes of an Azorius lawmage. "And I do indeed raise an objection."

* * * * *

One of the Azorius ministers stood to reply to Kos's challenge, but the man never got a chance to speak. The Grand Arbiter replied first.

"Lieutenant," Augustin IV said, "or do you prefer simply 'wojek'? I would call you 'avatar,' but you have proven quite a disappointment in that particular line."

"Oh, I don't know," Kos said. "I think I'm a real quick study."

"Curious choice of words," the Grand Arbiter said, "since all of you have been such poor students. So disappointing. So very disappointing. What makes you think I will let you object to anything that happens in these chambers?" The edge of the blind man's mouth turned up in a cold smile Kos could see even from his vantage point. "I put you in that body. I created you in your current state."

"I think if you could have destroyed me, you would have done it a few seconds ago," Kos said, "before I opened Murzeddi's fat mouth." He hauled his new bulk forward.

Obez had stopped shouting in his head a while ago, and Kos thought that maybe his anchor had given up. But as Kos's borrowed feet took him closer to the Grand Arbiter, the lawmage's mental voice reappeared. *You are going to kill both of us,* Obez objected.

You were *going to kill both of us,* Kos replied in kind, but he did stop moving forward.

We were supposed to pursue the cytoplast connection, Obez said. *You should have reported it and resumed the search for Szadek. There is no reason for us to die. For me to die.*

You're a coward, aren't you? Kos asked.

And you're a killer. You killed a guildmaster.

A crazy guildmaster. It's apparently my calling. And I'm not quite done yet.

Murderer, Obez replied, and Kos decided to give the lawmage the last word. Arguing in his head was exhausting.

The others followed as the Grand Arbiter watched with a look of growing amusement Kos couldn't quite understand. Finally, Feather landed beside him and removed her golden helm. She placed it before the Azorius guildmaster then took a position at his left hand.

That was when the hairs on the back of his neck—Obez's neck—started to stand on end. He got a good look at Feather, close up, at last, and he was shocked to see that although the similarity was uncanny—angels were all almost identical, magical duplicates of Razia herself, according to the tales—there were a few tiny differences. The way she stood. The shape of an eyebrow. The indescribable kindness Feather's face displayed, now totally absent. Kos had seen Feather almost every day for decades, and this was not her. It was another angel entirely.

But there were no other angels. Kos had seen the evidence clearly, if not with his own eyes then close enough for it not to make any difference. Kos's jaw dropped.

"Fonn," he said, "Pivlic, get the others and get out of here."

"What are you talking about?" Fonn said, drawing her sword. "We just arrived."

Kos whirled. "Do it!"

Even as he turned, Kos saw it was too late. The angel was breaking down into its writhing component parts. Millions of tiny blue-white worms swirled in a mass that was angel-shaped but was certainly no angel. The lurker—Krokt almighty, Kos had hoped to never hear, let alone think, that word again—gave up the angelic shape entirely, and its writhing collective body spread into a wall of worms that neatly cut them off from the only ground exit.

"No, you won't be going anywhere," Augustin IV said.

"But what about Szadek?" Kos demanded. "You said he—that I—broke the Guildpact."

"Why do you ask what is obvious, Lieutenant?" the judge said. "He—or rather, his immortal ghost—has been in my service since you so helpfully placed him there. With such a performance record, you were certain to eliminate Vig, which also serves my purposes. Szadek's body has been a pile of dust for over a decade, thanks to you it was child's play to finish him off in the dungeons. His ghost has been my slave ever since. A powerful creature to be sure but still *my* creature. Even as he led the ghostly armies against the angels, his absence here allowed the Guildpact to finish crumbling. Now there is no choice. Ravnica will follow a new law. Perfect law. The motion has been seconded, you know."

"But why drag me all the way here and feed me that line of—"

"Oh, it was no line," the Grand Arbiter said. "I spoke the truth. You could have destroyed Szadek. Other than myself, you might be the only one on Ravnica who could destroy Szadek. But your purpose—ah, that was something different, all part of the terrifying dissension that has wracked our world since you arrested Szadek and broke the Guildpact," Augustin said in mock horror. "When you handed Szadek to me on a platter and allowed me to enslave my ancient enemy with ease."

"But this will never work," Kos said. "The senators are sitting right there. They're hearing this entire confession."

"Oh, I assure you they're hearing something else," the Grand Arbiter said. "I could not allow your willfulness to destroy my vision. They are hearing how your renegade actions have brought about this destruction. Which is true, of course. But the Guildpact was flawed from the start. It was impure, a mongrel. Order that worked to preserve chaos. I knew this day would come, that one day I would be called upon to impose true order—true *peace*—for Ravnica. And you have given me everything I need to accomplish my goal."

"So your new law will be based on lies," Kos said.

"What laws aren't?" the Grand Arbiter said. "Have you learned nothing? If so, it cannot be my fault as a teacher. You all should have learned this by now, particularly those of you in the Boros Guild. All laws are arbitrary. It is that they exist and are enforced rigorously that is important. There is no abstract, objective justice. There is no nobility in human nature—or vedalken, elf, viashino, or miscellaneous nature, for that matter. There is only punishment—and fear of punishment—for disobeying the laws we lay out to preserve the peace." He finally broke into a wide smile. "You have served my purposes well enough, though your talk grows tiresome. I will give you and that pathetic band of yours ten seconds to prepare yourselves for death. Then my ally will begin to devour you. Szadek did not appreciate Lupul's power, and the dead Devkarin didn't either, though he could have. I assure you, I do."

"Dead?" Myc and Fonn said almost simultaneously.

Kos did not have time to comfort his friend or her son. Son! Kos could hardly believe *that*. Jarad's death was easier to grasp than the fact that he and Fonn had a child. He cast a look about the moon-and-glowsphere-lit chamber. A wall of solid, roiling lurker blocked the way out to the pavilion. He doubted he could get to Augustin himself without Lupul catching him, not in this out of shape body.

There was only one exit left, and even as he saw it the entire plan stunk of being led by the nose. Augustin had manipulated Kos all along. Why should the Grand Arbiter stop now?

But the only exit was the only exit. And there might be some kind of weapons in there. The engines might

"Yes, the Parhelion is open," the Grand Arbiter prodded. "Perhaps you would like to see your friend the baroness? Or the last angel, the one you saddled with that ridiculous moniker? I'd check the command floor. There is a slim chance they yet live. But be watchful for our ghostly friend the vampire."

"Come on," Kos said, though every ounce of experience he'd collected over one hundred twenty-five years told him he was barreling headlong into a trap. Augustin had just *told* him it was a trap. But if there was a chance Feather, the real Feather, was still in there. . . .

The others turned and followed without objection. True to his word, Augustin IV gave them exactly ten seconds before he ordered the wall of worms to follow.

* * * * *

I won't do it, Obez's inner voice said. *I am loyal.*

Were you listening? Kos demanded. *He doesn't give a damn what happens to you. You were a convenient tool. We both were. But there might still be time to stop him.*

Why? Obez said.

He used us, like I just told you. And I don't like being used.

So you will attack the only source of law and order this world has left?

I'm tired of debating, Kos thought angrily. He lifted the sword he'd taken from a dead angel and held the tip to Obez's heart. The lawmage's flabby body bounced against the blade as Kos ran down the corridor that, if the signage was accurate, led to the huge engine room. *What will it be?*

You wouldn't. You would be dead too.

Didn't take the first time. Why should it now? You, on the other hand—well, just try me.

Kos thought he heard a sound like an airless sigh and, finally, Obez's voice again.

I will try to find the Orzhov baroness for you, Obez thought. *That is the best I can do.*

I need Feather, Kos replied.

You need to understand how this works. Angels are pure magic. They look like flesh, blood, and bone—especially these ones on the floor here—but they are *magic. They're not a body with a soul. There's no place to put you.*

Okay, Kos thought. *Find me a human then. Now.*

Kos's inner eye went on a different path through the corridors of the Parhelion than the ones he used to jog down the one on the engine-room route. The inner eye, guided by Obez, passed through mizzium walls and grated floors for deck after deck before settling on the wide, flat surface of the command deck, dotted with ruined control stations and littered with wreckage and a shattered ship's wheel.

Unlike the "journey" through the greenhouse, this time only the shapes of the living occupants of the command floor appeared bright, blurry, and out of focus. The mizzium, metal, and wood were clear, as were even more dead angels. There were three living souls and one dead one. The dead one was a ghost, a tall, thin ghost with a form made of swirling, blue light immersed in a shadow. The outline of the shape was all too familiar. Szadek.

Teysa Karlov was seated on the floor below the remains of a jewel-encrusted console Kos couldn't have comprehended even when it was intact. She shone bright white in his ethereal vision and had one leg stretched out before her, the other one brought up and under her chin. Feather appeared as a blazing inferno with wings, like a phoenix. She stood at the empty wheel post, both hands behind her in a position that made Kos think she'd been bound with lockrings. The third living thing was not shining but only strong enough to manage a fairly dull, white glow rimmed with a red corona. It was . . .

Wenslauv? What was she doing here?

Dying, from the look of it, Obez said maliciously.

The fourth occupant was another lurker, a disturbingly pretty mass of glittering blue jewels in the shape of another angel.

All right, take us back, Kos told Obez.

You need to pick one, Obez replied. *I'm not a ferry service.*

"Kos, what are you doing?" Fonn asked. Kos blinked, lost the hold on Obez's roving eye, and realized he was about to walk into a wall.

"Are we still being followed?" he asked.

"I don't hear them," the ledev said, "hear it."

"It probably turned into something," the centaur scout piped in.

"Yeah, I'll bet it's still following us, but it looks like a bird or something. It could be flying," Myc volunteered.

"Stop helping, Scouts," Fonn said. "From here on consider engagement regs in effect."

"This way," Kos said and turned abruptly down the next corridor.

Just wait one second. First we need to get to the engine deck. And can you find that other lurker?

Silence.

Obez?

No, the lawmage admitted. *It might have found a way to join with that other one. Could have gotten ahead of us somehow. Or maybe it's become something—something inanimate perhaps? That might cause the trouble.*

Or you might cause the trouble, Kos replied. *You being honest with me?*

It's my body you're trying to get killed, Obez said. *Why the engine deck?*

Insurance, Kos said, *some weapons lockers. Won't take us a minute.*

You're lying to someone who is sharing a mind with you, Obez replied. *You're going to the engine room, and—*

I am.

I have to admit, Obez said, *it has a certain simple charm. I'd also really rather you thought of something else.*

It's the only way to be certain.

The plan settled with his host—for now—Kos led the small group of ledev and friends to a sheltered alcove in the bend of a sharp ninety-degree corner. "Fonn," he said, nodding to them in turn, "Obez—"

"Obez?" Fonn said.

"The owner of this body," Kos said. "He can see living things, and I'm picking it up a bit myself. I think the lurker isn't following us anymore. It's possible it's turned into something we can't see."

"You and Obez," Fonn said, "came up with that."

"Yes," Kos sighed. "Listen, can you keep the kids safe while we go take care of something?"

"We're not kids—" the centaur began.

"As you were, Scouts," Fonn said, and there was no more objection from the scouts for the time being.

"Who is this 'we' you speak of, my dear, old, foolishly mistaken friend Kos in a fat-man suit?" Pivlic said. "You did say 'we,' did you not?"

"We," he said to Pivlic, a plan coalescing that might just see his friends survive this even if he didn't. "You and I. We're going to check out one of the decks that might hold some weapons."

"You are a terrible liar in any body, Kos," Pivlic said.

Kos shot him a look that said "Not in front of the scouts, you idiot," or at least close enough that Pivlic clammed up and nodded.

"We'll stay here," Myc said. "We'll see you soon. We'll keep an eye on the—the thoroughfare here. Scouts, form up." Without so much as a questioning glance, the two older ledev trainees followed him into the small alcove —more of a closet— and sat in an orderly fashion.

Fonn nodded and said, "Why are you still here?"

Kos placed a hand on her shoulder. "Fonn, if that's true about Jarad, I just want you to know that I thought—"

Fonn's face looked a lot like it did the day Kos had told her the truth about her father's death, and it unnerved the wojek ghost.

"Never mind," he finished, "Take care, I will see you soon."

* * * * *

Fonn watched Kos and Pivlic dash down the corridor toward the engine room for a few seconds, and then turned back to Myc.

"We should move to either of these corners," she said, pointing to either end of the U-bend. "We stay close together, and we keep an eye on everything." She silently added "and everybody" with the guilty thought that she had taken her eyes off the scouts entirely too much. Any one of them could be . . . even Myc could be . . .

No, she told herself, not down that road. Not yet, her self said back, but just you wait. But despite the self-assurances, she still almost leaped out of her skin when she heard a new set of footsteps coming the same way they had. The soft steps, a shuffling gait, were still distant, but she could also make out humming.

The thing that had been Lily rounded the corner, softly carrying on her eerie humming. Fonn was sickeningly sure it was the scout. Her clothing was torn but still recognizable. Her face—gods, her face had been mutilated, eyes and mouth sewn shut. Her skin was deathly pale, already tight and dry. Her silk cloak, once emerald green, had been stained with blood and was now a deep black.

She heard the scouts let out a collective gasp, and Myc stammered, "No. No, Lily."

The dead girl continued to advance. Rather than face her, Fonn and the scouts, despite themselves and everything they had just been through, recoiled in horror. Fear rolled off of Lily in waves, carried by that pitiful humming, and sank into their bones.

Fonn's heart raced. She reached for her sword but found she could not draw it. Orval's teeth were chattering like it was the middle of winter, and Aklechin had begun praying again. And Myc—

Before she could stop him, Myc had drawn Fonn's silver sword and with a shout, charged forward and skewered the undead corpse of Lilyema Tylver through the heart.

No one, not even his mother, approached Myc for several moments as he sat, cradling the dead thing and sobbing. Finally, Fonn pulled him away gently, and Myc turned from the body. He handed Fonn her sword and set his jaw.

"Mom," he said. "It's okay. I know what I have to do. I have to defend us now."

"We'll all defend us," Fonn said. "We'll stand together."

* * * * *

"My dear old—" Pivlic said.

"Friend Kos," Kos finished. "Don't stall. Will it work or not?"

"According to what I know, which I remind you is entirely based upon idle reading, journals, you understand, and *not* from any kind of stolen information that would be grossly illegal to possess—"

"Stow it, Pivlic. You're not selling me a used zeppelid. I used to quiz Feather about this place on a daily basis, just out of curiosity. She told me about the flaw in the power source. It's vulnerable. I doubt she ever expected me to use that knowledge this way, but . . . well, we don't have a choice anymore. The world is upside down, Pivlic."

"At least you are still in it, my friend," the imp replied, "even in that kind of physical shape." He returned to calculations. "Now, if I can find the right leads and they have no safeguards, either magical or physical, against just such a well-known vulnerability—yes," the imp finished as they stepped into the cavernous deck and took a sweeping look at the reality engine, still mounted in place by six huge copper bolts. Tubes and glowing metal cables ran from the rather simple cylindrical engine casing, and even shut down they crackled and sparked with magic potential.

"Yes?"

"Yes," Pivlic said, "it will work. At best we would have perhaps twenty minutes to escape. If I can set it perfectly, perhaps as many as forty-five."

"So you're saying," Kos said, "you can do it."

"To think I actually helped pay for your funeral pyre," Pivlic muttered. "You could say please."

"Please, Pivlic," Kos said, "and please *hurry*."

There was little for Kos to do right away, so he took a short spin around the engine. Even here, dead angels littered the floor, mummified and scattered pieces of them everywhere. As he rounded the far end of the engine, he saw one that made his blood run cold.

For one, it was relatively fresh—not a mummy, though the angel was missing an arm and bore a grievously charred hole where her heart should have been.

It was the spitting image of the false Feather—the slightly different face of the angel Lupul had pretended to be, he corrected. And as the implication of the battered, unmistakable armor the corpse wore sunk in his bones felt icy cold. "Razia," Kos said to the corpse, "you were killed . . . Feather said it was ten years ago."

"What?" Pivlic called.

"It's Razia," Kos said. "She did die here."

The glassy eyes of the Boros guildmaster stared up at them, not accusingly—Kos always found that people who said dead eyes were accusing were usually the ones who had killed the owner of said eyes—but with a desiccated glare of surprise and regret.

Kos was still stealing glances back at the dead guildmaster as he helped Pivlic finish slotting the last of the cables, crystals, and control valves into all the wrong places. Wrong for proper operation, very right for what Kos had in mind.

"Did we get forty-five or twenty?" Kos asked.

"Pivlic always errs on the side of caution," the imp said. "But now we must go."

"No," Kos said, "you can fly out of here. That vent up there," he added, pointing, "should get you back to Fonn and the others. Get them out of here. I don't have time to run around. I've got to jump to the command floor. I'll get them out if I can."

Pivlic, to his credit, paused a full three seconds before he shrugged. "All right," he said, "I will meet you in the Senate chambers."

"Don't wait," Kos said. "Get out of the chambers any way you can and get out of this building. This is going to be a big bang, Pivlic."

"What about the lawmage?"

Yes, what about the lawmage?

"Wings feeling better?" Kos said.

"He almost broke one the last time I carried him, my friend," Pivlic said.

"He'll be good, won't you Obez?"

I hate you.

"Just get Obez, Fonn, and the scouts out of here. I'll be right behind you with Feather and the ones on the deck. I'll be wearing a different, er, suit."

"Good luck," Pivlic said. "I will, as always, do my best."

So will I, Kos reflected. But if Szadek is there, Pivlic, I don't know what I'm going to do.

I'm going to die, Obez thought.

You're eavesdropping again, Kos shot back.

* * * * *

Pivlic waited for the lawmage's face to go blank, then scooped the fat man up and spread his still-aching wings. He wished he had gotten into the habit of carrying teardrops whenever he did anything involving Kos.

A flicker of movement caught his attention behind the slack-jawed lawmage, something on the floor.

The dead Boros guildmaster was moving. No, Pivlic corrected, melting, into—

"All right, then, up we go," Pivlic said abruptly, launching himself and his burden into the air as the lurker roiled below, flailing at them with pseudopods, screaming from several different faces that appeared in the center of its writhing body. It was the lurker that had followed them, perhaps. Diverted to where Augustin expected Kos to go. And if Augustin expected this—

But Pivlic was certain he had set the engine properly. It would work. He had that much faith in his own abilities.

The last time Kos had left for body parts unknown, the lawmage had started talking almost as soon as he'd taken nominal control of his body back, which told Pivlic that Kos had made his "jump," or "leap," or whatever he called it. This time, Obez remained silent until they'd made it some distance down the vent shaft. Pivlic did not bother looking back. Either Lupul had followed or it hadn't.

Pivlic hated philosophy, though he admired the long-running scam of philosophy as a principle. Kos was making a philosopher out of Pivlic, and Pivlic didn't appreciate it.

* * * * *

Kos burrowed through the Parhelion, disembodied and on a beeline for the command deck. The four occupants were still in more or less the same places, though the weakening form of Wenslauv—another old friend he'd never counted on seeing again, and he hoped that he would have the chance soon to see her in better condition than this—was the one he'd finally settled on.

Feather would have been impossible. Teysa was trained to fight in the arcane, Orzhov styles, but Kos figured that would just put them at odds. The lurker was too risky. Even wounded, he believed he would have the best chance in a body that had wojek training. Besides, he owed Wenslauv more than one life. It was the least he could do to get her out under her own power if at all possible.

With a painful rush of breath and life, he blinked Air Marshal Wenslauv's eyes open on the command deck of the wrecked Parhelion. The first thing he noticed was that Wenslauv was more injured than he'd realized. The second was that Teysa had noticed him blink, and Feather also shot him a look. The second angel— the one Kos knew to be a lurker—stood facing slightly away from him. He couldn't tell, but he would have been willing to bet this one looked a lot like the corpse he'd seen on the engine deck.

There was no guarantee his allies knew he was here. As far as they knew this was just Wenslauv waking up. So she winked at Feather and formed the wojek hand signal for *situation normal, all botched up.* Feather barely reacted at all but blinked twice. Kos pointed Wenslauv's finger at Teysa, then himself. Then from Feather to the exit. He did not point at Lupul. He planned to be out the door before even the lurker could catch them. In Kos's experience—and he had more than most with the lurker, he guessed—it became those it impersonated to the extent that it used their eyes to see and their ears to hear. He was sure, well, almost sure, the lurker could not be watching him from the feathers of Razia's wings, for instance.

The one open question was how fast Feather could move with her wrists bound. If she did what Kos expected, he would launch Wenslauv's body at Teysa, grab her, and Feather would take off, pick them up, and head out the exit. It was a sound plan, and the only real one that made sense, so of course Feather would do it.

He nodded once, then twice, and on the third nod Kos shoved

off from the floor, feeling something tear inside Wenslauv's gut, but it wasn't enough to stop him from getting to the advokist.

Unfortunately, Wenslauv chose that moment to regain consciousness. She had been in something close to a coma when he'd taken over.

What the—

Wenslauv, long story. It's me Kos. I'm a ghost. I'm sort of possessing you. We have to get out of here or we're all going to die. Some of us twice.

What? Wenslauv's voice said. *Kos?*

Just—trust me on this one. Kos said. *We don't have much time.*

Okay, Wenslauv's voice answered immediately. *But you'd better stick around long enough to tell me this story.*

The exchange of thoughts took a fraction of a second, the time it took Feather to clear the wheel post and join Teysa and Kos. It was also the time it took for the lurker to melt into its familiar amoebalike form and for the ghostly shape of Szadek to catch sight of them and begin flowing toward them, a wicked smile on his ghostly lips.

"Teysa, it's Kos," he said. "Szadek—he's a ghost. You did that trick with the taj—"

"Kos," Teysa objected, "that was different. I was trained to use the taj, and—"

"Krokt," Kos said. "All right, you keep going. I'll catch up."

"No," Feather said, "we're getting out of this together."

"All right," Kos said and picked up a sword from a dead angel. "I just hope this works. I'm trusting Augustin, here."

The writhing mass of Lupul rounded the bend behind them as it made its way cautiously around the bulkhead. Szadek's ghost passed right through the lurker and drove straight toward Kos, his fingers outstretched and lined in ghostly light.

Kos, Wenslauv said, *I don't know that a sword is going to do any good. I saw that ghost—*

It's okay, Kos said. *I'm a special case.* Then he reconsidered that statement. Augustin had implied that Szadek's vulnerability to Kos was physical—but what if Kos used a weapon that *was* physical, to a ghost? *Wenslauv,* he thought, *tell me you're carrying—*

Third pouch on the right, counting from the buckle back, the voice said with an audible smirk. *And you can't be serious.*

I'm out of ideas, Kos said. *But what the Krokt. Procedure worked the last time.*

He just hoped that in doing so he didn't harm himself as well. But even if he did, it might be worth it if this worked.

The vampiric ghost caught sight of the silver disk in Kos's hands and laughed, the swirling worm-form of the lurker making the transparent shape even more distorted.

"Kos," Teysa said, "if you're going to do something, you might want to get around to it. Stop talking to the voices in your head."

Kos blinked then looked at the silver disk in his hand and at the face of the vampire that had haunted many of his nightmares for the last twelve years of the wojek's mortal life. Kos threw the disk on the deck in front of the charging ghost that had been the greatest threat Ravnica had seen before just recently.

The silver grounder sparked with blue lightning when it struck the ground. The lightning formed a cyclone of electricity that drew the vampiric ghost into its vortex, shrinking the shadowy figure more and more with each passing second. With a sound like a long, lingering electrocution, the grounder—one of the simplest and least-used artifacts in the 'jek utility belt—captured the guildmaster of the Dimir. Or what remained of the vampire, at any rate.

Kos slipped the grounder into Wenslauv's belt. The lurker was almost on top of him. Then he scrambled back to the others, where Feather crouched, ready to bolt as soon as Kos had finished.

Feather's feet hardly touched the floor. She already clutched Teysa Karlov in one arm when she reached out to take hold of Kos's borrowed body in a smooth motion. The angel spread her wings at last and immediately soared down the corridor the way they had come.

They almost made it. But instead of slipping off to lay a trap, this Lupul—unlike the one on the engine deck—got smart. It slipped back into its Razia shape and took off after them, wings driving the lurker's unburdened, lighter form faster than Feather could manage, encumbered as she was by advokist and wojek. Kos shouted a warning as the flapping Razia imitation extended a pseudopod hand and wrapped it around Feather's ankle. The lurker snapped the tentacle like a whip, and the angel was yanked off course and into the wall. Somehow the angel caught the brunt with her shoulder, sparing both her passengers and her precious wings. The blow knocked Kos and Teysa free of Feather's grasp and they tumbled to the floor, coming to rest not quite as far down the corridor as their winged friend.

Kos rolled Wenslauv's bleeding, steadily weakening body onto his back. The faux Razia grinned and drew a sword. Kos grinned back.

"What's so funny?" the imposter asked.

"I recognize this corridor," Kos said.

"Now!" Fonn shouted, and the scouts and their centuriad commander burst from the sheltered alcove in which they'd been hiding. Each one threw a fully charge bampop grenade at the lurker, which responded as usual by melting into a roiling mass. This didn't keep the explosions from incinerating millions of the worms and scattering the rest against the walls of the corridor.

The lurker was stunned, but could pull itself back together, Kos had little doubt.

He pulled himself to Wenslauv's aching feet and noted one of her boots was filled with blood. Kos felt the skyjek's belt instinctively and found a teardrop. He snapped the tip off and pressed it into the wound he had inadvertently reopened. The familiar rush almost made Kos lose both their balance, but Fonn caught him by the elbow. A short distance away the scouts practiced looking grim while furtively gaping at the splattered lurker. Fonn cut Feather's wrists free and turned to Kos.

"You going to live?" she asked. "That is you, right, Kos?"

"And a friend," Kos said. "Come on, we've got maybe five minutes to go before this entire place goes up. And I told you to get them out of here."

"I know," Fonn said.

"Hello?" Pivlic's voice said from a vent grate directly overhead. "Hello? Could you give me directions to the front door? This fat man is getting heavy."

* * * * *

The Senate chambers had been in ruins when they'd entered the Parhelion. Now the Senate, and from the look of it, Augustin IV's plans, where falling into ruin as well. The quietmen had arrived to impeach the blind judge. The Azorius guildmaster still sat upon his floating throne, but it appeared that his remaining lurker was fending off attacks from quietmen as well as the few ministers left alive. Several lay dead on the steps, whether slain by the Selesnyan enforcers or the lurker Kos could not say. He could not see Obez anywhere, but could sense that his anchor was still alive—and far from Prahv.

Smart thinking, Kos thought in Obez's direction. *Stay where you are, Obez.*

Who are you—? Wenslauv broke in.

Long story, Kos thought back.

Prahv was doomed. Kos had seen to that. Yet this was what Augustin had wanted, was it not? Open war between the guilds?

He reached down to Wenslauv's belt and produced the grounder, still crackling with energy. Perhaps the quietmen would finish Augustin. Perhaps they would not. But in his current state, Kos doubted the Grand Arbiter could withstand his old enemy. And if Kos timed it right, he would still be able to rid Ravnica of Szadek, too.

Call it insurance, Kos thought as Wenslauv realized where his thoughts were leading. Distantly, he could hear Obez's mental voice crying out in objection, but he ignored it.

"Your honor," Kos shouted. He thumbed the tiny release switch on the grounder's base. "Catch."

Kos hurled the small silver disk at the Grand Arbiter's feet just as Augustin turned his head to face Kos. The Grand Arbiter's face registered alarm for a split second, then the grounder's releases snapped, releasing the prisoner. Szadek's ghost sprang into being before Augustin IV with a howling shriek. The Grand Arbiter might have been blind, but he certainly recognized the sound, and the presence, of the vampire's spectral form.

"Kos, what the hell are you—" Fonn began.

"Doing my job," Kos said.

Szadek's ghost stopped shrieking and coalesced into a more stable shape. Without turning toward Kos, the shadowy phantom began to laugh.

"Augustin," the ghost said, "we have unfinished business." With that he lashed a spectral hand into the Grand Arbiter's chest. Blue lightning surrounded the pair, binding them together in place. The vampire's ghost continued to chuckle. Augustin IV screamed pitiably, writhing in place. All the while, the quietmen continued to batter Prahv and the other Azorius within.

Kos, you cannot do this, Obez shouted in his mind, still distant. *You will destroy—*

Yes, Kos interrupted. *I will destroy. But first I'm getting out of here. Then we'll talk about courage under fire, lawmage.*

"That ought to do it," Kos said to Fonn and the others.

"But you just released the—" Tëysa began.

"I know," Kos said, and winked. "And they'll both be occupied for another few minutes. We won't want to be here. Come on."

Kos waited until everyone was sprinting out of the building, as fast as their legs could carry them, then cast one last look at Szadek and Augustin, locked in a deadly embrace—one ghost, one mortal, both doomed.

"How long ago was it that you said 'five minutes to go,' Kos?" Teysa asked, panting.

"About . . . oh, damn."

There was an expectant pause. Kos pumped his legs, hoping they'd gotten far enough away from the blast to survive. "Perhaps I was wrong about the time," Pivlic said. "Pivlic is a businessman, not an engineer." Just then the explosion rocked the ground and all of the City of Ravnica. Pivlic would later estimate that had they departed just a few seconds later, the blast might have killed them all. As it was, the explosion flattened Prahv and sent a fireball into the sky that could be seen from the northwest pole. The shock wave shattered what few windows remained for a mile in every direction; left a crater the size of Thausstorin Arena; and threw Kos, Feather, Fonn, and the ledev guards to the ground—bruised, but alive.

CHAPTER 19

The Schism appears to have faded like a bad memory. Would that the memories of that fateful day the nephilim appeared would fade as fast. But as long as we remain, fellow citizens of Utvara, not even the immortal gods of the past can keep us from forging a new destiny. And your destiny includes half off all drinks at the new Imp Wing Hotel and Tavern, rebuilt and open under new management. Refreshment for the future of Utvara.

—Advertisement, the *Utvara Townsman*,
15 Paujal, 10013 Z.C.

3 Tevnember 10012 Z.C.

Fonn took her son's hand and ducked inside the labyrinth. She nodded at the hippogryph guards, who nodded back. They had obviously been told to expect her.

It was over. Feather, with the help of many teratogens, had hauled Rakdos's body—still alive, but in some kind of suspended animation—into the pit of Rix Maadi. Fonn had gone along for the ride, half-expecting the chance to take out some of her grief bitterly fighting the cultists.

The cultists were too busy fighting each other to fight the intruders. The angel and the teratogens dropped the demon-god into a deep slumber, perhaps for good.

She had requested leave from both the ledev and the wojeks for now. Fonn could no longer rely on someone else to help her raise Myc. But perhaps together the two of them could find a way to say good bye.

Golgari necromancy involved the transfer of a ghostly spirit into its own corpse. This did not return the dead to life, exactly, but retained as much of their mortal minds as the necromancer allowed. And Jarad, the guildmaster, had practiced the arts of Golgari necromancy a great deal since his sister's death.

Fonn and Myc walked hand in hand down the silent corridors, neither speaking, until they arrived in the center of the labyrinth.

"Hello," the guildmaster said. Jarad stood, the wounds on his body still evident. Though they had been cleaned up they would never heal now. The Devkarin had accomplished what few necromancers ever had—he forced his own ghost to return to his body and reanimated himself.

"Hello," Myc said. Fonn could not seem to speak and only nodded in dumb agreement. She had thought she could handle this, but seeing him there, not dead but no longer the man she had known . . .

"We have come to say farewell," she said at last. "Myc wanted to—"

"Mom," Myc interrupted, "Dad. It's all right."

"Myc, he's—"

"I am what I am, Fonn," Jarad said. "I am not that different than I was. But there are some things that—well, I think you are right. This is farewell for you and me. For now."

"But not for us," Myc said, and turned to Fonn. "He's still my father. Mom, I once said that I wanted to learn from both of you. And in the last few years, I've been devoting almost all my time to learning how to be a ledev. I think it's time for me to learn a little more about being a Devkarin, too. Not the zombie part, no offense, Dad."

Tears welled in Fonn's eyes, but she ignored them. She nodded.

"Are you sure?" she asked.

"Yes," Myc said. "Don't take this the wrong way, but I'm not eager to wield a ledev sword again, either. Not right away. Not after what

I had to do with one." He turned to the guildmaster and addressed his father formally. "Guildmaster, if you will have me, I would like to learn the Golgari ways. But understand this isn't a choice. I will serve both guilds. I think that—I think part of the problem with this world is that everyone is so locked into whatever role their guild gives them. Why do I have to be in one guild or the other?"

Fonn looked upon the boy with surprise—surprise that melted into respect.

"He is wise, isn't he?" Jarad said. His voice had lost whatever warmth it once possessed, but it was still his voice.

"All right," Fonn said. "Jarad . . . Guildmaster. Take care of him. And Myc, when you're ready to resume your training with the ledev, I'll be waiting."

She turned and left before Jarad could make eye contact with her again. The temptation to return to him was strong, but Fonn was not free to make the same decision her son had. She had already split her own obligations—to the ledev and to the wojeks. Myc would have to find his own path, and she would be there to help him when he needed it. And Jarad? Some things could not be overcome quickly. She would mourn the Jarad she had known, and perhaps learn to befriend the one that now led the Golgari. For now it was enough that the boy had a father again.

* * * * *

4 Tevnember 10012 Z.C.

At the edge of the devastated Utvara township, Crixizix the goblin stood silently. She had been here for almost a day, waiting and watching for some sign of the help she had called for to arrive. The containment team had never shown up, but the goblin had other resources.

While she waited, she stared at the capped caldera Niv-Mizzet had created before flying off into the unknown. Crixizix had felt no contact from the Firemind for days. Wherever Niv-Mizzet was, he did not want to be disturbed.

Utvara, however, would survive, despite her earlier dire predictions. Already some who remained had built simple shelters, while others had cleared out ruined homes and buildings, starting the cycle of civilization all over again. Eventually, they would need power, water, and all of the things a master engineer of the Izzet could supervise.

By the time the goblin saw the private yacht zeppelid break over the horizon, she had already reconstructed half of the Cauldron in her head. When Pivlic and the baroness touched down, she would be ready to begin rebuilding Utvara for good.

* * * * *

12 Cizarm 10014 Z.C.

"Welcome back, Kos," Feather said. "We were not entirely certain that would work."

"Feather?" Kos said. "Who am I— Where am I now?" It was a place at once familiar but different. Little things out of place, others gone entirely. People. And a sense that he'd been away, and not just because he'd been welcomed back.

"Look for yourself," Feather said and guided him to a tall mirror.

The face, the body, and clothing were that of Agrus Kos. All three were slightly translucent and carrying a soft, pale glow that came from no natural light source—well, except glowspheres, which were known for it.

"That's me," he said and heard his own voice. It echoed a bit more than Feather's in the guildmaster's office. Yes, that's where he was. This was the central sanctum of the Boros guildmaster in the heart of Sunhome, the Boros fortress that had been completely rebuilt—seemingly overnight from Kos's perspective. "Feather, what's going on?"

"It is a gift," Feather said, "from the new Azorius guildmaster. He has taken the name Leonos II."

"I don't care if he's taken the name Goblin H. Krokt—I don't want this," Kos said. "I'm— Don't you get it? I'm done. No more giant monsters, mad scientists, ancient shadowy villains. No conspiracies, no dromads, and no more dragons. I don't care what it is this time. I'm done. I am *dead*. Please accept it."

"Are you?" Feather said. "Done?"

"Feather, I don't know where I've been, but I daresay you've become glib."

"And a bit more diplomatic," the angel admitted. Then her expression became more serious. "Listen to me. No diplomacy. No glib. This form—your current and, if you like, permanent incarnation—is a gift, no strings attached."

"What made you think I wanted to go on living?" Kos asked.

"Can you honestly tell me you didn't?" Feather asked. "When you were merely an Azorius agent, you fought for your life just as hard as you did when—"

"I was *borrowing* those," Kos said, but even as he did he realized it wasn't really true. He hadn't been trying to save Obez's skin, nor the virusoid's. Maybe Wenslauv's, but they were old friends. Certainly he hadn't cared whether the god-zombie lived or died. Still . . . "All right, you've got me," he admitted. "But that doesn't mean— I mean, how does this work? Who can see me?"

"Everyone can see you," Feather said. "In fact," she added, tossing a dindin fruit from a bowl on the huge oak desk that dominated the room, "you can pick up, touch, and use any object you like."

Kos caught the dindin in one hand by reflex. He closed the fingers around it, and except for the fact that he could still see the skin of the fruit through those fingers it felt solid. He felt solid. He drew a breath.

If it was the illusion of breathing, it was close enough to his memory of the real thing.

He tossed the fruit back to Feather.

"There's something you're not telling me," Kos said. "You may be getting better at diplomacy, but I've known you too long."

"Well," the angel said, "I do have a—we have—an offer for you."

"A job," Kos said. "I knew it. What, has Niv-Mizzet decided to turn Vitu Ghazi into a scratching post?"

"What? No, Niv-Mizzet has left for—" the angel said. "Oh. That was a joke."

"Not a very good one, either. Now out with it," Kos said.

"The Guildpact as you remember it is gone," Feather said, "but we have signed a new accord. We are attempting to put something similar in place, an agreement that works on true interdependency, negotiation . . . in short, what the Guildpact was supposed to be but which the paruns felt had to be reinforced with magic. When that magic fell apart, so did a civilization that had grown used to relying on it."

"So the guilds? . . ." Kos said, curious despite himself.

"They are fewer in number by one," Feather said. "There is no need for a House Dimir to oppose the Guildpact's power because the power of the new accord is not in its magic but in the document. I must say I'm quite proud of it, though most of the credit should go to the baroness."

"Our baroness?" Kos said. "Teysa?"

"Yes, she composed most of it and helped me negotiate much of the rest," Feather said.

"You still haven't gotten to the job," Kos said.

"Yes," Feather said. "First, let me tell you something."

"Another something," Kos said.

"This one's simple," Feather said. "It has been two years since the Parhelion was destroyed, and the spell Augustin IV cast to anchor you to Obez faded with it. And in that time, there have been more changes than just the new accord. Step with me to the window."

Kos followed the angel to the edge of a large curtain that the angel swept aside with a flourish.

"What is that?" Kos asked, translucent mouth agape.

"That is Agyrem," Feather said.

"But that's a—" Kos had been about to say "myth," but the proof was before his eyes. It almost looked like the City of Ravnica had been copied and placed imperfectly atop itself. Translucent towers and busy, pale specters cut through the reality of the original central metropolis, mingling with the world of the living.

"It's not cut off from the rest of the world anymore," Feather continued. "The Schism is gone, but Agyrem remains here, a reality merged with ours, in a way, but also not there. I'm told it had something to do with the quietmen coming back, but whatever the cause it is done, and does not seem to be changing. Honestly, for the most part it's become just another neighborhood to most people these days, even if the inhabitants are somewhat transparent. But we—that is, the living—cannot truly interact with it, not physically."

"And . . ."

"And I need someone to establish the new Agyrem Leaguehall," Feather said, "someone I trust, with enough experience to hit the ground running. Someone who can not only see Agyrem, but can see and interact with its denizens."

"No strings, huh?"

"It is yours to refuse," the angel replied. "Your future is your own. And if you do wish to return to . . . nonexistence, it can be arranged." It was an offer, not a threat, but the word "nonexistence" gave Kos pause. He'd just spent two years not existing. And the more he thought about it, the less he liked the idea.

"There's still something you're not telling me," Kos said. "I can smell it."

"True," the angel said. "And that is why we need a Leaguehall in the city of ghosts. There is no longer an official tenth guild, but Szadek, and the Dimir, survive, in a way."

"In there," Kos said, pointing at the ghostly spires intermingling with the familiar towers of his home.

"Yes," Feather said, and looked somewhat ashamed. "He—his ghost—weathered the explosion in Prahv. It may be that this was his plan all along   he is in his element among the dead. It appears that there are too many ghosts for him to control them all, but he is gaining strength. And he is elusive. My forces cannot find him, let alone oppose him. For the sake of Agyrem, to say nothing of Ravnica, Szadek needs to be opposed."

"By me."

"By someone," Feather said. "And I can think of no one else more qualified."

"I'm a ghost."

"So is he." Kos eyed Feather skeptically then looked back out the window. Agyrem was huge, and from this vantage point he could not see where it ended and the "normal" city began. Indeed, many of the spectral towers were distorted imitations of the originals. He thought he could even make out a ghostly Vitu Ghazi not far from the solid one.

"Well," Kos said after several long, silent minutes. "It looks like I've got work to do."

The Year of Rogue Dragons

By Richard Lee Byers

Dragons across Faerûn begin to slip into madness, bringing all of the
world to the edge of cataclysm. The Year of Rogue Dragons has come.

The Rage

Renegade dragon hunter Dorn has devoted his entire life to killing
dragons. As every dragon across Faerûn begins to slip into madness,
civilization's only hope may lie in the last alliance Dorn and his
fellow hunters would ever accept.

The Rite

Rampaging dragons appear in more places every day. But all the
dragons have to do to avoid the madness is trade their
immortal souls for an eternity of undeath.

The Ruin

May 2006

For more information visit **www.wizards.com**